THE
INCREDIBLE
BRAZILIAN

THE
INCREDIBLE
BRAZILIAN

The Native

Zulfikar Ghose

THE OVERLOOK PRESS
Woodstock, New York

First published by Tusk/Overlook in 1983 by:

The Overlook Press
Lewis Hollow Road
Woodstock, New York, 12498

Tusk Books and Overlook Press Books
are registered marks of
The Overlook Press of Woodstock, New York, Inc.

Library of Congress Cataloging in Publication Data

Ghose, Zulfikar, 1935 –
    The incredible Brazilian

    I. Title.
PS3557.H6315   1984   823'.914   83-42920
ISBN 0-87951-200-8 (Hardcover)
        0-87951-195-8 (Paperback)

CONTENTS

I affirm that which is certain as certain, and that which is doubtful as such, that in an affair of so much importance, no one may believe more than is stated in this narrative.

Fr Cristóval de Acuña

If the explanation which dawned on me like a stroke of inspiration while listening to Lúcio's excited account of the discussions among my men in Goiânia is to be credited, then, it now occurs to me, it would have been a wonderful gesture of the gods if the first body in which my soul had resided had been that of Pedro Álvares Cabral, the Portuguese commander who led the first expedition which discovered Brazil in 1500, that blessed year of which, rather than of mortal humans, I can truly claim to be the offspring. But, as anyone with the patience to peruse this profoundly truthful narrative will discover, I am an honest man. I am not even given to flights of the imagination – if such ventures are still possible in an age of supersonic aviation. It is true that I am vulnerable (and who is not?) to fantasies; once, dressing up for the carnival in the costume of the Marquis of Pombal, that preposterously successful prime minister in eighteenth-century Lisbon, I found it easy to accommodate that empire builder's personality within my body simply by having made myself appear like him with a fastidiously meticulous attention to the details of my make-up – even to the extent of affecting the look of insolence so characteristic of people who enjoy immense power. I must admit that whatever task I have undertaken I have performed with a passionate regard for professional excellence. The spirit, I have often reflected, has the capacity of water to flow in directions one chooses for it; which compels me to add the cynical rider that sometimes it merely flows into the gutter. So it has been with me. Now my head has borne the weight of a bejewelled hat and now

9

been crowned only by the itching heat of the sun, between such extremes has my spirit fluctuated in its promptings of emotion. I am aware of the danger of fantasies, of adding spice to situations which were no more memorable than a frugal meal of rice and beans. I am aware, too, that since the reader is inevitably going to consider some aspects of my narrative as unbelievably impossible, I have the temptation before me of straining credibility still further by making incredibility a kind of literary convention, by suggesting, say, that the reader can only believe in my story if he first accepts the proposition that everything I have to say is unbelievable. That is an interesting notion, no doubt. But let me say it categorically once and for all: what ensues may seem incredible, but there is not one word of untruth in it.

Therefore (to return to the tantalizing proposition with which I began), I can only wish that I had been Álvares Cabral, for that would have given this story the kind of unity so beloved of novelists. Unfortunately, I must let the notion of ever having been Cabral pass as a pleasant little daydream. Regrettably, I was not even one of Cabral's company; it would have been fitting to have been Pero Vaz de Caminha, that impressionable clerk who accompanied Cabral and wrote, in a wide-eyed prose, reports of the New World to send to Lisbon. I can just imagine it. The months of hopeful praying, as well as of that profanity to which men sink in despair, while we coaxed the aggressive Atlantic to let us proceed a little farther and then a little farther. And then seeing the white shore and the great humpback of the jungle just above the beaches. Would there be hospitality and treasure there behind the menacing mask of the jungle, was this to be the answer to our prayers? Or would our profanity be revenged instead, would devils appear from behind the trees? Who knew then that what they saw was *Brazil*? Oh, I can imagine a great deal of what it must have been like to have been Cabral or one of his party. But what use are the embroideries of imaginative invention when one's material is already profusely patterned and is of the finest silk? So: I must admit that I was not even one of the lowest rank in Cabral's party, and consequently that aspect of Brazil's history, the arrival of the first expedition from Lisbon, is not part of my experience.

So much of Brazil is! I wait here on the border of Mato Grosso near a little town which supplies all my needs, I wait here for these difficult days, perhaps months, even years, to pass during which I must either submit myself to a cruel death or emerge as the prophet which I am now convinced is the ultimate role which destiny has contrived for me. These are not vain, pompous words, these are not the airy expectations of a crazed mind. I am a wanted man in more senses than one. When I see, while passing through some small town, a poster screaming out that Gregório Peixoto da Silva Xavier is wanted dead or alive, it is almost as if I were looking at another person's face. The finely wrinkled forehead, the large dark brown eyes, the severely straight nose and that mouth which must surely have an ancestor in Mediterranean peasantry, all proclaim a forceful personality. The Government, which puts up the poster, is making a fundamental mistake about the psychology of which the least sophisticated advertising agency could instruct it; that, far from tempting some peasant to earn himself a few thousand new cruzeiros, the poster has taken me right to the heart of the country, and made my image as compellingly saleable a product as a well-established detergent. It gives me not a little pleasure to regard the determined features of the wanted man on the poster. At other times, when, at a meeting on some farm whose absentee landlord is very probably lying with his latest mistress on Copacabana beach a thousand miles away, the peasants have cried out *Gregório, Gregório!* I know that I am wanted in the other, more important sense. My knowledge of my past makes me face my destiny with an equanimity which no one else in this world, certainly not in Brazil, is likely to possess. For I know that I am indestructible, who have, in one form or another, lived through four centuries. It could be that this is to be my last life after which my spirit, exhausted with the ecstasy of so much corporeal involvement, must find a rest

11

somewhere. While waiting here, talking to my companion Lúcio Barreto, I have until recently, when the explanation occurred to me like a stroke of inspiration, been puzzled by the immensity of my own knowledge of my country; for it has been much more than that acquired in a lifetime, however active and studious.

Lúcio is a simple man and he was quite convinced at first that my knowledge was a special divine gift, that it was a confirmation of my prophetic vision. I would have accepted such an explanation at the risk of appearing to lack in humility, at the risk even of seeming to acquiesce in the myth fast becoming popular that I am a special agent from heaven. There are people who believe this, and it must be said that people who are convinced that any spectacularly successful Brazilian is a special agent of the C.I.A. are bound to believe anything. I would have accepted, too, the status of possessing a prophetic vision, for with certain beliefs the limitation of rational explanation necessitates that pure faith be postulated as an ultimate arbiter. But what puzzled me was not merely the extent of the knowledge that I seemed to possess without ever having taken any pains to acquire it; it was the particularity of complete existences, precise images of having lived through definite epochs, that I found bewilderingly inexplicable. It was as though I had read the biographies of several men and that I had been convinced that I had lived their lives. Sometimes, I have found myself describing to Lúcio some past event – once I had him utterly engrossed in a vivid account of my love affair with Theresa Sylvestre – and even I have not thought until much later that my story has, strictly speaking, been an invention. Poor Theresa, such black eyes she had, she must have died at least a hundred and twenty years ago! And yet what love we made together beside the bamboos once until she went hysterical because a snake had appeared.

Ask me what it was like to be an ordinary Brazilian living in Rio de Janeiro at the time when shiploads of African slaves were chained in the streets until they were sold and I will give you a more precise picture than any social historian could possibly construct. Well, I suppose my memory of that time can hardly be called representative of the *ordinary* Brazilian, for no one could make a fortune trading in Negroes and remain ordinary. The experience was, to say the least, intoxicating. Ah, and what memory is it that makes my nostrils twitch as though a fly sat there, compelling me to drop my eyelids and to savour again the pungent odour of a sweating Negress whose munificent body seemed to prescribe that the act of love be pursued with gestures of imperial haughtiness? I could recall many things about Brazil's past with a particularity which no academic reconstruction is ever likely to achieve. I could tell you what it was to be one of the *bandeirantes*, pioneering companions, adventurers, men who in the darkest jungle saw bright horizons, setting out handsomely accoutred and gradually, after months of rain, after the year-long treks across insect-ridden swamps or snake-infested jungles, after the battles with the Indians, losing everything: losing their horses and companions, physically beaten but yet triumphantly alive, shrivelled and naked and possessing nothing but that horizon-searching look in the eyes, that searchlight intensity of vision. I could tell you, too, how much it cost, not just in coins and bank-notes, but in verbal compliments and presents of silk to the Madam of the house, to buy the privilege of deflowering a virgin freshly arrived in Manaus from Warsaw and fated, poor wretch, eventually to be made available to any drunken labourer from the rubber plantations for a few pitiful coins. Brazil! Who knows her, this wild woman with the blood of Europe and Africa in her veins?

I, Gregório Peixoto da Silva Xavier, know her!

If I had realized the truth about my memories much earlier, that is to say if I had known when I had time (of which I have so little now!) that my memory was not merely a gift, no strange freak of nature, then I should certainly have made a sustained attempt to perform what must surely be the greatest feat of historiography – given an eye-witness account

13

of four hundred years. Instead, I fear I must content myself with a hasty narration of a few episodes from my own life; and, alas, I shall have to neglect the graces of style which only a leisurely pace could afford opportunity for; and I must neglect, too, those considerations of drama and romance which are so dear to readers of fiction.

I wish I could say that this is a fiction, and there end the matter of this laborious prologue! The enforced obscurity of my existence is not a fiction. And the Brazil which I have known, from the days of sugar and gold and rubber to *this*, this moment of savage mutilation, is not a fiction. My present situation which is so closely linked to Brazil's present wrinkle-browed, grey-haired, tear-stained face is of such serious consequence to mankind that I cannot pass off the awesome truth of my story as an imaginative diversion.

The truth (which I must surely have known already) dawned on me when Lúcio returned from a visit to Goiânia one day. I am aware that by mentioning that city I have probably given away the approximate location of my hideout on the border of Mato Grosso. Still, Goiânia is a good two hundred miles from the border and, in any case, I am prepared for them when they come to get me. It will, I suppose, have to come to a confrontation – unless the bullet is aimed at my back. We shall see who is *wanted*! Lúcio returned, as I was saying, from one of his visits to the neighbouring provincial capital which he has to make on my behalf from time to time (our organization has to keep going even if I am obliged to live like a deserter in time of war!). As usual, Lúcio first described the proceedings. I listened attentively to discover what progress was being made by our movement in places as far apart as Belém and Porto Alegre. Ah, if I can survive the time while our movement, which has already taken root, begins to flower, to throw up its shoots like the sugarcane in Bahia! I questioned Lúcio in detail about the allegiance of our men in Goiânia, for I am very particular about matters of loyalty, knowing that one's closest friend may prove to be a traitor. And then, when we had exhausted the affairs of our organization, Lúcio went on to relate some of the other conversations which took place. I pay great regard to accounts of informal conversations, for they can often reveal some inconsistency in a person's character which might alert me to the possible presence in my organization of a potential betrayer. Well, one of the conversations during this visit was about death. I did not like that, this talk of death. It suggested that a fatalism was creeping in among my men. They must have been worried if they had begun to talk about death. However: the talk, according to Lúcio, turned to a discussion of what happens *after* death.

As expected, Emmanuel Xeria, who takes great pride in being a modern realist or a contemporary rationalist (you think up any damned label, and Emmanuel will stick it across his shining forehead above his merrily glinting eyes), declared that nothing happens after death, that you just disintegrate. Well, what did he expect but abuse, being surrounded by men who have never known any beliefs outside the Roman Catholic Church? Apparently, João Dias gave him hell – which is not too coarse a word to use since they talked at length about that particular place. But old Fernando Cardovil, who is forever pulling at his thin white beard, told them of a Hindu professor whom he had met once in São Paulo and of how the professor had explained the doctrine of reincarnation to him.

At that point I must have gone into a trance, for Lúcio told me afterwards that I had a strange look on my face, that I seemed no longer to hear his words, and that when I looked at him I did not give the impression of recognizing him. Lúcio has learned, from being with me for so many years, not to act rashly. He never panics in an emergency, is never surprised. Seeing me in a petrified state, my eyes apparently staring out into the darkness which had settled around the old farmhouse, he did the best thing he could: he left me and went into his own room to see that the machine-gun which he keeps next to his bed was in good shape.

Reincarnation! I must have known the word all my life.

But it seemed to strike me afresh with all its meaning when Lúcio uttered it in that context of the discussion about life after death. The precise memory of the events which is so alive in me suddenly acquired a fascinating explanation. I remembered – could it be? – all those things because they had actually happened to *me*.

Whether reincarnation is the lot of all mankind without its knowing, I do not know nor greatly care – although it must be said that as a theory explaining life and death, reincarnation has the beauty of something which can neither be denied nor proved. Just as one can neither deny nor prove the existence of God. Both theories are neat tricks of language with which people talk themselves into a comfortable state of mind. But I am not concerned with providing evidence for the truth of any theory. All I can say is that for some reason I have been chosen to *know* that I have lived in the past. Of course, if I really think about it, it could easily be that nature created me only this one time but did so with a store of memories of possible previous lives. But, as the reader can imagine, I am trying hard to avoid philosophical and theological controversy; I would readily enter into one, for I have always enjoyed argument and debate, but this is not the place for it. I am aware, too, that the whole thing could be a trick of the imagination. It may be that I am going mad in my isolation here in Mato Grosso. Any phenomenon which is the object of the mind's reflections is capable of infinite explanation. But then – considering this notion of reincarnation – I say: what does it matter? What I know I know. Neither proof nor disproof of any theory is going to change my knowledge. Well, then, let us, *for no other reason than to simplify matters* and to provoke a petty outcry among our pompous theologians (which will give me no small pleasure!), admit the possibility of reincarnation. I will give you two very good reasons why I am inclined to admit it myself.

First, black-eyed Theresa makes sense – ah, thinking of her now, after these hundred and fifty years or so, makes me swell with desire! And secondly, I now know that there could well

16

be some truth in the dream-like memory which keeps returning to me from time to time that I once married a girl called Nôemia Dutra dos Santos who turned out to be my own great-grand-daughter.

Book One

THE NATIVE

Chapter 1

'THE LADY, GREGÓRIO, IS YOURS!'

To show his affection to me, my father contrived that the celebration of his marriage to Augustina Rodrigues should take place on my fourteenth birthday; the fact that on the same day (or, rather, night), circumstances should lead me to the stifling room and the equally stifling bosom of Aurelia, the Negress maid who had been chosen for her good looks from a dozen young Negresses among the slave dwellings on the plantation to attend upon my new mother, is, I suspect, a measure of my father's generosity which he preferred to exercise in subtle ways. He was more blatantly generous on the same day when he designated Jari, a boy of my own age from the group of fifteen Negroes given to my father as part of his marriage settlement, as my personal slave. To me, therefore, my father's wedding-day was a day of several initiations, and not the least of my pleasures that day was the notion that danced in my mind, that my father in his bedroom and I in Aurelia's were enjoying the same experience.

Well, *that* cannot be wholly true. My father was a man in his forties, married for the third time, with five children already from his first two marriages and, as he was later to disclose in his will, he was the father also of seven children born to Negro women on the plantation; therefore, his experience that night can hardly be said to have been one which I duplicated even in its essentials. We were, it will be truer to say, equal in our respective dispositions in so far as each of us lay beside a woman.

But that was in the night. The day began with the kind of thrilling expectation which I had experienced in my childhood

21

only on such special days of festivity as Christmas and the feast-day of São João and that greatest day of celebration – the first day of harvesting the sugarcane when the procession from the fields to the mill, led by our own chanting, dreamy-eyed chaplain, signalled the commencement of frenzied activity in the kitchen and the tensing of emotions within us which would not be fully released until the dancing late at night.

'Get up, Gregório, wake up!' cried Tana, the thin old Negress who supervised the bedrooms and the kitchen. I saw the outline of her narrow shoulders against the light of the open door and, pulling a sheet over my head, made a gesture of dismissing her.

'Don't you know what day it is?' she called.

When women persist, it is like walking under a drizzle with no shelter in sight; but when a Negro woman persists, it is like being caught in a thunderstorm. It is, I have since learned, a matter of tone.

'Oh, our Gregório's so bundled up in his wicked thoughts, he doesn't know what day it is!' she mocked.

Although she could not see where my hand was under the sheet, I quickly snapped it up to give my chin a meditative rub, for Tana was said to possess powers of divining people's unspoken thoughts and I had heard it whispered that she had the capacity to communicate with the dead. If she had access to such mysteries, the sheet could have been no more to her than the surface of a clear, pebble-bedded stream. I pulled the sheet down and rubbed my chin vigorously.

'Well, well,' she went on, 'isn't that a lovely sight? Nine in the morning, half the day finished, and our young master has such tender eyes he can't bear to look at the sunlight. Do you squint, Gregório, on such a day as this?'

'Look, Tana, you can bring the sun in and hang it up on the ceiling,' I said, 'but please do me the favour and sell your tongue to the butcher.'

'Oh, what a way to talk! And on a day like this. Don't you know what day it is that you mock the saints with your

22

manners?'

'Yes,' I shouted. 'The day the cows walk on the river and the ants make honey and old Negresses pray to Saint Anthony to send them a lover.'

'Shame on you, Gregório,' she screeched back. 'It's the wedding-day, and what's more, it's your birthday, though why anyone should want to celebrate the birthday of so ill-mannered a young man I don't know.'

Saying that, she left the room. I threw the sheet away from my body and lay back looking at the pale blue silk canopy above me which had on it in gold thread a motif of flowers which could be distinguished individually or in groups of four – and, if you screwed up your eyes, in groups of sixteen or thirty-two – a kind of pattern that drove you crazy trying to figure out what exactly it was supposed to be.

Well, that was something to wake up for, my birthday, I thought, taking my eyes away from the infuriating pattern on the canopy and turning over in bed so that I could dangle my arm and touch the cool stone floor. Outside, in the verandah, Tana was shouting orders to the servants. I am sure the shouting was quite unnecessary. It was a trick of hers to make sure that I would not fall back to sleep, and as if she heard my thoughts and wished to confirm them, she began moving the furniture in the verandah, a procedure which entailed a great deal of noise. And my father's wedding-day, that was something too. I would have a new, young mother.

I had not seen my father's new bride, Augustina Rodrigues. She was being brought to our house from her family's planta-tion in Pernambuco on the northern shore of the São Francisco river. Sometime in the morning or early afternoon, one of our slaves would come running to say that he had seen them making their way towards our house in a glorious procession of horses, palanquins and hammocks borne by slaves. Well, that was something to wake up for, too. A procession. I have always enjoyed the dignified spectacle of a procession. I wondered what my father's thoughts were at that moment, whether he looked forward to a fresh fifteen-year-old virgin to give him more sons. I did not mean to be disrespectful to my father by imagining him in bed with his new wife, for the truth is that I was at that age when I could not see a married couple but the first thought I had was how the two would look together in bed; and I spent much of my time reflecting on how to contrive my own first experience, and the notion that anyone else, even my father, might be exercising as a matter of course what to me would be as momentous an occasion as a comet appearing in the skies to an astronomer preoccupied me with an engrossing fascination. My elder brother, Antônio, was no help at all. He was the one who had first told me about it when I was eleven, and whenever I asked him to help me get a slave girl, all he said was: 'Go try it on a hen first.'

Well, I had tried it on a hen. I had even tried it on a cow. While nature may be infinite in its scope, it imposes limits on boys eager to experiment. The hen was a mess. It struggled, trying to flutter its wings; it cackled so loudly I thought it was going to lay an egg right on the tip of my cock – not a fully developed egg either but one of those half-formed, quivering, yellow, red-veined balls you discovered in a hen when you slaughtered one – and in that moment I had the stupid fear that this little naked egg, translucent as a marble, would be stuck to my cock forever as a fit punishment for my sin and I imagined (in the same awful moment of the hen's cackling) a conversation with my future wife – Is this the egg, Gregório, which will become our son? asks this white-browed virgin, and I reply: Yes, my pretty little chick. What with its cackling and its attempts to flutter its wings and with these thoughts crowding in my brain, the hen escaped at the crucial moment, leaving me clutching grey speckled feathers in my sticky and wet hand. My precocious younger brother, Francisco, who had shown me how to do it, laughed and said it would be easier with a cow. At least, he remarked with a silly grin, I would be able to *see* where to put it in. O Jesus, I thought, we have a damn joker in the family, but in my relief at having escaped the egg, I forgave him the smirk on his face, and

24

enquired more about his technique with a cow. Well, that very afternoon we went to the corral, though I wished there had been an intermediate stage, such as a dog or a goat, for going from a hen to a cow was like learning to swim in the river in the morning and jumping from a ship into the ocean in the afternoon. It was a complicated manoeuvre, but I managed it with the help of a stool the cowhands used for milking; and in case anyone is wondering whether I had an audience of cowhands, let me say that I am not an exhibitionist and that, it being afternoon, everyone was having a siesta. When I say I managed the manoeuvre, I mean I managed it up to a point: to sit in a canoe is one thing but to be able to guide it over the rapids is another, and so it was with me and the cow. For no sooner was I in than the cow decided that its digestive functioning had reached its own inner climax and needed to be purged. The shock to me of the sudden pressure and the loud splashing which followed was considerable, and I fell clumsily. I could not have fallen at a more inappropriate place – just behind the cow's hind-legs. It all happened far too quickly for me to take any sort of evasive action, and before I knew it, I was covered from head to toe in the warm, thick green liquid from the cow's bowels. For some reason, Francisco thought this was hilariously funny. I told him sternly to fetch a bucket of water, and promised him that I would relinquish to him my right to have a first go at whipping my slave when my father presented me one, and he in return promised that he would not tell Antônio of the afternoon's accident.

The stone floor was cool to touch, but its rough and uneven surface offended my eyes. I already believed that I was more advanced than my brothers in matters of taste, and was waiting for the day when my father asked me if I had a wish he could grant. Yes, father, I have a wish (I would reply with the graciousness which came naturally to me when I spoke to my father), I would like our family's honourable name – Peixoto da Silva Xavier, how gloriously beautiful it is to pronounce! – to shine from every inch of our house. I knew

25

that he would reply with such words as: That is well spoken, son, your wish is a commendable one: how can I reward you for having such noble thoughts? Well, father, I would say, it occurs to me that the beauty of our name should shine from our house, and perhaps, if the suggestion meets with your approval, you could have the floor of my bedroom resurfaced with Italian marble. Such sentiments would never occur to Antônio. He had neither the tact nor an imagination creative enough to observe that the world into which he had been born in the privileged position of the eldest son required of him a demonstration that he was capable of exercising aristocratic prerogatives. Poor Antônio, he had no subtlety at all. Francisco, whose acquisitiveness extended more to knowledge than to material things, who could in turns be secretive and expansive, was the reverse of Antônio. There must have come a time – I was certainly aware of the situation by the time I was fourteen – when I must have realized that my role as the middle brother was one of trying to maintain a tacit alliance with Antônio against Francisco and with Francisco against Antônio without either knowing the precise nature of my allegiance.

I should have known that Tana's ordering the servants to move the furniture in the verandah was not merely the continuing of the alarm she had rung to keep me awake. For – slop, splash, scrub, scrub! – they were now washing the verandah floor. I rose, for the sound of several hard brushes scrubbing a stone floor makes my teeth feel as if a lemon had been squirted on them. I put on the English foulard dressing-gown with its olive-green flowery pattern on a background of ochre – a present brought by my father from his last visit to Bahia – and opened the door.

'Well, well,' – whose voice should it be but Tana's! – 'an early riser! The moon hasn't set yet.'

I thought of countering her appalling irony with a witticism about turning the verandah into the Amazon, but spared myself the labour and, instead, indicated to Joaquim, a broad-shouldered Negro, to carry me across the filthy floor to the dining-room. I sat at my place at the corner of the long rose-wood table and, asking Joaquim to inform the kitchen that I was ready for breakfast, leaned back in the heavy, ornate mahogany chair. Streamers of coloured paper, greens and pinks mostly, hung across the ceiling from the chandelier in the centre to points where the walls and the ceiling met. My eyes lifted to watch the gay colours had the effect of uplifting my spirit, and this reminder of the double significance of the day gladdened me immensely. Presently, Joaquim returned from the kitchen – much to my surprise – and said: 'Your breakfast will be a little delayed, Gregório.'

Not every slave was permitted to address me with such familiarity; Joaquim was an exception as I had grown up in his arms and he had taught me riding and taken me fishing.

'Late?' The morning had not begun well for me, and this further little annoyance so vexed me that I could say nothing but repeat in bewilderment, 'Late?'

'Ha, but it will be worth waiting for,' Joaquim said ambiguously and went away.

For once, I was angry with Joaquim, for although I knew that he was only delivering a message, he seemed to attract the immediate abuse of my frustration. Really, I did not have all day to sit around and wait for servants to attend on me at their pleasure. I was about to rise and go to the kitchen myself to see what recalcitrance was delaying my breakfast when I heard a slight commotion outside the door. Perhaps the drowsiness was still on me and my perceptions were some-what vague; but now I woke up, for what I saw had the effect of a bucket of cold water being thrown at my face. Well, well. A little procession entered the dining-room. It was led by my father who was followed by Antônio and Francisco and by my two little sisters, Sônia and Maristela; behind them came Tana, who carried something in her hands. My father came up to me, kissed me on both cheeks, saying: 'Happy birthday, my son.' Everyone joined in a chorus of greeting me and my father, raising a hand, said: 'You know, Gregório, this is going to be a busy day for all of us.' He gave me a friendly

27

wink when he said that. 'Normally,' he went on, 'we wouldn't celebrate your birthday so early in the day, but today I thought we should share your cake as a family group before the guests begin to arrive. Tana, will you please?'

As indicated, Tana placed the cake in front of me on the table. I was struck by the peculiar shape of the cake: it was neither round nor square, but a most irregular shape. I was too overcome by the emotion my father's speech had engendered in me to connect the shape with anything I knew. I laughed and said: 'What sort of a cake is this? Did the baker's hand tremble?'

'Ah, my boy,' my father said. 'Not the baker's hand, but God's. Look, here is Pernambuco, here is Bahia, and this line of blue icing, this is the Amazon.'

I understood. The cake was shaped like the map of Brazil, what little of the country that was then acknowledged to be Brazil.

'Well, Gregório?' my father went on. 'Which territory are you going to carve for yourself, eh? We offer you the whole of Brazil.'

My father's creative thoughtfulness so impressed me and filled me with emotion that I was unable to utter any words of gratitude, and was thankful that my sisters should again be embracing me and thus saving me from the embarrassment of a moment's speechlessness. In the confusion of renewed embraces, I even permitted Tana to kiss me. Finally, when I had cut the cake and offered pieces of it to everyone, I said: 'This is the greatest moment of my life, to be sharing Brazil with you. I do not think we desecrate the name of Brazil by eating it in this fashion. On the contrary, we are committing a holy act, for our country is so sacred to us that we want it to be inside us like a holy spirit. You, father, have done me the honour of giving me Brazil. Apart from expressing my gratitude, which I do sincerely even though my words are clumsy since I do not have your gift of speech, what can I say? I am overawed, overwhelmed by what you have given me. Here we sit sharing a piece of cake; but how can we share Brazil? We

28

can share it by saying that we believe in its future. The true meaning of share in this case is not to take and divide, but to arrive at a common agreement, that is, to share a belief, to proclaim that we believe in Brazil and will labour with what strength God has given us to perpetuate the greatness that is Brazil.'

My father led the applause when I had made this short statement of thanks, and I could see that Antônio was feeling quite uneasy while Francisco was quietly smiling to himself.

'Enough, enough!' my father exclaimed. 'You'll have us weeping soon! And this is no day for tears.'

Embracing me once more, he left the room with Tana to attend to the preparations. I would have loved to have spent the rest of the morning amusing my sisters, but I had no intention of having my brothers for company as well, for, although I do not deliberately avoid them and, indeed, often spend whole days with them, on this morning I was in no mood for Francisco's subtle tomfoolery and for Antônio's guileless aggressiveness. So, saying that I must have a bath and change, I left, thus foregoing my breakfast. The unexpected event of the cake had made me exceedingly happy, so much so that although the verandah was still wet and Joaquim was within hailing distance, I did not call upon him to ferry me across but used my own two feet to transport myself to my room.

I preferred to take my bath without the assistance of a slave – a sacrifice I felt compelled to make in order to save myself the embarrassment of allowing my nudity to be gazed at by a being with whom my relationship had necessarily to be that of haughty superiority. And that was difficult for me in those early years when privacy was invariably an occasion for participating in the procedures of adolescent ritual. On this morning, however, my mind was too preoccupied with my family relationships for the usual bodily wastage to take place. It pleased me – and yet filled me with anxiety – that my father should pay me the special attentions which he clearly neglected to do to Antônio and Francisco. I was certain that Antônio did not have the intelligence to perceive the peculiar family politics of which he must be the ultimate victim; but there was no doubt that Francisco, young though he was, not only saw what was happening but also had a clear notion of what it indicated. I hoped, however, that I overestimated Francisco's mind; that his jealousy would not be provoked provided he could be led to believe that he, in his turn, would receive special favours from my father.

After my bath, I decided to dress myself simply, and chose to wear a white cotton shirt the simplicity of which seemed to be emphasized by the adornment of Belgian lace at the collar and the cuffs. While I was putting on a pair of beige coloured drill trousers and, looking at my young man's appearance in the mirror, mentally congratulating the tailors of Bahia for accomplishing the difficult art of modifying European sartorial style for a tropical climate, I realized that I had not had breakfast. The cake had provided a wonderful and a memorable occasion to my mind, but my poor stomach did not care to be a witness to noble and holy sentiments. I walked down the verandah, which was now both clean and dry, in the direction of the kitchen, intending to order a servant to prepare me a dish of ham and fried tomatoes and make me a glass of hot milk. While I walked, I debated whether I should ask for two or three pastries filled with apricot jelly to follow the ham, but remembering that there were many rich dishes and delicacies to come on this day, decided that it would be wise to keep in reserve the better part of my appetite. As it turned out, I might as well not have thought of breakfast, for I heard a voice call my name. It was a girl's voice, sweet as an angel's. It was the elder of my two sisters, Sônia.

'Gregório!' she called from across the courtyard. 'The procession is coming!'

I ran towards her while she continued to say, 'I was coming to fetch you. Everyone's gathered outside the gate. My, how handsome you look! Didn't you hear the chapel bell ringing?'

I kissed her on the cheek and, holding her hand, walked

excitedly towards the gate under the harsh sunlight.

By the time we reached the gate, I was sweating and breath-less. We could hear the band playing before we reached the gate, and now saw the band ranged in two rows beside the entrance, the brass instruments glinting in the sun. The sweaty faces of the Negro players were comical as their cheeks puffed and blew. The wedding party was entering the house through these two rows of the players. My father stood greet-ing the visitors; some he greeted with a smile and a nod, some he embraced with loud words of welcome, and others he shook warmly by the hand. Slaves carrying palanquins put down their loads one by one. More guests emerged from the palanquins, parting the brocade or velvet or silk curtains under the awnings which had protected them against the sun and stepping out to the bright and now increasingly gay and colourful world. One of these was my father's prospective father-in-law, José Jerônymo Rodrigues, a man of my father's age except that his hair had turned grey at the temples and that, unlike my father, he had a moustache which covered his mouth giving him a grave air of weighty responsibility. Coming out of his palanquin, he flung his arms apart and approached my father with a generous gesture of affection. The two men embraced in a warm display of cordiality. At this point two slaves brought in and placed on the ground one more palanquin, and what a wonderful sight it was! The pure white silk of its awning with a border of flowers in the finest gold thread dazzled the eye; the arms of the palanquin, made of brasilwood and varnished until the wood seemed to be soaked in amber, were tipped with ivory; on the exposed part of the frame, just below the line of the curtain, oval pieces of jade had been inlaid into the polished brasilwood. For a moment, everyone's attention was held by this heavenly sight; and then we heard Mr Rodrigues say to my father, 'Look, what a prize I bring for you. Let me welcome to your arms and to your house, my daughter Augustina.' He stepped towards the palanquin and, parting the curtain, gently put a hand in and presently guided his daughter out. What I noticed

31

first of all about her was the blonde hair, for she hung her head down in her nervousness; next, I noticed how small she was and realized that I was a little taller than my new mother. She looked up shyly revealing a face white, smooth and innocent as ivory. She had thin lips and a small nose which was rounded at the tip and her eyes – O my happy father! – her eyes were blue. I could see that my father was deeply overcome by her beauty and I could sense that the hush which had descended upon the company, although the band still played on noisily and merrily, was the direct impact of this frail, beautiful young girl who seemed to come not out of the palanquin but out of some dream. My father bowed to her and again she hung her head down. At this point, meticulous as a master of ceremonies, Joaquim made a sign to the band and it began to proceed towards the chapel, playing a jolly marching rhythm.

The visit to the chapel was to say a mass as an expression of gratitude to the Almighty for having ensured that Mr Rodrigues and his party had had a safe journey across two hundred miles of Pernambuco and Bahia. I will not attempt to describe the religious service, for frankly I remember nothing of it since I spent the entire time in the chapel looking at our guests, especially, of course, at Augustina. Was there anyone in the chapel who did not furtively or openly stare at her? The Lord forgive me for what sins my mind committed in his presence. The chapel had always had the curious effect of persuading me that there existed outside it a world offering a multitude of delicacies to the sinful appetite; especially when I was at confession, recounting such peccadilloes as having used banana skin in the exercise of erotic experiment, especially at these moments when the worst sin I could confess to was embarrassingly trivial, I thought of the great potential of serious sins which awaited my excited participation. Later in life, I once argued with a priest that the Church's insistence that one confess one's sins made one think about sin in general and led one to dwell on sins one had not committed which had the effect, finally, of making the mind regard with a keen interest the subtle gradations of various sins – the mind now cuddling fantasies of lechery and now daring itself to contemplate the grosser acts of corruption and evil. As if an abstract notion of sin existed like a kept woman whose existence one did not acknowledge publicly and in whose arms one longed to be when away from her. Looking from one to the other of the assembled guests that morning, I wondered if anyone else's mind wandered from its devotions to have thoughts like mine. My eyes fell on the image of Saint Anthony, a brightly painted wooden figure whom I had always seen as a real person; his red, smiling lips, his rouged cheeks and his eyes, which, if you looked at them from any corner of the chapel, seemed to fix you with a gently expressed question, all suggested a benign forgiveness. I was happy to have Saint Anthony in the chapel, for whenever I looked at him, he seemed to say: 'Gregório, Gregório, when will you pray with me?' Now, I would whisper back, now! Excitedly, willingly. Each time this intimate dialogue took place between Saint Anthony and me, however, I found that the occasion which had brought me to the chapel – mass, or baptism or whatever – came abruptly to an end. I would shrug my shoulders at Saint Anthony and he would appear to give me a sly wink as I walked out with the rest of the gathering. As we walked out of the chapel on this morning, I wished I had had some breakfast, for I was feeling faint with hunger. Busy with my thoughts while the mass was being said, I had not realized that the oppressive atmosphere of the chapel was bringing on that peculiar weakness of the body that I feel when I have not eaten. Rising from my pew, walking down the aisle, and, finally, emerging in the burning sunlight had the effect of inducing a sudden giddiness in me, and I fell on the hard earth of the courtyard, spoiling my clean white shirt. I passed out, but noticed a second before passing out that one of the people who stood near me and looked at me with obvious compassion was Augustina. She has seen *me*! I cried to myself before I lost consciousness.

When I recovered my senses, I was in my room and Sônia

33

sat beside me holding my hand. My first thought was that I must change my clothes and join the party, and in that moment my mind ranged over the contents of my wardrobe, making a spontaneous attempt to choose a suitable shirt. I felt Sônia's hand press mine. She was obviously glad to see me return to consciousness, and I was so touched by her devotion that I, too, pressed her hand. Some feeling was mutually communicated with that brief gesture, for she quickly turned her eyes away, and I realized that my 'little' Sônia, who was not ten years old, was fast reaching womanhood and in another four or five years would be married and would be bearing her first child. I felt a profound love for her although she was only a half-sister, as was Maristela, both being the progeny of my father's second marriage.

'Sônia,' I said, moved by her devotion, 'why are you not with the wedding party?'

'You looked so pale,' she said, turning and bending towards me to place her cheek next to mine.

'I'm fine,' I said in a tone suggesting that she need not have any more concern over my condition and that she was free to withdraw, while I hoped, of course, that she would protest that I was paler than before and would press herself closer to me. 'I'm fine, you go and join them and I'll come as soon as I have changed.'

Although she was only a few years from womanhood, she was still child enough to take me at my word – whether to my regret at having been denied what further comfort she could have given me or to my relief at having been saved from a situation which might have compromised me with Saint Anthony, I was not sure which. In any case, she left, walking away lightly and spiritedly.

Well, I thought, what should I wear? The question prompted another one: What had Augustina been wearing? I had noticed her hair, her small, rounded nose, her ivory complexion; surely, I must have seen what she was wearing. It seemed important that I should remember at least the colour of what she wore – as if I wished to match with her! Oh,

34

come on, Gregório, I told myself, rising out of bed and pouring myself some water from the earthen pot on a side-table, she's come to get married to your *father* – what trick is this, Saint Anthony, my friend? – not to you! But I could not remember her dress and could it be – *You* brought her here, God – that I wished to look only at her flesh? I decided that some sort of penitence was called for after these thoughts. I could not very well wear black on my birthday, so I concluded that plain, unadorned white clothes of a coarse material would make the right gesture of atonement. To emphasize the sincerity of my decision, I promised Saint Anthony – I did not kneel down to do so (which is usually my custom when making promises to my saint) because I had barely risen on my two feet after having lain unconscious and I did not wish to risk collapsing on the stone floor – I promised Saint Anthony that I would go for a week without wearing those clothes which showed my strong physique and the delicate features of my face to advantage. What else could I promise?

I suppose I must have looked as inconspicuous as a slave in his best clothes when I joined the party, for no one noticed me enter. Several servants were going and coming, some of the guests were walking from one group of people to another, and in such a confusion, my entry attracted no attention. The party was in the principal drawing-room where the furniture had been rearranged so that three long tables, each capable of accommodating forty people, could be fitted in. It was apparent to me as soon as I entered that the feasting had commenced some twenty or thirty minutes ago – the time that I had spent in involuntary oblivion – for the guests were past the stage of formality and the empty dishes being carried out by the servants indicated that considerable quantities of food had already been consumed. The guests did not all seem content to remain in their allotted places, for some of them preferred to wander about, plate in hand, now chatting to one group and now to another.

All my thoughts about compromising my private pact with

Saint Anthony vanished when I saw the food. For what the tables had laid on them would be hard to find even in the house of the Governor General in Bahia. There were dishes made from turtles' liver and from fish; there was fresh roast beef – my father having sacrificed three of his precious cows for the occasion; and, as a further treat in beef, there was a dish of dried beef from Portugal; there was none of the daily fare of manihot and yam; the bread too was something special, being made of wheat-flour which came from Lisbon. And the variety of pastries, jellies and sweets was greater than I had ever seen. There were, too, dozens of bottles of Portuguese wine to buy which a man would need to sell three slaves if he did not have the money. I found myself a seat and began with the dried beef, soon alternating with mouthfuls of the roast beef. What a wonderful meat beef is! I wonder what happens to the teeth when they bite into beef and an exhilarating sensation is transmitted from the palate to that joyful part of the mind which applauds rare tastes. Salt pork, which is our most common meat, is too smooth; it does not have the grainy texture of beef which one can bite into, chew and swallow with a thrill. Eating that dried beef and munching the juicy, blood-rinsed roast beef, I thought how wonderful it must be to live in Portugal where one could have such a meal daily. When I had eaten a good plateful of the two meat dishes, I began to see the people around me for the first time, for hitherto I had been totally absorbed in the food. Well, right across me was my cunning little brother, Francisco; and do you think he had a kind word for me? Not at all, for he was eating away like a crazy rabbit, his eyes darting from one dish to another on the table as if he wanted to devour the lot at one go. And what do you know, eh Gregório, you're slow to catch on to these things, your advanced little brother is *drinking*. Not just taking the indulgent sip children are fondly offered by their parents, but he is actually draining great draughts of the Portuguese wine. Well, Gregório, here we go, too! So, I filled up my glass and, not being a barbarian like my brother, sipped gracefully from it before helping myself to another plateful of beef.

There was conversation around me, but I was unaware of it. We have a saying that a waterfall does not hear the rapids, and my position for some twenty minutes while I ate and drank was like that of the waterfall, for I heard nothing but my own mouth chewing the beef, legs of chicken, turtles' liver, and the sweetmeats. I even lost sight of Francisco although he sat there right in front of me, a disagreeable mass of uncouth flesh. At one moment I was aware of activity around my feet, and observed that there were some slave children dragging their naked little black bodies on the floor squabbling over bones; my father, in his generosity, permitted these children, some of whom were less than a year old, the freedom of the house on days of feasting. He was kind to the children and would often say that all the children on the plantation were his children. However, even their petty squabblings at my feet could not distract me from the sense of mission with which I was conquering the mountain of food on the table. If beef had made my palate vibrate with an ecstatic rhythm, the sweetmeats were making it dance. Of all the sweetmeats, my favourite was the one made from egg and coconut, butter and sugar. I ate so much of it – and remember now in retrospect that by the end of the meal I had lost my usually sombre sense of decorum and had begun to eat like my barbaric brother; instead of eating with proper regard to European etiquette, which my father had been at pains to teach me, I had begun to stuff my mouth with as much as possible, alternating the swallowing of solids with copious draughts of liquid in the form of the wine – well, I ate so much of the coconut sweetmeat that my teeth began to ache. I had to pause. I discovered a new thing, however: wine, which had first tasted rough had become smoother in relation to the beef; with the flavour of spiced roast beef in my mouth, the wine also became sweeter; but now that coconut, egg, butter and sugar coated my tongue and lined the rest of my mouth, the wine tasted coarser, even a little salty. This realization prompted me to try another plateful of beef to see if I could recover the smooth, sweet taste of wine. At this point there was a knocking on one of the tables, a moment's general commotion, and then a silence. I suppose it was that brief silence which made me realize for the first time that I had been surrounded by over a hundred people and wonder if many of them had been observing me eat; I hoped not, or, if they had been watching, that they had seen me at the commencement of the meal when my observance of etiquette was above reproach; or, if they had seen only the worst of my table manners, then I hoped that they had also observed that pig in front of me, Francisco, beside whose habits the revolting manner of eating of a thick-lipped, squelching-mouthed Negro would win the admiration of the Court in Lisbon.

Well, the silence was for my father who had risen to make his speech. It took me a moment to realize this, for my mouth was full of beef and all that the silence at first accomplished was to enable me to hear myself. But even at that age, I was polite enough to know when to be attentive to my elders, and so stopped eating at once and limited my indulgence to occasional sips of the wine, by now having restored myself to that degree of polished behaviour in all things which early in life I set as a standard for myself.

Addressing the guests with kind words which came as naturally to him as canoeing to Indian boys who live on the banks of rivers, my father said: 'This is a happy time for us. The Dutch have finally been kicked out of Pernambuco. The country is ours. It is a time for us to restore the damage done by the wars, and it is a time for us to rebuild our families, to make alliances to strengthen the hand of planters. But, my friends, it will reward us if we pause and reflect on what has shaped us. Let us look at the earth from which Time has scooped up the clay with which to fashion our fragile forms.'

How I loved my father's well-chosen phrases, the deliberate excellence of his speech! How I congratulated myself on having so lofty a model to imitate!

He went on: 'It was a little over a hundred and fifty years

38

ago that that brave general from Portugal, Pedro Álvares Cabral, first set foot on this country and discovered Brazil which he called the Holy Cross to add to the glorious Portuguese Empire. That is common knowledge. We honour the memory of Cabral, we applaud his valour. Each new acre of our soil which we till and plant with sugarcane is one more wreath respectfully and affectionately laid at Cabral's tomb. If Cabral magically and miraculously – but in a sense which to us is real and true – conjured Brazil out of the great ocean like a dream to fire the imagination of Portugal, then it has been the ordinary Portuguese who, pursuing that dream, has made a reality of it. We must applaud those humble peasants and artisans and merchants who sailed down the Tagus, abandoning the centuries-old settled ways because their eyes saw a horizon which seemed to be a vision of the gates of heaven. One such soul, possessed of the fire of this vision, was my dear and beloved father. Some fifty-five years ago he left his native Algarve and sailed down the Tagus. It was the year of new hope, for it was the dawn of a new century, and what expectations do not people build at times when the Christian calendar suggests a moment in history when a fresh beginning may be made? The year 1600 filled my father with an optimism which he had never experienced before. He used to tell me about Sagres, the little town from where he came. He used to tell me of the country around Sagres. It was a wind-swept land where even the fig trees were incapable of supporting themselves but had to lean heavily as if they would flee from the wind. He used to tell me of the ocean, the same ocean which so tenderly kisses the shores of Brazil, how it flung its fury at the rocky coastline of Cape Saint Vincent. My father had been a fisherman. He had challenged the ocean's fury with his wits and with the strength of his body until the tragic day when the ocean plucked one of his companions from the boat, sucked him into its all-devouring mouth. My father had been a farmer, he had cultivated rice on a small plot of land until a year of drought turned his land as hard as baked clay. And so he chose Brazil. I bless his memory for the choice he made. He could have chosen India or Africa, but he chose Brazil. And this is why I recall his sacred memory now, on this sacred day. We, many of us here, are Brazilian-born. Brazil is our country, and we must honour our ancestors who gave us this wonderful gift.'

A spontaneous burst of applause obliged my father to pause. I took the opportunity to put a dainty little sweetmeat with a dried apricot at its centre into my mouth and to reflect that my father was speaking to me. He was telling me who I was and, in recounting his memory of his father, he was indicating his relationship with me.

He silenced the continuing applause by raising a hand, and resumed his speech: 'In this sense, those of our ancestors who came here and put the land to use were Brazilians before they were Portuguese. Lest I am misinterpreted, let me declare that I have the highest regard for the Crown, and that in talking of ourselves as Brazilians I do not imply disrespect to the rights of the Crown. I am not, as is the habit of planters, grumbling about the taxes.'

There was laughter at this point, for the elderly men among the guests enjoyed the reference to their own favourite topic of conversation.

'No. I am loyal to the Crown and will, if necessary, swear my loyalty in front of the bishop of Bahia. What I mean, however, when I say that our ancestors were Brazilians and that we are Brazilians, is that a man belongs to the land he cultivates. Alas, I cannot say that of the most recent arrivals from Portugal, the *mascates*. They think that by acquiring a little wealth by being money-lenders and middlemen they can call the tune. They think the land belongs to them because a few landlords owe them money, never realizing that the land can only belong to those who have given it their labour, that the land can never be bought. My friends, let us never forget our prominent position in the society which we have created, a position which God has seen fit to favour us with.'

There was more applause which compelled my father to remain standing silently for a moment or two. Certainly, he could not have expected his criticism of the *mascates* to have been met with silence, for there must have been among the guests planters who were being harassed by these middlemen and money-lenders, and, certainly, everyone present was aware of the growing conflict with the *mascates* who were being talked about as though they were a type of despicable foreign invader. I noticed, however, that one man, Domingos Cardoso, who sat a few places from my father, clapped his hands very softly, seeming rather to go through the motion of doing so than actually giving the expressed sentiment his wholehearted approval; his eyes looked down gravely, and perhaps it was the ugly wart on his right cheek which stuck there like a fly sitting on a rotten mango that bothered him.

My father went on: 'Not only must we not forget our position in the society of Brazil, but also we must take care to protect and promote this position. That is why this marriage is important. We are uniting two established families; we are strengthening that class of people which can be called the original Brazilians. Sometimes, when I am out in the fields, observing the slaves at work, I have a vision of the Brazil of the future. A land, a mighty land which extends from the great Amazon in the north to the Rio de la Plata in the south, a land conquered, subdued and settled, a land divided into plantations. For how can a country prosper unless its resources are put at the disposal of those who can best exploit them? And who are they, but the planters? And in my vision of the future of Brazil, I see the land in the hands of its rightful owners, our sons and our grandsons, and so on for generation after generation. Marriage, my friends, is an important and a sacred institution which we must employ in the creation of true Brazilians of tomorrow. That is why I began by saying that this is a happy time, a happy day for us.'

My father sat down while the applause rang loudly through the room. Well, it was a wonderful speech to make on his wedding day, I thought to myself as my eyes fell on his bride who sat two places from him, the intermediate place being taken by her father. I realized that it was the first time that I

41

had seen her since entering the room, and I wondered at my father's calm self-control, the poised dignity of his bearing in her presence. How those blue eyes flashed across the room! I was convinced that had I been in my father's position, I would not have invited all those guests or, had custom obliged me to do so, I would have gone peremptorily through the ceremony of feasting so that I could be alone with the soft-cheeked, thin-lipped Augustina to see if she were indeed made of flesh and bone and was not an apparition. But, Gregório, what thoughts are these? Look, Saint Anthony, I had no such thoughts for a good hour, an *hour*, for I ate and drank and listened attentively to my father's wonderful speech. Will that hour cross out a minute's evil in my mind? Help me, Anthony, my friend, my saint.

At this point a strange thing happened. I was leaning back in my chair, the glass of wine in my hand. With the chair lifted on its two hind legs like a playful horse, I brought the glass to my mouth to take another sip. At the final moment, the glass slipped out of my hand, and in that panic which comes over us when we drop something, I lost balance. The chair tipped back and I crashed against the floor, my head banging rather nastily on the hard stone surface and my shins knocking against the table. What seemed to amuse me as I fell was the fleeting sight of my stupid brother, Francisco, who had obviously drunk too much and whose head had collapsed on the table, his mouth open and secreting the messy saliva of a silly child. Well, I collapsed and passed out. I did not go completely unconscious at once, for I could hear people around me. Someone said: 'Poor Gregório, first sunstroke and now he's drunk.' I could not distinguish who it was that made this unconsidered statement although, forcing my eyes open, I saw blurred images of people, and nor could I identify the voice, for I wanted badly to tell him that I was not drunk, that it was just an accident that I fell back. Some-one else said: 'We'd better carry the poor fool to his room.' And another: 'Pity, he's going to miss the ceremony.' And yet another: 'Ceremonies mean nothing to children.'

I would have liked to have known who this pompous fool was, for I would have liked to have told him what I thought of adults who considered young men to be children. Well, soon they were carrying me out. I wanted to protest that nothing was the matter with me, but, hard though I tried to kick my legs and to flail my arms, my body seemed to have gone dead. The next thing I knew was that they had dropped me into my bed, and left me alone there. For a few minutes I thought I was going crazy with anger at the foolishness of adults, for the room seemed to be spinning round and round, but then soon I fell asleep.

How long I slept, I could not discover since I did not know at what time I had fallen asleep; but somehow I managed to dissipate the major part of the afternoon in a state of total oblivion. When certain indistinguishable noises outside my room scratched at the window-panes of my mind, making, as it were, a little opening for some light to tinge the opaque unconsciousness of my sleep – ha! do I use these words now or did I command them then, learning a graceful fluency from my father? – I half opened my eyes and remained as I was, unmoving in bed. I could not tell for some time whether it was morning and the noises which I heard were the usual morning ones, and it was not till I realized that I was fully dressed that I recalled the circumstances which had brought me to my room. Now I became aware of a heavy dizziness in my head and attributed it to my excessive consumption of beef and the coconut sweetmeats. I could feel the food rise in me and induce a nauseous flavour in my mouth. My tongue was dry. I reached for a glass of water from my bedside table and just at the moment when I had picked up the glass, the door opened and my father entered, leading his bride by the hand.

'Ah, still drinking, eh, Gregózinho?' he remarked. 'Well, don't you have anything to say to your new mother?'

I swallowed some water clumsily, spilling some of it on my shirt-front, an action most untypical of me, and I regretted the fact that it should have happened in front of Augustina.

43

I was sorry, too, that she should see me in the state I was in – my clothes crumpled, my hair no doubt in a mess, and now here was this water beginning to trickle down my chest. I tried to say something, but my tongue, which had always served me well in the expression of melodious sentiments, seemed suddenly to be made of lead.

'You see, Augustina, how spoiled my children are?' my father remarked to my dismay. 'See what's happened to them while they've lacked a mother. They've become ill-mannered drunkards. They don't have the grace to rise and bow when their parents come to their room.'

Augustina smiled coyly and did not herself say anything. I hoped she realized that my father meant to be witty with his remarks which, surely, he could not have intended her to take seriously. He spoke on: 'This wastrel here, Gregório we christened him even though he's given every indication of being nothing more than a pagan barbarian, a horrible heathen in matters of religion, he's the second son. He's as vain as a peacock and as wilful as a canoe in the rapids. But I love him. He's the future of Brazil. Sons, Augustina, sons is what this country needs.'

Well, I was touched by this speech, and was particularly glad that my father should refer to the care I took over my appearance and that he should think that my character possessed the important quality of determination.

'And do you know,' my father proceeded to speak to Augustina, 'it is this scoundrel's birthday today? Well, why don't we give him a surprise? Go send for one of the boys among the slaves you've brought with you. We'll present him with a slave. Your gift to me will be my gift to my son. What better bond between us?'

Augustina went out for a moment during which my father peered at me anxiously as though he feared for my health, and said: 'Ha, you silly bastard!' He seemed to raise his hand as if he wished to pinch my cheek affectionately, but just then Augustina re-entered, and he turned to hold her hand. A moment later a tall Negro boy came and stood beside the door.

'Come here, boy,' my father said. 'What's your name?'

'Jari,' the boy said.

'You, Jari, are to serve this young man you see, yes that's a man all right although he looks pale as a girl. Gregório is to be your master. Yes, yes, that's him all right, don't gape, he's not dumb and deaf or an invalid, he's just drunk himself sick. And your first duty, Jari, is to throw a bucket of cold water on your incapacitated master, have him dressed, get him some food if he can bear to eat any, and then bring him to the dance.'

As soon as he was left alone with me, Jari, following my father's instructions literally, went and fetched a bucket of water and flung its cold contents at my face before I, who had been hypnotized into inaction and disbelief by this idiot's not being able to see a joke, could take any evasive action. The water certainly had the effect of making me jump up and of releasing my tongue from the weight which had held it.

'You damn fool,' I shouted, rising and slapping him across the face, 'don't you know that was meant as a joke?'

He hung his head down in shame, and to impress him with my authority, I slapped him once more. Just then another idiot arrived on the scene, my brother Francisco who had the catlike capacity of appearing unexpectedly at places, especially where he was not wanted.

'I heard you've been given a slave,' he said, smiling and looking at Jari as though he were measuring him up for some dark purpose.

'So?' I said, suggesting what did it have to do with him.

'I just remembered the cow,' he said.

'What cow?'

'The same cow,' he said.

'Oh, *that* cow,' I said, remembering my promise to him.

'Well, shall we do it now? He might as well get it over with.' I must admit that I was not unexcited by the notion of administering a whipping to my slave, and agreed though not without taking a moment to ponder the question so that it

45

would be clear to Francisco that I made my decisions for myself.

A few minutes later, the three of us were standing outside the stables, having picked up a whip of tapir hide. Jari was beginning to whimper and was holding his arms tightly against his sides as if he wished to disembody himself from his back.

'Since he's my slave, I make the rules,' I said to my demented brother.

'No backing out now, Grego,' he said. 'You wouldn't want Antônio to laugh at you, would you?'

'Look, Francisco, I'll whip you first before I let you whip Jari if you speak like that. Remember what I promised. I promised that I'd let you be the first one to whip my slave. That's all I promised. And now I'm keeping my promise. Here is the whip. But wait, listen to my instructions first. You may give him one lash, no more. And your lash must be such that no mark should appear on Jari's back.'

I gave him the whip, which he took, and, turning his face away from me, spat into the earth, saying, 'That's going to be a great thrill, to whip without drawing blood. That's not what I mean by whipping. And I know that that's not what you mean by whipping either.'

'I'm keeping my promise, that's all.'

Meanwhile, Jari was observing the two of us with a mixture of fear, hatred and profound interest. His jaw sagged and moved nervously as though he were shivering.

'I whip as I want to whip, even if it's one stroke,' said my stubborn brother.

'No, you don't,' I said. 'You don't have to prove you're a barbarian, I know that already.'

'That's an insult,' he said.

'That's the damned truth,' I remarked casually.

'Why you . . .' he shouted and was lost for words as a rage overcame him. In his rage, he raised the whip and made to strike me with it. His sleepy alligator's eyes seemed to open suddenly and become the searing green eyes of a jaguar as he swiftly moved to strike me. At this moment, Jari, perhaps seeing a chance of salvation for himself, or perhaps taking an early opportunity to show his loyalty, leaped on him, gripped his wrist and attempted to release the whip from Francisco's enraged grip. Francisco had that temporary strength which comes from strong emotion and struggled with the larger and more powerful Jari for a moment or two. But Jari, supple-bodied and skilled in the art of physical combat, knocked Francisco over with the elementary device of inserting his right leg between Francisco's legs from behind and levering him off the ground with a deft flick. Francisco fell and dropped the whip and Jari, picking it up with one swoop of his body, handed it to me. Francisco lay on the ground, quivering with anger and seemingly on the verge of tears.

'Serve you right,' I said, 'trying to strike your elder brother. As for you, Jari, it is my duty to thank you for protecting me from my enemies. But wait, there's no need to start kissing my feet. It is also my duty to punish you for having taken the liberty of attacking my brother. Go and stand against that wall and be ready to be whipped.'

Jari went obediently and, I detected, proudly, for he recognized that I was a just master whom it was his privilege to serve. I could see that Francisco, too, was impressed, and as I walked towards Jari, Francisco followed me. I gave Jari three lashes of moderate strength. I did not draw blood, for I did not wish to hurt him. The three clear white lines which appeared across his back, however, evidenced that I had inflicted upon him just the right amount of severity so that he would not think that I was a weakling: so that he would know my potential strength and at the same time have a measure of my compassion. Francisco watched me with obvious envy, and I recognized that in spite of his subtlety he was still a child in that his emotions shifted from moment to moment depending on what he looked at or experienced. Feeling sorry for him, I said: 'All right, Francisco, don't ever say I was unkind to you. Here's the whip. Go on.'

For a moment, he could not believe that I could be so kind

47

to him. And then, taking the whip, he swung it at Jari's back. It was a weak and an ineffectual stroke.

'Come on,' I said, 'what's this? You're not taking a mule to the fair. Go on, whip him properly. Look, you don't have to swing your bloody arm as if you're throwing a stone into the river. Use your wrist, let the power come from your wrist and forearm.'

'Enough,' cried Jari who had begun to sob.

'You'd better shut up before I give you three more,' I said to him.

But Jari had collapsed and was crawling towards me.

'I shan't warn you again, you black bastard, stand up and take your beating, or I'll give it to you properly this time.'

'O master . . .' he moaned, clutching my ankles and beginning to wet my feet with his slobbering lips.

'No, none of this nonsense,' I said, kicking at his jaw so that he recoiled, involuntarily drawing away his hands from my ankles to hold his jaw. 'Go on, Francisco, beat the bastard while he's grovelling in the dust.'

'No, no,' cried the stupid black.

'Go on, Francisco.'

Francisco raised the whip and cracked it down on Jari's back while he was on his knees. As the whip touched him like a stroke of lightning, his knees gave way and he fell on his stomach.

'Go on, go on, one more.'

Francisco, as if he had discovered a new pleasure, cracked the whip once more.

'That's a perfect one,' I applauded him.

'Yeah, that felt good,' Francisco said.

Together we pulled Jari up on to his feet and helped him into the house. Francisco quickly found an excuse to leave me alone with my slave, and this was a typical trick of my crafty little brother, for he no doubt anticipated that I might ask him to help wash Jari's back and rub some ointment on it. Well, I let him go, considering that I had taught him a thing or two about the proper use of authority. As for Jari, I was

48

anxious for him to know that he had not been beaten for an offence but that the beating had been a necessary initiation to establish the master-slave relationship which would exist between us until that day when I gave him his freedom. Had I beaten him for some crime, I would not only have been more severe but I would also have left him to recover by himself; in short, I would have abandoned him to his deserved suffering until he came to me offering me his life if I did not forgive him. But the light-hearted whipping which he had now received was a sport which it was my privilege to exercise; and therefore, it was my duty, when the game was done, to help him recover from what little pain he had had to endure. I was impressed by the manner in which he participated in the sport; his whimpering, his slobbering at my feet, his tears were all authentic. I knew that I could trust him.

I washed Jari's back with a wet towel. He cringed, arching his back when he felt the pressure of my hand behind the towel.

'Come on,' I said, 'this is nothing.'

'You were good, master,' he said. 'You had a firm stroke.'

'Firm, but not vicious,' I warned him. 'Remember that the firmness can take on a terrible power. Remember that before you attempt something stupid.'

'Yes, master,' he said. 'You had a beautiful stroke.'

I applied the ointment to his back, strongly rubbing it in, and said: 'Now, you can wear your shirt and go to find something to eat. Since it's my birthday, you can have a free evening. But tomorrow morning, I want you outside my door at sunrise whether I'm awake or not. Tomorrow I'll tell you your duties.'

As I washed myself and debated what I should wear, it occurred to me that one way or another I had missed the most important events of the day, especially the wedding. Well, I resolved, deciding to wear a brocade tunic over simple cotton trousers, I should make amends by giving a good account of myself at what remained of the festivities.

And what remained was the best part, the dance. I suppose

49

that when I walked into the drawing-room, where a band of five Negroes played a lilting tune, I must have looked as conspicuously elegant as a swan gliding up a river on which the other creatures are mere ducks, for I noticed that several eyes were turned towards me. A number of couples were dancing with an air of solemnity, the most graceful among them Augustina's two elder sisters and their well-groomed husbands. Before I could find a suitable partner, a hand touched my shoulder and a voice said: 'Well, if it isn't young Gregório, at last!'

I turned round and saw that I was being addressed by Mr Rodrigues, Augustina's father. There must have been a momentary look of puzzlement on my face, for he said: 'You are Gregório, are you not? The second son?'

I did not like that, the second son; but I supposed he needed to identify me somehow, and therefore hoped that he did not intend the definition to imply any diminishing of my status. My doubts, however, were soon dispelled, for as I smiled assent to his question, Mr Rodrigues went on: 'I was certain you were Gregório although we have not been introduced. I did observe a weak young man lying in the dust outside the chapel this morning, and I also caught a glimpse of a pale looking youth collapsed on the floor at the end of lunch. But this handsome sight, this tender physique, this is something I *had* been prepared for. Yes, my boy, you are famous in my household. Whenever your father has come to pursue his wooing of Augustina, he has talked at length about you. I knew what you looked like before I saw you. But, how thoughtless of me! Let me introduce myself.'

'There is no need to, sir,' I offered gallantly. 'I would know you even if I were to encounter you in the heart of Amazonia.'

'That's well spoken, son. Although I can't think how you would do so, that's very well spoken.'

'I may not, if I encountered you in the jungle, recognize you as Mr Rodrigues, but I do not doubt that I would recognize a gentleman of aristocratic bearing, one who had brought the gift of industry to the lazy Indian tribes.'

'My word, the young man has wit! He is no mere pretty puppet.'

'I thank you, sir, though you make me vain by flattering my vanity.'

'Promise me one thing, Gregório.'

'I can promise you anything my body is capable of performing, which is to say, sir, that I cannot promise you the world.'

'Ha, you rogue, you're quick with words.'

'And my limbs, too, I hope,' I quickly added.

'Are you?' he asked, leaning back as if to scrutinize me carefully. 'No, no, you're too unmarked for me to believe you're quick with your limbs. Come, come, don't blush. But we'll soon remedy *that*.'

I knew what he was talking about, the same subject which had resulted in my making myself appear a fool in front of Francisco, the subject which was making me begin to feel ashamed of myself. To distract Mr Rodrigues from any teasing which he might commence, I said: 'You wanted me to promise something.'

'Yes. Promise me that you will visit my house.'

'It will give me great pleasure to do so.'

'Are you not curious as to why I should want to invite you particularly? For let me tell you, Gregório, that I have not extended this invitation to anyone else, certainly not to your brothers. Although I should add that any member of my son-in-law's family is certainly welcome to my house. But what I implied was that I have deliberately, after careful thought and having a good reason for doing so, invited you, that I wish you to come; whereas anyone else of your family may or may not come as he chooses: it will be my pleasure if he does, but not my loss if he does not.'

'My happiness permits no curiosity,' I said although I was desperately curious.

'That, too, is very well spoken, son. But, Gregório, I notice a lady across the room who is bored standing alone. Either you or I must go and dance with her. Shall we toss a coin to decide? Let chance make the next move between us.'

'I do not gamble with my destiny.'

'Oh, that's beautiful! In that case, my seniority will decide. The lady, Gregório, is yours!'

'It is my pleasure to obey,' I said, bowing and walking away, wondering anxiously why he had made me promise to visit him at his house. As I made my way through the dancing couples, I observed the lady with whom I had been commanded to go and dance. I did not know her name and only vaguely recognized her to be the wife of one of the guests. She was short and plump, her black hair lifted up behind her neck so that her chubby cheeks seemed positively fat. Just before I could reach her, however, I saw Domingos Cardoso, the jelly-like wart on his right cheek wobbling as he walked, step up to her and invite her for a dance. I looked back to see if Mr Rodrigues had noticed this little turn of destiny, but he had disappeared out of sight. I continued to walk in the direction of what was now a blank wall and, reaching it, stood where the lady had been standing.

The band now played a lively rhythm, and I noticed that my father, stooping graciously, for his new wife barely reached his shoulders, was leading Augustina lyrically across the floor and setting, as he did in most things, an example for those who wished to acquaint themselves with civilized elegance. Augustina had changed to a dress of purple silk which flashed, as she danced, reflections of the many-candled chandelier, so that her flowing movement across the room seemed to my astonished eyesight to be the flowing of a river which reflects fragmented sunlight. I was too absorbed in admiring this enchanting couple to entertain thoughts any more of my own keen desires or to remark to myself that my duty at that moment was to be dancing, too. Suddenly, my father stopped dancing and, clapping his hands, attracted everyone else's attention. He said nothing, but taking Augustina's left hand in his right, he extended his free hand to the lady who happened to be nearest him, and thus began the arc which soon developed into a circle of linked hands. All those who had not been dancing, joined in too, including me; the

52

band took this as a cue for really fast music, and in a moment the entire company was whirling around, pausing, whirling around in the opposite direction, pausing, clapping hands in the air, bowing now to one and now to the other partner, and thus proceeding in a most articulate confusion of beating breasts, happy faces and sweating bodies. Only one thing spoiled my own ecstasy. While Augustina's left hand was held by my father, her other hand was clasped by my elder brother, Antônio. I did not wish to deny Antônio his pleasure, but I did not like the complacent look on his face which suggested that as the eldest son he had a natural right to hold his new mother's hand. I would have liked to have believed that his presence next to her had been accidental, but I knew my brother too well to think of his actions as being the result of coincidence. Oh, he has been quite shameless in his petty expressions of power and yet he has little notion of what his position represents. For the moment, however, I was prepared to forget the indecency of his presumption that he rightfully belonged where he stood.

As if we were not sufficiently dizzy with dancing, the band suddenly changed rhythm, introducing a new and wildly exciting melody. I had never heard anything like it before. The drums seemed to predominate over the string instruments and were beaten with such a fury that I felt that the beating was a furious knocking at my heart. At first a profound giddiness overcame my spirit and then my mind seemed to clear itself of everything and there was only the wild beating, only the throbbing which was now the tensing of the veins at my temples and now the veins at my groin and now all my flesh which was bursting, alive, throbbing, throbbing. Da-da-dum, da-da-dum, da-da-dum. God, the drums were driving me mad. We all seemed instinctively to abandon our bodies to this music, we flung our arms, our legs became the wooden legs of puppets whose strings were attached to the drums. The circle disintegrated and without any formal asking and acceptance, each man had a willing, committed partner. Mine was a lady, Mrs Barballo, wife of the planter from Olinda, the distinguished José Barballo who was also a councillor of independent views. Mrs Barballo was plump, her breasts, lifted high up by her corset, appeared to wobble; her parrot's beak of a nose shone at the tip; her black hair which she had brushed so assiduously was beginning to crinkle with sweat; but she was delightful. For the moment, I loved her completely, adored even the flabby flesh of her arms as she flung them above her, for there was such a lovely twinkle in her eyes. Had I possessed the temerity or, if you like, the gross foolishness of persuading her with that language of lovers which at that time I found it impossible to utter before a woman although I often rehearsed it (most convincingly it seemed to me) when alone, had I managed to entice her out into the darkness or, better still, the privacy of my room, then I do not know what extremity of sin I would not have committed had she but only half permitted it. I would have kissed the hair under her armpits, had she wanted me to, I would have rolled my tongue over the sweat there and drawn it into my mouth. It seemed to me that her twinkling eyes had the capacity to look into my heart, or at least into my mind, for she said, sighing and for a moment letting her head collapse on my shoulder: 'This heat is too much, Gregório, I'm going to take the air in the garden for a while.' And taking her head away from my shoulder, she looked into my eyes, smiled sweetly, pressing my hand at the same time, and walked away.

Well, Gregório, what can this mean, eh? Is this how lovers in crowded company hint to each other? And if she did mean to hint, what was I supposed to do? Follow her out at once or allow a respectable interval of time to pass before doing so? I have to admit that there were many questions to which I desired an immediate answer; and, in retrospect, I must also state that youth, which is universally considered to be a wonderful time of one's life, has always seemed to me a period from which it is best to grow out as soon as nature will permit, for youth entails more frustrations, heartaches, blundering cluelessly and commitments to utter foolishness than age entails incapacity to engage in those fond activities which are supposed to come easily to youth. Well, I decided that I should follow Mrs Barballo to the garden and see whether her words had been an invitation. The dancing was proceeding with a gaiety which was becoming increasingly a general abandoned state of mind, and I slipped out unnoticed. Sufficient light fell on the garden from the lights inside the house and from our bright Brazilian stars for me to be able to distinguish the shapes in the garden. For I clearly saw two shapes which I discerned to be human beings, and, standing beside a tree, I waited long enough to be able to discover that the two shapes were those of Domingos Cardoso and José Barballo – *her* husband! They were walking up and down on the lawn and were obviously absorbed in some serious conversation. It was difficult for me to hear what they were talking about, especially as music filled the air, the windows and door being open. I picked up one or two phrases when they strolled near to where I stood but missed the real import of their expressions as they turned back to continue pacing the garden. What I picked up was to do with taxation, credit and reforming the social structure of the country. 'The landlords must learn to pay,' I heard Cardoso say. I was relieved that they were busy with such unimportant matters, for, this being so, Mr Barballo could not be aware that his wife was somewhere in the garden waiting for me. I must say that I enjoyed the irony of the situation before I began to wonder where she could be and how I was supposed to reach her without attracting the attention of the two men. I decided that the obvious thing for her to have done must have been to go as far away as possible from her husband which meant she must be among the decorative bamboo trees at the far end of the garden. I determined that I could use the cover of the trees which fringed the garden and find my way to the little bamboo grove without being seen by the two grave gentlemen. The trees which I used for cover were planted along a verandah which had behind it a number of rooms which were used mainly for guests. A little candle-light came from these rooms, but the light was not strong enough for anyone to notice that I was in the garden, whereas one or two rooms, the doors of which were open, offered me clear view of what, if anything, was happening in them. In one room I saw a Negro woman standing in the doorway talking to someone inside. I stopped but could not hear anything. Presently, the Negress went away, revealing Mrs Barballo who came up to the door, half closed it and withdrew to the room. I must have forgotten that she had said that she was going to the garden, for all I thought now was that this was her way of making me come to her and that she had obviously got rid of the Negress who no doubt attended on her. So, I leapt up the verandah and went and stood by the door, looking in without being noticed by her. She sat at a dressing-table, making up her face. This, I felt convinced, was in preparation for me; so, I let her conclude the artful prettying up of her face before making my entry. She sighed loudly, putting down a powder-puff. Poor woman, I thought, she must desperately want me to come and was about to enter when I heard footsteps in the verandah. I quickly drew back and jumped into the garden. It was the Negress returning with a jug of water in one hand and a glass in the other. It was now clear to me what had happened. Mrs Barballo had come out in the garden, and, seeing her husband, had realized the foolishness of any amorous encounter in the garden. She had then decided to go to her room where she had found her maid and consequently she had had to pretend that she had a headache and wanted to rest. Well, I thought I should wait, for she would presently send the maid away.

A few minutes later, the maid walked out and while she was closing the door after her, the light suddenly went out in the room. It occurred to me now that either Mrs Barballo took me for an experienced lover who knew the meaning of each little action or that she had indeed gone to bed without any thought of me. I must have stood there for a good ten minutes debating what I should do; and, to be quite candid, I was clueless and did not know whether I should have the temerity to fling the door open and jump into her bed – which, for all I knew, might be expected of me – or, doing so, commit a ghastly blunder in case I was not expected and so ruin my name and heap scandal on my father's house. I went up to the door and, being either courageous or insanely foolish, slowly opened it. I held it slightly ajar and listened. There came from inside the room the sound of profound and contented sleep as signified by loud and rhythmic snoring.

When I look back on that moment, I cannot help expressing relief that the decision was made for me by that appalling sound which brought to my mind a frog rather than a woman's body; for chance led me to a happier encounter that same evening.

I walked back towards the drawing-room, hoping to fare better with a new partner. My father saw me enter and called me to him. He sat at a table, Augustina beside him together with her father.

'Been out watching the cows, have you?' my father asked.

'No, sir,' I replied, 'merely seeing if some of our guests who find it more congenial to be in the garden did not need any refreshment.'

'Good lad,' he said. 'Well, you can do a little job for your mother. Go to Aurelia, that good-for-nothing Negress I've presented to Augustina with the hope that she might learn some manners from her new mistress if not also the meaning of work, go and tell her that she need not sit up for her mistress, that she is excused for this one night. And I suggest you better go to bed after that.'

I wished them all good-night and withdrew, regretting that I could not dance any more that night. As I was turning away, I thought I saw my father turn to Mr Rodrigues and wink at him. Well, even if he did wink, it did not signify anything, for my father is a man of a great sense of humour and will make a joke of anything.

I went and found Aurelia. She had a small, windowless room to herself, and she was sitting on the edge of her bed sewing buttons on a dress. She was squinting at the dress, for there was only one candle in the room and that, too, was behind her back.

'My mother won't need you tonight,' I said to her.

'Who will then?' she called back, and I realized how right my father was about her bad manners.

'What do you mean?' I asked with some severity in my tone.

'Am I needed or not?' she asked, and there was a laughter in her voice.

'Don't be bloody stupid,' I said. 'The message is quite simple. My mother won't need you, that's all.'

She fell back on to the bed, laughing softly, and then sat up again, saying, 'Who will need me?' And laughed some more, a little hysterically this time.

'What's the matter with you?' I asked as she fell back again.

Tired of this silly game, I was about to leave when I saw her for the first time. So far I had looked at a Negress slave, a maidservant whose function in life was to attend upon my mother. Now I saw *her*, the young woman. I was standing in the doorway and seeing her laugh, I shut the door behind me, and said: '*I* need you.'

She stopped laughing. She put her sewing away under the bed and stood up. She placed her hand on my shoulder, felt the stiff texture of my brocade tunic, and passed her hand down my back, coming closer to me so that her breasts touched my ribs.

'First of all,' she whispered in my ear, 'we shall have to see if it is a *man* that needs me.' And she put her hand on that place where my boyhood had suddenly grown into the hardness of a lusting man.

Chapter 2

A HEROIC PERFORMANCE

The chapel bell was ringing so loudly that in my disturbed sleep I wondered what day it was, whether it was some feast day when the chaplain would call the world to rise and genuflect before the glorious memory of some saint. But it was scarcely daylight outside and ardent though our chaplain was to take every opportunity to impress us with his zealous piety, it was too early even for him to be calling the house to some service. Father Soares was a hard man on those among us who showed signs of slacking in our public expression of religious fervour, but he admitted that God who designed that man should partake of fowl, fish and beast could surely not penalize man for the heavy slumber that befell upon him as a consequence. Father Soares always praised God for the meat he was served and, one hand stroking his paunch and the other held in front of his yawning mouth, invariably rose from the table – whether after lunch or dinner – to retire immediately to his bedroom. The bells were maddeningly loud. I turned my head so that I could bury one ear in the pillow and was about to put my hand to the other ear when an arm rubbed across my shoulder and a hand clasped my ear. Jesus! Where was I?

For a moment I panicked but with my usual self-control did not utter a sound. Then a voice whispered, *Aaah!*, a long drawn-out sigh, and I realized that I was, of course, in the embrace of the muscular, smooth-skinned arm of Aurelia. Outside the bells continued to ring loudly and urgently. Aurelia pressed herself closer to me as though wanting to protect me. I slid down the bed a little so that my head was at

59

the level of her bosom and, pressing myself there, I succeeded for a moment or two to close my ears to the ringing bells. I felt as though we were lovers of acquaintance far longer than a night's duration. I felt quite at home there pressed against the warm breasts, one nipple squashed against my cheek. I have never described to anyone my first night with a woman, and I must say that I have no intention of ever doing so. It is not that I cherish it as a particularly private experience, for I have to admit that neither the hen nor the cow nor all my fantasies had quite prepared me for this night's encounter. And as a boy what do you do with your shame when at the woman's first touch you come bursting out with your damn pants still on? But Aurelia was kind; she was generous and understanding. Among her many felicities was her subtle use of her tongue along the sensitive veins, an action which had the same effect as a snake-charmer's pipe which roused a limp snake out of its basket – as I had heard Veríssimo, a soldier in my father's service, describe when talking of his days in India. And, with her tongue there, I would have burst out again into the empty air, had she not quickly jerked her head away, withdrawing that delicious hot breath of hers, and asked if I wanted a glass of water. With all her art, whether employing her hands, her mouth or her breasts, with all her guile, sighing now and now talking of something frivolous with which to distract my impatience, she guided my inexperienced fumbling and made out of it the calculated moves of a sophisticated lover.

She moved, and the squashed nipple against my cheek fell against my mouth. The chapel bell still rang furiously outside and I could also hear people running around and shouting to one another; the sounds, however, were of confusion, and although I was curious to know what was happening, to ask me at that moment to take my mouth away from the munificence offered it would have been like asking me to give up breathing. Aurelia raised her head a little to observe me at her breast. The little light which came from the chinks in the shut door was sufficient to give an outline to her face and for

60

there to be a gleam in her eyes. She had a Negress's perfect white teeth, but her hair, being masses of thick waves rather than tiny curls, suggested that an alien blood had entered her ancestry at some stage. The confusion outside was intensifying and I could hear some of the shouts clearly. 'Get all the men out,' came one cry several times. At one moment I thought I heard my father shout: 'Wake up all of them, we need every man and boy.' And then I clearly heard him call across some space: 'Antônio, you come, too, and I want those lazy brothers of yours. Time you learned what life is all about. Go on, hurry.' In the meantime, I had moved up from Aurelia's breast and was kissing her with the passion of a soldier who must leave his beloved and go to war. I pulled myself upon her, but she delayed me, teaching me the ecstasy of postponement. The bell was ringing more furiously than ever; the shouting seemed so universal that it was impossible to hear what was being said; there were people running around; there was a noise of doors being banged upon, and, seemingly far away, the cries of animals – or, at least, what appeared to be animals. Aurelia probably realized that the circumstances were not propitious for me to learn the delights of postponement, that lovely lingering that maddens the body and exhilarates the mind, and took me in. Her mouth was open wide and seemed to be devouring the area between my upper lip and the tip of my chin, her tongue strong against the roof of my mouth; her woman's smell, with the night's sweat potent on her, enchanted my nostrils, a smell so animalistic that I found it a wonderful stimulant. Just when I was about to discharge, I heard a woman's voice outside ask: 'What's going on?' A man answered: 'A battle, there's an invasion of Indians.'

I passed out at the mention of Indians. Aurelia held me in her embrace for a few minutes and then eased my weight off her body and, picking up a rag, cleaned herself. I felt drowsy and weak.

'Aren't you going to help?' she asked. 'My strong hero?'
'Eh?'

'Come on, let me help dress you.'

A few minutes later, conspicuously dressed in my brocade tunic, I willed myself to walk out. The purplish eastern sky was turning pink, I noticed, and even that weak intensity of light hurt my eyes. My legs seemed sore and so lacking in strength that I found it difficult to walk with any firmness. The people who had been running around outside the room had all disappeared in the direction of the main gate from where all the noise was coming now. I decided that I should go to my room and change into something more suitable for the battle.

The effort of walking to my room fatigued me greatly. I simply had to rest. Entering my room, I quietly closed the door behind me and threw myself on the bed. I hit my face against something hard which I soon realized was the hipbone of someone lying in my bed, and this someone, I immediately realized, was a woman. While I instinctively put a hand to my forehead, which had taken the worst of the blow, the woman rose, holding her hip and giving out a short scream. The woman – help me, Saint Anthony! – was Mrs Barballo.

I must admit that the first thought I had was that she better know some subtler method than Aurelia's way of snake-charming me into erectness. But Mrs Barballo grabbed hold of my shoulders and began to cry.

'I'm sorry,' I said. 'I didn't know there was anyone here.'

'Oh, it's Gregório!' she exclaimed, seeming to recognize me for the first time, and began to sob profusely.

'Why, did you expect anyone else?' I asked, wondering if there were not some mistake, but telling myself nevertheless that she was experienced enough to know what she was doing. All that business about going to the garden and then to her room had been a clever ploy, I now thought. But I was glad that I had not gone into her room, for coming from Aurelia to Mrs Barballo now revealed the latter's ugliness to which I had made myself blind while dancing with her. Ah, Gregório, you're learning quickly! I must say that I hated Mrs Barballo while she held on to my shoulders and wept, for she seemed

62

to me to be guileless, tactless and even crudely selfish, coming to my room and waiting up for me. Why should she assume that I wanted to make love to her? As if I were a plaything for her, a willing instrument for the satisfaction of her lust! She must be desperate, I thought, endangering her marriage and her honour – and as my father's guest, too!

'Oh, I've had a terrible night,' she said. 'Simply ghastly.'

'I'm sorry,' I said.

'Why did you come?' she asked, suddenly stopping to weep.

'What do you mean?' I asked, glad that she had withdrawn.

Two thoughts occurred to me. One, that she might not know that this was my room – which had this puzzling implication: how was I to discover where I should find her? And two, she knew it was my room and that implied that she had come here expecting me and, not finding me, would want to know where I had spent the night. I must say I wished I had joined the battle in my brocade tunic.

'I'm sorry I disturbed your sleep,' I said as a kind of hypothetical answer, an experiment intended to discover what the hell was going on between Mrs Barballo and me.

'That's all right, Gregório,' she said. 'I'm glad to have someone to talk to. What was all that noise about just now? Never mind. It's over now. There's always some noise in the world. People must have something to shout about. You don't understand this, my boy. But there's a lot of shouting in this world. My husband is a great shouter. You think it's fun being married to a councillor in Olinda? I can never shut my ears enough. Last night it was just too much, all this talk of changing this and changing that. I just couldn't take it any more.'

Well, that seemed to explain things and now that it was clear that I had been accusing her falsely of harbouring an unbearable lust for me, I was somewhat disappointed. I even began to be curious about what might have transpired between us, and looked for a moment across her body, my glance taking in the points of interest from her mouth to her ankles. Certainly, there were possibilities, but, really, Aurelia was a queen beside this peasant. I let her talk and took leave of her as soon as opportunity permitted it. Out again, I decided the best thing to do with my brocade tunic was to remove it and leave it on a chair in the verandah. The sun had now risen and I, who had seen so well in the darkness for much of the night, found the intense light distort the objects of my perception. However, stripped to the waist, I slowly walked towards the noise of the battle, looking for a possible weapon on the way.

Apart from twigs and, if I had gone to the kitchen, a carving knife, there was nothing by way of a weapon in my path. I hoped that my father's Strong Seventy, his little army of specially trained Negroes, would adequately deal with the Indians, leaving me an interested spectator. The Strong Seventy were trained by an old Portuguese warrior named João Veríssimo who had fought against the Dutch in recent years. Veríssimo was a wonderful grey-bearded man of some sixty years, having begun his soldiering days in Lisbon and seen action on the Malabar coast of India. He had a six-inch scar across his stomach where, he swore, the Prince of Calcutta himself had stabbed him with a sword whose handle was encrusted with rubies. My father often taunted him by asking how was it that the Prince of Calcutta was fighting on the Malabar coast which was on the other side of the vast Indian land-mass, but Veríssimo swore that he had held on to the sword seeing that it had precious stones on it and had later presented it to the King in Portugal. Well, we accepted old Veríssimo's stories, for he was popular with the Strong Seventy and drilled the Negroes regularly to keep them fit for combat should the occasion rise. Fire-arms and ammunition being expensive, only ten soldiers were equipped with them; the rest used spears and daggers, except for six who had been given special training in bows and arrows. Veríssimo learned the bow and arrow technique from the Indian slaves on our plantation, but he had refused to use Indians in his army, saying that since most of the attacks we could expect would be from Indians, it was no use pitching their brothers against them. Whereas whenever two adjoining plantations warred with each other over some disputed land, Negroes were willing to fight their neighbour's Negroes since the Negro, being more advanced than the Indian, had a sense of loyalty to his master. Old Veríssimo had many theories and many stories, but now he faced a real test, Indians at our gates.

And there he was himself, on a black horse, wearing a chain-mail tunic and a helmet which reminded me of drawings of Alexander the Great, old Veríssimo, as if he confronted the Persians. Two of the soldiers who had shotguns were positioned on a high lookout, two others had climbed up a tree some distance away, and they were all shooting away. I could not see any Indians, however, but noticing a ladder against the tree on which the two soldiers were, I climbed up the ladder, and saw an astonishing sight. At the centre of the open space in front of the gate a cart drawn by two mules was slowly proceeding up a path; on the cart stood six Negroes who were expert with bows and arrows, and they were shooting arrows simultaneously into the distance in front of them. About forty or fifty yards away was a copse of trees, but all their arrows did not reach that far and those that went farther seemed to disappear into the foliage. On either side of the cart were fifteen to twenty soldiers, spread out in a single line, their spears held pointed in the direction of the enemy. They were all chanting some ferocious war-cry, while Veríssimo trotted up and down the line of soldiers in the rear, urging them on, brandishing his sword in the air. Some fifteen soldiers had been left out of this exercise, and these stood at attention in front of the gate. Veríssimo suddenly ordered his advancing army to halt. The shooting soldiers suddenly stopped firing. For two or three minutes there was a silence, a stillness. Veríssimo came galloping back and spoke to my father.

'I would advise and request you, sir, to withdraw behind the gate,' Veríssimo said, speaking loudly enough for every-

65

one to hear. 'The enemy does not perceive our strategy and is about to be drawn into the open. The battle will be bloody. It will be no sight for innocent eyes, and I would hate to bear the awesome guilt of unnecessary injury to anyone of your worthy family. Leave the fighting to the soldiers. War is our business.'

'No, no,' my father said. 'We want to be here to support you. Numbers is our strength.'

'Sir,' said Veríssimo, 'this is a matter for the military. Ten good soldiers are better than a thousand civilian men. I can cite famous cases from history to prove this point. Untrained numbers only lead to confusion. Confusion is the enemy of discipline, and where discipline fails, there an army loses. I beg you, therefore, to trust in my judgement and my experience. When I served the Crown in the war on the Malabar coast. . .'

Veríssimo did not finish his sentence or, if he did, no one heard it, for a great screeching scream which seemed to come from a thousand throats filled the air and in the same instant a horde of Indians came charging through out of the trees. The shock of this sight was such that I fell off the ladder and suffered a cut on my chest against a sharp stone. I paid the cut no attention since I was anxious to regain my position on the ladder to see what was going on, for, from my position on the ground, all I observed was a mass of bodies running in several directions, some falling to the ground, and a glimpse of Veríssimo charging in a direction which seemed to me to be inappropriate, though it is possible that by falling I was momentarily confused about the points of the compass. When I stood up, holding the ladder to support myself since I was a little dizzy from the fall, I noticed with some shock that an arrow had become stuck to the tree and realized with great horror that if I had not fallen, the arrow would have been stuck somewhere in the area between my navel and my ribs. I decided not to climb up the ladder. I looked towards the scene of action. All I could see was a long wall of men, their heels raising little clouds of dust, trying to push a barrier

66

against the attacking Indians. It occurred to me that we had made a disastrous mistake, for we had come out into the open while the Indians had remained under cover until they had decided to surprise us. And worse, we were all out there in the open whereas the Indians very probably had reserves in the neighbourhood. I noticed then that the fifteen or so soldiers of the Strong Seventy who had been stationed by the gate still stood there as if nothing in the world was happening to disturb their equanimity; and just when I was looking at them with some admiration for the discipline Veríssimo had instilled into them, an arrow pierced one in the chest and he collapsed. This was too much for his companions who dispersed, most of them to the direction of the crowded ranks in the distance, and two inside the gate. I thought that the best service I could perform would be to apprehend these two cowards and followed them into the house. Entering the gate, however, I noticed that they were running at a considerable pace and it seemed foolish for me to be pursuing them, and I decided it would be best if I reported them to Veríssimo later on. So, I turned round and, picking up the spear of the fallen soldier, wondered whether I should not join the scuffling that seemed to be going on some fifty yards away. I stood for a moment, looking at what was going on but could not really make out exactly what was happening. Convinced, as the saying goes, that it is foolish to jump into a river without first testing to see if it is free of piranha, I walked back to the gate and climbed up one of its posts. What I saw was a circle of bodies in the distance and it appeared that our men had completely surrounded the Indians and were mercilessly butchering them. Well, that was quite a turn of events, I thought; either several of the Indians had retreated, or in the sudden shock of first seeing them when I was on the ladder, I must have had the illusion of seeing many more than there actually were. I debated whether I should go and join the slaughter of the Indians which was evidently going on with Veríssimo now galloping round in circles, vociferously urging his soldiers and whoever else was there to show no mercy.

Just then a shower of arrows flew out of the copse of trees, made a graceful arc across the sky and swooped down on our men, taking them completely by surprise and probably killing three or four, for I saw at least half a dozen fall. A new confusion arose, for as the men realized that the first batch of Indians had tricked them into gathering in a small concentrated group in order to facilitate this attack, they began to disperse rapidly in various directions. One group of soldiers – perhaps ordered by Veríssimo, I could not tell for there was a great deal of noise – made a mad dash towards the copse and then halted – perhaps seeing the instant death that awaited them there; for a moment later they made a determined dash back. Now, Veríssimo did a militarily sensible thing: seeing the confused dispersal of his troops together with what must be called the civilian element of our forces, he galloped up and down haranguing his men until he managed to have them standing at attention in two lines in front of the gate some five yards from where I was. The six who were originally in the mule cart were also made to join the formation. The civilians in the meanwhile had retreated to various points of shelter, which is to say they had crowded around the three trees near the gate. Veríssimo began to lecture his soldiers. 'Order,' he called, trotting up and down and looking each man in the eye. 'Order, discipline.' That is all he said, but the two words, repeated several times, seemed to be sufficient to make some of the men perceptibly raise their heads a little as if it were an indication that they responded with pride to their leader. The enemy, however, seeing that our back was momentarily turned, so to speak, now made a fresh charge, and I saw another batch of Indians come screaming through the copse. Well, well, I thought, this is not altogether a happy day for us; for clearly the Indians were strong in number, and could afford to throw out many of their men as bait. This time, however, there was no panic, no sudden rush. In fact, this time, none of us moved, though I must confess that of all the ideas to occur to my mind at that moment when it seemed that we could all very well be killed,

I had the thought that, well, if I'm to die, at least I've accomplished the great experience of having been with a woman. Hearing the Indians, Veríssimo turned round but he, too, waited and watched. The Indians halted in their advance and for a minute or two there was a silent confrontation of the two forces. I counted the Indians. They were twenty in number. Veríssimo made no move, but sat firmly on his horse. There was another scream from the copse and a fresh group of Indians came rushing out; these, too, halted when they were beside the first batch. Still, Veríssimo made no move. The waiting was becoming unbearable and just when I was beginning to think that we ought to attack or come inside the gate and lock the Indians out, what should I see but one more batch of Indians! I counted thirty-five in this group, thinking that the Indians were too clever and experienced as warriors to be bringing out their entire force into the open: either they had gone crazy as a consequence of Veríssimo's unpredictable tactics or they were bluffing or they had many more supporters in reserve. I must say that my normally logical and perceptive mind was becoming somewhat confused, seeing all these sudden and unexpected changes. Well, the confrontation continued, and I could well imagine what would happen next: more Indians would come out and their massed forces would stand in front of us for some time and then suddenly make a wild attack. For the first time, I realized the awful implications of the battle; up to now I had been bemused by the possibility of death, but now I realized that were we to lose, there would be a massacre, arson, rape and looting. Just when I was contemplating the consequences of these happenings and wondering whether I would survive, an unexpected event took place. Even Veríssimo was taken by surprise.

The two soldiers whom I had earlier seen run into the grounds of the house and whom I had taken to be cowardly deserters, now did a heroic thing. They returned on horseback, followed by eight or ten more Negroes on horseback and leading a string of some thirty or so horses. These eight or ten Negroes comprised the band which had led the wedding party through these gates on the previous day, and now each member carried his musical instrument and seemed ready to play it. The two soldiers who led this magnificent sight turned their horses aside so that the band could now lead the horses. The soldiers who had earlier been inveighed by Veríssimo to learn order and discipline were now commanded to mount the horses, so that we now had a cavalry troop of some thirty or so. No sooner was the cavalry in order than the band began to play, and Veríssimo, giving the impression that he had planned this stratagem himself, trotted up to be at the head of the two-fold line led by the band which was now playing a brisk, brassy rhythm. It was a wonderful sound, it was the sound of Brazil – noisy but melodious, friendly but determined to be independent. It touched one's heart and it made one want to march or run or dance. It was a music which committed the body to boldness of action. I can tell you it had the Indians wondering what the hell was happening, for they were hypnotized by the sound. The mounted band continued to play and to proceed in the direction of the Indians until it was some twenty yards from them – a very courageous act, I thought, wondering whether I would ever be as brave as the man who beat the drums, a great grin on his face. As soon as the band halted, Veríssimo ordered his mounted men to charge at the Indians, who now turned on their heels and began to flee, thus offering easy targets to the spears of the mounted soldiers. The entire action could not have taken ten minutes, at the end of which time a good many Indians lay dead on the ground and what remained of them had fled through the trees. Veríssimo ordered four of his soldiers to go as scouts through the trees and to determine if any Indians still remained, and made a triumphant return in the direction of the house, holding his head high and his jaw firmly clenched. He ordered all his men to line up in front of the gate and to come to attention, and counted them. We had lost seven men, the Strong Seventy had been decimated; but, as Veríssimo put it when giving the news of the fatalities to my father, the Strong Seventy had won a glorious victory in which every calculated tactic had worked. My father slapped Veríssimo's shoulder with an affectionate regard and announced that we should all go in and eat a hearty breakfast.

It was the largest and the noisiest breakfast that I have ever attended. Everyone recounted his story of the battle to everyone else, and my father made a short speech in praise of the Strong Seventy's bravery and courage and asked everyone to give a standing ovation to Veríssimo. Our brave commander stood up to acknowledge the applause and made a gallant answer in which he thanked everyone for his support and told a story about a battle on the coast of Africa in which he had fought.

After breakfast, my father ordered some slaves to clear the bodies from outside the gate; a mass grave was dug for the dead Indians and our own casualties were to be given an honourable burial – under the stone floor of the chapel where members of our own family were buried. My father announced this intention of burying our dead Negroes in the chapel with great solemnity and, indeed, the announcement was received with gasps of astonishment, especially by the wedding guests. 'I want it to be known,' my father said, 'that those who have died fighting to defend us are to be considered free human beings whom we love as dearly as we love our own family.' This noble sentiment sent a current of admiration throughout the household.

While we were leaving after breakfast, each to go and attend to his wounds or rest after the fatigue of the battle – and I must say I could barely stand on my feet after this most extraordinary morning coming hard upon the most hectic night I had ever spent – while we were all leaving, my father, seeing me, called out: 'Hey, Gregório!'

I went up to him and as I walked towards him, he said: 'Did you have fun watching all that?'

At that moment he saw the cut I had sustained on my chest, and said: 'What's that, Gregório? You're injured! Come on,' he shouted, 'where are all our women-folk? My boy here has been wounded and no one seems to pay him any attention.

What was it, Gregório, an arrow?'

'It's nothing,' I protested.

'Come on, it might have been a poisoned arrow. You'll die a slow painful death, my boy. Where were you fighting, up at the front?'

'I was only watching,' I said weakly.

'Come, come, there's no need to be modest about your achievement. I remember seeing you with a spear. Ha! There you are, Tana. Look, Gregózinho here's been badly wounded, it looks like a poisoned arrow. Please see that he gets thoroughly washed; put some of that herb potion on his wound and send him to bed to rest.'

I would have told my father the truth that I had cut myself falling from the ladder and not sustained any wound fighting but I noticed that Tana was looking at me with admiration and tenderness and it occurred to me that if she was to be impressed by the slight cut on my chest, then the lie was worth maintaining if only to buy a few days' peace from Tana's constant nagging. So, I surrendered myself to her ministrations, and was presently put into bed, a bandage tightly wound around my chest.

I slept the rest of the morning, and was woken up by my slave, Jari, who said that my father wanted to see me if I felt well enough to get up. I asked him to fetch me some cold beef and bread while I washed myself and put on some clothes.

My father had called a meeting in his study, and welcomed me warmly, saying, 'Ah, here is our hero! Come in, my boy, join the men.'

My two brothers, Antônio and Francisco, were seated at the table on my father's left. On his right sat Veríssimo, and I took a seat next to him.

'How are you feeling?' Veríssimo asked.

'Fine,' I said. 'It was nothing.'

'Spoken like a soldier!' Veríssimo said. 'You have courage, young man, you have a heart like a rock.'

'Well, Gregório,' my father said, 'I've called this meeting following an excellent suggestion made by Veríssimo. We have today endured a savage attack by barbaric Indians. We have lost seven of our brave soldiers. Eleven more people, including yourself, have been wounded. But we have come through. We won the battle decisively although it was apparent that we were outnumbered.'

'By three to one,' Veríssimo put in.

'It has been a heroic performance,' my father went on. 'First of all I want to impress upon you three, my sons, the consequences that might have befallen this house had we lost. By now, all our throats would have been cut. Vultures would be pecking at our entrails right now. The house would be smouldering, having by now been burned down. Whether the savages would have been kind enough to our women and killed them forthwith I very much doubt for it is most likely that they would have used the women for their pleasure first, for that is the way of all invaders. So, our first duty is to gather in the chapel this evening and say a special mass. But we have to think of the future, too. We have not only to compensate ourselves for the slaves we have lost – and I must tell you, my boys, that losing seven Negroes is no small matter, for apart from the monetary value of each one, we have also lost seven potential breeders of more slaves – we have also to show the savage tribes that we mean business. Veríssimo's idea is that we should send a party out to hunt Indians. By doing so, we shall be showing the Indians that we are determined to remain the masters of this land and also be adding to the numbers of our slaves. What's more, if we can capture Indians, we have the opportunity of converting them to Christianity, thus doing them a favour by saving their souls.'

'When do we go?' Antônio asked.

'In a week or so,' my father said. 'Veríssimo will plan out a campaign and you will go under his leadership.'

'Who all will go?' I asked.

'I hope you will have recovered in a week,' my father said. 'It is an important experience which you ought not to miss.'

'I would go now if necessary,' I said, 'but who else?'

'The three of you under Veríssimo, together with however many soldiers Veríssimo thinks it necessary to go with you.'

'Father,' I said, 'if I may make a suggestion. It is right that Antônio and I should take part in this expedition, but is not Francisco too young?'

'I'm big enough!' Francisco cried out before my father could reply.

'The question is not of size or age,' my father said.

'I agree,' I said, 'it is not merely a matter of age. But, father, let me respectfully remind you of the old story you were so fond of telling me when I was a child, the one about putting all your eggs in one basket. If we were all to go and if something were to go wrong, you might not have a son and heir.'

There was a brief pause as my father pondered the importance of what I had said.

Veríssimo broke the silence with: 'Gregório has said something very shrewd which we in our enthusiasm had overlooked.'

'Yes,' my father said, shaking his head in deliberation.

'The question,' I said, 'is not about the youngest or the eldest, but who should be left behind to uphold the family's name. I suggest Francisco. Perhaps someone else has another suggestion.'

Well, so it was agreed that Francisco should stay at home, and my father left the other details – date of departure, what supplies to take, and so on – for Veríssimo to work out with Antônio and me later. As we were leaving, Francisco came up to me and said: 'You double-faced coward!'

I must say my little brother is a tiresome creature. However, I am a patient human being, and said to him: 'Francisco, consider yourself lucky. The jungle is a dangerous place.'

'You're a coward,' he said.

'Look, Francisco, don't be a bore,' I said. 'If you think it's going to be fun hunting for Indians, just realize that it isn't a game.'

'Yeah, and lying cowards won't win either.'

'I don't know what you've got on your mind,' I said. 'If you're trying to pick a fight, wounded as I am, I'll happily oblige if you care to come into the garden.'

'Wounded!' he mocked, laughing.

I was glad that the others had walked on, leaving the two of us in the verandah, for Francisco went on, 'You fell from a bloody ladder. I saw you. I was sitting right above you in the tree.'

'All right,' I said. 'So, you saw what happened. But know this. I didn't ask to be made a hero. Before I could tell anyone I'd cut myself falling, everyone assumed I'd been hit by an arrow. If you tell them the truth, as I tried to but no one would hear, then you won't be hurting me. They like to think they have brave sons around them, and you'll be hurting them by depriving them of a hero.'

'You're a coward and nothing else.'

'Francisco, it's no use trying to provoke me. If you want to go hunting Indians so badly, then I'd be glad to step down in your favour. What else can I offer?'

'I hope you're really hit by an arrow,' he said. 'I hope it's a poisoned arrow and I hope it pierces your heart.'

Imparting this curse, he wandered off, leaving me disgusted with his behaviour. The moral I learned from this little episode was that in future I should keep an eye on my brothers, for clearly I could not trust them. Although Antônio had not treated me badly, there was no doubt that he would hear the story from Francisco when it profited Francisco to tell him about it – for Francisco had a habit of hoarding bits of information to use as blackmail when an opportunity arose – and Antônio, not having Francisco's meanness, could be immediately vicious if not destructive. I am sorry to have to say that, all in all, I had a right pair of bastards for brothers. I turned my thoughts to the more interesting prospect of the adventure on which we would be embarking. I wondered what weapons Veríssimo would give us, and hoped that mine would be a shotgun. The notion of firing into the running body of an Indian and seeing it drop dead thrilled my imagination.

For most people in the house, the next few days were a continuation of the wedding feast, but for me it was a time that had to be killed before setting out on the expedition. And yet, we did not remain idle, for Antônio and I had frequent conferences with Veríssimo and, once he had decided that we should be carrying shotguns, we also spent afternoons in shooting practice. For this, my slave Jari was most helpful, for he suggested that we might use the scores of unwanted kittens and puppies which were forever being born among the slave dwellings, and himself volunteered to round up as many stray creatures as he could find. With three slave boys to help him, Jari soon collected two baskets full of kittens, packed in like yams, and about a dozen puppies, and we went to the sugar fields where we spilled the kittens among the lines of cane and first, for fun, let the puppies loose among them.

The kittens all crowded together while the puppies collected in a group and stared at the kittens; it was difficult to say what they thought of each other, for the kittens were frightened of the puppies and the latter were at least bewildered by seeing so many kittens in front of them. Instead of any battle developing between these two groups, all that happened was that the kittens huddled closer together and the puppies seemed to become bored and began to show curiosity in the cane around them. We all withdrew some twenty yards, and Antônio and I decided to have a competition: he would shoot at the puppies and I at the kittens, and we would see who killed more. Jari and his slave companions thought that this was a wonderful idea, and Jari suggested that we should have ten shots each, at the end of which one of the slaves would go and count the dead creatures. We agreed to the rule of the ten shots and appointed Jari as a referee between us. He drew a line in front of us by dragging his heel across the earth and said that neither of us must jump that line. Asking us to take aim, he lifted his head to indicate that we should commence firing. Antônio, having had some experience of shooting before, completed his ten shots while I was still firing my sixth. My slowness gave me this advantage, that I could tell that he had shot two puppies and now all I had to do was to make sure that I hit at least two kittens. I deliberately took my time – which made Antônio mad, especially as my eighth shot got a kitten in its nose – and when it came to my final shot on which the competition depended, I aimed with great care and kept my finger on the trigger for a minute or two until I had Antônio swearing at me for keeping him standing. Well, I was not going to be panicked into missing my target, and so I said to him to stop complaining as he was disturbing my concentration and began again the slow business of taking my aim. Finally, I fired, and hit a kitten right in its side so that it went skidding along the ground for some ten yards. Two of the slave boys ran up to make a tally of the dead, while I said to Antônio: 'The rules said ten shots each, there was nothing about how soon we should fire the ten shots.'

'If you take that long,' Antônio said in a mocking tone, 'they will have cooked and served your liver by the time you take the first shot at them.'

'Ah,' I said, 'but we're not shooting Indians now, are we?'

'That's what we're practising for!'

The slaves returned with the dead creatures. I had killed two kittens as cleanly as one cuts a melon with a knife; the one I had hit in the nose looked rather silly with its head shattered while the eyes still seemed to look on. I had also injured one, a white and black kitten which had been hit high on its left hind-leg. Antônio's score was exactly the same, two puppies killed and one injured. Jari looked at the two injured animals, and said: 'We can decide who is the winner by seeing which of these two dies first.'

'It might take hours,' Antônio protested.

But Jari had another idea. We all walked to a tree where Jari asked one of his friends to climb up the tree, from where he was to throw down the kitten and the puppy from exactly the same height. The boy quickly climbed up and the two creatures were passed to him. He threw the puppy down first. It fell on its side. Jari picked it up, felt it for a moment and then told us that it was still alive. The boy next threw the kitten down. Its fall was lighter, and it seemed to discover a little life from some secret reserve, for it clearly made an attempt to balance itself as it fell. Jari passed both the creatures back to the boy in the tree and asked him to try again. Well, the boy tried four times, and it was at the fourth attempt that the puppy died, for this time it luckily fell on its head and although its heart was still beating when Jari picked it up, it stopped doing so just when Jari was about to pass it back to the boy in the tree. Well, the game now depended on my kitten, and it could still end in a tie if the kitten would do me the favour of dying on its final fall. I could see that Antônio and Jari were as enraptured by the suspense as I was and we instinctively moved back to make room for the kitten. The boy let it fall. Plop! Jari ran forward to pick it up. Just then with a great beating of wings and a loud screeching cry, an eagle swooped down, caught hold of the kitten with its beak and flapping its wings mightily, soared up again, giving Jari one hell of a shock and for a moment petrifying all of us. Antônio, with some presence of mind, took a shot at the eagle, but it was out of range. Jari recovered from his shock to whisper to us: 'It's a tie.' The eagle, however, had given us an idea and we thought that we should next practise shooting at birds. All in all, this aspect of our preparation for the expedition provided us with a great deal of excitement and fun.

And then there was Aurelia. If I could have had my wish, I would have seen her every night and every afternoon, too, for who knew how long I would be away on the expedition? It was not easy for me to be visiting her room whenever I felt so inclined, for I had to be on my guard against the spying of my brother Francisco not to mention the eyes of all the other servants who invariably milled around the part of the house where Aurelia's room was. In the confused and drunken atmosphere of the wedding-night, no one had known who did what. But now there were many idle eyes around the house. Also, Aurelia had her own duties to keep her preoccupied since she was my new mother's maid. My only hope was to steal to her room in the middle of the night, and this I did on the second night after the battle.

I suppose that since I woke her from her sleep, she did not show an immediate pleasure in seeing me. She let me in, saying, 'Oh, it's you,' and fell back to her bed while I closed the door. I had imagined a pleasant little scene in which I would whisper at her door, 'Aurelia, it's me, Gregório.' And she, opening the door, would also open her arms to me so that, embracing her, we would together fall into bed. But none of this, for she fell back into bed alone and seemed to go to sleep – as if she were a mother who had opened the door to let in not her lover but a vagabond son. Well, I pulled my clothes off, and jumped into bed with her. 'Softly!' she whispered, visibly annoyed at my exuberance, and turned round so that her back was to me. She was wearing a kind of loose gown, and I pulled it up so that her buttocks were exposed. She made a moaning sound and her hand shifted as if unconsciously and pulled the gown down. Although I was annoyed by this, her wonderful sweaty smell and the mere proximity of her body were producing a tumescent excitement in me and, seeing that the backs of her thighs were uncovered and closely pressed together, I pushed my loaded little rifle-snout between them where no sooner did it come into contact with her warm flesh than it exploded.

'Jesus!' she exploded too. 'What's this, my bedroom or your damn bathroom? What do you take me for, a stone floor, a gutter on which you can spill your muck? If this is what you want, why don't you go up to the corral where the cows don't mind what you do to them?'

In hurling this abuse at me she had turned round. The shock of the abuse as well as the fear that the noise might attract someone's attention suddenly made me burst out crying. That stopped her instantly, and as she was leaning towards me, I put my right hand round her back, pulled her on me so that my head was buried under her breasts where I continued to sob uncontrollably. This was too much for her emotions which swung from violence to tenderness and she

79

spontaneously pulled her gown up so that my closeness to her bosom would be more meaningful. At least it was an effective way of stopping my open-mouthed sobbing. The only danger now was that I might suffocate, and even as I was trying to shift myself in such a way that my nostrils would have access to some air I said to myself, What better way of dying than to be choked by Aurelia's breasts?

My left hand found itself touching the inside of her thighs and came into contact with the sticky wetness which I had deposited there a few moments earlier and which (I praised Aurelia's magnanimity at ignoring it although it must be giving her some discomfort) had been trickling all around her smooth flesh. I decided to make amends to her, and rising so that I could lie with my head at the level of her knees, I slowly kissed her thighs clean. Her fingers gently stroked my head, for she seemed obviously to be enjoying what I was doing, and being unable to bear any longer the proximity of my breath to the centre of her own heat, she gradually and with deliberate slowness so that she could prolong the expectation of thrill pushed my head so that my mouth could be where it gave her the greatest pleasure. My tongue played among the little hairs like a snake working his way through grass and found the damp areas where the flesh was soft and moist. And now, since my waist was at the level of her mouth, she began to attend to me, beginning with running the tip of her tongue along the veins which had become swollen with palpitating blood and then taking the tip between her lips she slowly drew all of it into her mouth.

Well, the night turned out to be a happy one after the unpropitious beginning. One thing I learned that night was that many acts which are publicly considered to be obscene are in private immensely beautiful and gratifying and conducive to fostering a feeling of profound love between the participants.

I did not see Aurelia after this night, for on the two succeeding nights there were magnificent dinner parties for the wedding guests and Aurelia was kept busy while I, spending most of my days training with Veríssimo, for he insisted that we learn the elements of soldiering, and then joining the evening feasts, was too tired to wait up until Aurelia was free from her chores. Also, some instinct told me that I should now store up my energy for the demands which would no doubt be made on it in the coming days.

There was a special mass in the chapel on the morning that the wedding guests departed. Father Soares did not look too pleased saying it, for it was unusually early in the morning since the guests were anxious to reach the house of a neighbouring plantation twenty miles away where they expected to spend the night. I looked at the guests, one by one – Augustina's father, Mr Rodrigues, who had made me promise to visit his house; Domingos Cardoso, who had struck me as a strange man, something of a misfit in this company, and yet he was often in conversation with my father for, being my father's agent in Bahia, he was responsible for shipping our sugar to Lisbon; then there was Mr Barballo, who had ahead of him the long journey to Olinda where he would no doubt make his famous speeches to his fellow councillors; and his wife, Mrs Barballo, looking at whom now made me smile to myself for my own desperate thoughts of a few days ago. My eyes next fell on my mother who looked solemn as if she had determined to herself that she would command her household with authority. I was surprised to realize how quickly she had adapted herself to her new role, how easily she had changed from a girl to womanhood, for no one looking at her now could deny that that frail young body was built upon the sturdy frame of a strong-minded woman. I recalled now how, two days after the wedding, she stood at the kitchen door instructing the servants in a loud voice about what a low opinion she had of their cooking; and I observed, too, how one look from her was sufficient to shut Tana's constantly busy mouth. I looked at the other guests, most of them landlords from Bahia and Pernambuco, and their squat little frowning wives, stern matrons all. And then I realized that Saint Anthony was watching me, and I must admit that for a moment I felt ashamed, for I recalled having made certain resolutions and promises, and here I was in a shirt with an embroidered collar and feeling that contentment of body which only a young man who has enjoyed the love of a satisfying woman can achieve. Saint Anthony seemed to be shaking his head disapprovingly while I remembered also the small matter of the wound on my chest. Vanity, I thought I heard Saint Anthony say in a sad voice, vanity, deceit and sin: son, let me tell you about hell. I can see you arriving there in your brocade tunic, your hair greased and immaculately combed, your body perfumed. Ha! First you'll be stripped. Your brocade and your silks will be thrown into the fire being prepared for you. Then arrows will be aimed at you, and one by one the arrows will be shot at your body. They will stick forever to your body, creating wounds which will let out blood forever. Apparitions of beautiful naked women will approach you and excite you and just when they are within touching distance of you, they will change into monstrous vultures who will peck at those parts of your body with which you have given yourself the greatest pleasure. The tongues of flames will lick your body, burn you, but they will not consume you. Oh, Gregório, do you now expect pity from me?

I had to admit that Saint Anthony's abuse was justified; but what atonement could I offer? If Saint Anthony had suggested a penance to me, I would have undertaken it there and then. Instead, he seemed to turn his head away from me. I was considerably shaken by this experience and wondered if I should not confess my sins to Father Soares; but seeing Father Soares mumble the Latin words as though his mouth was full of beans, I felt no respect for him. To him my confession would be too scandalous for belief. The least I could resolve, then, was that in the following weeks while we hunted for Indians, I should conduct myself as a true Christian: I would be prepared, in the name of Christ, to murder those Indians who did not submit to baptism and to our way of life. I was greatly cheered at having made this noble resolution even though Saint Anthony did not care to turn back his gaze at me, and when the guests assembled outside to take their leave, I was prepared to meet them with a brave face. There was one moment, however, which made me feel awkward; and that was when Mrs Barballo, ignoring the hand I had offered her, reached for my shoulders, embraced me tenderly and implanted an explosive wet kiss on my cheek, which, luckily, made me blush so that Mr Barballo said aloud, 'Ho, ho, the young man is not used to kisses as yet!'

By that afternoon, the house had returned to its normal ways and everyone changed into such poor clothes that, had the guests returned, they would have wondered if the plague of poverty had not descended upon the house in the few hours of their absence. Even Augustina, having packed away all her silks, wore cotton clothes which soon became grubby; and, what is worse, she did not seem to care how she looked. My father, wearing only a pair of dirty trousers, returned to supervising the work in the fields, sweat making rivulets down his hairy chest, and his stomach curving out in a billowing bulge like the sail of a ship in a high wind. I wandered aimlessly about the house, looking for something to do. I would have loved to have gone out on shooting practice again, but Veríssimo had put a stop to that, with my father's approval, since he wanted to conserve our ammunition. My slave Jari followed me about until I got sick of his presence behind me and told him to go to the corral and to fetch me a glass of milk straight from a cow's udder, just to give him something to be busy with for at least half an hour. Routine in the house meant utter boredom for me, and I was glad that evening when Veríssimo summoned Antônio and me and announced that we would be leaving on the next day for our expedition and that we would be accompanied by fifteen of his soldiers. The only person who did not like this news was Father Soares who was again obliged to rise early to say mass for us before we left. Perhaps it was to be a sign, although we did not heed it as such since it was too early for us not to be excessively courageous, but the first misfortune of our expedition occurred within two hours of our leaving the house.

Chapter 3

FLIGHT FROM THE INDIAN WOMEN

Before our departure, Veríssimo had us all lined up in front of the gate, having persuaded my father that he should inspect us before we left. The fifteen Negro soldiers stood proudly at attention, and I must say that I was quite pleased with myself to be standing at the head of the line with Antônio. We, too, wore the uniform of a green shirt and a green pair of loose trousers, for it was Veríssimo's idea that we should not look distinctly different from the soldiers because if we did, we would be taken for leaders and would therefore attract special attack. Veríssimo's reasoning had seemed to us to be sound and since self-preservation was as strong an instinct in us as in any mortal, we readily agreed to submit ourselves to the temporary indignity of being dressed as plainly as the Negroes. My father stood in front of us, and, embracing first Antônio and then me, said: 'My sons, you are going to that part of Brazil which the hand of civilized man has not yet tamed, for it has not so far experienced the whip of discipline. There, the savage lives wild, making sounds rather than speaking a language, hunting rather than tilling the earth. He is a creature of wilful and uncontrolled energy. He bends his knee to superstition and not to God, and believes more in the fulfilment of his body than in any manifestation of his mind. My sons, this is the creature you must subdue for the labour that is his destiny to perform. You are going on a dangerous mission, my sons, and I say with an open heart, Go in the name of Christ and you will come to no harm. Go with pious thoughts, go with prayers on your lips, and my prayers will go with you.'

He then proceeded to shake each soldier by the hand, stopping in front of two or three to address personal remarks to them. Of course, the wives and children of all the slaves were standing watching this moving ceremony, and some of the women were in tears and, indeed, were I not wearing a soldier's uniform, I would have found it difficult to control my own emotions. The horses, which the stablehands held some distance away from the ceremony, seemed relieved when we mounted them for they had been restlessly stamping their hoofs, raising dust, and had already begun to sweat. When we finally left Veríssimo, loudly shouting his commands as though he wished to impress the King of Portugal on his throne in Lisbon, led us away in a strict formation, he at the front with Antônio, followed by eight pairs of horses in a double line. He led us on at a brisk trot, determined no doubt to impress the audience, which gazed after us, with the urgency and the importance of our mission. I was glad that I had refrained from visiting Aurelia during the previous three days, for I am sure that I would not have been able to withstand for long the strenuous ardour with which we were expected to follow our leader. Although we were aware that we were being watched from the gates of the house, none of us looked back to wave one more goodbye, for Veríssimo had strictly instructed us that we should not do so, that, instead, we should keep ourselves firmly mounted, that we should present to our beholders backs so rigidly straight that our backs would seem to be made of iron, for that, he insisted, was the stuff soldiers were made of. Once we were out of sight of the house, however, Veríssimo allowed us to relax and to ride more naturally, but warned us that we should always be ready to assume the disciplined posture of true soldiers whenever there was the likelihood of our being observed.

The country we were passing through was familiar to me. On our right extended my father's land. The sugarcane plantation stretched out to as far as we could see, the rich, rising green spotted with the black dots of the Negro slaves moving about in the slow rhythm peculiar to them. On our left, however, the vegetation was thinning out, leaving the earth as a vast arid plain, dry, hard. Although nothing moved on this barren land, dust appeared to be rising along its surface as if the heat of the sun had the effect of physically pounding the earth. The contrast was such that I was overcome with feelings of great admiration for my grandfather who, coming to this dry land, had created a fertile plantation out of it. I had never seen my grandfather, but my father often mentioned him, dwelling especially on those aspects of his character which he thought were worthy of our emulation. I liked best the story about grandfather's departure from Lisbon.

He had come from Sagres near Cape Saint Vincent, and while waiting for a vessel in Lisbon had found himself spending evenings in certain houses which provided drinks and card-games among other amenities. Well, having been nothing in his life so far but a peasant and a fisherman, and this being his first visit to a city, and Lisbon at that, my grandfather was easily duped by a man named Pareira. Pareira apparently called himself a merchant and passed himself off as a man of experience and considerable wealth. Pareira worked on my grandfather for two days, giving him the impression that he was to be trusted implicitly and meanwhile discovering my grandfather's story and also the fact that my grandfather had the peasant's habit of carrying all his money. On the third evening, the two were drinking together when a golden-haired girl with the kind of figure which would make a man fifty miles away frantic with desire walked past the table, her gown brushing grandfather's chair. Naturally, my grandfather's eyes went red as he stared at her. She disappeared, and Pareira remarked nonchalantly, 'A virgin from France, it's her first night here.' This only maddened grandfather still more. 'How much?' he cried.

'Shh,' answered Pareira, 'not so loud. It's the privilege of counts to offer her estates, my dear sir, she's beyond the price we merchants can afford.'

'But how much?' cried my grandfather, prepared for the moment to give up all his dreams for the embrace of this girl.

'Why, I wouldn't be surprised,' Pareira went on, 'if a count is expected later in the evening. Ah, I can just imagine it, for I've seen this happen before. She will go now and soak herself in a bath of perfumed water. She will wear a robe of the finest transparent silk, letting the golden tresses of her gorgeous hair fall across those sweet rising breasts which no hand of man has ever touched. She will stand at the foot of the bed when the count will enter. Price? Not for you and me, my dear sir.'

'But how much, how much?'

'Suppose it was as much as all the money you had in the world, so what? Do you think a count is going to take what a peasant has touched? But wait, I have an idea.'

'What?'

'Just let me think a moment. Ah, yes. Suppose I went and made a deal with the Madam. Suppose I could persuade her to give you the count's privilege and then trick the count into believing that the girl's still a virgin, for women have ways, subtle secrets in these things.'

'Yes, yes.'

'And suppose, too, that I could get her to make a price which you could afford, something which will still leave you enough money with which to go to Brazil. What about that, then?'

'Yes, yes!'

'I'm afraid I shall be laughed at for making such a proposition. But, for a friend who appreciates the genuine article, I'll try.'

And so Pareira went away and disappeared behind the scenes for a few minutes during which my grandfather ordered and hastily swallowed two more drinks.

Pareira returned beaming and told my grandfather that he had been able to make a deal for him. Just when my grandfather was about to go to the room to which Pareira had described the directions, Pareira said to him, 'Wait, don't rush off and lose everything!'

'What do you mean?' my grandfather asked.

'Obviously, you have little experience of such places. The first rule you must learn is that you never take into the girl's room more money than you need to pay her, for however new and innocent the girl to this business, the people who run her life know what they're up to. And I can tell you from bitter experience that it doesn't pay to take chances.'

'What should I do?'

'I suggest for your own good that you leave your money with someone you can trust. If you had any relatives in Lisbon you could leave it with them but even if you did that would take time and we have to think about the count, or you could...'

'Look, you're my friend, you hold on to it,' my grandfather said hurriedly, taking out his little sack of money, counting out the coins he needed, and thrusting the rest into Pareira's hands.

Clearly, my grandfather had behaved precisely as Pareira had anticipated. He did not give it any thought, marching off in the direction of the girl's room, for at this stage there was only one notion in his mind. And to make his condition worse, what should he see when he entered the room but that the girl was standing there at the foot of the bed wearing a fine transparent robe, her golden hair falling across her breast. Had he had any doubts about Pareira, they would have vanished with the fulfilment of that apparition. Well, the girl skilfully kept him engaged for a full twenty minutes although I can well imagine that the only thought he had was to tear at her breasts and let his lust explode as quickly as possible. When he had finished, the girl managed to delay him for another five minutes by weeping and saying something about how she would have to deceive the count. Finally, my grandfather took leave of her and, returning to the table where he had left Pareira, found that his trusted friend had vanished with all his money.

Losing the money, he, of course, missed the boat to Brazil

88

when there was one. Having nothing to live on, he took jobs helping out the local fishermen, now mending their nets and now painting their boats; it was a miserable existence, for all he received in payment were a few scraps of fish on which to survive. But all this time, he worked on his revenge. He found out where Pareira lived and made a note of some of his habits. Two months passed, and my grandfather made friends with the master of a ship which was setting out for West Africa with the intention of capturing slaves for trading to Brazil. He tried to persuade the ship's master to give him a job on the ship so that he could work his way across the ocean. The master made a deal with him; he would take my grandfather to Africa and there, if my grandfather could catch ten Negroes, he would be offered free passage to Brazil; if not, then he would have to work for his passage, and the only job available was that of a supervisor of the slaves, a job which required a tough man who knew how to use a whip.

A day before the sailing, it was clear that the ship would leave Lisbon late at night. Perhaps it was something to do with the tide at the mouth of the Tagus, perhaps it was to do with the prevailing winds. Anyway, the information was important for my grandfather. He joined the ship early in the evening, taking with him three large fish as a present to the master. Consequently, for one generosity elicits another, the two had dinner together. After the meal, the captain went about his business, preparing to sail down the river, and my grandfather went out and stood on the deck. He had brought with him a thick long rope, and this he now tied to a railing and then let it trail down the side of the ship until it fell into the water. Having done this, he discreetly left the ship, knowing that he was taking a monstrous risk. Someone might see the rope and haul it up, or some other uncalculated event might take place. But he needed to take the risk, for without it, he saw no way of taking his revenge.

He ran all the way to Pareira's house. He waited outside the house from which he heard a woman calling at a child.

Punctual to his habits, Pareira emerged to walk to the nearby square from where he took one of the several directions. My grandfather pursued him softly, inconspicuously, waiting until they were in a dark, deserted street. When that moment came, my grandfather, quietly catching up on Pareira, suddenly gripped him by the neck from the back and, reaching a hand out, stabbed him thrice in the stomach, each time dragging the knife out at an angle so that Pareira's flesh as well as his internal organs were ripped open, while saying: 'It's me, remember the French virgin?'

Pareira fell dead. My grandfather ran back to the jetty from where the ship had left some fifteen minutes earlier. He took a rowing boat and rowed himself down the river and caught up with the ship which was slowly manoeuvring its way out of the mouth of the Tagus. The rope still hung limply from where he had tied it, he was relieved to see. He grabbed hold of it and pulled himself on to the ship. Having examined himself for any bloodstains, he went up to the bridge where the captain was plotting the course. 'Just thought I'd say goodnight before I retire for the night,' he said to the captain.

Well, I suppose I must have been quite lost in remembering the story of my grandfather's momentous departure from Lisbon, for we were slowly jogging along beside the fierce glare from the dry plain on our left and I had noticed nothing untoward until I was suddenly brought back to my senses by the rest of the party having stopped. It could not have been more than two hours since we had left the house and yet it seemed that we had been travelling for a long time. I, for one, absorbed in my own thoughts, had not seen the three figures with the mules who sat under the shade of a tree on the roadside and who, consequently, had been unnoticed until we were within a dozen or so yards from them. The mules grazed, though there was so little grass there that the poor creatures seemed to be doing no more than kissing the earth. The three men, who from their dress appeared to be friars, sat under the tree eating dry bread. On seeing us, they stopped eating and stood up, making the sign of the cross and greeting us in the name of Christ.

'God be with you,' Veríssimo called back.

Antônio and I pulled up our horses next to Veríssimo while our fifteen soldiers remained some distance behind, for, like us, they must have assumed that once the greetings were exchanged we would continue on our way. We stared at the friars for a moment out of curiosity and surprise, and the one who sat in the middle of the three said: 'As you can see, we are holy friars. We have travelled from Olinda and have been sent by the holy church to take the word of Christ to the darkest corners of Brazil. The word of Christ is all we know and all we have. The charity of the planters sustains us, giving us food. We bless the planters who are making Brazil a fit home for Christ. When we go into the jungle in search of souls, the planters provide us with provisions; and when we return exhausted from the jungle, the planters give us shelter for a few days before we proceed with our work.'

I was greatly impressed by this speech and said to the friar: 'Holy father, perhaps you do not know that at the end of this road is the house of the most generous planter in Brazil, my father. I beseech you to go to his house where you will be welcomed with open arms. For him it will not be charity but a holy duty to have you as his guests. Is this not true, Antônio?'

'Yes, yes,' Antônio said in a hasty mumble, obviously somewhat embarrassed that the initiative had come from me.

'You are very kind,' the friar said. 'Indeed, we shall go there. But can I invite you and your party to share with us what little we have? And you can tell us where you are going in this warlike fashion.'

Veríssimo, who had been carefully scrutinizing the three friars, now said: 'We do have to stop shortly to refresh ourselves and to rest our horses. We are happy to take this opportunity, for there is nothing more enjoyable than to share one's rest and food with men of the Church.'

Well, that decided it, and I must say that I was glad to alight from my horse and stretch my legs a little. The Negroes who carried our provisions placed them on the ground and although the friars insisted that we should eat what remained of their bread, we soon persuaded them to share some of our meat. As we ate, Veríssimo described to them the purpose of our expedition. The friars listened with interest and approval, one saying that he hoped to be around when we returned so that he could baptize the Indians we captured.

'No, no, don't consume your water,' one of the friars said when Veríssimo ordered a Negro to hand out half a glass of water to each member of our company, for that was the measure he had decided we were to allow ourselves. 'We have plenty of water,' the friar went on, 'and besides it does not matter if we finish our supply since we are so close to your house. Why, half a glass, you can have two glasses each of our water, and save yours. I can tell you water is going to be the most precious item of your provisions.'

We gratefully accepted his offer, and each one of us drank a good two or three glasses in the course of the next twenty minutes while we ate and talked. Seeing that two or three of the Negroes had stretched out on the ground and had dozed off, Veríssimo, perhaps feeling a little tired himself, suggested that we could have half an hour's rest before we proceeded. I was glad at the suggestion, for I was thinking what a hectic life I had been leading in recent days and what little sleep I had had. The Negro soldiers quickly found comfortable places in the shade to lie on, and as Veríssimo himself was preparing to lie down, the friars rose, one of them saying, 'We will say goodbye before you have your rest, for we must be on our way to the noble house you come from. We can hope for no greater pleasure than to pay respects to the master of your house. It will be a privilege to visit him. Friends, we wish you well on your expedition. May Christ go with you.'

Presently, the three of them mounted their little mules and rode away towards the house. They looked a slightly comical sight, the three large bodies on the mules, and as I watched them trot away, I fell asleep.

I was the first to wake up, and, to my horror, I realized

that it was totally dark. At first I did not know where I was, for it took me a moment or two to recall the circumstances which had led me to where I was. I had a passing fear that I was alone in some dark jungle from which any escape was impossible. But soon, becoming accustomed to the darkness, I saw the other bodies beside me, and remembered how we had all stretched ourselves on the ground for a short rest. I had no way of knowing what the time was, no way of determining whether it had only just got dark or whether it had been dark for many hours. A panic overcame me and I began to shout, 'Veríssimo, Veríssimo!' I had to shake him violently by the shoulders in order to wake him, and soon the two of us were shouting at and shaking the others one by one.

'What has happened?' we all seemed to be asking simultaneously when we had more or less come to our senses, and some of the Negroes were also asking, 'Where are we?'

'A moment ago it was barely noon,' Antônio remarked, 'and now it is night. What has happened?'

'We just didn't wake up!' one Negro exclaimed, for some reason finding the situation funny.

'Something went wrong,' I said, suddenly having a sense of what had happened. 'Otherwise, how could *all* of us have slept on for so long?'

'What do you mean?' Antônio asked.

'Try to think,' I said, a little impatient at the stupidity of my elder brother. 'We all fell asleep almost simultaneously, and not one of us woke up until now. I don't think that's natural, do you?'

'How could it be?' he asked. 'I mean how could this unnatural thing have happened?'

'The friars!' Veríssimo shouted out. 'They tricked us, we've been robbed!'

'It was the water,' I cried aloud, 'the water they gave us to drink, there must have been something in it which put us to sleep.'

'Yes,' said Veríssimo. 'It was a clever trick. They weren't friars at all, but robbers. My bag of coins has gone.'

'The meat has gone,' shouted a Negro who had been in charge of the provisions.

'My money's gone, too,' Antônio said.

'It's a wonder they didn't kill us all,' I said. 'We must be thankful for that, at least.'

'I'll ride to the house,' one of the soldiers said. 'I'll go kill them.'

'Don't be so damned stupid,' I said to him. 'They never had any intention of going there.'

'We shall have to return,' Antônio said.

'No,' Veríssimo said with loud emphasis. 'We do not retreat. If we've been taken for fools, we do not go back and declare the fact to your father. That is not the way of soldiers. We have not been beaten, only tricked. We do not retreat.'

'But, Veríssimo,' Antônio persisted, 'we have no money, we have no provisions. How can we go on?'

'We have our bodies,' Veríssimo said. 'We have our wits. We have our horses. It is not the way of soldiers to give in after the first little setback. If we don't have food, we find it.'

'What if we don't?' Antônio asked.

'Antônio,' I said, 'what kind of a coward are you? Veríssimo is absolutely right. I can see that it is tempting to go back to replenish our supplies just because we are so near home. But we waste time that way, and what do you think everyone is going to think of us? They're going to have a good laugh at their little army which is so brave and clever it can't go five miles before it has to return because three crafty robbers have tricked it so easily. If you want humiliation and if you want to be branded a coward, go back. I say no, I say that we should follow Veríssimo's judgement.'

Antônio did not answer, but began to sulk, while Veríssimo, emboldened by my affirmation of faith in him, ordered us to rise and resume our journey.

'In the dark?' one voice asked.

'Yes, right now in the dark,' Veríssimo shouted back. 'You should be quite safe at any rate, no one will see your black face in the dark.'

94

This put the Negro soldiers in a good humour, and soon we were all mounted on our horses and on our way. It was a novel experience for me, to be riding out at night; the cool night air was a change from the heat of the day, and although there was no moon, there were plenty of bright stars to give us some light. We rode quietly, and I kept thinking of the phoney friars – no doubt the others were absorbed by the same thought, too – and hoped that one day we would come upon them and inflict upon them the revenge they deserved.

The next five days of our journey passed without any extraordinary event. Of course, we had problems, especially that of finding food, but the ingenuity of eighteen men is not inconsiderable and it is sufficient to say here that we managed to feed ourselves in one way or another. On the third day we had come to a village and we debated whether we should trade in one of our horses for food. We decided against doing so, Veríssimo concluding the argument with, 'Better to eat him when the time comes than to sell him for a few pounds of dried meat.' Instead, he persuaded a merchant to give us meat and bread in return for a show that we would put on. Within half an hour, Veríssimo not only devised a show in which ten horsemen displayed a complicated pattern of movements, a kind of elaborate dance on horseback, but he also managed to rehearse the horsemen so that their subsequent performance was flawless. It was an enjoyable entertainment and the merchant was pleased to part with more meat than he had agreed to when the bargain was made.

So far, having crossed into the state of Pernambuco, we had been travelling through a dry barren plain, but on the fifth day we came to a shallow river which could easily be forded by the horses simply walking across it. It was late in the afternoon, and Veríssimo decided that we should compensate ourselves for the five days of long hours on horseback by spending the rest of the day beside the river. He had our unanimous approval, and within minutes all of us, including the horses, were gaily splashing in the river. The water was no more than thigh-deep, and we just floated about in it once we

95

were tired of playing such little tricks as coming up on someone and ducking him. In the evening, we lit a fire on the bank
of the river and sat around it while Veríssimo handed out our
meat ration and chunks of dry bread. While we ate, stories
were exchanged, and I was amused to observe that some of
the Negroes had a good knack for relating anecdotes. When
we had eaten and exhausted the story-telling, two Negroes
began to sing sad ballads, from which I remember one pretty
little tune with the words:

> O woman, you drive me insane,
> You know I'm married to the cane.
> Leave me, woman, leave me alone,
> I'm sick of your mutter and moan.
> Look! Round my neck is the iron chain
> Which keeps me married to the cane.

I suppose I liked this verse then and still do now because
the Negroes seemed to be confessing that they loved their
work in the plantation more than their wives. Soothed by such
gentle strains, such hypnotic melodies, we were all soon overcome by sleep. Veríssimo, Antônio and I in our hammocks
slung between trees, and the Negro soldiers on the ground,
the fire flickering youthfully, we were that evening a contented company whose members had discovered that comrade-
ship which comes from sharing common hardships. Of course,
our hardships so far had been few, and had mainly to do with
finding food after we had been tricked by the false friars; but
still, for me at least, who had been used to demanding and
receiving food at a moment's notice, the notion that food was
something precious for which I depended on the wits of my
companions filled me with a thrilling fear. The thought that
we could conceivably starve had a strange attraction.

When I awoke the next morning, I enjoyed the sight of the
early sunlight picking out the leaves of the tree above me.
I noticed something move and realized that it was a bird, a
large bird, a vulture, I suddenly recognized, that was circling

above the tree. I observed next that the vulture was only one of several which were silently and seemingly stealthily floating just above the top branches of the tree. Leaning up in my hammock, I saw that Antônio was sound asleep and that Veríssimo, although quite unconscious, was involuntarily brushing away some insect which appeared to be intent upon entering his mouth. I pulled myself up and climbed down from the hammock. A heap of ashes lay where the fire had been and the Negro soldiers were fast asleep nearby. I walked towards the river, deciding to wash myself, and as I did so, I suddenly stopped as my body was shot through with fear, for I had become aware of what I had seen a moment before: arrows stuck out of the bodies of some of the Negroes as if little flag-poles had been planted there. I suppressed the scream of horror and of fear which rose to my lips, realizing that I might be watched by the people who had shot the arrows and who might at this very moment be taking their aim at me. I threw myself to the ground and slowly found the courage with which to look around; I could see nothing except the trees and the vultures which circled above them, but I had heard sufficient stories about the subtle ways in which Indians camouflaged themselves to feel sick with fear. I wanted to cry out to Veríssimo, but decided that the situation called for both tact and discretion and that it would be wiser if I gradually crept up to where his hammock was. As I slowly moved up towards him, crawling on my belly and pausing in between each forward thrust to look around me, I had the irresistible urge to evacuate my bowels. This, I felt convinced was unnatural in me, that losing my normal control over such matters was probably a consequence of the sickness I was feeling; but I was unable to suppress the urge by rationalizing it, and nor did I feel strong enough to rise and run down to the river. Indeed, the very thought of running down to the river suggested to my mind an image of myself running, bent at the knees, and some twenty arrows singing through the air and ripping open my back; and hardly had this image occurred to my mind when explosions began to boom through my buttocks. I tore at my pants, which were already soiled, and sat up to let this matter of nature take its course now that it had begun without my collusion.

'What the hell are you up to?' I heard Antônio call. 'I suppose you want me to step right into your shit!'

I made a sign to him to be quiet, realizing that in my attempt to crawl to Veríssimo's hammock I had reached Antônio's and, of course, it must strike him as a nasty practical joke for someone, especially his younger brother, to be laying a pretty little trap for him when he descended.

'I'll get you for this,' he shouted out while I continued to make desperate signs to him to be quiet – which he probably interpreted as meaning that I did not wish the others to wake up and see me in my present posture. 'Christ! You stink! Just wait you little bastard, you think you're so damned clever, I'll get you.'

'Look,' I called, my voice half-choked within me while my bowels continued their perverse piece of exhibitionism, 'look there.' I pointed weakly to the dead Negroes.

The noise had woken Veríssimo, and now he began to talk loudly, 'Why, Gregório, couldn't you do the decent thing and go to the river-bank?'

I began to cry. This was too much for me and I suppose that in that moment of despair I thought that death would be welcome, and so I pulled up my pants and, the damned shit still bursting out of me, I ran down to the river. There I sat down and cried. I cried until both my bowels and my eyes were exhausted. I felt utterly miserable. And realizing now that no arrows had been shot at me during all this commotion, I felt all the more wretched that I had not been able to face fear calmly and that my fear had manifested itself in a manner which was bound to lead to ridicule and taunts of being a coward. I threw myself into the river and managed to find more tears to shed.

When I went back, Veríssimo had obviously realized what had happened, for he was now standing by the ashes of last night's fire and was talking to the soldiers who had woken up.

Four had not, for they lay there, each in his own blood, although someone had removed the arrows. Veríssimo was saying: 'The question rises, why did they spare the rest of us? Let me put it in another way. Were we the Indians, and had we come upon a party of whites and blacks, we would have known at once that we looked upon a dangerous enemy. The enemy lay asleep, the enemy was at our mercy. Why do we decide to kill only four? Why not eliminate the entire company?'

There was a pause as each man puzzled over the question, as each man stood or sat there in a pool of fear, his mind confused by images suggested by the fear.

'To frighten the enemy,' Antônio said. 'To make us afraid because they have shown us that they have the power and the arrogance to come right into our camp and do what they like with us and to go away.'

'Yes, yes,' said a Negro named Anselmo who had a deep scar across his right cheek. 'To show us they have us at their mercy.'

'No,' said Veríssimo, ponderously shaking his head. 'They cannot be so foolish. For to let the majority of us escape is to invite danger for themselves; whereas had they killed us all, no one would have known for many months what had happened to us. Now they must know that having killed four of us they can only expect the rest of us to be provoked into hunting them out to take our revenge.'

'You mean to go on?' Antônio asked, and I must say that although I am no coward, I felt like asking the same question.

'Yes,' Veríssimo said. 'As long as I have one soldier left, I shall command, and my command is never to retreat.'

'But we still don't know,' Anselmo said, 'why they let us free.'

'I know,' I said. 'Obviously something must have made them think that someone had woken up. Perhaps someone moaned in his sleep, or something, and they fled.'

'That is likely,' Veríssimo said. 'Clearly, there could not have been more than two or three sent here specifically to butcher us all, for two or three rather than a whole lot of them would be likely to do the job more quietly and also be able to slip away easily if anything went wrong.'

'How did they do it?' Olympio asked, a Negro whose head was completely bald and already glistened with sweat. 'How could even one of them come here in the dark and be as soft as a cat and not even make a horse stamp his foot, not even make one little false move?'

'You don't know the cunning of the Indian,' Veríssimo said in so matter of fact a tone that the horror of his implication plucked more sweat from my body.

'The question now is,' Veríssimo said, 'what is to be our next move? I suggest we all wash ourselves in the river, have a breakfast, and in the meanwhile I shall plan our strategy. We have also to bury the bodies and say a Christian prayer over them.'

'If I may suggest it,' I said, 'we should appoint two soldiers to keep guard over the camp.'

'A good suggestion,' Veríssimo said. 'I was going to make it myself. From now on we shall have two guards on duty, each man serving in rotation, so that someone will be awake twenty-four hours of the day.'

The first two guards were appointed and the others began to make their way to the river. Antônio called to the men, 'I should go upstream, friends, Gregório has been shitting in the river.'

There was some uncouth laughter at this very poor joke which I pretended not to have heard, for if there is anything I abhor it is vulgarity.

Two or three hours passed while the bodies were buried and while the men washed and ate and finally collected the equipment together. Veríssimo was pacing up and down, staring at the ground and now and then looking up at the sky. He did not seem to want the men to hurry, and when anyone tried to speak to him, he impatiently brushed him aside and continued to frown at his own thoughts. I sat by a tree, waiting and wondering what was to happen to us. I looked across

100

the river which we had crossed; a dusty, dry plain extended to the horizon there, reminding me of the previous day when we had slowly trudged across it, weary and thirsty, until we had reached the river and had joyously plunged into it. On this side was the fairly thick vegetation on the river's bank; a dry area with patches of grass lay ahead of us and in the distance I could see more trees. Soon, perhaps within three or four miles, we would be on the edge of the jungle. We would be entering a world of which the Indians knew every contour, every little dip in the land, and of which we knew nothing; we would be among trees which would be to us like the walls of a narrow cell and which were to the Indians the sentinels of freedom; the jungle's herbs which gave to the Indians medicines with which to cure themselves of sickness we would not dare touch with our lips for fear that we sucked at poison.

Veríssimo stopped pacing up and down and, taking a map out of a leather pouch at his hip, unfolded it and began to examine it. He frowned and sucked at his teeth, tapped his tongue on the roof of his mouth and shook his head. The wrinkles on his forehead seemed to deepen as he stared at the map. In the distance Antônio was tightening the saddle-straps on his horse. Some of the soldiers, having nothing to do, squatted on the ground and exchanged gossip. It was becoming hotter; not only the heat but also insects were thickening the air. Finally, Veríssimo put his map away and, giving the impression that he had been granted some private revelation, ordered the men to mount their horses and with a great air of confidence, which suggested that he knew precisely what he was doing, led us in a north-easterly direction. It was the direction I had been looking at earlier and it had seemed to me the inevitable course for us to take.

Although we reached the trees which I had taken to be the edge of the jungle within an hour of leaving the river, we were nowhere near the jungle. Indeed, the trees were short and dry and not at all profuse; and in fact, it was worse territory to be riding through than the barren plain, for there

101

one could at least proceed in a straight line whereas among these trees one had to wind one's way and yet gain none of the advantages that one would expect – shade, moisture, perhaps pools of water. As it was, we did not come to another river for two more days and did not reach the real edge of the jungle for several more days – by then I had lost count of time, and could not have told how long it was since we had left home. I thought of home at nights, lying in my hammock, listening to strange and frightening sounds, which were strange because during the daytime we saw no creatures apart from birds, and frightening because with the falling of night a multitude of beasts seemed to be miraculously created. Thinking of home filled me with a heavy melancholy, and I have to confess that my thoughts were less of my father and my new mother and more of Aurelia; what's more, thinking of Aurelia, I hoped that the darkness provided me sufficient privacy in my hammock, for I could not, on several nights, resist imagining that I embraced her body and, doing so, turn in my hammock and squeeze out my growing passion for her.

We had no more misadventures during these days although it was suggested that the Indians could very possibly be following us stealthily. One of the four horses which were now free, following the death of the four soldiers, provided us with good meat for several days, and we kept replenishing our supply of water whenever we came to a river. The principal question which now occurred to some of us, though no one dared mention it to Veríssimo who seemed to be possessed of some fantastic vision, was for how long were we to continue. One day Antônio said to me, 'This trip is a bore.'

'Come, come,' I said, 'don't forget our mission.'

'What mission?' he asked, managing to convey a bitterness of tone.

'To take our revenge on Indians for having attacked our house, to avenge the bodies of the four Negroes, to capture Indians to add to our father's property, to capture Indians to turn into Christians. Why, the Pope will bless us when he hears!'

'Nonsense,' said Antônio. 'How many of us are there now? Fourteen. Suppose we capture Indians, how many are we going to capture? Two, six, a dozen, twenty? And how are we going to keep them meek and quiet while we take them back home? We have iron collars for fifteen or so, but how are we going to make them wear them? By telling them to be good Christians and to learn to love the whip with which we discolour their backs?'

'Why, Antônio, how can you have so little faith!'

'What's it got to do with faith?' he cried. 'Look, the Indians are a savage lot. They're going to eat us before they let us baptize them or whatever we think we're going to do to them.'

'Veríssimo knows what he's doing,' I said while admitting to myself that I had not thought of the possibility of being eaten by the Indians.

'Veríssimo's an old man,' Antônio said. 'He probably has some mad idea that he's back in India or Africa or some place where he was a dashing young soldier. He's just playing a game with his imagination. What does he know about the jungle? Nothing. He can't tell one tree from another. He's so ignorant of insects, he can't tell a fly from a mosquito.'

'That's not true!'

'Maybe not,' Antônio said, 'but what I mean is he's generally ignorant about this land.'

'No, Antônio, we've got to trust him. He's our leader. And besides our father wanted us to come on this expedition, he wanted us to follow and obey Veríssimo.'

'Our father's back home, he doesn't know what the jungle's like, he doesn't have to sleep in a hammock wondering if a snake is not uncoiling down on him.'

'Antônio, this is Brazil, this is our country.'

'This is a knife, its point an inch away from our flesh.'

There our dialogue abruptly came to an end, for it seemed that our views would remain irreconcilably opposed. Perhaps he felt secretly the need I experienced to undertake a heroic action; and perhaps I felt – well, I'm willing to admit that I

103

did – a grave fear that we were foolishly journeying towards death and that the cause for which we penetrated more and more into the jungle was a ridiculously unimportant one. I have to admit that privately I, too, began to despair.

The jungle began to thicken around us, slowing us down, for vines and creepers covered the ground and the trees left little space for our horses to go through. One day we were making hardly any progress, and Veríssimo ordered the men to cut down the vegetation to make a small clearing in which we could camp. While the soldiers began to hack at the trees and bushes, Veríssimo, Antônio and I stood aside taking sips of water.

'We're almost there now,' Veríssimo said, looking at his map.

'Where?' Antônio asked.

'Where the Indians are,' Veríssimo said.

'How do you know they are there?'

'Well, Antônio,' Veríssimo said, 'I hope you don't take me for a fool. I have, I think I can say without boasting about it, served the King in serious and bloody wars with some honour. You didn't expect me to come on this expedition without finding out the facts first, did you?'

'Once we were tricked by thieves,' Antônio said tactlessly, 'and once we were nearly massacred by the Indians. Sure you know all the facts!'

'Antônio,' I said, 'how can you be so ignorant of the ways of war? Chance can interfere in the plans of the most skilful general, you should know that. A soldier's duty is to support his general whatever happens.'

'What will we do,' Antônio persisted in asking another foolish question, 'when we're near the Indians?'

'Ah,' Veríssimo said, generously taking Antônio's question seriously, 'no general will describe his strategy in advance.'

At that moment a tree crashed down near us, making us all jump back. It missed us by several feet, but our sudden consciousness that it was falling in our direction a moment before we actually realized what was happening produced a retrospective fright, and a second after it fell, leaving us safe, I imagined it falling again but this time crash straight on my head and cracking my skull open. Veríssimo swore at the Negroes who had cut the tree down and went off in their direction. But before he could walk two or three paces, an extraordinarily dense cloud of tiny insects sprang out of the vegetation and exploded into a vicious whining sound as if a million little wings vibrated in anger. I lost sight not only of Veríssimo but also of everything else as I was forced to close my eyes on the tens of thousands of insects which crowded in on my face. Soon I was slapping my face wildly and screaming like one who has gone quite crazy, aware, while I did so, that all my companions were suffering the same fate, for I could hear louder screams than my own. The insects seemed to be attacking my face in waves as if my face were a fort which they needed to topple or die themselves in the attempt. I found myself flinging my arms wildly about me while at the same time trying to slap my face as frequently and as hard as possible. The insects began to attack my hands and arms and, reaching my ankles, began to travel up my trouser legs. In my hysteria, I was aware that the menace of the insects was not that their bite was painful but that it was frightening, horribly frightening. And soon I had to cease screaming, for my open mouth had attracted hundreds of them and I was trying to cough them out while realizing the painful knowledge that my nostrils were being closed, too. If I had had a hundred arms to wave about me and a hundred hands to slap at the air around me, I would not have succeeded in allaying to any appreciable degree the monstrous numbers which attacked me, nor the pain which I was suffering, nor the horror which I felt. I began to run around, mad as an enraged bull. But not seeing anything, I crashed into a tree so fiercely that I rebounded off it and fell on my back, being simultaneously victim to how many hurts I could not tell in the frenzy in which I was, but remember feeling a sharp pain in my forehead as well as bruises in several parts of my body. At the time, however, if I was conscious of anything it was that if the

105

insects did not kill me with their pinching and biting, then I would soon die of suffocation. My hysteria seemed to spend itself when I fell back, for now although the insects did not diminish, I just lay there hoping that if I had to die then let it be a quick death. My screaming had given way to whimpering just as my hysteria had given way to resignation. I heard the screams and shouts of some of the others and vaguely wondered how my brother was when I heard the horses. For, clearly, the horses had been as enraged and rendered as crazy by the insects as I and my companions had been, and now they had apparently begun to run around wildly in the narrow area in which we all were and to make such a terrifying sound that for a moment I was petrified into forgetting my own suffering. Soon, however, not only was my suffering brought back to me but a new danger appeared, for as I listened to the horses rushing around, I felt the hoofs of one so near to me that it was only a matter of luck that he missed stamping me into the earth. I stood up and for a very brief moment opened my eyes. I saw a grey darkness, for the vicious cloud of insects still lay heavily around me, and in the greyness I saw the dark forms of the horses going round and round, making a high-pitched sound. I hopefully flung myself forward and banged against the tree from which I had earlier rebounded, prepared to suffer more bruises provided I could find some escape from the fury of the horses. My eyes again shut, I groped my way to the back of the tree, and was thus safe from the horses. The insects came with me as if they were part of my clothing. Having saved myself from the horses, I now found some energy with which to renew my attempts to slap away the insects, and again I began to scream and fling my arms about the air. In the meanwhile, the din from the narrow area which the soldiers had been trying to clear continued fearfully. And suddenly, the horses stopped. It was incredible in the situation in which I was that anything should come to a stop, and it took me a moment or two to realize that the horses had stopped. Although the cries of the men continued, there seemed to be a total silence when the

106

horses became quiet. I was so amazed that I opened my eyes. First I saw the wonderful fact that the insects had vanished, and then I saw the new horror: three soldiers lay bleeding on the ground, stamped to death by the horses. One of the soldiers still had across him a horse which lay on its side upon the soldier's stomach, so that all but the soldier's head appeared to be crushed under the horse's weight; his head seemed to be stuck on the horse's back, the mouth open, oozing blood, the eyes fixedly looking up as if they saw some maddening vision up on a distant tree. Three other horses lay dead on the ground; two had cracked their skulls against trees and one had apparently been choked to death by the insects. Seeing him, I wondered how I had not been choked to death, too, and became aware now of my own immediate discomfort which consisted mainly of the presence of the insects inside my trousers, my shirt and some in my ear-holes and nostrils.

Soon, we were all gathered together, using rationed amounts of water with which to attempt to clean ourselves. Veríssimo walked about, examining the horses, and I could see from where I stood that some of the horses were still suffering from the shock of their recent experience if they were not also lying injured. I was not surprised when Veríssimo announced that seven of the horses would have to be shot. He instructed the soldiers to do so at once, but I suggested that it would be best if the horses could be taken away for we should try and not panic our remaining horses into another stampede. Veríssimo agreed with my suggestion and asked Anselmo and three other soldiers to take the horses down the path and to shoot them as discreetly as was possible in the difficult circumstances in which we had found ourselves.

'Well, general,' Antônio asked, 'what next?'

Veríssimo ignored him and ordered a soldier to inspect the food supply and to report if any of it had been damaged.

'Antônio,' I said, 'this is no time for quarrelling.'

'Quiet, puppy,' Antônio said to me.

107

'You don't have to call me names,' I said. 'We're all in the same trouble, and it doesn't help to get angry.'

'Look, go and yap at the trees, will you?'

Veríssimo, who had been listening to this exchange while pretending that he was too busy to have any patience with Antônio's kind of nonsense, said: 'We've lost three more men, reducing our company to a total of eleven. We cannot afford to have disputes. As for your question, Antônio, what happens next is up to all of us. Your opinion will be as important as anyone else's. For the immediate, however, I can say that we shall have to spend the night here. The insects attacked the food and thousands of them seem to have got stuck to the meat. We shall have to spend tomorrow doing what we can with the dead horses.'

Just then, as if to give a gruesome emphasis to Veríssimo's point, we heard shots in the distance and knew that the soldiers had fired at the wounded horses. Veríssimo's quiet tone and firm reasoning seemed to calm my petulant brother down, and when the soldiers who had gone to kill the horses returned, Veríssimo suggested that we all busy ourselves at once with the several tasks which needed immediate attention: burying the dead, lighting a fire on which to roast a horse, and putting up the hammocks.

The first two tasks took up what was left of the day, and as night fell, we sat round the fire, discussing the situation in which we found ourselves. I could have predicted that Veríssimo was determined not to turn back, that he was going to give us no option but to continue our pursuit of Indians.

'We're going to make a fine sight,' he mocked at my brother's suggestion that we return, 'when the eleven of us straggle back through the gates of your father's house. The wives of the seven soldiers who have been killed are going to spit at our faces and cry, demanding for what purpose did their husbands give up their lives, what was the purpose of our going forth in such splendour when we had to return like cowards? And what will we say to them? That we returned because some insects bit us? Because some Indians surprised

108

us in the middle of the night?'

Clearly, Veríssimo had a most moving effect on the soldiers who still suffered from the shock of having lost their friends. And their faces indicated that they agreed with their leader. Veríssimo, noticing this, went on: 'Where are the Indians? they will ask when we return. Did you not bring back *one* Indian? they will ask. And we lost seven of our men while you did not even *see* an Indian? What are you, soldiers, or children playing hide and seek in the jungle? My friends, you will have to answer all these questions when you return if that is what you want to do now. And as for your father,' Veríssimo added, addressing the remark to Antônio and me, 'to which corner of the house will we turn in which to hide our shame when he asks us to give an account of ourselves? Or will he generously laugh away our failure and say, Ha, ha, it is nothing to have lost my horses, it is nothing to have lost my slaves provided I have cowards as sons. No, my friends, I tell you, it will be the height of foolishness for us to return empty-handed.'

'And what is the alternative,' Antônio asked, 'never to return at all? Quite frankly, I'm not interested in being a hero if that means I will die here of insect-bites. All you're concerned about is the prestige of soldiers, all that bothers you is that you might be called a coward. But what guarantee is there that we're going to capture and take back enough Indians for everyone to be happy that the losses have been worthwhile? None at all. There are eleven of us left. The jungle may have a hundred, a thousand, a million Indians. We just don't know. If anyone gets captured, I know who it will be. And I know exactly what will happen to us, too, when we're captured. What is the point of it all? What kind of heroism is this which demands that suicide be its precondition? I say, no. We have had enough. Seven lives have been lost for no purpose, let us not lose any more. Let us return. Let us suffer the shame. Soon, everyone will forget about it. Soon, we will live our own lives in peace.'

I have to admit that there was some sense in what Antônio

had to say, and I could see that the soldiers were beginning to look worried. Being simple-minded, it was too much for them to be given one set of convincing arguments and then to be told the opposite which seemed also to be convincing; that there could be more truths than one on any given situation was something which was beyond their comprehension.

'And what's more,' Antônio went on, 'we're soon going to run out of food. We thought we could use the horses for food, but look at what happened. We've shot seven horses today because they were wounded, and all we can manage to do is to cook one, for it is impossible to cook seven in this place and even if we could do so, we would find it difficult to carry all that food through this jungle; and even if we could carry it all, most of it would become putrid before we needed to eat it. So, all we do is to waste our resources. And don't tell me that, when we run out of what little we've got left, all kinds of fowl will present themselves for our delight. Look, the jungle is thick, and we haven't come across even a simple fruit we could live off.'

The soldiers, confused by conflicting rhetoric, were becoming restless, and Anselmo said: 'Yes, master, what you say is true. We must go back.'

For one of their own kind to say this inspired the other soldiers, and they all began to demand that we return. I could see from Veríssimo's face that he was angered by this demonstration; for he believed in his own absolute power, and for anyone to challenge his judgement was not only to cast a doubt on his qualities of leadership but was also to denigrate sacred military principles. By a stroke of inspiration, I suddenly thought of a way of saving the situation.

'To return,' I said, 'does not necessarily mean that we return at once to my father's house. Our first consideration is that we should retreat to a safer place than we are in at present. Our second consideration is our honour. We shall feel ashamed if we return directly and have nothing to give but news of the death of seven of our soldiers. Therefore, I suggest that we do the following. We march back to some of

110

the villages we came through. You will remember how we performed at the villages for our food. Well, we could perform for money. We could live in safety and yet we could accomplish the task for which we set out. We could make enough money with which to buy Indian slaves. All we would need would be about ten slaves and we could march back to the house in triumph.'

Even as I spoke, I realized that my scheme was not entirely capable of success. For the Indians would cost more money than we could probably earn in a short time and remembering, too, that we would have to pay for our food, the possibility of our saving any money was remote. But to my surprise, everyone enthusiastically welcomed my scheme, including, I was astonished to see, Veríssimo – which seemed to suggest that he was glad to be persuaded that we should turn back and that all he needed was a trick with which to save his face.

Well, the next day we began our retreat as soon as we had packed the hammocks and had the horses ready. It had taken us several days trudging through the gradually thickening jungle for us to reach the spot where the insects had attacked us; leaving it, the jungle should obviously have thinned out gradually, but it did not seem to do so. I thought that this was merely a trick of the imagination, for I could not to any precise degree remember what exactly the jungle looked like. Also, since we had all agreed to return, we seemed to be anxious to see the end of the jungle and our pace was far quicker than it had been when we had come. One day, it must have been four or five days after we began our retreat, we were proceeding down a slope where the jungle was so thick that we had to walk, leading our horses by the hand, for it was necessary to hack down the branches in our path to make way for the width of the horses. As we slowly made our way down the slope, we noticed that there was a river in the distance, for there was more light there and soon we could see the sun's reflections on the river. At that moment we knew that we had completely lost our way, for we had not crossed

111

this river before. In our disbelief, we approached the river in complete silence. It was a good quarter of a mile away and we were still in the jungle which was thick enough for the river to be totally obscured at times. As we came closer to the river and looked down upon it, we noticed some white objects on its banks. All of us seemed to stop simultaneously as we recognized that the white objects were Indian women, completely naked, bathing on the river's edge or combing their long black hair.

I do not doubt that all of us had the same thought when we first saw the Indian women – were they really there on the river's edge, innocently bathing without any regard that they might be witnessed by strangers, or was it some vision that we saw? If what we saw was real, then our expedition had fortuitously succeeded; we had found an Indian settlement. But now we had to come to terms with the next aim of the expedition: to capture the Indians. For the moment, however, we feasted on the vision, the beautiful bodies of the Indian women; we were too far away to observe the warm subtleties of their flesh, but we were near enough to realize that the Indian woman's body is a fine delineation of basic beauty. And in this respect, too, there could be only one thought in our minds. Inevitably, memories of Aurelia came to my mind, and my limbs engaged themselves in a moment's fantasy with the slender figure of one of the Indian women whom I looked at while I recalled Aurelia's breath at my mouth. I would have passed out, standing there, had not Veríssimo quietly ordered a retreat.

We obeyed hypnotically and did not open a questioning mouth until we were a good mile away from the spot where we had momentarily stood petrified both by fear and by incipient ecstasy. As might have been expected, the first person to speak was my brother.

'What's the strategy now, general?' he asked, persisting with the habit he had formed recently of referring to Veríssimo as the general. 'What do we do now? We wanted to find Indians, and now that we've found them, the first thing we do is to run away from them as quickly as we can!'

'Antônio,' I felt compelled to say, 'that is a most unfair statement. What did you expect, for all of us to charge down at once, or let our horses give away our presence? Military bravery doesn't mean that we should present our naked chests as easy targets. Sometimes one needs to retreat before advancing.'

'That is very well spoken,' Veríssimo said. 'Gregório is a born soldier. His logical mind has perceived something of my intentions. Well, soldiers, fate obviously did not wish us to leave the jungle without accomplishing the noble task that brought us here. That is the only reason I can think why the good Lord thought it fit that we should lose our way. Since we had given in to the cowardly notion of retreating, the Lord took pity on us and has shown us where the Indians are.'

'Why don't you go and capture one or two?' Antônio asked.

'Antônio,' Veríssimo replied, 'the good Lord will forgive our mistakes, but will have no pity on any foolishness we might be led to commit.'

'It seems to me,' I said, thinking to myself how wonderfully patient Veríssimo was with the stupidities of my brother and that the least I could do was to give my support to the old soldier, 'that what we need to do is to pitch ourselves here for tonight, and then we should spend a few days sending scouts around this territory to discover first of all the nature of the enemy. And then, we could decide how best we ought to attack.'

'Precisely,' Veríssimo said. 'Gregório, your thinking is so clear and militarily sound, that I think that when we get back I shall suggest to your father that he send you to Lisbon with my warmest recommendation to the King that his majesty accept you as a soldier in his army.'

Antônio laughed as though what Veríssimo had said were a joke, but no one paid any attention to him, for Veríssimo went on: 'Gregório has in fact outlined exactly the plan I had. We shall stay here for at least two days which we will

113

use to discover all the facts we can about the enemy. And then we shall be ready for action.'

After the next day's scouting, we discovered a strange fact: there were no men in the Indian settlement on the banks of the river. This information excited a certain amount of mirth among the Negro soldiers, two or three of whom joked among themselves that they could now lead a life of luxury and lechery.

'The men have gone hunting, that's all,' Antônio said, making one of the very few sensible statements that he did on the expedition. 'How the hell do you think they've had all those children, by magic?'

Anselmo suggested that Indian women made more useful slaves than the men, and there was no reason why we could not capture as many women as we could cope with and take them back rather than wait for their men to return. 'And what's more,' he added with a twinkle in his eye, 'women are like the land and can give an annual crop.'

'Just because they are women,' Veríssimo said with some deliberation, 'does not mean that they'll submit without a fight. Don't think it's going to be easy.'

Veríssimo described the plan. We were to invade the village on the next day, an hour before sunrise in the grey light of the early morning.

Leaving the horses behind, we slipped into the village in the early morning dark. We formed ourselves in five pairs, which left Veríssimo alone by himself. The idea was that we would stealthily go into the huts and attempt noiselessly to capture a woman each. If we could accomplish this without arousing the rest of the village, we would retreat to our position in the jungle; if not, then we would try to bring back two or three women as hostages. I found myself paired with Anselmo, and the two of us softly approached our target. The sun had not yet risen, but there was beginning to be light in the sky, and we could clearly see the hut some thirty yards away. I was relieved that there were no dogs and yet was puzzled about this fact. Maybe, I thought, Indians had not learned to keep domestic animals. It seemed unnatural to me that people who lived in the jungle should not keep dogs, and the notion of a people being in any sense unnatural filled me with intense fear, suggesting that they possessed some magical qualities or some supernatural powers. Of course, I said to myself as I walked, all my present thoughts are the working of fear, and I wondered how I could be analysing myself so coolly and yet suffering the thing which I could analyse and pondering almost objectively. This thought made my fear all the greater, and with each step I took, a drop of sweat seemed to fall loudly. That, too, I thought about, the sweat falling, and said to myself, Of course it's not making any noise, how can it be, a drop of sweat can't make any more sound than a feather falling; but I can tell you I heard the drops fall as though they were the round balls at the end of drumsticks and the ground a loudly echoing drum. I don't know what Anselmo was feeling right then, and I didn't ask him. Well, we reached the hut. This was a simple structure of thatched leaves with a wide-open entrance; it was merely meant to be a protection against the rain and the sun and not what we call a home. We stood at the entrance, trying not to be too conspicuous, and looked in. It took us some time to realize that there was no one there, that the hut was totally empty. Without saying anything to each other, we moved to another hut, some ten or fifteen feet away. My fear worsened as I walked, for I was now thinking of what might have been happening right now if someone had been in the hut. Having to go through the process of walking to a hut all over again brought up a sickness within me. I had never known fear to take on so powerfully physical a presence within my body. But this hut, too, turned out to be empty. As we stood beside it, the light having now increased, it occurred to me that the two huts were empty not by some accident, and I suddenly had the feeling that *all* the huts were empty and that there could be only one reason why they were so: the Indian women knew of our presence in the jungle and had prepared a trap for us.

While I suffered these chilling thoughts, Anselmo and I

continued to look into more and more huts; I observed that we walked now without the fear that we might attract someone's attention. Such apparent carelessness at least ought to have indicated that my general fear had diminished, but unfortunately that was not so; in fact, it had increased, for the question asked itself again and again, What was the trap we had walked into? Well, as we moved from hut to hut, it happened that the others in our party had been doing precisely the same thing, and soon we all found ourselves beside the three huts which were closer to the river than any of the others. A muffled laughter came from Antônio, who was no doubt determined to prove himself a cretin before our expedition ended. I walked straight to Veríssimo and said: 'It's a trap, we'd do best to retreat as quickly as we can.'

'Gregório,' Veríssimo said with an unnecessary display of his authority, 'I have already commended your military insight. We are now in the field of battle and I suggest you allow me, your leader, to make what decisions my experienced reading of the situation leads me to make.'

Antônio laughed aloud, and Veríssimo turned sternly to him and said: 'As for you, Antônio, I wish you to remember that passing moments of indiscipline during a march or an encampment are one thing but that any kind of behaviour which in any way departs from the strict code of the army is greatly to be reprehended and will be dealt with later with appropriate severity.'

'Christ!' Antônio exclaimed, 'what army? Don't forget, old man, you are a servant of my father.'

This was obviously a foolish statement for Antônio to have made and I was sorry to see that it was not merely a statement which had unfortunately slipped out of his mouth for which he might later be sorry, but that, on the contrary, he seemed distinctly pleased at having made it. To divert Veríssimo's attention from this unforgivable rudeness, I said to him: 'Sir, we await your military command; the situation is one of extreme danger.'

Saying this, I only reminded myself of the ghastly situation

116

we were in and, in the silly way I have of connecting one event with another, remembered the time in chapel when I thought I simply had to run out and go to the lavatory to evacuate my bowels and yet felt it would be a shameful and an irreligious thing to do and stayed there suffering from the awful knowledge that if the service did not end in five minutes I would explode right there in the pew.

Antônio giggled, making me wonder why he was behaving in so silly a manner. I think now that he had gone hysterical, that he had seen what none of us had yet noticed in that murky morning light. And what he had seen was a long line of Indian women standing on the opposite bank of the river. I am glad to say that I was man enough to overcome my fear for a moment to say to myself, My God, what a beautiful sight! I have seen nothing like it again. The totally naked women standing in a line along the river's edge in that grey early morning light – if ever my perceptions approximated to the image of a dream, it was at that moment. Antônio, I noticed, was not looking in the direction of the women, but he was still giggling and bursting out with moments of soft laughter. He had seen something else.

Behind us, among the trees, on the slope, stood Indian *men,* a crowd of them, and it seemed that more were coming down the jungle. Those whom we could see clearly were armed with bows and arrows. And even in that moment of recognizing that my death was at hand, I had the most absurd thought: I thought that Aurelia stood on the other side of the river, beautiful and naked, beckoning me, and that I knew that I must go to her while I also knew that no sooner would I take my first step towards her than an arrow would pierce my back. This strange fantasy aside, it was obvious to all of us that unless a miracle occurred, the moment of our death had arrived on this grey dawn in the middle of the jungle. Was this, I wondered, the Brazil my father had sent me out to experience?

The miracle did not occur. For a few moments, we simply stood there as if we had become statues. The light was in-

117

creasing; at least I could now clearly see that the Indian men outnumbered us at least five to one, though how many more there were behind the trees I had no way of determining. Then, Anselmo saw our chance.

'The canoes!' he whispered as if he was himself astonished at his own discovery.

There were four small canoes on the river beside the bank. Seeing them, gave us hope, a feeble hope, for in our hearts we knew that as soon as we took a step, the Indians would shoot. I did not doubt that they were perfect marksmen, but it suddenly occurred to me that if the Indians had deliberately deserted the huts and had carefully planned trapping us, then they would not have made this error of leaving the canoes where we would find them and probably attempt to use them.

'I think,' I said softly, keeping my eyes on the Indians, 'they mean us to take the canoes. I don't know why they should want to let us go, but I think they've left them deliberately.'

We began to step back towards the river, keeping our eyes on the men with the bows and arrows. I was right! They did not shoot, but merely observed us keenly.

'Three men in each of the first three canoes,' Veríssimo whispered. 'Gregório and I will take the fourth one.'

Even as we were slowly trying to escape from the Indians, I began to imagine alligators and piranha that were probably waiting downstream to devour us to death. But now that the situation was more extreme than it was ever likely to get, I felt freer, even a little relieved to know that this was the nature of suffering. Well, no sooner than did we all begin to paddle down the river than the Indians began to shoot. I had been wrong – I was happy to admit – about their being good marksmen, for their aim was so appalling that I was willing to believe later that they had merely attempted to scare the hell out of us. Certainly, we didn't smile back at them when the arrows began to fly, for we paddled like madmen. Anselmo, in the first canoe with two other Negroes, set a fast pace and there must have been a good thirty feet between his canoe and ours. It was almost comical to find the arrows falling limply into the water around us, and I must say that I was already congratulating myself on the fact that there were no alligators and piranha in the river. Just then an arrow pierced the right shoulder of one of the Negroes in Anselmo's canoe. I saw him lean over sideways in a slow action, as if I was again in a dream, and fall with a sudden acceleration of rhythm and go crashing into the water; the moment he went over, which happened both slowly as well as all too quickly, and had the effect of unsettling the balance of the canoe, Anselmo and the other soldier toppled into the water, too. I saw the two of them try and snatch at the canoe which was rapidly drifting away from them and I could see that unless one of the other canoes raced up to them, the two would be drowned together with the wounded soldier whom I had already given up for dead, for he seemed to be making no attempt to save himself. Antônio was in the second canoe and it could not have been more than ten feet away from the one in which Anselmo had been; at first, Antônio's canoe looked as if it was making for the direction of Anselmo and his unfortunate companion, but then it changed its course and began to go away from the two in the water. I could not understand this action, which looked like a miserable act of inhumanity all too typical – I was prepared to believe – of my brother. But as Veríssimo and I proceeded down the river and as I thought we might yet save Anselmo and his friend, I noticed that the water around them had crimsoned with the blood of the wounded soldier, and a moment later I realized why Antônio had changed course.

Piranha, which are maddened by blood and rarely attack otherwise, had sprung up from the deeps of the river at the smell of the wounded soldier's blood; already, the wounded soldier was nowhere to be seen, and as I desperately tried to follow the circuitous route established by Antônio, I could see that Anselmo and his companion were being rapidly bitten at by hundreds of little piranha. I was also aware that the arrows, which had earlier fallen limply into the water,

119

were now swishing past powerfully. Obviously, the Indians knew what we did not, and had waited to get us where they knew the piranha were. Just as this explanation occurred to me, I saw one more astonishing sight: the three Negroes in the canoe in front of us were paddling away furiously, inspiring me with the intensity of their action, when suddenly and simultaneously – and this simultaneity was the astonishing and nearly incredible part – each one was hit by an arrow at almost the identical place just below the neck and, as if the three were taking part in some well-drilled action, they turned over on their sides and collapsed into the water, each one in exactly the same manner. I wondered if the Indians had now taken to sport, if they were now showing how absolutely we were at their mercy. Fearing more piranha, I again changed course, hoping that rapid changes of direction would also help against the fantastic aim of the Indians. And veering suddenly left, I now saw that just at that moment the sun had come up and that I was approaching a bend in the river. I noticed a moment later that the arrows had either diminished or were being aimed wildly now. More fun and games, I thought, for I could not believe that the Indians who were shooting with such deadly perfection a moment earlier could suddenly begin to miss the mark wildly. There was a spot on my back where I expected a poisoned arrow to stick itself at any moment, thus fulfilling my vicious little brother Francisco's vile prophecy, but fortunately the Indians seemed so drunk with their own power that their mark had gone crazy. Seeing the sun again, I realized what had happened. It was one thing they had not considered in their calculations to send us to our bloody and horrible deaths, for the sun shone straight into their eyes now – as indeed it did into ours, though a little obliquely. Still, we did not need to see where we were going. We just wanted to get the hell out as fast as we could, and that is what we kept on doing, the two little canoes, the five of us who were left.

I felt sorry for Veríssimo who sat behind me in the canoe. Thirteen men had been lost as well as all the horses; if he survived and was not to be accountable in the near future to his heavenly master, he had his earthly master to satisfy. Obviously, whatever Antônio was likely to say on the matter, I would defend Veríssimo, for it was clear to me that our losses were not the consequence of any decisions taken by Veríssimo. I realized that these thoughts were both premature and irrelevant, for we were still struggling to flee from the Indians who might well be pursuing us stealthily. The river, containing wide, looping bends, obliging us to paddle for a good hour to travel a distance which along a straighter line would scarcely have taken us fifteen minutes, gave us the illusion of escape without really taking us very far. But we paddled on regardless, without thinking what hazards might not lie ahead of us. Several hours later, convinced that we had not been pursued, we decided to stop, especially as there was a little clearing on the bank of the river where it would be easy to disembark.

We collapsed on the little patch of land, exhausted and hungry. This was to be our condition for the next ten days or so. We decided that we should proceed down the river until we came to some settlement rather than risk attempting to find a way through the jungle. The river at least guaranteed that we travelled in one direction – albeit in a winding, wasteful manner. There was little conversation among us, for our discourse during these days was mostly the silent one with hunger, fear and despair. I noticed, looking at my friends, that little hollows had appeared on their faces; their cheeks had sunk in and their eyes seemed to have retracted, giving prominence to bony sockets. I supposed that I would look a stranger to myself, for I had not seen myself in a mirror for many weeks, possibly for some months. It was impossible to say for how long we had been away, and certainly the exercise of trying to determine it was totally irrelevant to our existence now. Time meant nothing to us; space was all, unending, thickly vegetated, dark space, which remained fearfully quiet all day but roared at night with the cries of beasts. Even that place beside the river where I had woken to see

121

four of the soldiers lying dead now possessed the attraction of home; and as for home itself, we dared not talk of it because of an unspoken superstition that were we to mention it, we would thereby forfeit what slim chance we had of reaching it again. It makes my forehead sweat again, thinking of that time when we drove ourselves on down the river, fighting exhaustion and hunger, and seeing no hope of ever emerging from the dark world which encompassed us.

Indeed, we did not all survive. By the time the Jesuit missionary found me beside the river and managed to coax the fever out of me, I realized as I recovered under his care that, could I succeed in returning to my father's house, then I would be the principal heir to his name and property.

Chapter 4

TWO PRIESTS

Unlike the others who died, Veríssimo did not suffer from
delirium; yet it was clear that some poison had entered his
blood, that the level of his blood was lowering like water
lowers down a well until the bucket cannot reach it any more.
His voice became quieter, his mind reflective. He did not say
what had happened to him, whether some insect had bitten
him or whether he had recognized that failure must be faced;
and that failure, too, which was not merely a passing setback
but one which was now the unalterable condition of his
existence. The amusing, anachronistic, grey-bearded man who
to us seemed to live in some glorious past of his own imagination and who often elicited our sympathy, admiration and
sometimes pity and who nevertheless inspired at least me into
a high regard for principles of honour and discipline, this
old-world soldier in our midst, now appeared to be a tragic
figure, one who had made an unfortunate mistake at some
point in his life and had consequently seen some private vision
collapse. As we had paddled down the river, I had begun to
become aware that the man behind me was making less and
less of an effort; what I first observed to be weariness in him
soon manifested itself into a nearly total loss of energy. A
time came when, coming to dangerous rapids which were
followed by a sheer drop in the river of some fifty feet, we
simply had to abandon our canoes and start walking as close
as possible to the side of the river. This is where it became
clear that Veríssimo had no energy left at all, and he himself,
recognizing his own extreme condition, begged us to leave
him behind to die.

There were three of us left, apart from Veríssimo: Antônio and I and a young Negro called Cristóval. It occurred to me as an irrelevance that it was strange that all that had survived of our party was its oldest and three of its youngest members. Of course, we refused to grant Veríssimo's wish to be left alone to die. At first I tried to help him walk by letting him support himself by having his arm across my shoulder. But he made so little progress in this manner that we next tried to have him supported between Cristóval and me; so that there were moments when Veríssimo was merely being dragged along, his legs making no attempt to negotiate the ground. Antônio, despite all his quarrels with Veríssimo in the past, was not without humanity and also tried to help, so that the three of us could take turns in supporting Veríssimo. And it was Antônio who came up with an interesting solution to ease this problem: he cut down two bamboos, and, standing about three feet in a straight line behind Cristóval, he placed the bamboos in two parallel lines across Cristóval's and his own shoulders. The two then bent their knees to lower themselves and I helped Veríssimo to fall across the bamboos on his stomach; Antônio and Cristóval, straightening themselves up, were able to carry Veríssimo with greater ease than had been possible earlier. Poor Veríssimo, he must already have been at an advanced stage of suffering, for the bamboos must have been uncomfortably hard against his stomach and ribs and the slightest jolting must have hurt.

We made very little progress in this fashion. Although we had been walking for three days since abandoning the canoes, the roar of the rapids and the waterfall seemed to be as intense as it had been when we were near there. I do not know what gave us the energy to continue. We had not eaten any proper food since fleeing from the Indians, and lived on a variety of things which we found in the jungle, including mouthfuls of ants and the bark of trees.

One day I had thought I smelt meat. I was convinced that I was imagining things. This was some time before we came to the rapids and the waterfall, and Cristóval's companion Negro had just died and we had asked Cristóval to take him away and to bury him. Burial, of course, did not mean a grave, for we had no tools to dig with, but only that the body be left on the ground covered with leaves. When I smelled what I thought was meat, I rose and walked towards the place where the smell appeared to be coming from. I came upon Cristóval who had managed to light a fire and held above it a forearm torn from his dead companion who lay only partially covered in leaves not far away. Unseen, I stood behind a tree and watched Cristóval. Soon, he began to eat. I noticed that when he took his first bite he shut his eyes. Perhaps the taste encouraged him, for he soon began to nibble at the meat as if it were the leg of a goat. Finishing, he threw away the bone, and was about to rise when he saw his companion's nose and mouth sticking out from among the leaves which he had heaped on his face. Cristóval began to cry softly, and he sat there making low moaning sounds. I must say that when I had seen him bite at the meat, my mouth had watered as if I were some poor beggar at the door of a rich man watching some feast from which I was excluded. But now, observing Cristóval's recognition of the horror which he had created for himself, I withdrew, myself feeling sick.

'I think there will be no need to carry me any further,' Veríssimo said one day in a voice so low he could have been talking to himself. 'The time has come when I must make my peace with my Maker,' he went on gloomily. 'He sent me forth into battle and now He calls me to make a final retreat. We must all lose the battle in the end, Gregório, we must all bow down our heads when the great conqueror, death, stands above us, his axe poised to strike us down.'

I must say that this speech was already too much for me and I was near to tears. The old man had a way of saying the most obvious thing and yet engaging one's profound sympathy. What from another person would have appeared to be empty statements were from him basic truths before which it was necessary for one to genuflect humbly.

'Retreat, ha!' he continued. 'Battles, victories! Is it neces-

125

sary that I should take my delusions to the grave? I've lived long enough to believe fully the myths that I've put forward about myself. Antônio and Gregório, and you Cristóval, I pray to God that you will all survive. Promise me one thing, you who are like my children. Promise me that on the day you emerge from this unending jungle, you will go straight to a church and falling on your knees will first offer your thanks for your own deliverance and will then say a prayer for me, an old sinner. Promise me that you will take my confession to the holy church and will repeat these words of mine. Ha! This jungle is nothing, this pain is nothing. And if you see your father again, too, Antônio and Gregório, tell him of my confession, of my sin.'

We were quite lost for words, especially as it seemed that Veríssimo was on the verge of some momentous revelation and could possibly be dead before he made it.

'I'm not the soldier I've said I am or have been,' he declared. 'I never saw the coast of India or of Africa. As a youth in Oporto once I killed a man. There was a lady, a wine-merchant's wife, who allowed me the favour of her affections. Perhaps she was enchanted by my strong, young body; perhaps she tired of her husband's long absences into the country or she found him wanting in certain respects. All I know is that I myself was enchanted by her. Nothing flatters a young man more than to be offered free access to an older woman's arms. Her most secret sighs escaped from her lips when those lips were close to mine. I was at that age when men believe that no woman in the world could ever possibly want to look at any other man; the very idea that there were women in other parts of the world who had to live and die in complete ignorance of my wonderful body was a source of considerable amusement to me. I felt sorry for the poor creatures. And of course, once a man gains admission to the heart of one woman, he believes that all other women are available to him, and I began to grow adventuresome, seeking out new affairs while maintaining my attachment to this lady who remained as a kind of fixed standard by which the success or failure of my other affairs had to be judged. However much I enjoyed the pleasure of making love to women superior in beauty to the wine-merchant's wife, I found that it was for her that I experienced the greatest passion. But young men are boastful, conceited. And one night while I lay with this lady of my passion we began to have a lover's quarrel over some trifle, and I declared to her that I was not dependent upon her affection. To make it worse, I even referred to her age. She answered back angrily, whereupon I retorted, Look at those breasts of yours, they'll be down to your waist in a couple of years. Friends, if I can give you one piece of advice, it is this: never, never be cruel to a woman in respect of her body. Beat her, if you like, deny her your company if you like, but never say that she has a wrinkle on her cheek or that her beauty has diminished in any way. And what could this gracious lady do when I told her the cruel truth about her breasts? She banished me from her company for a start, but when her husband returned, insinuated that I had tried to rape her and that I would have succeeded had she not had the presence of mind to scream and catch a servant's attention. The husband decided it was his duty to avenge his wife's honour. Give me water, Antônio, just moisten my lips. I'm dying. Well, it ended with my murdering the husband in self-defence. It happened in the house and the wife was the only witness. She could have covered up for me, she could have made me her slave. Instead, she went into public mourning, announced to everyone that she had greatly loved her husband and that I had murdered him in order to rape her and to rob her house. This sudden change of her loyalty I had been unprepared for. I fled, that's all I could do, run away, lose myself among the ruffians and pick-pockets of Lisbon from where I made my way to Brazil. What I have done here is another and a longer story, but soldiering, that has been only one more of my adventures. It was never a profession. I've never had a profession other than deceiving people, other than running away from incriminating circumstances. I was too old when I came to your father's house for working as a labourer or even as the kind of handyman which so many illiterate immigrants end up by becoming. All I could offer him was a new deception. All I could start was a new game. Well, it worked for a time. And it would have worked until I died. There's not much to soldiering. Any fool can be a soldier. There's more to farming which requires skill and patience. And this is where my soldiering has brought me, to a painful and an ignominious death. I deserve it, dying here in the jungle, far from what comfort the presence of a priest might have given me in my last moments, far from any kind of home I could have called my own.'

The moment that Veríssimo died, Cristóval went delirious. Perhaps he was reminded of his companion's recent death which had led to his cannibalistic meal; or perhaps his mind had gradually been disintegrating under the pressures of our existence in the jungle. But when Veríssimo concluded his speech and, attempting to rise from the ground as if he wished to reach a hand out to each one of us, fell back and died, Cristóval, his eyes bulging out, began to howl and to run around. I tried to hold him, but he screamed loudly at being touched and slipped out of my attempted grasp and began to run wildly. Antônio came up, too, and we both made a dash for Cristóval, thinking that together we could hold him down and perhaps give him a drink of water. Cristóval, seeing us approach with our eyes fixed on him like two cowboys approaching a recalcitrant bull, gave one loud howl and ran into the jungle. We did not pursue him, knowing he would not get far. We could hear him howling as he seemed to run on and on. A little later, the howling stopped. We went after him and took some time finding him. We wished we had not tried to do so, for he lay sprawling against a bush, his stomach cut open with a knife and his head bleeding from knocking against the hard thorny bark of some tree. Antônio and I silently retraced our steps, not wondering if it had been a miracle or a coincidence that we were the only two left, but wondering, rather, who would be the next to die.

A day later, while we tried to make a path through the

jungle not far from the river, Antônio said: 'It must be fate, don't you think, which has kept us two alive so far. Is it possible that we should survive the rest of the party and not continue to survive until we reach home?'

'We have no control over anything,' I said, not really knowing what to say and thinking that he should not have mentioned home.

'Where did we go wrong, I wonder.'

'It's too far back for us even to begin to think about it,' I said.

'Poor Veríssimo,' Antônio said, 'he wasn't the fool I'd always thought he was, he wasn't even the mad and impassioned soldier. He was just a fraud. A frightened old man pretending hard to be brave.'

'I don't think we should ever mention it to father.'

'Yes, let his secret die with him.'

I was beginning to feel something of a love for my brother, a feeling which was new to me, for our past relationship had been one of mutual jealousy. Naturally enough, at home I had resented his superior status and had often schemed to have his name discredited while he had obviously disliked me and been suspicious of my cleverness. Now we depended entirely on each other, and spent our time exchanging stories of our childhood, stories which became distorted as each of us unconsciously attempted to show that we had always been happy together and that there had never been any rivalry between us.

The river had settled down to a steady flow and we again began to walk along its bank where it was less necessary to hack out a path for oneself. We debated whether we should attempt to construct a canoe but having nothing except a small knife between us, it would have taken us weeks even to cut down a reasonably sized tree, and the idea was nothing more than a topic with which to keep our minds engaged for an hour or so as we debated the possible techniques of making a canoe.

One day we heard the splashing of oars in the river.

Although we had been aware of an unfamiliar sound, we had paid it little attention. I rather think that our senses and powers of discernment had been greatly blunted by the condition that we were in, for I am surprised when I think back on the occasion that we managed to recognize the sound as that of someone paddling up the river before we actually saw that someone.

Instinctively, we withdrew into the vegetation, so that we would be unobserved. Gradually, the sound came nearer, and it began to be obvious that there was more than one canoe. In fact, there were five. I don't know why we should have expected that the occupants of the canoes should be white men – explorers or missionaries or whoever could have had business in these inhospitable parts – but I remember being greatly disappointed that they were not white men. Instead, they were Indians, beating at the water with short but powerful stabs.

Seeing the Indians going up river suggested several implications, and all of them were of a sinister hue, the worst being that we were still far from any kind of civilization and that if there was any kind of settlement farther down the river, it was bound to be an Indian one. There was the implication, too, that since the settlement was likely to be on the river-side, we would need to go into the jungle to avoid it. We dared not calculate the chances of our not being seen by parties of Indians out hunting in the jungle.

Convinced that we had no choice in the matter, we continued. Half a day later, we came to a junction on the river where a tributary came down to meet it; what we saw in fact was a meeting of two rivers, for we could not tell which was the main river and which the tributary, both the rivers being of equal size.

'Now this is interesting,' I said to Antônio. 'If we could know which river the Indians came up on, we could risk going down the other.'

'Why should that be?' Antônio asked. 'There's no reason why both the rivers should not have Indians living on their banks.'

'True,' I said. 'What we need is not the sure knowledge that there are no Indians along one river, but some sign which would make us think that there might be no Indians along it. Something, in fact, to give us the confidence to proceed. There can be no guarantee of anything. All we can hope for is a lessening of the odds against us.'

Antônio suggested we stay there for the night since it was late enough in any case. We would decide what to do in the morning. It was a picturesque spot when I think back on it, though I suppose that at the time I had no eye for natural beauty. I did remark, however, that the land had flattened and that, unless it was a delusion to which we were no doubt susceptible, the vegetation seemed a fraction thinner than it had been.

It was in the middle of the night that Antônio went delirious. At first he began to moan, reminding me of the way in which Negresses moaned when they lost a child, and I said: 'Antônio, what's the matter, Antônio?' I did not think he could be going delirious, for I thought that he was probably having a bad dream or that the hunger was getting too much for him. He did not answer, but continued to moan, gradually becoming louder. 'What's the matter, Antônio?' I asked again, going to him and touching him on the shoulder. He began to cry, making a wailing sound that filled me with fear, for it suggested that whatever was wrong with him was of a nature which could not be alleviated with whatever help or comfort I could offer. I stroked his cheek affectionately. 'Go to sleep now, Antônio. We'll be fine tomorrow. We'll come to a big town where we'll eat meat.' He began to scream and pulling himself away from me, sprang up to his feet.

'Antônio!' I called after him. 'Don't move, whatever you do, don't panic. Antônio!'

I stood up, too, walking towards him so that I could hold him. But he began to stamp his feet and then to run around, his screams becoming long drawn-out howls.

'Antônio!' I called. 'Come to me. Look, Antônio, I'm frightened, come hold my hand like you used to do, remember,

131

when there was thunder and I was a little boy and frightened of the thunder and you used to hold my hand, saying it's nothing, it's only thunder.'

But my words had no effect on him, and I realized that either he did not hear me or that he was in some mental state in which words meant nothing. I tried to run after him, but it was too dark and, from his howling, I could tell that he was running around wildly. I could not see where he was, but now his howling was to my left and now to my right. I do not know how he managed not to crash against a tree. Perhaps he did bang into trees, perhaps he did tear his flesh on the hard thorns on the shorter vegetation. I could not tell anything, for I was myself going mad with his howls which tore through the night. Suddenly, he stopped. I waited for a few minutes, wondering whether he would soon resume howling. But he did not.

'Antônio,' I called softly, 'where are you? Just make a small sound, Antônio, and I'll come to you.'

But he did not make any sound. I walked here and there among the thorny vegetation, but did not come upon him.

I saw him the next morning. He was not far from where I had spent the night sitting up, frightened and beginning to feel a cold shiver by the morning. Large ants were making elaborate journeys on and into his body. His open mouth had already been eaten into and blood had trickled from it. His eyes were open and fixed at that point in the darkness where they had seen some terror before ceasing to see anything. I could not make myself touch him to close his eyes, for the ants were entering there, too. I turned away, shivering and feeling sick, and walked towards the river. I stood on the edge of the river, wanting to stoop down to wash myself, to cool the heat I was beginning to feel within me. And half stooping, I felt as though I was about to collapse, as though I would fall into the river if I moved a little closer to it. I seemed to go dizzy and remember telling myself, I mustn't fall, I mustn't fall; and then, checking myself, I withdrew a couple of paces. No sooner than I felt safe, I collapsed, my knees involuntarily giving way. All I remember feeling for a long time after that was the intense heat within me which seemed to be threatening to tear my flesh open and the breeze that played in the sweat that was pouring out of my body, making me shiver with cold. And for a long time I kept thinking that the ants, the ants were finished with Antônio and were coming towards me. I do not think that I was conscious enough even to realize that I, too, was dying.

I have no recollection of how or when my body was picked up, placed in a canoe and transported down the river to a settlement where Father Gabriel Prado was in charge of a Jesuit mission. For when I regained control over my senses, I was in a dark hut with a boy standing beside the hammock I was in, fanning away the flies and the insects. It did not strike me as unusual that the boy was an Indian. Seeing me open my eyes and show some interest in my environment, the boy ran out and called the priest.

Father Prado was a short, paunchy man, his skin having gone brown through constant exposure to the sun. He had a small round head which was completely bald, and his eyes seemed to stand out like a frog's. He smiled at me, nodding his head as if in approval of some expensive object which he was willing to purchase.

'Very good,' he said, clasping his hands in front of his paunch and continuing to nod his head in little jerks, 'very good. The herb works.'

Obviously, he was talking to himself and seemed more concerned about the success of some experiment he had made than about the fact that my eyes had opened for the first time in many hours, if not many days or, indeed, several weeks. I had no way of telling for how long I had lain unconscious.

There was a crude little table in the corner of the hut, a rough plank of wood held up on some logs, and a similarly crude stool next to it. Father Prado sat down on the stool and began to scribble something on a piece of paper. If he was writing a letter, he must have had a lot of news to give, for I guessed that he sat there for a good half an hour. I wondered what sort of excitement there could be in his life that he could not stop writing.

When he came to see me again, he brought with him a glass full of some liquid and, putting it to my lips, urged me to drink. I took a sip and turned away, for the liquid was bitter.

'You'll have to drink all this, my son,' Father Prado said, smiling devilishly, it seemed to me.

I made a sound indicating revulsion, and he said: 'Yes, yes, I know it's bitter. Believe me, son, it has the breath of Christ in it.'

I took some courage at the mention of Christ, concluding that at least he was not a false priest and being reminded of the three friars who had tricked us in the first few hours of our expedition, and, holding my breath, took a draught of the medicine the priest offered me.

'That's better,' he said, and again I wondered if he was not an evil man in disguise, trying to find a subtle way of killing someone, but again he allayed my doubts as he went on to say, 'Ah, my son, you're brave. What's more, you're strong. But whatever your strength, without this potion, you would be dead by now. Ah, this discovery will go to Lisbon. It will be the glory of Portugal. Why, it will go to Rome! The Church shall take the credit for it.'

Resolving to do my best for both my rulers and my religion, I took one deep breath, held my nostrils tight between a fore-finger and thumb and drank the rest of the contents of the glass.

'Bravo!' cried the priest. 'You will be a saint, young man. If this continues to work the way it has in the last three days, why, you'll be on your feet in another week.'

I frowned over the implication of doubt in his statement, the *if* which could conceivably be fatal.

'Now,' he said, withdrawing the glass, 'you just keep your mouth tightly shut and I'll bring you something which will give you a better taste.'

He went out and soon returned with another glass filled with a yellow liquid. I put my lips to this glass with a look of scepticism on my face, and he said: 'Don't worry, this is sweet. Go on, sip it slowly and it will take away the bitter taste.'

I followed his instruction, and soon began to lick my lips, for it was the delicious juice of some fruit.

'Enjoyed that, did you?' he said. 'This gives you not only a sweet taste but will also bring back your strength. I know you're dying to eat meat and bread and everything else. Well, my son, it's too early for that. You'd die if you ate meat. You've probably not had any meat for months, is that right? I thought so. Your face is that of someone who's had to keep running in the jungle. You were too afraid of dying to stop and look for food. Or, you didn't know how to go about finding food. The jungle is rich, my boy. It has everything. But for one who doesn't know where to look and what to look at, it's just like a desert; only worse in that you can't find your way. Now you just stay there. Sleep as much as you can. Slowly, you'll be able to have everything you want. Ever had turtles' eggs? We'll start you on that in a couple of days. Don't you worry. That other man we found with you, we buried him. There was little to bury. Nothing but bones. The ants had had a feast on him. You're lucky he lay dead near you, otherwise the ants would have made mince-meat out of you. If not the ants, then something else. You think the Indians are cannibals. Everything in the jungle depends on everything else. Take the ants away, the foliage will choke the jungle. Take the foliage away, and where will the panthers and the jaguars go? And so on. You're just lucky to have made it.'

He left me with feelings both of gratitude and despair. Obviously, I was overcome with gratitude at realizing that I had been saved and that this priest had had the skill and the resources with which to relieve me of whatever sickness had come over me. Whether it had been simply exhaustion and hunger I did not then know. And I felt despair because of the condition I was in, absolutely helpless, not knowing where I was, how much more I had to suffer before I reached home.

In a few days I had recuperated sufficiently to be taken out of the hut so that I could sit in the shade and amuse myself with looking at the people who came and went in the open space which was surrounded by huts in a wide circle. Although I had not considered it unusual that the boy who attended to my needs inside the hut and assisted Father Prado by looking after me was an Indian, for there was no novelty about someone having an Indian slave, I was astonished to see on coming out of the hut that we were in an Indian village. Indeed, if there was anything unusual about the place, it was the fact that Father Prado lived there and behaved as if he were perfectly at home. I was soon surrounded by children who made such a din around me that I had to ask Father Prado to tell them to go away. In the distance I heard the mothers of these children call and, seeing that the women were naked induced a sudden surge of blood in my groin – a sure sign that I must be recovered.

'Ah, you mustn't mind the children,' Father Prado said, shouting some words at them nevertheless so that they went. 'Children are the same everywhere. You leave them alone and their curiosity is soon sated. You scare them away and they'll hang about in corners, sucking their thumbs, wondering what they're missing. And still we go on the same all over the world, screaming at children, telling them to go away. Well, since you've told me all about your ill-fated expedition, you can see now why I didn't make any comment. You didn't know until now that you were in an Indian village. In your usual plantation master's son's manner you assumed that the world belonged to your class of people and that it was inconceivable that there might be a place where your race and class would not be in power. Well, I didn't want to tell you where you were. I wanted you to see for yourself. It's beautiful, isn't it? No, I don't mean the trees and the sky. I'm not a poet drooling over sunsets. You know what I mean. Everything, even those naked women. Why, I'd say especially those naked women. Beautiful's the word, perfectly beautiful. Now don't

136

get me wrong. You may believe me or not, but I've never had any kind of relationship with those women, apart from helping now and again with a childbirth or some illness. Believe me, I'm not that way inclined. And that's not simply because I'm a priest. You must know the reputation of our priests in these matters. Well, this is a silly subject. All I was saying is that it's just beautiful being here. There's many a priest I know would want to clothe the women and the children first thing. A disastrous mistake, I think. Why impose your order on another society without first trying to see how that society works? Let me tell you how I came here. My home town is Coimbra in northern Portugal. I grew up there, studied there, and became a priest there. I suppose I would have stayed there all my life. I had no interest outside theology except for the peasants who always fascinated me for the simple reason that my family was of that human condition, peasants, whose job it was to keep going up and down on the land, winter and summer, tilling, sowing, harvesting, year in and year out, up and down, up and down. Somehow, I think I know why but it's too complicated to explain easily and briefly. Well, somehow, I became involved with the life of the mind, especially of that nature which takes it upon itself to serve mankind in some humble way or the other. Well, I didn't like it. There seemed to me to be something false, something hypocritical about it. And sure enough, soon I was being accused of possessing intellectual pride. When I pointed out that I spent months among the peasants, trying to bring into their existence those meanings of life and faith which I felt I was beginning to see, when I remarked upon this, I was accused of being boastful and of implying that I should be rewarded with worldly advance. To every authority in Portugal, whether it's the Church or the Court, or even some little judge in some village trying a man for stealing a goat, one statement comes easiest of all when faced with someone like me – off to Brazil with him. Or, off to India with him. And so off to Brazil I came. So, you see, young man, why I like being here. The truth probably is that I like it because I have no choice and simply must remain here. Ah, whoever has a choice in this life! Did you think you had a choice the moment you left home and set out on this expedition? You take one step, and a whole lot of actions follow which you hadn't anticipated. Chance or fate, accident or God, who knows what has saved you so far? Had I not been the provocative priest I was ten years ago, I would still have been in Coimbra and you would still have been on the river-bank, that is if the ants had left anything of you. Or, it may be that someone else from somewhere else had found himself here among these Indians and it could even be that that someone else would have been me. Everything is possible because everything is ordained. Remember that God is the greatest coincidence of all. This is heresy, of course, but I'm intrigued by possibilities. Well, here we are in Brazil. But what is Brazil? The hundreds of square miles which are your father's plantation? The cities of Olinda and Salvador? Are they Brazil? And the land to the south and the land to the west, going on for thousands of miles, is all that Brazil, too? And this? This little village in the jungle, is this Brazil? If I asked you to go and look for Brazil, could you find it for me? Of course, such questions can't be asked. A country is what an emperor decides it is; or what an army decides. We have frontiers drawn up if the sea or a great chain of mountains don't maintain natural boundaries for the state. Can a country like Portugal still exist as Portugal even if all the people in the world who call themselves Portuguese were to perish simultaneously? Surely, there'd be nothing but land, an empty area. And isn't that the condition of most of Brazil at the moment? A great big land we assume is Brazil, but which is really a great big emptiness. Now, let me tell you what I think a country is. Or, what makes a country into that country and none other. It is not the notion of property. Come on, are you listening? That kind of statement ought to make you scream in protest, for you're the heir to one of the largest properties in Bahia. Well, let me repeat that what makes a country is not the notion of property; and actually, I don't mean the kind of property you can own or a hundred big landowners can own. I mean that sense of property which a nation has over another nation. To give you an example: if Portugal had invaded China and grabbed hold of a few provinces, it could not have proclaimed that it possessed a land which it proposed to call Brazil. It would have possessed a land which was part of China. Here Portugal has been able to proclaim Brazil because there were no Brazilians here. There were assumed to be a few savage tribes, people of no consequence, people either to be converted or massacred. For all practical purposes, the land had to be empty and convertible into property for it to be Brazil. Yet, I think this is a fallacy, for this conversion amounts to no more than an expansion of the territory which is Portugal. Therefore, again for practical purposes, we're not yet in Brazil. We're only in Portugal which has become enlarged. This land will become Brazil when Portugal will again become Portugal. That is why I have no interest in converting the Indians. They're like the peasants in Portugal. They really don't have any say in the matter. I like to live among them, that is all. I suppose this is my vanity. They never question me. They tolerate me because I'm useful to them. I like them because they're simple enough to accept what help I offer them. This allows me to make my discoveries of medicinal herbs, and perhaps one day when I have catalogued as many herbs as I can find, I'll send a box full of my notes to Lisbon. Or perhaps I shall just throw it all into the river. No, I've not lost my religion. I believe I'm closer to Christ than I ever was. Indeed, I believe that I serve God best by not being among people who believe in Him. Which is a great contradiction, isn't it?'

There I sat, out in the open, every day for some six or seven days, watching the children's games or keeping a bemused eye on the women about whom it must be remarked that they appeared to be better preserved than some of our own Portuguese or Brazilian women. I don't know even now what it is about an Indian woman that keeps her skin from wrinkling and sagging for far longer than is the case with our women. The men on this settlement were busy with fishing and hunting expeditions; parties of them would return, engendering a great deal of excitement among the children, and after a night's rest would go away again. Each party returned with a good haul of fish or with a couple of carcasses of some beast, so that almost every night was the occasion for a small feast.

On one of these occasions, Father Prado said to me, 'Notice that the Indian is generous but not extravagant. His generosity is an instinct; what he has must be shared by the community, and in this respect it is not generosity that drives the Indian as much as an instinct for survival – for he can only survive as a tribe and the concept of individuality is meaningless to him. As for extravagance, that idea just does not enter the life of an Indian. Only those races have learned extravagance who have organized a part of their population into labour and then proceeded to exploit it; because such organization results in surplus and, once you possess such plenty, what better thing can you do for the furtherance of your own reputation than to hand out your surplus which you don't have any need for yourself, but to hand it out with a great show of doing everyone else a great favour. We love ostentation, we love mankind to say we are generous, hospitable, extravagant, and so on, all the laudatory words. And this is the difference between the two types of culture, ours which we assume is an advanced and a civilized culture and the Indians' which we presume before observing it is backward and primitive. But the point is this. The Indians haven't arrived at the words we have. And the reason is not that they're backward, but that they don't need to arrive at such words. When I first came here, I had the missionary's usual zeal. I wanted to teach them as rapidly as possible such words as love and forgiveness. But I soon realized I was a damn fool to be attempting such a thing. They've evolved their own way of life, and it's a life of rituals and magic chants on the one hand and a communal sharing of all their resources on the other. It's a perfectly balanced existence. Theirs is a completely harmonious and an integrated world. They have no need for love and forgiveness, nor do they have any need for Christ. Yes, you may express astonishment at such a statement from a priest, but that's the inescapable truth. I found it hard to reconcile myself to this fact, for I've been trained to believe that a world without Christ is unacceptable. But seeing the Indians' way of life and observing it to be altogether superior to our own, I said to myself how can I try and inculcate upon their minds the tenets of an inferior way of life? Yes, inferior. Obviously, this startles you. But tell me, do you see any poverty in the lives of the Indians? No. Do you see any disparity between one Indian family and another? No. For clearly you do not see one family live in a mansion and another on the edge of the gutter which comes out of the mansion carrying its filth. Do you see one Indian standing in the shade, a whip in his hand, watching another Indian toil in the sun? No. Do you see one Indian envy the lands of another? No, because all the land belongs to all of them, for the notion of possession has never occurred to them. But, you will say, all this is to do with the body, and, you will ask, why is it that I have carefully not said a word about the spirit? To which I answer, observe the way we live. What dominates us and victimizes us is the sense of property and wealth. Most of our laws are to do with property and wealth. Everything in our laws which defines the relationship between two or more people is concerned with stating which party may possess what or how much in relation to the other party. A man cannot get married, but he enters into a relationship of property with a woman. A man cannot have children but the relationship to his property of each child has to be defined by law and even God cannot help the child who does not happen to be the eldest son. A man dies and the law is concerned with his property. Where, I ask you, is the spirit of religion in all this? I sometimes wonder if people in Europe don't see God as some kind of a remarkably astute lawyer who is also a very clever banker. As I've told you, I came to Brazil because I was sent here. I didn't have any choice in the matter. But when I came, the Church gave me my instructions. Go and baptize,

I was told. Get more souls for Christ. And I must say that I was eager to do so, I was determined to show them that I could do a fine job for Christ. It's like some damned competition, some race. But I believed then what I'd been told about our country's history. Portugal's great mission was to conquer as much as she could of the world and do its territories the favour of converting them to Christianity. I was innocent enough and involved passionately enough with the Church to believe that this was the sole reason for acquiring countries like Brazil. Yes, obviously I was aware that we'd get some commercial advantage from these conquests and discoveries, but I was as convinced as anyone else that that happy day was fast approaching when the entire world would be converted to Christianity. And there are priests out here, even in this jungle, who believe just that and go about converting. I've seen them at work, I've been one of them. The method is a slightly devious one since the priests discovered that the Indian just could not grasp our noble words like love. Well, what do they do? They succeed first of all in getting established in an Indian community and start performing little miracles, saving a child from snake-bite or some such thing. As soon as they've won the Indians' confidence, they begin the business of conversion. It doesn't work, not always, and some priests have devised a subtle system. They teach the young boys to sing hymns or they teach them to dance in feminine ways. The trick is to get the boys so to enjoy singing or dancing or whatever activity the priest can think up that with the years the boys come to loathe the activities of their fathers. So that when they grow up, they're incompetent at hunting and fishing and just stay there with the priest. But the real conflict between these boys and their fathers comes when it's time for them to be taking part in their old magic rituals. The boys just don't see the point and the brasher ones among them even ridicule their fathers for the fancy dress they wear for their rituals. And of course, the ridicule of one generation for the other destroys whatever is considered sacred within that society. So, what happens? A generation of weak-willed, emasculated young men grows up to find it has to carry on the business of its community. And of course, they're incapable of doing so. Beginning to learn the words of Christianity, they lose the instincts of their tribe; they don't know enough of the first, and they've lost too much of the second; they're totally confused and utterly in the hands of their priests who now proceed to make them work on the land, a kind of work which their race has never before attempted in its history. So, you have your souls for Christ, but all you've succeeded in creating is a bastard race which will soon be obliged to compete with the people whose kind of life it's been compelled to adopt and, not being equipped to meet the competition, it'll probably try to revert to the ways of its ancestors, and finding it difficult to rediscover the lost ways, will become so confused as to go insane and will simply die out. This doesn't bother the priests just as the master of a slave-ship is not bothered by how hungry or sick or deformed his slaves are as long as they have some breath in them when they're unloaded at Salvador. Quantity is all. In a hundred years or three hundred years, there won't be any Indians left on this land because my fellow-priests would have taken good care of their souls by then. I knew one priest who, finding it difficult to convert the Indians, put his faith in those who were ill. He would tend them and a moment before they died, as many of them did, he baptized them. This had a comical sequel. For the Indians, observing that whenever someone died, the death was preceded by this strange ceremony of the priest chanting some words and sprinkling water on his head, soon concluded that the priest was some evil spirit who had access to some special water with which he could kill people. One day, just when he was about to baptize an Indian, two Indians snatched the holy water from him and making some howling sounds poured the water over the priest's head. But the priest of course did not die. This scared the Indians so much that they ran out and, getting the entire tribe together, hastily abandoned the settlement.'

I must say that I found Father Prado's thinking both

143

illogical and confused. Even at that age, I was certain that a destiny ruled the world and that whatever happened had a meaning; it was clear to me that the destiny of the Indian was to be the slave of the white conquerors of Brazil, for why should destiny decide that a European power should become the master of a country without making it master also of the primitive tribes of that country? Frankly, Father Prado's talk about the Indian culture having its own virtues didn't convince me at all; for he had missed the basic point that it is man's lot to be always trying to improve himself, and obviously the Indian was at that stage from which he would gradually rise to the higher level which our race had already attained through superior intelligence. The Indian was fortunate in that his development would be accelerated now that we were in Brazil to make him our servant and, by doing so, to instruct him in the values of a higher culture. Obviously, I didn't say any of this to Father Prado. He was kind to me and I did not want to contradict him; also, I felt that having been among the Indians for so long, he had himself lost touch with the reality of the European immigrant's life. I must say that I felt rather sorry for the old man.

It was decided that as soon as I recovered my strength sufficiently to travel, I would be taken down the river on a canoe by Father Prado himself since he needed to make one of his periodic visits to a village where there was an established mission. 'There,' Father Prado said, 'you will notice how the Indian youths are being trained to reject the ways of their fathers.'

The village was called Glória, and a priest by the name of Father Boscoli was in charge of the mission there. The first thing I noticed about Father Boscoli was that he was a younger man than Father Prado; he had a hooked nose and eyes that never fixed themselves on any one object: when he talked to you, Father Boscoli kept looking over your shoulder or the head, glancing, too, from time to time, up at the sky, always giving the impression that he was either expecting a strange revelation at any moment, that he had long expected the revelation and wondered if it were not behind some cloud, or that he was constantly on the lookout for evil. Father Prado left me with him, waving aside with a fat little hand my expressions of gratitude.

Father Boscoli's church was made of wood. It was a small frame construction, and a table with a white cloth on it served for an altar; a wooden figure of Christ, which Father Boscoli said he had carved himself, was placed on the table together with a cross fashioned out of iron. While he was showing me the church, there was the sound of distant chanting outside, and we went to the door. 'My choir,' he said.

Presently, a group of twelve or fifteen boys entered the courtyard, the boy at the front carrying a wooden cross. The boys were all Indians, aged between eight and ten, and wore white cotton smocks. Their hair was cut short, and if one closed one's eyes and heard them sing, one could easily be deceived into thinking that one were in the cathedral in Salvador.

'These are my little angels,' Father Boscoli said. 'You won't hear a sound so sweet anywhere west of Rome.'

'What do their parents think of them?' I asked, remembering Father Prado's explanation of how the priests went about converting the Indians.

'Their parents are enchanted,' he said. 'On feast days I invite the parents to a concert here in the courtyard. They sit there enraptured with the beautiful hymns.'

That was sufficient to convince me that Father Prado had been talking nonsense, or that he had been distorting the truth, for it was clear that he himself had had no success with converting the Indians. As the choir boys went past us, and into the church to continue their devotions, Father Boscoli suggested that I go into his house if I wanted to rest before dinner. The setting sun was throwing a bright red glow in the sky when the good priest showed me to his house. There, he introduced me to a middle-aged woman called Maria who kept house for him. Maria's face was so wrinkled it looked as though spiders had been busy turning it into an intricate web.

'Have you cleaned out the room for our guest, Maria?'
Father Boscoli asked her.

Maria looked at him with her sharp, searching eyes as
though to scold him for ever doubting that she was in any
way negligent, and said: 'Angela's been doing it. She must be
finished by now.'

'Very well,' Father Boscoli said. 'Please show this gentleman to his room, then, for he's had a tiring day down the
river. We will eat in an hour. And, Maria, make sure the
meat's well cooked. I don't want to lose my teeth yet!'

Father Boscoli returned to his church and Maria, making a
grumbling sound, led me down a corridor to a room. There,
a girl with long black hair and wearing a grubby shirt which
barely reached her knees, was placing a sheet on the bed.
When we entered the room, she was bent forward, facing the
door, so that her small breasts hung down and could be seen
through the shirt which was open at the neck.

'Angela!' Maria said in a scolding voice. 'Haven't you
finished yet? Come on, off with you!'

Angela stood back, startled, and revealed herself to be
slender and handsomely shaped. I thought she was probably
fifteen years old, sixteen at the most, and I must confess that
in that moment before she walked out, very slightly swaying
her hips, I had the fantasy of seeing her come into the room in
the middle of the night and lie next to me. The fantasy continued and became more elaborate, inducing my hand to enter
the shirt at the neck, when Maria left me in the room. I closed
the door after her, hoping to lie down and have a short nap,
but my hand seemed to come into contact with Angela's soft
little nipple. Unfortunately, such dramas in my mind have
only one kind of epilogue; if I presently exhausted myself, at
least I had proved to myself that I had recovered completely.
Although my breathing was heavy, that, I told myself, was
how it used to be in the days before Aurelia. As my eyes
drooped with this addition to my exhaustion, I remarked that
it was a good thing the floor was made of earth, for it would
soon dry off. I had not wanted to wet the good Father Boscoli's

sheet.

Later, at dinner, a man named José waited on us, and Father Boscoli explained that he was Maria's husband and that Angela was their daughter. José had committed some crime in Portugal and had been deported. He had begun to make a living for himself in Olinda, but had fallen into bad company and been led again into a criminal life. Father Boscoli had rescued him from a severe fate and had brought him and his family to Glória, making them his servants and thus ensuring that he would have at least three Portuguese companions with him albeit of such a lowly situation.

'The trouble is,' Father Boscoli told me in a whisper while José was gone to fetch the meat from the kitchen when we had finished soup, 'he's impotent. I wanted him to have more children as I want everyone in Brazil to have more children, but he said to me one day, Father, he said, it's no use praying, I just can't do it. What? I asked, you want a priest to show you how? It's not that, he said, not caring for my joke, you see I'm not made that way by nature. Then how about Angela, eh, I suppose you're going to tell me that was a miracle? No, Father, he said, it's not like that. You see when Maria was a young girl, she was very beautiful and it happened, well you know, what happens when you're young and beautiful, and she was big with Angela and there was nothing for her parents to do but to find her a husband since she stubbornly refused to tell who Angela's father was. Maria's father was a hard man, a peasant in the mountains of Castelo Branco, and he beat her till she went blue, but still she wouldn't tell. Well, Father, there I was in the same village, known by everyone as having been made incomplete by nature. It was a great shame to Maria and a greater shame to her family. But her father saw it as a punishment on himself and so he inflicted the greater punishment on Maria of marrying her to me – José went on with his story. It was done secretly, said José, and the old man, giving me what savings he had, shedding his own tears on the coins he gave me and trying not to look at his daughter, sent us to Lisbon where soon Angela was born.'

147

José entered the room and, placing a plate of meat before us, withdrew to the kitchen.

'So you see, Gregório,' Father Boscoli continued, 'each man carries his own cross. There's many a quiet face, outwardly calm and composed, which masks a great deal of private suffering. And this mystery of other people's lives is of absorbing interest to us, we're always willing to listen to someone's story or to look at someone's heart to see how badly it's been bruised.'

The meat was dried beef and although it had been well cooked, it tasted putrid. The only way in which I could eat it was to take a deep breath, put some in my mouth, and swallow it as hastily as I could without letting its taste come into contact with my palate.

'As for the Indians,' Father Boscoli said, 'there are two matters which need the country's urgent attention. First of all, we must bring as many Indians into the Christian fold as possible and secondly, we must make as many Indians as we can capture work as slaves in plantations like the one you have described run by your father. Obviously, those who work in the plantations can be assumed to have been converted already, and those who are being converted can be assumed to be potential slaves. I find there are cynics who say that our only motive in converting the Indians is to provide free labour for the plantations and thus, indirectly, an easy wealth for Portugal. What these cynics do not realize is that we are doing an immense favour to the Indian in the first place by giving him a chance in this world of rising to our level of civilization and, in the second, by offering the Indian a fulfilment in the after-life which he could never have contemplated had he been left alone for a million years. And there's another thing which the cynics tend to overlook. It would be unpardonable for us to live in a country and to deny its native savage tribes the advantages of our own knowledge of heaven. It is like knowing how to cure the victims of a plague and letting an entire village die of the disease when you could have saved some of its population. It is like knowing a well is poisoned

148

and letting children come to drink its water. Believe me, my young man, it would be the grossest sin we could commit if we knowingly allowed the Indians to exist as savages when we could bring them both civilization and the promise of heaven. And obviously, what's the best way but for the Indian first to submit himself to the apprenticeship of labour? When a young man wants to become a builder, he doesn't paint a sign to put outside his house declaring that a new builder is now available. No, he is first required to learn his skills at the hands of a master. He becomes an apprentice and it is not until he has proved himself, not until he has shown that he, in his turn, is capable of being a master that he can command the respect of his community for his skills which he has demonstrated as possessing the insight of experience. Similarly, how can anyone expect the Indian to assume the responsibility of being a Christian human being until he has shown that he can perform the humblest tasks? No, my friend, I fear the cynics are being foolish. By making the Indian our slave, we are exercising the utmost charity. We're giving him the greatest chance his race ever had.'

I was relieved when the meat dish was taken away by José, for I was convinced that it was sending out a gradually increasing smell, so that I was finding it difficult to concentrate on the wise statements my friend Father Boscoli was uttering for my benefit. I was delighted to eat two bananas for dessert, for they were ripe and fragrant and succeeded in exorcising the awful taste of the dried meat.

'Ha, Brazil!' said Father Boscoli, smacking his thick lips so that I could see his tongue roll the pulped banana in his mouth, a quite revolting sight, I must say, although I did not mind it since he was so kind and intelligent a man. 'What, I wonder sometimes, is this country which we're creating? The very sound of it is something special. You can say France or England or Spain or India or China, it makes no difference, but when you say Brazil, ah, you have to say Brah-zil, shutting your eyes slightly as if you experienced some ecstasy simply by saying Brazil! For, surely, there's no country like

149

Brazil! Were Portugal to conquer all of India or of Africa, that would not excite the imagination although it would be a tremendous feat. For India and Africa are known, and for Portugal to conquer them would be to add further chapters in their histories. Whereas Brazil, is not Brazil like the world being created for the first time? Is not Brazil like the most beautiful young woman you ever saw, waiting to be matched to the most eligible man in the world? What wonderful off-spring will they produce! And you, my young man, you are one such suitor for this land. You must make it your business to woo her and to wed her and to give her the handsomest sons you can, for she deserves them.'

I must admit that I was most inspired by this speech although there was no channel into which I could immediately direct my inspiration. So that I said: 'Yes, Father, I will love this woman. When I left my father's land for this expedition, all I knew was that I had a home and that the home was a small part of Brazil. Now I know something else. Now I know that there is Brazil and that, and that only, is my home.'

I am far from sure what I could have meant by expressing such a sentiment, but the good Father was pleased with what I had to say and blessed me before he retired for the night. I, too, went to my room and, lying back in bed, thought how fortunate I had been not only in being saved from the fate to which all my companions had succumbed but also in the coincidence which had led to my acquaintanceship with Father Prado and Father Boscoli. Obviously, while I felt grateful to Father Prado for having saved my life, I was sorry that he was a failure in his profession and did not really understand what was meant by improving the Indians' condition. But Father Boscoli was a man of such commonsense and gentle humility that I congratulated myself in having met him.

We had retired early and since I had rested a little before dinner, I was not all that sleepy. I lay thinking of our tragic expedition and of those moments which had been its worst. I lay thinking, too, of my brother Antônio who had fruitlessly given his life for no worthwhile cause. Poor Antônio! Perhaps fate had intended that I should succeed to my father's property since I had the best aptitude for that position. Certainly, I could not imagine Antônio, whose tactlessness had been all too obvious in his remarks to Veríssimo, having much success in doing business with the merchants of Bahia.

The house had gone dead quiet; even the sounds of washing-up which had been coming from the kitchen had stopped. The cicadas had usurped the kingdom of sound. And I lay in the darkness of my room, thinking of this and that, not being able to sleep. Poor Veríssimo! A miserable adventurer, that's all he had been; not even one who by risking a deception hoped to achieve a sudden fortune: instead, his deception had been the necessary precondition to his survival. I thought I heard a sound in the passage outside my room, but paid it no attention. My thoughts wandered to my parents, filling me with the thrill of happiness that with luck I would soon be with them. There was a shuffling in the room next to mine where Father Boscoli slept and, fearing that there was a burglar in the house, I rose and stood against the wall, my ear next to the wall. I thought I could hear Father Boscoli's voice in a whisper and the smacking of his lips as though he still tasted the banana he had eaten at dinner, and, concluding that there was no danger and that perhaps he had an unexpected visitor, I returned to bed.

But no sooner was I again in bed than I noticed that a light had appeared in the room. Looking at the wall, I saw that there was a crack in it and that the light was coming through it; the crack, when I rose and examined it, was not bigger than the width of my little finger and yet it let in the light as if a bright moon shone through a window; and no doubt this was the effect produced by the total darkness in my room, a darkness so intense that the weakest source of illumination gave the impression of brilliance. The crack was high up on the wall, above the level of my head so that I could not look through it. I thought I heard Father Boscoli smack his lips again and that there was in his room the remonstrating voice of a woman. I could not hear what was being spoken and debated for a moment whether I should put a chair against the wall and peep into Father Boscoli's room. There were good reasons why I should not, I thought. I was his guest and had no business to be peeping into his private life. I was supposed to be asleep. I would soon be leaving his house probably never to see him again. This last reason, I thought, was not a reason for preventing myself from peeping through the crack but a good reason why my conscience need not be bothered by the imprudence of my action.

Well, there was the chair and there the crack in the wall; I needed only to lose my fastidious scruples. I think now I knew what was going on in my mind which I as yet had refused to admit: I knew, without letting myself think about it, that what I would see through the crack would not be some extreme urgency, some matter of life and death which required a woman to visit a priest in the middle of the night, but, alas, that manifestation of human weakness which made a holy man break the vows of his profession. And what kept me undecided about pulling the chair up against the wall was a struggle between the desire, on the one hand, to witness the union of a man and a woman and, on the other, the fear that by doing so I would lose the faith I had in Father Boscoli's goodness. Losing my righteousness, however, I tip-toed towards the window where the chair was, and picking it up quietly, carried it across the room and placed it under the crack, having, at that moment, a wild fantasy of Father Boscoli's buttocks in the air.

I paused to suppress my amusement which threatened to make me burst out laughing; I chided myself for having such irreverent thoughts of the holy man. Well, I softly climbed up the chair and found that I was now too high and needed to lower myself by bending my knees – a posture which was going to be decidedly uncomfortable if the performance, whatever it was going to be, went on for some time. Just when I managed to get my eye next to the crack, I heard the woman say, 'I'm ready now' and in that moment while my sight was

152

becoming used to the light in the room and trying to establish its authority over the chaos of images which sprang to greet it, I heard Father Boscoli say, 'All right, then,' and, with those words, blow out the candle.

I almost cursed aloud in my frustration. Hoping either that my eye would become accustomed to the darkness and be able to distinguish shapes or that the couple might decide to light the candle again, I waited for a while longer. I knew after a few minutes that there was no chance at all of my eye ever seeing anything in that darkness, not even a weak tracing on a blank paper which might afford me some imaginative gratification.

There were sounds, but they only served to increase my frustration. It was too annoying to have an aural sense of what was going on and not be able to confirm it with my eyes. The worst thing was that I myself had become excited, and, finding no vicarious outlet, was, for the second time that day, obliged to employ the willing service of my hand. Dazed from this experience, for which the floor had again been the receptacle, I pulled myself up on to the bed and began slowly to be overcome by sleep. Suddenly, there was a commotion outside, and I woke up with a start. There was a loud knocking on a door, which seemed to be the door to my room but I soon realized it was the one to the next room, the one in which Father Boscoli lay. A woman's voice, which I recognized to be Maria's, was shouting: 'If you're in there, Angela, come out now, come out before I break this door down. And you, Father Boscoli, if you have my daughter in there, let her come out at once before I call all the neighbours in and show them what kind of a priest we have here bringing Christ's own sweet word to these barbaric parts. José, what are you standing so dumb for, why don't you say something? She's in there, I'm sure she's in there. Angela, do you hear me?'

I heard the door open and Father Boscoli's voice say, 'What is it, Maria, my child? What has woken you up at this time of the night? I hope it was not some nightmare.'

There was the silence of astonishment from Maria, and

Father Boscoli went on, 'Something has troubled you, Maria. Do you want to come into my room and pray with me?'

I enjoyed that, it was like pretending at cards that you had an unbeatable trump when in fact the card you held was worthless.

'No, Father,' Maria replied meekly.

'Well, then,' Father Boscoli said, his voice so calm he could have been saying mass, 'why don't you sit down on that chair and José will bring you a drink of water. Will you do that, José? Thank you. Now, tell me what has upset you.'

'Angela,' said Maria as if she were describing the symptoms to a doctor. 'She's not in her room. It's not the first time, I know she goes somewhere, maybe it's some lover. But, Father, who?'

'Maria, you are aware, are you not, that I know your story, that when you were the age Angela is now, you had a lover who made you pregnant. Whenever a woman has an experience like that, she fears that her daughter will turn out to be exactly like her and suffer the same fate. This is nothing new, Maria, your history is the history of all women who have fallen to temptation. But Angela strikes me as a sensible girl. If she's out, then she's probably in the church where it is cooler. There's one thing I do know about Angela which you don't: she has a nun's devotion to Christ. Thank you, José. Here you are, drink this up and go to sleep.'

'But if, Father, if.'

'If what, Maria?'

'If something should happen to Angela.'

'What do you mean?' Father Boscoli said. 'You don't think she'll fall into the river or something, do you?'

'No, not that. If. Well, suppose there is a man who discovers she's in the church at night and follows her there, and if something happens then.'

'Maria, you're still worrying about your daughter turning out like you. Try and be charitable.'

'I know, Father, but there's no man here she could marry. You're the only proper man here, and you. . . .'

154

'Of course, I'll marry her. She's a Christian, she shall marry in church and who will marry her there but I who am the only priest?'

Father Boscoli laughed at his own weak play on words and, putting Maria in a lighter, more relaxed mood, sent her back to bed. He shut his own door very carefully and I imagined him lying back softly in his bed and caressing Angela's breasts.

Although I remained awake for some time, straining my ears to listen to whatever strategies or demonstrations of affection were taking place in the next room, I could not hear anything to which I could accord an interesting interpretation. I wondered for how long Father Boscoli could carry on his affair with Angela without some consequence or the other asserting itself in the near future; and Maria, though both credulous and easily exploited, surely had the correct instinct about her daughter's escapade. I wondered, too, if Angela enjoyed the attentions of Father Boscoli or whether she felt constrained to accept his mastery in the house. My speculations about the future of these people were futile, for on the next day circumstances led me to leave Glória with greater hope than I had hitherto experienced of reaching the civilized parts of Brazil and, especially, of returning home. I thought, when I was on my way down the river again, that that was how life was: it took you among people, showed you a little of their lives and then, without the beginnings ever continuing, it took you away to some other place, among some other people, leaving you to imagine an infinite variety of endings to those beginnings which you had briefly witnessed. I thought, for example, how Father Boscoli could possibly become dominated by some scheme which entailed a conspiracy between Maria and Angela; or how he could be blackmailed by the entire family; or how he could probably live happily for many years a life of open sin with the connivance of Maria. But then, on the other hand, a thousand other things could also happen. What does it matter, eh? I asked myself on the boat down the river, life goes on similarly

155

in a million households, there is some quarrel here or some great affection there, one thing or another happens.

On the day after my night at Father Boscoli's house, a large boat had been moored on the river-bank in Glória and a party had alighted to replenish its supplies. It turned out to be a party of explorers who had gone up the river in search – they said laughingly – of El Dorado. I found out later that their interest was more in science than in treasure and that they had spent their time collecting plants and making drawings of animals and insects that they found on the way. Now they were on their way back to Salvador which they hoped to reach by following the river into the ocean and then heading south. Realizing that I had not thought to ask either Father Prado or Father Boscoli what the name of the river was, I now asked the explorers. A very pale-skinned young man who had a fair beard, said, expressing surprise that I did not know where I was, 'Why, don't you know? The São Francisco.'

I was astonished. If the São Francisco is as far as we had gone, then first of all instead of going north, which is what we thought we had been doing, we had ended up by going south-west; secondly, we had never been more than two hundred miles from my father's property; and thirdly, if, as the pale-skinned young man informed me, we were only two days' journey from the ocean, then we should pass through my step-mother's father's property in another day, for the São Francisco ran through the plantation of José Jerônymo Rodrigues.

Chapter 5

A MARRIAGE PROPOSAL

When I alighted at the landing-stage on the plantation of José Jerônymo Rodrigues, I could not have been happier had I arrived at Lisbon. Long before we reached the landing-stage, I had reminded myself again and again of the invitation which Mr Rodrigues had extended to me at my father's wedding; I was even more keenly intrigued now than I had been originally about the special nature of the invitation.

From the landing-stage on the river to the house in the middle of the plantation was a journey of two days on mule-back. There was a house on the river-side where a Portuguese peasant family, in the employ of Mr Rodrigues, lived and looked after the exporting of sugar from the plantation to the port of Bahia. There I was hospitably received and after a good night's rest, was offered a mule and the company of one of the sons to take me to the master's house. I felt a great freedom during these two days, an exhilaration which came from the knowledge that I travelled without my former companion, danger.

We reached the house at the end of the second day when night had fallen. I did not know how late it was, but as we approached the house, we saw that the lights in most of the rooms had been extinguished; and although we could have spent the night in one of the several houses and dwellings which had been built for the slaves, I was determined to reach the master's house, for I was sick of spending nights wondering about the next day's destination. I had no real reason for thinking so, but I felt as though I was very near to an important junction in my destiny; and this notion being uppermost in my mind, I did not wish to delay my arrival any longer.

A servant stopped us at the main door to the house, and looked dubiously at me when I told him who I was, reminding him of the recent marriage. He said with not a little irony in his voice, 'Well, let me tell the master and see if he wishes to entertain any strangers at this time of the night.'

When he went away, I realized something to which I had given no thought: that my clothes were in shreds, that my hair grew wildly about my head, and that I had not washed myself during the last two days. I was beginning to doubt if Mr Rodrigues would recognize me when I heard his voice in a passage inside the house. And as he came in my view, I heard him call, 'Is that you, Gregório?'

'Yes,' I called back loudly as if wanting to reassure the whole house that I was no vagrant.

In another moment, Mr Rodrigues and I were standing face to face.

'It's too dark here,' he said, 'but who could have those eyes, eh Gregório?'

And he embraced me, saying, 'Well, this is a wonderful surprise. What have you been doing since I saw you, hunting Indians? Come in, come in.'

As I entered, he said to the servant, 'Gilberto, look after that young man, will you, and bring something for our guest to eat and drink. Well, Gregório, let's go into my library, that's the only room that's properly lit. I've developed a habit in recent years, sitting up late and reading. It's just impossible to sleep the older I get, and a man who's twice been a widower has no more appetite for the usual nocturnal pastimes. There's nothing like a book.'

I was dazzled by the light when we entered the library. There were two multi-branched candelabra, one on a desk on which there was also an open book, an ink-stand and some paper, and the second candelabrum stood on a tall, graceful stool beside a window. Behind the desk was a plain white wall with a wooden cross on it, while the wall in front of the desk had bookcases standing against it.

The servant, Gilberto, came in and gave me a tray on which were a plate of rice and beans and a glass of water. He bowed as I thanked him and softly withdrew from the room without turning his back to us until he had reached the door.

'Indeed, a most wonderful surprise,' Mr Rodrigues said, watching me with his bright eyes. 'It's been a long time since we last met and you promised me that you would visit my house one day.'

'Do you remember that, too?' I asked.

'Indeed, I do,' he said, smiling and nodding his head.

'You say it's been a long time. How long?'

'What can you mean?' he asked as if my question were not a simple one but somehow mysterious.

'Just that,' I said. 'How long has it been since that day? How many weeks or months have passed since then?'

'Ah, are you suggesting that you're so young that the passage of time means nothing to you?'

'No, sir, that's not it. I shall explain.'

'Well, it's not been all that long, though I had, indeed, hoped you'd visit me earlier. Still, nothing has been lost by the delay. But, to answer your question, it's been nearly eight months since my daughter Augustina became your stepmother. Surely, you'd know how much time has passed simply by looking at her? She's big now, I hear, very big, and I hope it will not be too difficult for her in another month or two. Poor thing, she's still very young, you know; hardly older than you, and she has such a weak constitution.'

'I have not seen her for eight months,' I said.

Mr Rodrigues expressed astonishment and I proceeded to tell him my story, slowly eating from the plate in front of me. I finished the rice and beans long before I finished the story, and Mr Rodrigues called Gilberto to take the tray away.

When I had concluded my narrative, he said, 'What shall I say? Shall I congratulate you, which I do, for having survived a most dangerous and, I must say, a most foolish undertaking? Or shall I sympathize with you, which I also do, for having lost your elder brother? And I'm the first to hear all this!

Your father will be beside himself with grief. The eldest son gone, and for no reason at all. And Veríssimo, a blundering old fool, but a likeable man nevertheless, and all those slaves, all those horses. It's a great loss. But isn't destiny a great thing, Gregório? Of course the whole thing was a mistake, but mistakes are part of our destiny, mistakes take us into alleys which we would have turned away from were we guided only by prudence. You are the only one to have emerged alive from this most disastrous expedition. There must be a reason.'

I was silent, for I had exhausted myself with telling my story; and somehow the incidents which I had borne with magnanimity or with stoicism or had simply suffered seemed much more frightening now that I had reconstructed them. In retrospect, my imagination seemed to magnify each danger as it attempted to convey its atmosphere.

'You're tired,' Mr Rodrigues said. 'Let me ask Gilberto to show you to your room.'

'But should you not tell me something?' I asked.

'What?'

'The reason why you importuned me to visit you?'

'Oh, that. That can wait till tomorrow. It's not so important. I don't see how anything can be important after your terrifying story. Especially after the realization that you've miraculously been saved when you, too, could have been . . . oh, but it's too horrifying. Tomorrow we will have breakfast together, and I will show you my property during the morning. And tomorrow you must find time to write to your father. I'll get a horseman to deliver your message. The news must be broken to him somehow. And it'll be easier for you to write, easier, that is, when you get home.'

After breakfast the next morning, Mr Rodrigues and I rode out of the house to look at his property. Out of courtesy to my host, I did not point out the fact that I had been riding across his plantation for the last two days and had seen much more than he could possibly show me during the morning. But I had been mistaken, I soon realized, if I had thought

160

that looking at his property meant simply riding around the land and looking at the sugarcanes growing. What he had to show me was something I would not have noticed had I travelled alone on the route that he had planned for me. First, we came to a large wooden building which I took to be a house for slaves, but from which came, as I could not help remarking, the strange, chanting sound of children. Mr Rodrigues showed me into this house, which turned out to be a large room; the children's chanting grew louder as we stood and observed them.

'This,' Mr Rodrigues informed me, speaking very close to my ear, 'is my school.'

His explanation was unnecessary, for I could see that the children were reciting something in chanting, sing-song voices. I could not understand what they were saying, for if they spoke Portuguese, it was not the Portuguese which I understood. The teacher, conscious that the master observed him and that the master had with him a visitor who must be given a favourable impression, stood exaggeratedly erect and, beating a cane in the air to keep time, conducted the merry chanting of the children who seemed to be aged between five and twelve and were, of course, all boys. I had never been inside a school before, but somehow I felt convinced that this was not how schools were in Portugal; and yet I felt thrilled to be present there, hearing all those boys so solemnly and determinedly repeat again and again the phrases that were so incomprehensible to me.

As we rode away from the school, I asked: 'But what were they studying?'

'Why, couldn't you tell?' Mr Rodrigues said with some alarm as if to wonder whether his school-teacher were not incompetent that a stranger could not tell what was being taught. 'Latin, of course. The boys were conjugating a verb.'

'Oh, yes, of course,' I said somewhat hastily and confusedly. 'But why Latin? The boys are all slave children, aren't they?'

'Precisely,' Mr Rodrigues said. 'They are all slave children. I have two reasons for wanting them educated. First, a

161

demanding study keeps them out of mischief, and, second, although some of the older boys could easily be helping in the fields, I want them all to be educated so that they may develop their minds and thus be better equipped to serve me when they're ready to do so. Also, I would like my Negroes and Indians to see that they are different from us not simply because we're the masters and they the slaves but because we have behind us a culture which has made us what we are. Education is the only way in which I can make them see what this culture is; and the more of it they can see, the more will they understand us. And this understanding is important, I think. I don't believe in keeping the slave a slave by keeping him ignorant and enmeshed in his world of fears and superstitions. If he is to be my slave, I would like him to be so because he understands me and wants to be my slave. I prefer to have his love rather than his servile obedience, for I know that the latter kind of attachment entails resentment which can lead to ill-will, even to rebellion.'

'But why Latin?' I repeated my earlier question although I was greatly impressed with Mr Rodrigues's argument for the education of the slaves.

'Is there anything else worth studying?' he remarked. 'You know, sometimes while I'm sitting in my library, reading softly aloud to myself, I wonder if one of these sixty or seventy boys will grow up one day to find an interest in books and whether he will sit there like me, beside the candles, reading Virgil and convinced that he can hope for no higher pleasure. Isn't it strangely foolish, the kind of dream each one of us lives with?'

We had now arrived at another building, which in its outward structure was nearly identical to the school.

'This,' Mr Rodrigues said, allowing me to enter before him, 'is something quite different, and after what I've just said about the need to educate the slaves, you will probably see no logic in having both the school and this. For this, Gregório, is a distillery, and what you're looking at now is the slow maturing of a very potent liquor which those men there are distilling out of the canes. Why do I make liquor on my land when I could so easily suppress it and keep my slaves sober at all times? Let me tell you, Gregório, if you have not already learned this important lesson. Never suppress anything. If you suppress the manufacturing of anything, it only leads to people making it illicitly; whereas if you make the thing yourself, you can both satisfy the people as well as make a little profit; the most important point, however, is that you keep things under your control. In this way, you give people what they think is freedom and yet you keep all the power in your own hands. Nor should you ever suppress ideas. Should anyone begin to discuss something which you abhor, don't, whatever you do, declare that the subject is never to be mentioned again on your land. Instead, proclaim the fact that it is an idea which you yourself have had and ask the people to come and talk about it in public. And then, if you have the subtlety, either let them exhaust the idea until it becomes worthless or destroy it by ridiculing it. And so it is with this liquor. I don't, frankly, care for it myself, preferring a civilized glass of wine to any of this hard country stuff which can be a killer if taken too much of. I see a glint in your eyes, you rogue, would you like to try a sip? Perhaps later, after lunch, it's too early in the day. Ha, I remember at my daughter's wedding, during the feast in your father's great drawing-room, yes, yes, I wasn't blind, I saw you gulp down glass after glass of wine and then collapse on the floor. Oh yes, I can see that you're quite interested in all this!'

I was very surprised to discover that he had such a good memory of how I behaved at my father's wedding-feast, and he went on, while we walked between the two rows of earthen jars and observed the men at work along the far wall: 'But to return to this question of why I should provide liquor for my slaves. Well, let me say that I don't believe in denying anybody a little pleasure if this is indeed what he calls pleasure. Also, the slave, so far in the history of Brazil, is treated as if he were a mule which one has to flog and flog to get the maximum work out of. Of course, the less we have to spend on the slave by way of providing him with food and clothing without impairing his ability to give the most he can in labour, the more money we make. This at least is the belief among our landlords, and it strikes me as a pretty naïve belief. Because, it seems obvious to me that the slave's output is not the consequence only of how much fuel one can put down his throat, but also of whether or not he is contented with his condition. In other words, it's our job to see that he is not denied a measure of happiness. And another thing. You've never done a hard day's work. Ha, you don't have to protest, I can see that from your slender limbs, at best you've perhaps stood and watched the slaves at their labours. Well, if you ever do half the work an ordinary slave does in a day, you'll find that there's no greater relaxation than to drink a glass of liquor and to sit back. Now, do you see why this distillery is as important as the school? All my planning on this plantation is calculated to give the slave a positive development.'

While I was impressed by his reasoning, I asked, 'But isn't there the danger that some of the slaves are going to get addicted?'

'Ha, you're sharp,' he commented as we walked out of the building. 'As a matter of fact, I did think of that, and as a precaution the liquor is strictly rationed.'

'But,' I said, 'surely there must be some who don't like the liquor and sell to those who can't do without it?'

'Good God, you are most incredibly sharp! I hadn't thought of that. I shall have to make a few discreet enquiries to see if that might not be happening. Gregório, it's a pleasure to have you here. It's most useful to have your kind of intelligence on this land.'

I wondered what he could have meant as we rode away. We made a circuitous way back to the house, stopping on the way to look at the saw-mill, the granary and the chapel. At each of these stations on the way to the house, he explained the importance of each to his scheme to develop the slaves into intelligent and creative human beings.

'Isn't there a danger,' I asked when we were finally riding

towards the house, 'that the slave will become so developed that he will no longer want to be a slave?'

'And a very good thing too!' Mr Rodrigues cried somewhat vehemently, and I must admit that I was not a little shocked both by his suddenly aggressive tone and by the implication of what he had said. 'Why on earth should these people be my slaves? What have I done that I should be their absolute ruler? Of course, I love my land and I enjoy the wealth it produces for me and my family. But the land, Gregório, is enormous. A tenth of my land would satisfy me if my avarice were a hundred times greater than it is. And why can't I organize this land and the people I have collected on it in such a way that the land is as generous to the people who labour on it as to the people who simply by some good fortune or the other are its first masters?'

'I agree with you,' I said, though I must admit that I had all sorts of doubts in my mind, 'but can you answer one other question which is nagging me? Suppose the slave begins to appreciate the advantages of the kind of life you and I enjoy, will he not then want to usurp us?'

'Oh, Gregório, you talk like those people who're afraid of ever leaving their houses in case the burglars take advantage of their absence. Come, you must show a little trust, otherwise what are you going to give mankind? We're all entitled to our little measure of avarice, jealousy, possessiveness, selfishness, and the general exercise of vanity, but I wish that there were some force which compelled us to make room for a little trust. Not charity. Charity is only one way of making a public and an ostentatious expression of our possessiveness. But trust. A most difficult concept.'

As we alighted from our horses, I was filled with an exhilaration and experienced the thrilling sensation of inspiration, for obviously Mr Rodrigues had taken me round his property not merely to show what it was like but to impress upon my mind a certain pattern of behaviour, a moral. My inspiration, however, was slightly soured by the suspicion at the back of my mind that the good-will which Mr Rodrigues wished to express towards the slaves was misguided.

'You will no doubt want to wash and rest for half an hour or so before we meet for lunch,' he said. 'I'll ask Gilberto to bring you something cool and refreshing to drink. None of that hard stuff, eh?'

I smiled appreciatively at his joke, and he added, 'My daughter Alicia will be joining us for lunch. I have one request to make of you. Please do not address any words to Alicia.'

With this ambiguous request, he left me and wandered away into the house. As I went to my room, I began to think that there was a great deal which was mysterious about Mr Rodrigues. All that I had heard about him before had not suggested several of the idiosyncrasies which seemed to be the dominating features of his character. I had imagined him to be like my father in all but the very personal circumstances of his existence, for I took the two men to be representatives of a very specific culture, each committed to upholding a very specific type of life. And yet, already what little I had observed of him showed him to be as unlike my father as Father Boscoli had been from Father Prado. I wondered if my father knew the true Mr Rodrigues, the one who for some reason had chosen to reveal himself to me. As I prepared myself for lunch, soaking my hair in water so that I could comb it down satisfactorily, it occurred to me that there was either something saintly about Mr Rodrigues or something devilish. I was too young to realize which. And the mysterious manner in which he had mentioned his daughter Alicia. Not the least of the mystery was that her name had never been mentioned during the days that my father was engaged to Augustina, a time when there was a lot of talk of the Rodrigues family, a time when every member of his family had exhaustively and with great fervour been discussed by my father. He had described Augustina's two older sisters and the families into which they had been married. He had talked of Mr Rodrigues's deceased wives and how he had once met the second wife. He had, with touching pathos, described how Mr Rodrigues's first wife had borne two sons and seen them both die and had died herself of a broken heart. But he had never mentioned a fourth daughter; certainly, he had never mentioned the name Alicia.

A few minutes later my speculations came abruptly to an end as I sat down for lunch with Mr Rodrigues, taking the chair to his left and seeing that to his right and directly opposite me sat a young girl. The resemblance to Augustina was unmistakable even though I could not see her eyes which were turned to her lap. I guessed that she must be thirteen or fourteen years old. Just when I was sitting down and was in that posture of leaning slightly forward while about to make contact with the chair, she looked up for a moment. Our eyes met and she quickly turned away to look again at her lap. Her eyes were blue; if anything, they were a shade darker blue than Augustina's. I was overwhelmed, for here was the same delicate perfection I had observed in Augustina; only there was a greater aura of innocence about Alicia, there was a sadness about her flawless pale skin. To prevent my mind from venturing into fantasies, I looked at Mr Rodrigues and apologized for having kept him waiting. He waved a dismissive hand with a charm that seemed to come instinctively to him, and said, 'Ha, let's get on with the soup. Alicia, let me serve you first.'

He picked up Alicia's plate whereupon she looked up at him, and he said, 'But let me introduce you two! Alicia, meet Gregório, your sister Augustina's step-son. Gregório, this is my daughter Alicia.'

He accompanied this statement with gestures of the head while filling Alicia's plate with soup and putting it down in front of her. She looked nervously at me and seeing that I smiled at her, having raised myself a little from my chair, she smiled back though I thought that I detected a moment of hesitation and confusion on her face.

'I hope you'll like this soup, Gregório,' Mr Rodrigues said, now filling up my plate. 'Plain vegetable soup. Wholesome stuff. This is all I eat for lunch, this and a little bread. But don't be alarmed, young man, I know of the appetite of youth.

167

You will have a plate of meat presently. Certainly, you need to eat a good amount of meat. Your adventures in the jungle have plainly kept you undernourished. But I'm getting old for such things. I have an imbecile doctor who prods my body with his fingers from time to time. You know what he told me the last time I complained that I felt exhausted all too soon? He said that I needed a strong diet. He recommended that I begin the day with three raw eggs beaten into a glass of hot milk. And not with sugar either, but some damned herb which turned the mixture into a vivid orange. I was supposed to follow this with undercooked liver which was to have no salt on it. All this for breakfast. He had wilder ideas for the rest of the day. For lunch I was supposed to choose from among the kidney, the tongue and the heart of an ox, and if I needed greater choice, I could ask for stewed ox-tail or for boiled tripe. Whatever I chose was to be heavily spiced. What, I asked this imbecile, was the philosophy behind all these suggestions? Honestly, the craziness of our quacks bewilders me at times. He said, "It must be obvious to you, Mr Rodrigues, that it is the smaller organs of an animal's body which do most of the work. When people eat beef, they take a slice off a cow's rump, say, or they go for the meat in the neck. Now, all these parts are inactive, they're just dead matter which the living body has to carry, not absolutely dead, of course, but it is clear that the kidney or the liver is a much more active part than the mere layers of flesh on the cow's body." Well, Gregório, you can imagine his argument, you can imagine what kind of idiocy had taken shape in his mind. I didn't realize at once that I had a fool for a doctor, for I followed his lunatic instructions for three days. After that I suffered the worst constipation I've ever experienced. I didn't even send for the idiot, but decided for myself that the only way for me to survive was to follow a simple but wholesome diet. And here you are, having to suffer not only my account of my troubles but also the diet which I have no doubt must appear excessively insipid to one not used to it.'

I protested that I had enjoyed the soup enormously – for I

168

had finished it by now – and that I particularly liked the flavour of cloves in it.

'Ah, cloves!' Mr Rodrigues said. 'Now there you have something which is really helpful to the body. There's nothing like cloves to keep the digestion in good shape. Why, every morning I chew half a dozen cloves while drinking a hot cup of milk. And coriander, now coriander is one of the most important little plants in nature. One of my favourite dishes is chopped brain fried in olive oil with lots of cloves and black peppers crushed into it, and just when it's cooked, sprinkled with chopped fresh coriander. Ah, what a wonderful flavour coriander produces!'

A servant took away Alicia's plate, for she too had finished, and replaced it with a plate of meat before performing the same service for me, too. Mr Rodrigues ate his soup slowly and seemed to chew the vegetables with the care one gives to fish which might have bones in it.

'My Alicia,' he said, extending a hand and patting her head affectionately so that she looked up and smiled brightly at him, 'she likes a small slice of meat for lunch. Don't you, my dear?'

She did not answer him, and I thought that she was covering up her excessive shyness by absorbing herself in the meal as if it were a difficult task which demanded all her concentration.

'You must bring out some of your embroidery, Alicia, to show Gregório how clever you are. Yes,' and now Mr Rodrigues addressed me, 'she's my cleverest child. And she has the tenderest heart. One day I came across her in the yard, a cat in her lap, tying a bandage round the cat's left paw. Apparently, she'd seen the cat limping and seeing what was wrong was trying to help the poor creature. My other children would probably have kicked the cat into the fields.'

Alicia, hearing these complimentary allusions to herself, seemed all the more determined to keep her mind shut to the conversation, for all her thought was directed to cutting thin slices of the meat and putting them very gently into her

169

mouth. When she finished, Mr Rodrigues patted her on the shoulder, saying, 'You can go and rest in your room now, Alicia.'

She rose, and, casting a quick look at me, smiled. She walked away, taking light, slow steps, and I observed that she was slightly taller than Augustina and that, consequently, her figure was better proportioned.

'You have a charming daughter,' I said, hoping that I was not being too presumptuous in paying Mr Rodrigues this compliment.

'And to think,' he said, obviously either not interested in the topic I had raised or tactfully ignoring my presumption, 'that only a miracle has brought you here! Isn't it most extraordinary?'

I did not reply, for I felt somewhat rebuked at his changing the subject.

'Your father is going to be most hideously depressed,' he went on. 'This is a time when landlords can't afford to lose a fraction of their resources. Brazil, Gregório, is opening up. Portugal is sending out not only men but whole families. Eager and hardened businessmen are pouring into Salvador by the shipload. And when merchants come to a new country, they don't think of cultivating a piece of land, they look around and see what's most profitable and then begin to plan how they can take over. Obviously, anyone coming new to Brazil doesn't even have to open his eyes to see that the most profitable establishments are the plantations. And these merchants are clever, damned clever. I know of one merchant who persuaded a landlord that he could increase his profits if he set up two more mills on his plantation and that this could be easily accomplished by borrowing money from the merchant. The merchant seemed most eager to help. Of course, no sooner was the transaction concluded and the mills built, than the merchant wiped away the affable, sycophantic smile from his face and put on the mask of a fierce dog and soon hounded the landlord into bankruptcy. These things are happening and you, who are now the elder son, must understand what they signify. Not only Brazil, but the entire New World is opening up. I've heard that the English have established themselves on the islands off North America, and what do you think they're beginning to cultivate there? Sugar! So, for how long do you think Brazilian sugar is going to hold its price? The world is expanding, changing, bursting with a new energy. The old stability – which, if you ask me, is another word for stagnation, inertia, lack of purpose, downright laziness – has gone. Everywhere men's eyes are alert. Which is why we have to commit ourselves to experiment, change and progress. Did you mean what you said just now?'

'What?' I asked, suddenly surprised by the question which had no relation to what he had been saying.

'About Alicia,' he said, 'that she's a charming girl.'

'Yes,' I said and perhaps my tone suggested an eagerness in my voice which I ought to have kept under check. 'I hope it's not improper of me to compliment you on the charm and good manners of your daughter.'

'Good God no! Alicia is an angel and I love her dearly. Anyone who sees her value as I do wins my regard for expressing his opinion. For Alicia, I intend to find a husband who will not just be a handsome young man with good prospects but who will also demonstrate that he is capable of dedication in the face of misfortune.'

Later that afternoon, as I lay in my room, resting from the heat of the day, I pondered these last sentences of Mr Rodrigues. There was something ambiguous about what he had said and I could not understand precisely what it was. One thing, however, was certain: Mr Rodrigues had come as close as he could, without saying it in so many words, to offering me his daughter in marriage. I could now understand why he had been so solicitous that I should visit him, for obviously I, rather than either of my brothers, was of the right age (if Mr Rodrigues did not also detect superior qualities in me) for Alicia. But there *was* some mystery about Alicia, my mind insisted, for I could not forget that she had never been mentioned, and nor had she, unlike the other sisters, been brought to my father's wedding. There was something I did not know, and it occurred to me that Mr Rodrigues had been very careful in his choice of words while he talked about her.

Alicia did not join us for dinner, and Mr Rodrigues explained that she had been taken ill with a slight fever. It was quite unusual for her to be ill, he added, for she was a healthy girl. I did not suggest that a doctor be called, considering that Mr Rodrigues had spent most of the time during lunch maligning his doctor. Indeed, the subject of Alicia seemed promptly to be dropped after Mr Rodrigues had mentioned that she was a healthy girl. Although I vaguely hinted on one or two occasions that I would be prepared to be drawn into a discussion of his daughter's future, Mr Rodrigues, for some obscure reasons of his own, completely neglected my concealed offer. Whether it was some eccentricity in his character or whether he proceeded by some premeditated design, it was impossible for me to tell; all I could do was to remark to myself with some astonishment that Mr Rodrigues was an alarmingly unpredictable man, that he was not at all the dignified and witty man I had met at my father's wedding; although his dignity was not, of course, in question now, what I had seen at the wedding was a public façade: the private man was withdrawn on the one hand, and an actively concerned land-owner on the other. He was absorbed both in his books and in the welfare of his slaves. But beneath these levels which I was beginning to discern just below the mask I now looked at there was another level, and I was convinced that this other level was one of anxiety, fear, possibly even one of extreme despair.

'What I want to tell you, Gregório,' he said when we had finished dinner and adjourned to his library, 'is that we should possess a certain vision.'

'What do you mean, sir?' I asked.

'If Brazil appears to us as a naked woman,' he said, suddenly shocking me with the choice of his image, 'then we should not be ashamed to look at her. If she is beautiful, then we should thank God and enjoy her beauty. If, however, she appears deformed or in any way lacking in certain physical charms, we should have the courage to look at her. And even the most perfect beauty, Gregório, must lose its excellence, for the wrinkles will come whatever precautions we take to prevent them. Therefore, what we need to pray for is the strength to abide by this woman whatever happens to her. But there is this important difference between the country Brazil and this rather silly notion I have suggested by comparing her to a woman: what happens to the woman will happen without our instigating it, at least there are certain matters, well, the wrinkles for one, over which we have no control. But what happens to Brazil is largely in our hands. The way she goes, whether she becomes a grand old lady or an obscene slut, will be our doing. But enough of this comparison! You get my point, don't you?'

'I understand,' I said. 'Brazil's destiny is in our hands.'

'Yes, but there's something else you must not forget. It's true enough that the destiny of every country is in the hands of its people, but Brazil we recognize to be something special. For the truth is that Brazil does not as yet exist.'

'How can that be?' I asked. 'We're sitting in the middle of Brazil.'

'Yes, but what are we? Landowners, simply landowners. And for most of us, the land could be anywhere in the world as long as it is ours. And what do we do with the land? Exploit it as much as we can for no other reason than that our wives may be able to buy silks from France. Everywhere I look I see men grabbing land and abusing it in all kinds of despicable ways. And everywhere, too, I see men who have acquired the land debase their fellow-men. No one is acting with vision. We are all behaving like children who have been given the freedom of a pastry shop.'

'But the country is large enough!' I protested.

'I do not doubt that the country is limitless in its resources; but what I wonder is what will happen to men who grow up thinking that thoughtless exploitation is the only way. That is why I say, let us act with vision, and not do what's happening all over this state. People burn up the jungle here, grow a crop for one year, and then move on, burning up the jungle somewhere else. Or they cut down the timber in one part and move on, cutting up the timber there, never pausing to replant an area. Without vision, I fear a greater barbarism than mankind has ever known will be the future of Brazil. You said this afternoon that you found my daughter Alicia charming. Are you still of the same opinion?'

'Why, indeed I am,' I replied, once again slightly bewildered by his sudden change of topic.

'Be careful, Gregório,' he said, 'I wouldn't want you to go back to your father and tell him that you've fallen in love with his sister-in-law.'

If he had accompanied this last statement with a laugh or even a smile, I would have enjoyed the joke, but I could see that he spoke in absolute seriousness.

'I can observe charm,' I said, 'even beauty, without wishing to possess it. As for your daughter, sir, I applaud her beauty without presuming to think that I am worthy of her affections.'

'Oh, do stop being so pompous, Gregório!'

'What can you mean, sir?' I asked, somewhat alarmed by his sudden exclamation.

'You have a fine way of talking,' he said. 'You have a way of speaking exactly what you do not want to say, and as for what you do want to say, you keep that nicely withdrawn like the claws of a cat.'

'I'm sure I don't understand you,' I said.

'There you are! My meaning is perfectly plain.'

'Then tell me,' I said, almost challenging him, 'what it is you want me to say.'

'You will soon be going home, you will soon have to meet your father and to give him the most tragic news he's ever had to hear in his whole life. Would it not help to alleviate the tragedy by having some good news to give him, too?'

'Certainly it would help.'

'Then there's no reason for us to tease each other with

riddles,' he said. 'I would like you to answer one other question.'

'Anything you ask,' I said.

'Suppose someone near to you, someone you loved very much, were to be suddenly struck by some dreadful disease, would you have the patience to look after that person with the same affection as you had before the person was struck by the disease?'

'Certainly, I would,' I replied.

'No, I don't think you've understood my meaning. Rather – please forgive me – I don't think I've made myself clear. Let me put it in another way, then. Suppose one night somewhere in the jungle you thought you had come to some hidden treasure, that it lay there glittering on the ground; and suppose, at daylight, you discovered that it was not a treasure at all, but some deception induced by the moonlight: would you be disappointed?'

'I would be inhuman if I did not experience that feeling.'

'Yes, yes, that's true enough. But would you have the strength to overcome the disappointment?'

'Yes, I think so.'

'Well, then, you're the man.'

He seemed to stop in the middle of a sentence, for his conclusion did not come to me as any kind of revelation. I was more puzzled than ever. He pulled a book out from a shelf and, walking up and down the room, turned some of its pages, looking at a few sentences and murmuring them aloud. The sound was incomprehensible to me. He put the book back and resumed his seat.

'Do you read?' he asked.

'Not with any mastery,' I said. 'My father believes in actions rather than words.'

'Most unwise of him,' he said. 'You should learn to read well. I would like to think that one day these books will give someone as much pleasure and comfort as they do me. Well, Gregório, you have answered all my questions. No doubt you have a question or two for me?'

175

'Well, sir, you puzzle me,' I said in a frank tone. 'When we met at my father's wedding, why did you ask me especially to visit you?'

'So that we could sit, as we are doing now, and have a quiet conversation.'

'And these questions which you have asked me this evening, what is the significance of them?'

'Gregório, you know something which even your father does not know. You know that I have a daughter, Alicia, Augustina's sister. There is a good reason why Alicia has never been mentioned before. Nor has she been seen by anyone outside the family before today. Naturally, you've been puzzled by a good many things. I asked you this morning not to address any words to Alicia. I asked you this for the very simple reason that she is deaf. You must have noticed that whenever I spoke to her, I touched her and drew her attention so that she could follow my gestures. She could not hear me, of course, but she has developed a way of understanding what I say to her. And, as you must know or at least guess by now, people who are deaf from a very early age are also dumb. Until this year, Alicia has been an embarrassment to me and to her sisters. Her sisters considered that their own chances of marriage were in jeopardy because of Alicia. You know how people are, unaccountably superstitious. They think that if there's one person in the family who is in any way deformed or lacking, then there is something wrong with everyone else in the family. That there is some curse on it. But after Augustina's marriage, I've only had Alicia in the house. And I've begun to realize that she is the most beautiful of my daughters, that she has a profound understanding of nature, that, instead of being an embarrassment to my family, she is the most valuable gift I have to give. You have seen for yourself, Gregório. Do you not agree with my judgement?'

'I do,' I said, though my voice was a little weak, for I was beginning to realize that I had been put into a corner. I saw now why I had thought that there was something devilish about Mr Rodrigues, and I wondered now whether I thought

176

of him as a scheming father who was anxious to find a husband for his unmarriageable daughter or whether I thought of him as a benevolent patriarch who sought an alliance in order to bring two vast properties together, and did so with the subtlest diplomacy. I had other thoughts within the same moment: that there was no reason for me to think that Alicia was unmarriageable, that, instead, she would probably make a wonderful mother of most beautiful children that we would surely have, that, by having this thought, I was already presuming that I would agree, that I would eventually be the master of one of the largest properties in Brazil when I inherited both my father's and Mr Rodrigues's land.

'And do you agree with my notion,' he asked, 'that Alicia deserves a husband who is not only devoted to her but also has the capacity to rule over his property as if he were ruling over Brazil?'

'I do,' I said, as if in a trance, for the statement came to my lips before I could think of formulating a suitable answer.

'And are you that man?'

'I am.'

'Well, then, you have good news to take home. I shall write a letter to your father, announcing your engagement.'

'You have two other daughters,' I said, 'apart from Alicia and my mother.'

'Yes, but they're married already.'

'I know,' I said. 'But who is to inherit your land?'

'Are you attempting to bargain with me?'

'No, sir, I would not presume to do that. You showed me your land this morning, and I was impressed by what you're trying to do for the slaves. Don't you think your work should be carried on?'

'Indeed, I do. Are you suggesting that you are the man to do so?'

'If I have the qualities you seek in Alicia's future husband, then I also have the qualities which will be necessary to run your land according to your own far-sighted plan.'

'Either you're very smart or you have abundant confidence

177

in yourself. In either case, I am impressed. My land will go to Alicia's husband.'

'Then I am your man.'

That very evening, when I said good night to him, Mr Rodrigues sat down to write a letter to my father so that I could take it with me, for at the conclusion of our conversation I declared that there was no need for me to prolong my departure and that I should leave for home the next morning.

He gave me the letter after breakfast the next morning just when I was ready to depart. I was about to say good-bye to him when he said, 'Just wait a moment, will you?' and went into the house. He returned with Alicia, leading her by the arm.

'It would be improper to leave without saying farewell to your fiancée,' he said.

Alicia stood there in the verandah, pale and slim, the morning sun falling in her dark blue eyes. I noticed, too, something I had not remarked on the previous day: that her hair was not blonde like Augustina's, but had a reddish glow to it. I glanced, too, I have to admit, at her breasts, and was not disappointed, considering she was no more than fourteen. Her mouth slightly open, she stood there staring at me as though she were a vision of perfect beauty. I shook hands with Mr Rodrigues and then, turning to Alicia, said, 'Good-bye, my dear,' and, putting a hand on her shoulder, surprised both myself and her by softly kissing her on the cheek. I did not look again at Mr Rodrigues, but hastily walked away, congratulating myself on my daring. A stablehand had my horse ready in the front yard, and soon I rode away with that beautiful image of Alicia as the mirage which to pursue. It took me five days of hard riding to reach home where I was astonished to discover that news of our tragic expedition had preceded me although I had not written the letter Mr Rodrigues had suggested. I was received with tears of joy and with greater weeping for Antônio. The only person who did not cry was my younger brother, Francisco, whose demeanour seemed to suggest that he suspected that I had plotted everyone's, and especially Antônio's, deaths on the expedition. When the weeping died down, I was able to confirm that Augustina was big with child. Ah, well, I thought, it doesn't matter now, I'm the eldest whatever happens. And then I had a surprise. Aurelia, too, was pregnant.

Chapter 6

AURELIA'S DOWNFALL

Blaming himself for the tragic outcome of the expedition into the jungle, my father seemed to withdraw from the management of the plantation. He spent much of his time in the chapel, kneeling in his pew, his head bowed. Once I observed him in the chapel without his knowing. I noticed that he had taken away the cushions on which it had been his habit to rest his knees while kneeling. His hands clasped in front of him, his head weighted down as if by some tremendous guilt, he remained in that posture for a long time. I could see his lips moving, but the solemn silence of the chapel was not disturbed. Two or three times he raised his head, and the light caught his eyes as he looked up at the statue of Christ. Seeing his tears, I could not bear to watch his agony any longer, and left him to his prayers, tears smarting my own eyes. The birth of Augustina's first child, a son, assuaged my father's grief; at least he was temporarily diverted from the immensity of his suffering. It was with great pride that he named his son Antônio as if his former eldest son had been returned to him.

Aurelia, too, had a son some twenty-four hours before Antônio was born, and my father decided that a good name for him would be João Veríssimo. Of course, I, like everyone else, applauded this decision and did not reveal the true story of old Verissimo's life. I must say that I was quite proud of little João Veríssimo, for he had a tiny brown face and fine black hair. I was pleased to admit to myself that he looked like me, though, of course, I hoped that no one would notice the resemblance. Within a few days of the babies being born, however, the servants began to whisper that the two boys looked remarkably alike in their features, that each had the unmistakable forehead of the da Silva family. It took me some time to realize what this rumour implied: that each boy had the *same* father! I was sure that this unfortunate rumour had been begun by the old Negress Tana who, I had begun to notice, seemed determined to take her revenge on the many severities inflicted upon her by Augustina.

Obviously, the rumour reached Augustina who was most disturbed by it – naturally enough. I wished I could have reassured her that little João Veríssimo was my handiwork and that she need not becloud her face because of his existence. But events took a turn for the worse. Little Antônio passed away and took his place among the angels after three weeks of earthly existence. There was no consoling my mother that Antônio in his pretty blue silk crib should die while João Veríssimo seemed to thrive in Aurelia's squalid little room. Much as she had disliked the coincidence of the two births, Augustina now hated Aurelia; for, probably convinced in her mind that her husband had fathered the bastard, Augustina saw the death of her own child as a weakness in herself: if something had gone wrong, then her own frail body had contributed to it whereas the larger Aurelia had given birth to what was obviously a healthier child. As if to confirm this, Aurelia seemed to go about the house in a haughtier spirit, making sure that everyone saw what a fine physique she had for bearing children. I disliked her for doing this, for her behaviour entailed her supporting the lie that her child was indeed my father's, giving her a spurious superiority among the slave women. In fact, I was disgusted by the supercilious way in which she went about, humming merry tunes to herself, and one night I sought her out to tell her what I thought of her behaviour.

I had, in any case, been looking for an opportunity to be alone with her, for I associated the satisfaction of my desires with her lascivious body. I must admit that I had moments of doubt, for I asked myself how I could desire a woman who cast a slur on my father's character, hurt my mother, and

181

took advantage of everyone's feelings at a very trying time in my family's history. But I desired her as men desire strong liquor, knowing that it is bound to do them harm. All my fantasies in the jungle and during the final stages of my journey home had been of her. I simply needed to affirm to myself that the vivid images in my mind of our experiences together which had occurred before the expedition could still be realized. I wanted to touch again the curving contours of the shape which my imagination had attempted to hold close to itself while I lay in my hammock in the jungle, my stroking hand grasping for that intense ecstasy which made brighter the vision and yet finally more frustrating the reality.

For a month, I had not been able to see her when she was not surrounded by other slave women who seemed to envy her condition. We had said nothing to each other since my return, and I must say that I found the proud glint in her eyes when she looked at me across a room rather offensive. It had been no use my visiting her room in the middle of the night, for when I ventured to do so once, I discovered that Tana, who for some reason had decided that Aurelia's giving birth to a boy was an important event, had put a bed in the verandah outside Aurelia's room and herself slept there in case Aurelia needed any help at night. And as I tip-toed away from this sight, I heard the baby begin to cry inside Aurelia's room. I simply had to wait. Finally, Tana gave up her solicitous presence outside the room, and I took my chance one night and paid Aurelia a visit.

'Shhh . . .' she whispered, 'you'll wake the baby.'

'Jesus,' I cried, 'is that all you care about?'

The baby was in a cot next to the bed on which she lay, and already that odour from her body, a mixture of sweat and the various kitchen fragrances which she could never wash away, was making me want to lie next to her at once and commence fulfilling my fantasies.

'Mind what you say,' she said. 'You have no business to be here, and if you're going to make a row, I'll make a louder row, and that won't be nice for you.'

182

'Aurelia, how can you talk like this?' I asked, sitting down on the edge of the bed for the room was too small and I felt awkward standing.

'Look, Gregório,' she said, 'I have the baby to nurse, I have the kitchen to work in, I have your mother to attend to, and she drives me hard, I can tell you, I can tell you she's going to tear me limb from limb one of these days, the way she looks terrifies me, and I'm tired after all that, just damned tired. Do you understand, Gregório?'

'Aurelia,' I said softly, 'I've been away from you for nine months, for nine months I've thought of you and your beautiful body, for nine months I've said to myself that if I survive, if I get back, I shall go straight to the arms of Aurelia.'

She seemed to be moved by this little speech, for she was silent for a moment. So that I went on, 'Aurelia, I've thought of you day and night, I've dreamt of you and in the middle of my sleep I've called out your name, Aurelia, my tongue has called and my hand has groped in the dark for your beautiful shape. . .'

Just then the baby began to cry, and although she had not remonstrated when I was beginning to stroke her leg, which was under the sheet, while making my romantic speech, she now sprang up, saying, 'Now, look what you've done!'

She gently picked up the baby from the cot and returned to bed where she lay back again and, uncovering her breasts, began to suckle the baby. I was both greatly touched by this beautiful sight and maddeningly excited by seeing her full, round breasts.

'Aurelia,' I whispered, 'Christ be praised for this beautiful vision, our baby at your breast. I am proud to see you hold my son and nurse him with such affection. Does not the father deserve to be absorbed into this vision?'

'What do you mean?' she asked.

'This,' I said, moving up and putting my head to her free breast and rolling my tongue about it in search of the nipple which I liked to pretend I could not find so that an ecstasy could be provoked in both of us when finally I did.

183

'Gregório, don't!' she exclaimed a little loudly, rudely pushing my head away. 'Please, Gregório, none of that.'

I was dismayed, even momentarily angered, but I decided to wait, to let the moment pass and to work again at the slow business of arousing her desire for me. She seemed all too absorbed in the child, and it occurred to me that my relationship with Aurelia at present would have been much happier had I not been so fertile ten months ago.

'I'm sorry,' I said, accepting the humiliation as if I justly deserved it, and changed the subject. 'Are you glad,' I asked, 'that little João looks like me? He has exactly my eyes.'

'He should,' she said, 'you both have the same father.'

Now this angered me. It was one thing for her to be acquiring a prestigious position among the slaves by flaunting the notion that she had had a son by the master of the house, but she did not need to impress me.

'Aurelia,' I said, trying to be as calm as I could, 'I have not liked the way you've encouraged the rumour that João is my father's son. My mother has not liked it for obvious reasons, but it has seemed to me to be a cheap trick. You don't gain anything but a moment's fame by such a trick. But what you do in the household is your business for you will have to be accountable to your Maker when the time comes. What you say to me in private is another matter. You insult me by telling me that João is not my son but my half-brother.'

'Don't come to me with your pious preaching,' she said. 'What makes you think that you alone have the privilege to tell the truth? What makes you think that whatever a black maid says is bound to be a lie? Ha, you make me sick!'

'Come on,' I said, 'don't tell me that my father tired of his new bride in two days and took to sleeping with you.'

'What do you know about how babies are born?'

'Saint Anthony brings them down in a sack.'

'I know what you think,' she said, ignoring my irony. 'Just because Antônio and João were born within a day of each other, you think it's impossible for your father to be the father of both. You think that obviously the two children

184

were conceived on the same night, more or less, that it happened on your father's wedding-night while he was with your mother and you were with me. That is so nice a coincidence that you can't believe it could be otherwise. But let me tell you, young man, I know more of what happens inside my body than anyone else. And let me tell you that João happened one night before you came to me that first time on that wedding-night. You don't have to believe it, what do I care! But your father came to me the night before he got married. What's up, Mr da Silva, sir, I asked, how can you want me one night before your wedding to a sweet young white virgin? And you know what he said to me? He said, he wanted to be gentle to his new wife, he didn't want to frighten her with exploding in her straightaway after not having done it for so long. And so he had to explode in me. Three times, too, just to make sure, I suppose, that when it came to the nervous little bride, he could show her gently, just to make sure he'd have everything in full command. I didn't mind it; in fact, I was pleased, flattered even, to be with the master, and what's more, he was good. He joked, too, talked of how nice the Negresses were. And we had other jokes, too, if you want to know. Why, I think I'll tell you. What does it matter? The fact is, Gregório, you were one of his jokes. Poor Gregório, he said, he's going to be fourteen tomorrow and he's had no experience of a woman. It's a disgrace, he said, a son of mine a virgin at fourteen. Send him to me, I said, joking. Well, why not, he said, and I said, Sure, I'll open the door to him. And that's what happened, didn't it, didn't he ask you to come to me with some message?'

'This may be true,' I said ruefully, for I was much saddened by her account, 'but it proves nothing about the paternity of that child.'

'Well, then,' she said, 'tell me this. There's been a rumour now for two weeks that João is your father's son. Why, in all this time, has not your father said one word to deny the rumour?'

'Obviously,' I said, 'he believes it's his son because he slept

185

with you the night before the wedding. Just as I believe that it's my child because I slept with you on the wedding-night and again later.'

'And who's the one who can tell for sure? Obviously me. I know whose it is for I know exactly when I got pregnant. Now will you please go and let me and the baby get a little sleep?'

Greatly saddened and embittered, I rose out of her bed, wondering what I should say. Nothing, I decided, thinking that I was not going to suffer any more humiliation from the tongue of a slave whose sexual charms I would soon have tired of in any case. Going out, I swore at myself for lowering myself to the position where a mere servant thought she could do what she liked with me; silently, as I walked towards my room, I abused myself for not having pursued the traditional prerogative of young men of my class and rank, to use slave women for one's pleasure and to discard them without allowing one's emotions to come into play; instead, I had involved myself in the degrading thoughts of a love affair. Instead of using her as a mere receptacle for my lust – which any common black girl is proud to be – I had dragged myself down by my worthless demonstration that I depended on her. I hated her little bastard, and was convinced that she either lied or flattered herself by saying that it was my father's child and not mine. Yet, now that I had no intention of ever again attempting to make love to her, I was glad that everyone believed that João was my father's bastard. Had the paternity been attributed to me, I would have had to put up with all sorts of coarse humour for which, I must say, I never had any patience.

Coming up to my room, I found my slave Jari asleep outside my door. I gave him a kick, saying, 'Wake up, you bastard, and do some work for your master for a change.'

He shook himself in his sleep, involuntarily putting a hand to his hip where I had kicked him. I gave him a harder blow with the inside of my foot and he woke up with a start. I bade him follow me into my room where I undressed and lay in

186

bed and asked him to massage my back. Softly, as if he was still asleep, he prodded my back with his fingers.

'Come on,' I called, 'you can do better than that, or do I have to wake you up with a whip?'

'I'm awake, master,' he cried, beginning to work vigorously so that I felt his bony hand pluck the tiredness out of my muscles.

'Jari,' I said, 'what do you do when you have a pain in that part of your body where no ointment can offer relief and no amount of gentle massaging can be of any help?'

'What do you mean, master?'

'You know damn well what I mean, there's only one part of the body which fits that description.'

'Massaging help that, too!' he said, joking cheerfully. 'You want to try?'

'Cut out the nonsense, boy,' I said. 'Is that all you've got to say about it? Don't tell me that's how you get rid of the pain!'

'There are hens, master.'

'Oh, do shut up!'

'Well, there's cows, too.'

'I said shut up!'

He worked silently on my back for a moment or two and then said, 'There's girls in the slave quarters, dozens of them. You want me to get you one? I've had four.'

I turned round, pushing him aside so that he stood up, and looked at him. He wasn't joking.

'You want me to?'

'What kind of girl?' I asked.

'Black, brown, or Indian. Thin or fat. Tall or short. How do you like them, master?'

'You mean to tell me that you could go now to the slave quarters and come back with a girl for me?'

'Sure.'

I did not believe that it was so simple, but I said, 'All right, then, just to see if you're telling the truth for once, go and fetch me an Indian girl. Not too fat and not too thin, either.

187

I don't care about her height.'

'Okay, master,' he said, going out and giving me the impression that it was as easy a matter to fetch a girl as it was to get a glass of water.

No sooner had he gone than I began to have fantasies of the Indian women I had seen on the river-bank, standing there naked while we paddled away frantically in the canoes. I remembered, too, how I had been excited even in those moments of terror and flight by the fine beauty of the Indian women. Images of those women began to float about me, the white, smooth skin of their breasts seemed to swell against my cheeks. This was too much and I felt as if I was about to explode, and went running to the bathroom where I quickly sprinkled water on my face and soaked my hands in the cold water in order to calm myself down. Then some evil voice in me said, Just touch it once to see how good it feels, just pull the skin over a tiny little bit to get a foretaste of what you're soon going to experience with the Indian girl. I had never known myself resist this particular temptation, and even as my hand reached for the swollen veins I knew that my hand was not going to be content with a tiny little bit but was going to go the full throbbing distance. Well, a few moments later, I returned to my bed, utterly spent, and, collapsing against my pillow, fell asleep.

Much to my annoyance, Jari woke me sometime later, calling, 'Master, master!' as if the house were on fire.

'What, where?' I called, somewhat confused.

'Master,' he said, 'you didn't tell me it was after one o'clock at night. It was impossible, there were so many dogs jumping out of the darkness. Give me till tomorrow, master, and I'll get you the prettiest Indian girl you ever saw.'

'Oh, go away, you lying shit-face. Remind me tomorrow to give you a good whipping.'

'No, no, I promise, I'll get you one tomorrow. In the afternoon if you like. In the *morning*.'

'Tell me tomorrow. Get out now.'

Perhaps his failure at this late hour was a good thing after all, for I was too exhausted even to think and fell back to sleep promptly. Later in the night, I heard his hushed voice again and woke up slightly startled to see his bent body over me, his face very near mine.'

'Master,' he whispered, 'I have her out now.'

'Look, what the hell are you talking about?'

'The Indian girl,' he said. 'I woke up early, it's maybe five in the morning now, but I woke up thinking you were going to whip me and I should do something about it. So I went and found the girl.'

'You bastard,' I said, smiling at him. 'Go, send her in.'

'You want me to light a candle?'

'No, I can see in the dark.'

He went out, and I heard a shuffling of feet and some whispered words. A girl entered and I saw Jari stretch his arm in and pull the door shut. I rose and held the girl by her shoulders, for she had halted in the middle of the room, perhaps finding it too dark. She had something on which seemed to be a frock, and my hands, busily exploring its openings, discovered that it barely reached her knees and that it was the only garment she wore. I pulled it up and stroked her small, tight buttocks, passing my hand to the front to stroke also the soft hairs there.

Presently, I lay beside her frail body, for she appeared to be very thin, and her breasts were so small I seemed to be able to swallow them whole. She said nothing, nor made any kind of sound. If I paused in my caressing and kissing of her body, she lay limply as though she was not at all capable of being excited. I decided to stimulate that area among her soft hairs which I knew no woman could experience passively. I think a sigh escaped her lips, but otherwise no kind of manipulation or the working of my tongue along the contours of her body had any effect on her. Enough of this, I said to myself, deciding I might as well finish the business which was rising towards its climax within me.

'Well, girlie,' I said, 'here I come.'

Leaning on my elbows, I lay upon her, and then moved my

189

right hand down to draw her legs apart, a procedure for which a knee also came in useful. She seemed to get the message and put her legs in the proper position.

'That's a good girl,' I said, thinking perhaps she needed a little encouragement. 'Now, you'd better help. Take it gently in your hand and put it in.'

To my astonishment – for she had been so uncooperative so far – she was soon holding it in her hand and pulling it towards her; I had almost expected her to remain completely detached.

'That's my beauty,' I said, encouraging her some more. 'We didn't want a damn rape, did we?'

But now, try as we both might, the damn thing wouldn't go in. She pulled and I pushed, but it just would not work. Good God, I said to myself, she's a bloody virgin. I pushed her legs out wider, I moved my knees together and then held them apart, and she kept trying to pull in the right direction as if wanting to do her best in effecting the insertion. While I was beginning to be infuriated by this frustration, I was, at the same time, getting closer to my climax. And, bang, there it was, all out on her soft hairs, and there I was a moment later, collapsed on her, absolutely exhausted. She wriggled a little, and I let her move away from under me. I passed out completely. When I woke up, it was broad daylight and she had gone. Later, when I saw Jari, he had a stupid grin on his face and he said, 'Was that good, master?'

'Shit, no,' I said. 'I couldn't even get it in.'

'You said you could see in the dark,' he joked.

'She was a bloody virgin,' I said. 'I couldn't break her in.'

Jari began to laugh aloud, and I asked, 'What the hell's tickling you, for God's sake?'

'She's no virgin, master,' he said. 'I screwed her yesterday afternoon.'

I whipped him for that. He cried aloud for mercy, which is his usual cowardly habit whenever I whip him.

'Don't ever bring me anything which you have soiled first,' I said to him, leaving him lying in the dust, the whip marks striping his back.

The whipping did him good, for after that he was careful to bring me girls he had not touched himself. At least he never told me about it if he had, and so this particular appetite in me no longer drove me to distraction with craving as it had done in the past. Also, of course, I learned not to be dependent on Jari to procure girls for me; soon, I, too, learned the simple tricks, the clever little ploys, so that I was astonished that there had been a time when it was difficult, almost it seemed impossible to find a partner of the same species.

It was during these weeks that I became well acquainted with my mother, Augustina, with whom I had hardly exchanged two words before going on the expedition. The bearing of a child had been so painful an experience for her and – as I discovered later – she had lost so much blood in the process that she needed a long time to recover. She had begun to make some progress, which was obviously helped by the joy of seeing the child at her breast, when the baby's sudden death seemed to work on her like a new and a greater loss of blood. The shock was such that she lay, silent and disdaining all food, in the darkness of her room. It was at this time that I began to see her, feeling that, as the eldest son, it was my duty to help my mother, particularly as my father had still not emerged from mourning for the loss of my brother Antônio.

I found that I could hold Augustina's interest by narrating incidents of the expedition. At first she found my stories sufficiently distracting to pay my presence some attention; later, she became deeply interested and pressed me for more of my adventures whenever I concluded giving her an account of some particular episode.

Now the interesting thing was that that despicable slave girl, Aurelia, served my mother, and was often present in the room when I told my stories. I was glad to notice that my mother took every opportunity to abuse Aurelia and to call her names, and even more glad when I once insulted Aurelia indirectly by saying in her presence that all slave girls were sluts and discovered that my mother smiled approvingly at me for doing so. One day, when I finished describing one of my adventures, my mother begged me to tell her one more. As it happened I could think only of the adventure of the night I spent in Father Boscoli's house, and wondered whether this might not be a little too spicy to be telling one's own mother, even a step-mother. I decided, since I could think of nothing else the more I tried to think of something else, that I should tell it, and so asked her if the maid could be sent out since the adventure I had in mind was not for the ears of lowly slaves who had nothing better to do than to spread malicious rumours. I was delighted to see that Augustina not only immediately shouted at Aurelia to go out but also that she was glad of what I had said, for when Aurelia had gone out, my mother said, 'That girl is the worst bitch I've ever come across. One of these days when I'm strong enough, I shall knock her teeth out with my shoe.'

'Oh, please, mother,' I said, 'when you do that, let me be a witness. It will give me great pleasure to see justice done to her.'

'Certainly,' she said. 'And I'll do more than knock her teeth out, I can tell you. She thinks she's a great beauty. I'll teach her the consequences of being proud.'

Well, a week later when I saw my mother, she said excitedly, 'Gregório, today you're going to see something. I've been planning it, and today I feel strong enough to do it. Why don't you sit in that chair in the corner and watch when Aurelia comes back from doing my laundry.'

I did so when Aurelia came to the room.

'Oh, Aurelia,' my mother said, 'how pretty you look with your hair gone all stringy with sweat! A little work brings out the best in you. The sweat on your face gives it a fine polish, and the smell when you're around is just like a perfume!'

I must admit that I was a little embarrassed to hear this poor attempt at irony; it sounded false and was not the language that seemed appropriate to my mother's sweet face.

'Come here, Aurelia,' my mother went on to say, 'sit in

front of this mirror, and let me show you how beautiful you can look.'

Aurelia, probably sensing that she was being attacked by an insidious abuse, looked confused and did as she was commanded. In any case, being a slave, she had no choice but to obey. My mother stood behind her and taking up a brush, began gently to stroke Aurelia's hair.

'We'll start at the top,' she said, brushing back Aurelia's hair and then parting it in the middle. 'Now isn't that an improvement?'

Even I could see that it was and Aurelia, probably beginning to believe that no malice was intended, slightly nodded her head in agreement.

'But,' said my mother, 'it's too long, it doesn't become a modern girl like you. Let me just trim it for you.'

She picked up a pair of scissors and trimmed the edges of Aurelia's hair, saying, 'Look, how much neater it is now.'

Aurelia seemed hypnotized by this beauty treatment, and my mother said, 'I could make you look really beautiful. Would you like me to do that?'

Aurelia nodded assent once more, being quite incapable of speech for some reason.

'Close your eyes, then,' my mother said. 'One doesn't notice the difference when one watches the changes step by step. If you closed your eyes, I'd give you a lovely surprise. No, I don't think you're going to have the will-power to keep them closed, you're going to peep without my knowing. Let me tie a handkerchief round your eyes, that way you won't be tempted.'

Aurelia submitted to the handkerchief being tied round her eyes, and my mother, taking up the brush and the scissors again gently worked on her hair as if she were doing Aurelia the greatest of favours.

'You know, Aurelia,' she said, 'when I was young, my sisters and I used to play at making each other beautiful. You remind me so much of my elder sister, sitting there quietly but excitedly, wondering how lovely you're going to look

193

when I've finished. Your hair is so thick! It will be nice if you could make little rings at the temples, and take it up at the back, like the ladies do in Lisbon, but it needs to be thinner for that. Let me thin it just a little bit. That would do the trick. Then it will be more manageable, and it won't go all fuzzy when you sweat. Sweat isn't nice on a young lady, is it? If I thin it a little from the top, then there'll be room for your head to breathe, the breeze will be able to play in your hair and keep your head cool. That will be nice, won't it? No, don't move, I don't want to cut your ears! Now, if to look really pretty, you're going to put your hair up, then you don't need so much of it at the back, so I'll cut some of that off. I always say that nothing looks more messy than thick curls of hair sticking out of an otherwise well-made hair-do. And you don't want to look like a sloppy old maid, do you?'

Thus, talking away and snipping away, my mother gradually cut Aurelia's hair until there was nothing left but the short prickly hairs standing erect as on the head of a boy who has just had his hair cropped.

'Now we're ready to reveal the great beauty,' my mother said, putting both her hands to the handkerchief. Holding the handkerchief in front of Aurelia's eyes, she pulled it down with a sudden jerk in such a way that she made deep scratches on both of Aurelia's cheeks, drawing blood and permanently marking her face. Aurelia screamed with pain a fraction of a second before her eyes opened and then, seeing both the blood on her face and her cropped head, began to shriek hysterically. She jumped out of the chair and made for the door, but my mother, surprising me with her agility, tripped her so that she fell on her face.

'Oh, no,' my mother said, 'you don't go yet. I haven't finished with you. You wouldn't want your lover to see you like that, would you? I have to make you perfect for him.'

Aurelia, flat on the floor, held on to my mother's ankles and began to beat her head against my mother's feet. I was quite amazed by my mother's strength, but then realized that she was very young and that even if Aurelia were stronger than her, my mother had the advantage of being the mistress of the house, and were Aurelia to strike her mistress, then she would be dealt with as one deals with a diseased dog. Pulling her right foot away from Aurelia's hand, my mother swung it back at her face, hitting her hard on the mouth with the tip of her shoe. She repeated the blow several times while Aurelia writhed and wriggled on the floor, her blood falling in drops from her mouth, as if someone had carried a leaking pot of water across the room in a haphazard manner and it had left drops in a crazy pattern. When Aurelia finally rose to her feet and began to stagger out of the room, I saw that her lips had been cut open and that her front teeth had been knocked out. Blood still trickled from her mouth and filled the two lines scratched on both her cheeks. She went away, but her wailing could still be heard as she walked crazily towards her room. My mother asked me to go and tell Tana to come to her room and to clean it while she went and had a bath.

I was mistaken if I thought that my mother had taken adequate revenge, for this episode was only the beginning of a far more horrific mutilation of Aurelia's body. Being a slave, Aurelia could neither run away nor refuse to submit to my mother's attacks. She was no better than a prisoner in this respect, and I must say that I was proud of my mother who began to command total respect from all the other slave women in the household. It was clear to everyone that Aurelia fully deserved her fate, for the greatest crime a slave woman could commit was to suggest that she was good enough to usurp the authority and the position of the mistress of the house. Poor Aurelia! Although my sympathies lay entirely with my mother, I felt a little sorry for Aurelia, but only during those moments when I recalled my first night with her. My mother did not say it in so many words, but by dropping hints to Tana, she succeeded in spreading the story that her own baby, Antônio, had not died a natural death, that there had been little blue marks on its neck when it was found dead, that the marks suggested that the fingers of a girl had pressed there and choked the child to death. So that soon everyone was prepared to believe that Antônio had been killed by Aurelia in order to have her own son, João, closer to the heart of the master of the house; and consequently, the mutilation of Aurelia's body was accepted by everyone as a just punishment. I noticed that even my father did not object or attempt to persuade his wife that Aurelia had suffered enough. I understood many years later why he had not said anything, for I, in my turn, found myself in a similar position and discovered that it was best not to interfere in the quarrels of my wife with her maid and that if one maid had been made unattractive, it did not matter, there were others who could satisfy me.

I did not witness any more of the mutilation, but I heard about every little detail; for one old Negress had taken pity on Aurelia and had begun to look after her in her suffering, and she would tell Tana of her condition and soon the story would spread. I have to admit that some of the details seemed unbelievable, but there was no reason why the servants should have invented any of them; if proof were needed for the truth of what was being whispered, one had only to look at Aurelia. Perhaps the most extreme of my mother's actions was to cut off Aurelia's nipples; at first, the servants said that it was to deprive little João of his mother's milk, but later it was rumoured that my mother had had the nipples cooked with the meat prepared for my father's dinner, for it was a charm she needed to employ to win him back to her bed: in this manner, my father would consume and then purge himself of that which kept him from his wife.

If my father needed to be charmed back to my mother's embrace, I did not think it was because he had tired of her, but simply that he had taken upon himself the burden of excessive penance, part of which probably entailed a severely disciplined abstention from his wife's bed. On the other hand, my mother's triumphant revenge over Aurelia now needed the climax of her becoming pregnant again in order that the household's full confidence in her be restored.

One day, Tana, having come to my room to make my bed,

said to me, 'Ah, Gregório, the trials of being the master of a house are many, but they do not match the trials of being the mistress of the house. Will you, too, treat your wife this way?'

'What are you prattling about now?' I asked, aware that she had some gossip to reveal.

'What can a woman do,' she said, 'when the master spends his time either praying in the chapel or wandering alone among the fields, watching the slaves cut the cane?'

'I'm sure a woman has a lot to do running the household,' I said, hoping that my answer would bring her to the point.

'Yes,' she said, 'but there's a lot more than giving orders to the servants. What good is a house to a mistress if she has no sons of her own to bring up in it?'

'Look, Tana, if you're talking about my mother, you should know that she recently had a son, that the son unfortunately died, and that it is probably too soon for her to be having another one.'

'Ah, how little you know about women! Especially of what goes on in their minds. If you want to know the truth, your mother would like nothing better than to be pregnant again.'

'How do you know?'

'Gregório, I have been in this house since the days of your grandfather. I know what young wives do when they think that their husband's mind is wandering from the pleasures their bodies have to offer. I have seen one enter a chapel in the middle of the night. I happened to be in the chapel since I was then mourning the death of a child I had had. Yes, I had a child once, Gregório, don't be surprised. I was once young and beautiful, too. Well, while I was praying in the chapel and beating my own breast because of the unhappiness with which it swelled, the chapel door creaked and I saw the mistress of the house enter. She did not see me since I sat at the end of a pew, beside a wall. She knelt in front of the saints, one by one, and prayed, and each time she finished the prayer, she rose and, embracing the saint, lifted her skirt so that her legs were naked against the saint. She rubbed her legs against the saint's as though the saint could impregnate her. Some of the saints were high on windows and she had to climb up for her little act, and some, such was her determination, she lifted off their pedestals in order to embrace them with her skirt raised. And when she came to our dear Jesus, she lifted him up and laid him down on the ground on his back, can you believe it! And then, pulling her skirt right up, she lay on him, and beat down upon him with her thighs and I'm sure if anyone had entered the church then and seen this performance he would have thought there was a pair of illicit lovers there on the floor. And this was not all. There were other charms which she pursued in order to win back her husband who had begun to love a black slave. There was the traditional charm of using her own blood, the blood women cannot help losing once a month, in which to cook the meat for her husband. She did that on a feast day when he expected a special dinner, and he got it, that special dish, which I had to serve. I remember seeing him smack his lips after the first mouthful and say how delicious it was. I knew then that she was going to succeed. And she did. About ten months after that meal, she gave birth to a son.'

'I don't believe it!' I exclaimed, though I knew that a lot of life depended not only on superstition but also on the methodical performance of such rituals as Tana had just described.

'I don't care whether you believe it or not,' she said, 'but let me tell you one thing, Gregório. If she had not done the things she did, *you* would never have been born.'

'I believe you even less!'

'No, Gregório, you should know by now that there is no point in lying about the dead. I've told you the truth so that you would know something about being a woman.'

'Why should you care whether I know anything about women or not?'

'Gregório, I am not blind and I am not deaf although I may appear totally senile to you. It is a good thing what happened with Aurelia, but be thankful that it's over.'

'What do you mean?' I asked, wondering whether she spoke of Aurelia in connection with my mother or me.

'You should realize, young man, that strict privacy is not possible in a house full of servants. Even if you think that the door is shut and everyone else is asleep, there are other ways for news to announce itself. Don't forget it's the servants who wash the dirty linen. The colour of each stain tells its own story.'

'Tana, you're talking a lot of rubbish.'

'Rubbish! Ah! That's a sure sign that I'm talking a lot of sense. Whenever people say you're talking rubbish, you can take it that you're saying something they wouldn't like anyone else to hear. No, my young master, you can be quite sure that everyone knows that you have lain in Aurelia's bed. All I am saying is that you should be glad it's over and that you're free. The worst thing for a young man is to be involved too closely with one woman, especially with one slave woman. It can ruin the house.'

She left me with that portentous statement, and I must say that I felt both a fool and at the same time extraordinarily wise. The history antecedent to my birth intrigued me. What a way to come into the world, I thought, when all the saints and Christ himself contribute to your conception!

That same afternoon my brother Francisco turned up and asked if I would like to join him in an interesting game.

'What kind of a game is it?' I asked, rather bored by the prospect of having to pursue some childish affair, for since the time that I went on the expedition, I had grown more and more distant from Francisco. He was still a boy and I had become a man in the fullest sense of the word.

'You'll see,' he said in his idiotic manner of letting his mouth hang open in a knowing smile, and I must say that Francisco was the only person I saw in my whole life who could manage to look worse when he smiled.

'Oh, come on Francisco,' I said with obvious impatience, 'I'm not a kid to be joining you playing robbers or something.'

199

'It's not that,' he said, 'it's a game you'll enjoy. I promise you you'll enjoy it.'

'All right,' I agreed reluctantly. 'I'd better not be disappointed.'

'Sure, you'll enjoy it,' he said as we walked out of the house. 'It's your kind of game.'

'What the hell do you mean?'

'You'll see,' he said. 'It's a game you play every day. Or almost every day.'

'Look,' I said, 'I'm going right back to the house if you don't at once tell me what the hell you're talking of.'

'Gregório,' he said in the manner he had of suddenly appearing very wise, 'you seem to be going out of your mind. I hope Aurelia didn't give you the pox.'

'Francisco, what are you talking about?'

'Come on, Gregório, everybody knows.'

'Knows what?' I asked.

'Jesus, do I have to spell it out for you? That you've been screwing Aurelia, that's what. And all the other girls Jari gets for you.'

'How the hell do you know?'

'Oh my God, you're so damned innocent! The girls tell their friends, the friends tell the elders, and so it goes round. And sooner or later one or two of them, of course, get pregnant. That's what everyone wants, more sons for the house, more sons for Brazil. So, everyone is delighted that the young master of the house is busy creating the peasants for the future. Shall we go on now?'

'All right,' I said, moving on with him. 'Francisco, tell me one thing. How old are you now?'

'Ten. Why?'

'You know an awful lot for ten.'

'I keep my eyes and my ears open and my prick ready.'

He laughed in a diabolical manner and added, 'I thought I'd got the pox three months ago, but your slave got me a jar of liquor. That hurt, Christ, it hurt, pouring it over just like that, it bloody burned, but I guess it saved me.'

'Who was that with?'

'The big poxy one, Aurelia, who else?'

'Oh, come on Francisco,' I said, sure that he was merely pulling my leg. 'The whole world knows she was pregnant then.'

'Of course she was. That's why she sat on me. It was the only way, I thought I could manage it from the back, like a dog, but she felt tired that way. So, she sat on me. You want to ask your stupid slave to get you some of that liquor. Have it ready to pour on your cock every time you do it. It burns like hell, but saves you from the pox.'

'Thanks for the advice,' I said. 'I didn't know there was liquor on the plantation.'

'Gregório, the things you don't know are more than the ants in this world. The slaves make the liquor in their houses. How else could they have it? God help this house when you become its master!'

I ignored his absurdly expressed sentiment, for we were approaching the corral.

'What the hell are we going to do here?' I asked. 'Screw the cows?'

'That's right, big brother, you're learning.'

'Oh, come on. I told you I didn't want any of your childish nonsense.'

'Don't go mad before seeing what the cows look like,' he said. 'At least have a look inside the shed first.'

I realized what the game was as soon as I entered the shed. Inside, joking and laughing, stood Jari and three Negro boys, and huddled in a corner sat seven Negro girls, each one of them stripped naked.

'Now,' said Jari, who seemed to be familiar with a good many games. 'The idea is this. Here in the cowshed we have seven pretty little cows. We are the bulls. Each bull must mate with as many cows as he can. The bull is allowed five minutes rest after each mating. Five minutes, no more! After that he must find another cow. The bull which mates the most number of times is the winner. Okay? Let's start!'

201

Leaning on their hands and resting on their knees, the girls positioned themselves like beasts and five of them were soon mounted. The two who were left acted as referees to make sure that no bull was cheating. Needless to say, all kinds of attempts were made to simulate cow-and-bull sounds; there was a great deal of mooing.

'You haven't passed out,' one of the referee girls shouted when she saw Jari withdraw, 'put it back in!'

I was glad she spotted Jari's trick of feigning a climax, for that was the obvious way to win the game, to pretend that you had discharged and then immediately to penetrate another cow. Well, the referee alerted us all to the trick and consequently no one dared to try it since the subsequent referees squeezed each organ as it emerged from its coupling to make sure that it had concluded its performance.

After my third cow, I felt that I couldn't possibly go on without a longer rest than five minutes. Indeed, the only bulls that seemed to have any vitality in them to continue were Jari and Francisco. While the three Negro boys and I lay exhausted on the floor, Jari and Francisco proceeded to couple for the fourth time with the cows. Each moved in a slow motion, as if he were rowing a boat across a lake. We all watched closely to make sure that each stroke was firmly and fully executed, and I must say that I was quite astonished at my little brother who seemed to be a professional at the game. They were taking a long time to complete this round while we watched keenly. Jari again tried to get away with simulating a climax, but we forced him back in again. The performance was becoming more exciting for the spectators than the participants; for the latter it was becoming the agony of never reaching an end while we were beginning to give our vociferous support now to Francisco and now to Jari, urging each on to faster action. We were so absorbed in this drama that we did not hear the door open.

'Get up all of you!' cried a voice, suddenly taking us all by surprise.

It was my father. I saw Jari and Francisco hurriedly pull

202

themselves out and noticed that Jari quickly went limp while Francisco's little member remained erect. Well, we looked pretty silly, all of us naked, and all except Francisco thoroughly exhausted. The girls again huddled close together, trying hard to hide their shame – which seemed absurd to me since they had been quite shameless in front of us.

'Gregório and Francisco, get back to the house and wait for me outside my room,' commanded my father. 'I'll deal with you others right here.'

Francisco and I could hear the lash of the whip and the cries of the black slaves as we walked away from the shed.

Later, when he had taken us into his room, he said sternly, 'I would like you to know this, my sons. Had I not come upon you by surprise and had I never known what you had been doing, I would not have minded if any of those girls had at some time in the future given birth to children, especially to sons. I want to tell you that slaves and their children are the most valuable property a plantation has. What you were doing is nothing new in Brazil. Wherever there is a big house with a master and his sons on the one hand and the slaves and their children on the other, the same type of game, or some variation of it, is played regularly. There are many masters who play it themselves and encourage their sons at it. At a time when credit is tight and taxes are heavy, the best thing a man can do it to invest in multiplying his slaves. If we follow the logic of this reasoning, then it seems that what you were doing is not something for which you should be punished. Instead, you deserve my thanks. But no. There has been too much sin in this house in the past. I am now beginning to pay for my sins; this house is beginning to pay for its sins. Remember that whether the sin is committed by me or by you or by the lowliest slaves, the consequence of it is suffered by the house. Therefore, I will not tolerate your sinful actions. I have already punished the slaves, and now you will have to take your punishment, too. I don't intend to whip you, but to punish you in a manner from which you might learn something. From tomorrow, you will be present in the chapel from

203

sunrise each morning and will say mass with me. You will remain in the chapel after breakfast and spend at least three hours each day for a month, either praying or meditating silently in the chapel under the supervision of Father Soares. You may go now.'

Francisco immediately slipped out of the room, but I stayed behind.

'Do you have anything to say to me, Gregório?'

'Yes, father.'

'Well, say it then, and get it over with.'

'Since my return from the expedition, nothing but tragedy has filled your heart and your mind. I have not dared to break the news which I have carried with me since returning, for it would have been an intrusion on your grief. Perhaps the time is now right.'

I gave him the letter which I had picked up from my room on the way from the shed to my father's room, for I had thought while I walked that I should use the moment not only to make good my promise to Mr Rodrigues but also attempt to restore to my father the gaiety which he had lost since the loss of his son. I saw the surprise in his face as he read the letter.

'Perhaps I should explain,' I said, 'for you have not heard of Alicia.'

'You're mistaken, my son. Augustina has told me about her. I shall write to Mr Rodrigues.'

'But what do you think, father?'

'It is too early for you to marry yet,' he said. 'But you have to get married sooner or later. Yes, certainly yes. The two plantations together will make you one of the richest men in Brazil. And you'll have a dumb wife who will never nag you and who will be deaf to all your scolding.'

'She's very beautiful,' I said.

'Well, what more do you want?' he asked and I thought I saw the good-humoured face of a year ago. 'I must go and tell Augustina about this. She'll be pleased.'

Perhaps my news was instrumental in bringing my parents

together again in an intimacy which, as the entire household had been observing, had been lacking in their life since the death of little Antônio; or it could have been some charm. Whatever it was, my mother was pregnant again.

My father's prophecy that I was destined to be the richest man in Brazil was not to be fulfilled; for within the year a number of events left me first the master of my father's plantation and then totally destitute. When I look back on it, one event seems to have pursued another with the headlong pace of a waterfall; but in fact, within the context of daily existence, each tragedy occurred slowly and painfully so that the termination of each came as a kind of relief. One had to endure silences and solemnity; one had to live with a downcast face, waiting, waiting for the better days to return. It is not a time that I enjoy looking back on except for the brief period when I was the master. It pains me now even to think of this tragic period in general, and it would be excruciating to have to recall it in detail: therefore I shall record it as briefly as possible.

First, just when my father's good spirits had returned to him and he was looking forward to negotiating the terms of my marriage to Alicia, we heard that Mr Rodrigues had had to mortgage his plantation in order to meet some debts he had incurred in Bahia. A month later we heard that the terms of the mortgage were such that Mr Rodrigues could not hope to get back his land for his heirs. Next, my mother, her pregnant condition made worse by the news of her father's downfall, died in childbirth. She lost a great deal of blood during the delivery and was hardly conscious enough to discover that the child had been still-born; perhaps she did hear this sad news, for her condition deteriorated soon after the birth and she died within a few hours. Amidst tears, we speculated that she might have had the strength to recover had she had the child to look forward to. The grief was perhaps too much for my father, for within a month of burying his wife, he suffered a heart attack and died.

I was, of course, overcome by all this gloom around me and

205

felt as though I had inherited a kingdom just when all the neighbouring countries had massed their armies on the frontier and were ready to invade my lands. Even as I was being proclaimed the new master of the house, I was aware that my rule would be brief. Therefore, I was determined that it would be a splendid one, and at once sent a message to Domingos Cardoso, whom I was prepared to retain as my agent since I had no reason to believe that he had not served my father well, saying that he should arrange for the best Italian marble to be sent to the house in order that the drawing-room and my bedroom could be done according to my taste. While I was busy with matters of managing the plantation, I did not realize that my brother Francisco had not been seen in the house for some time. One day Jari told me casually that Francisco had left, that he had put some of his belongings together in a bundle, taken a horse and gone away without telling anyone where he was going. I must confess that rather than being perturbed, I was greatly relieved. I could guess why Francisco had left: he could not tolerate his status as a younger brother and preferred to make his fortune elsewhere. Good luck to him, I thought, deciding, too, that I should arrange the marriages of my two sisters who deserved a good future, so that I could be alone: I had the dream of building my own paradise for myself. Jari was my companion and adviser, and I was amused to reflect that the affection which I hardly ever felt for my brothers I experienced spontaneously for Jari.

With Jari's help, I succeeded partially in the pursuit of my dream. White marble gleamed upon the floors which my feet honoured with their tread. My white horse was decorated, emerald green silk ribbons intertwined with the reins, spots of red dye making a pattern of flowers on his flanks, my name tooled in gold on the saddle. The slaves paused in their labour and bowed low as I rode past, my whip of tapir hide in my hand ready to sting the back of any slave who did not know how to show respect to his master. I sent four Negroes to Salvador to learn to play the violin so that, when they returned, I had music in my dining-room while I ate. My dinner was served by seven naked Negro girls aged between fifteen and seventeen who were trained to stand in statuesque poses in between courses; and, of course, frequently I chose to complete the indulgence of my appetite by taking one of the girls to my bedroom. Whenever a girl did not come up to my expectations or whenever I had had enough of her, she was dismissed to be replaced by another. In this manner not only did I manage to make each meal into a memorable occasion but also accomplished the astonishing fact of making fourteen girls pregnant in one month, thus increasing my property in a most enjoyable fashion.

All the slaves on my plantation as well as the landowners of neighbouring plantations soon knew what was going on. The latter were clearly envious, and I heard that one had decided to institute a similar procedure in his household, a decision which led to his wife mutilating the bodies of three of the slave girls. My slaves were overawed by what they heard their master was doing. To make sure that the slaves did not become degenerate or slack, I established my Sunday morning whippings: three of the slaves were appointed as overseers and their duty was to bring before me when I emerged from saying mass in the chapel those slaves who had been guilty of neglecting their labour or who had committed any immoral action. These were made to stand facing the chapel wall so that I could personally whip them. Father Soares, whose indolent ways I was also determined to cure, was ordered to be present at these whippings so that he could lecture the slaves on the importance of hard work and of virtue.

At this time I had several offers of marriage. I rejected them all, thinking that those aspects of my existence which marriage would satisfy were already more than adequately achieved. Even Mr Rodrigues sent me a long letter, written in a most florid hand, the prose full of the most intricate figures, reminding me that I had made a promise to him concerning Alicia. I sent him the brief reply he deserved, simply stating that a landowner has land before he has children, that it was universally understood that he no longer had his land to give and, therefore, it was presumptuous of him to be offering his daughter.

As I saw it, my life at the moment was perfect. I considered myself the most fortunate man in all Brazil since by the age of sixteen I was not only my own master but also thought of as a most eminent and desirable young man, especially if the person thinking of me happened to have a teenage daughter. This wonderful mode of existence lasted just under a year; and then, whether it was nemesis or simply the inevitable course of my destiny I cannot affirm, but I suffered a double setback.

The first was a personal matter, an affliction which struck every Brazilian of my age. I had expected it to strike me sooner or later, but had half hoped that, since everything that had hitherto happened in my short life had seemed to suggest that I was somehow unique, I would escape it. Then, experiencing an acute pain while urinating one day, I realized that I had not escaped it, and there, as immediate confirmation, I could see pus oozing out with my urine. Soon, the condition of this tender organ deteriorated and I began to discover marks on parts of my body, the marks which branded almost every Brazilian youth. I decided that I would need to go to Salvador to seek a doctor who could help me.

No sooner had I taken the decision to go to Salvador when Domingos Cardoso arrived from that very same town and presented me with the second catastrophe. Apparently, I was so grossly in debt that even if I could increase the production of sugar by tenfold and find the highest price for it, I would still not be able to meet my creditors. Nor did it help me to be informed that the price of sugar had fallen in Lisbon since sugar had begun to be produced in the Antilles and there was a great surplus of it in Europe.

'Who are my creditors?' I asked Cardoso in disbelief.

'The moneylenders, who else?' said morose-faced Cardoso while I looked at the wart on his right cheek.

208

'I never borrowed money.'

'How do you think you paid for the marble, for the wine, for all the gold trappings you kept ordering? Let me try and explain something to you about money. What you have is a plantation, right? Right. And all that you produce is sugar, which you do once a year. I sell the sugar for you in Bahia from where the merchants export it to Europe. Now, all the money you earn is earned on one occasion in the year. But it often happens with a landlord that he runs out of money within six or seven months, sometimes within a couple of months, of earning it. But his plantation has to go on, and since on paper he is potentially very rich, there are money-lenders who will give him as much money as he needs to meet his expenditure until he can produce his next crop of sugar. Moneylenders, of course, don't exist to do landlords a favour but to make money for themselves. Usually, a landlord can pay back in time or he can keep a cycle of borrowing and paying back going in such a way that although he never has a sizeable amount of ready cash at any given moment he is always rich because he has access to limitless credit. There are two exceptions, or two types of failure which lead to bankruptcy. One is when the crop is so much below expectation that the landlord is obliged to borrow larger sums than before, thus committing himself to the likelihood of continuing indebtedness. The other failure is the result of mismanagement and extravagance. In this case, the landlord lives a fancy life, pays no attention to his sugar, and when at the end of the year his earnings are a fraction of what he has spent, he can no longer survive as a landlord. It's as simple as that.'

I had listened very carefully to Cardoso for no other reason than to distract myself from the pain in my groin, and I must say that I was quite bored by his theorizing.

'Enough of why these things happen,' I said impatiently. 'Tell me what is best to do now.'

The choice he offered me was either to continue to be the nominal master of my plantation or to give it away completely. If the former, I would be a kind of a slave, working for ever for the moneylenders who would allow me a very basic existence and for whose pleasure I would have to vacate the best parts of my house, and if the latter, then I would have to leave the house with nothing except the clothes I wore. I was not even to be allowed a horse. This struck me as an absurd joke, but even while Cardoso was talking on in his gloomy voice, I resolved what I should do.

I decided that life on the plantation would finally only bore me with its repetitiveness even if I could continue to live in the fashion of an emperor. What seemed to be my downfall I now saw as a sign of a new beginning, for it offered me the freedom to be myself without any of the obligations which came from being a landlord. To hell with Cardoso and his moneylenders, I thought while he moaned on and on about the legal complications of my indebtedness, I will take my white horse, I will rip up the floor of the chapel to see what treasure might not be stored there, I will go away and start a new life somewhere else. I will go to Salvador for a start and see what can be done about this damned Brazilian curse between my thighs.

Well, the taking up of the chapel floor produced no treasure. All that turned up was a skeleton which might have been my grandfather's, and I must say that I was greatly amused to see the hollow sockets in the skull and that ape-like grin. There were several skeletons of babies, too, but not one had been buried with as much as a gold ring.

When I left for Salvador, it was in the middle of the night, for I was convinced that Cardoso must have bribed some slave to keep an eye on me and to make sure that I smuggled nothing out of the house. Since I had very little money, I decided reluctantly that Jari should accompany me on the best available horse other than my own: so that in Salvador I could sell the two horses as well as Jari and thus have some capital with which to begin a new life. In pursuing this scheme, I overlooked the obvious fact: that Salvador was where the moneylenders were and that even in a crowded city they would discover that I had arrived with some property to which I no longer had any right.

Chapter 7

THE ASSAULT

When we were half a day's ride from São Salvador do Bahia and were resting our horses beside a river, we saw, emerging from the stunted vegetation of the bush, a thin figure of a man who was completely naked. Jari, convinced at once that the man was an Indian, aimed his gun at him.

'Don't shoot,' I whispered to Jari, for, although the man was some distance away, I could already see that he was not an Indian. For a start, he was too dirty to be an Indian, and his hair, which hung down in thick curls to his shoulders, was light in colour. His body had patches of black on it as if shadows had stuck there permanently. The drunken gait of his walk suggested that he was nearly exhausted with fatigue. As he came closer, I saw that his eyes had a wild look as if they had ceased to observe the immediate phenomena in his vision.

'He's no Indian,' I said to Jari, boldly deciding to walk towards the man.

He stopped when he saw me, and stared dreamily as if he did not quite believe what he saw.

'My name is Gregório,' I said, offering him my hand. He shook his head as if to suggest that he understood and that he was pleased to know me. He took a step forward, attempting to raise his hand to grasp mine. The effort was too much for him, and he collapsed. With Jari's help, I carried him to the river bank, and, scooping up water, sprinkled his head.

'Why don't we throw him into the river?' Jari suggested.

'No,' I said, 'the shock would be too much. He'll come back. Look, already his mouth is twitching and his eyes are

212

trying to open.'

Gradually the man regained consciousness. The man seemed to me to be about sixty years old. His flesh hung loosely about him, suggesting that once he had been muscular and heavy, and that he had lost a great deal of weight from sheer hunger. His hair, which had grown to his shoulders, was, however, thin at the top, and the skin of his face had that webbed texture which is characteristic of white people who have spent many years in the tropics. Emaciated though he was, he still struck me as being broader and heavier than me. As he regained consciousness, he sat up and looked at us and seemed to smile. He glanced around at where we were and, seeing the river a foot away from him, jumped into it.

'That's what we should have done to him in the first place,' said Jari as if his point had been proved; for the man seemed to have revived completely when he emerged from the river a few moments later. The black patches I had noticed on his body had been dirt, for now he appeared completely white, although, of course, his body had tanned considerably under the sun. His hair, now that it was clean, was white and, being wet, hung down straight as a little girl's.

'Ha!' he said, 'I haven't seen water for two months. You wouldn't have any food on you by any chance?'

We had some bread and dried beef which we offered him. He ate slowly, gently, as if he held some treasured object in his hands, revolving the chunk of bread as though it were a precious stone. He drank water in little sips and constantly kept looking at the river as one would at a marvel.

'Where are we?' he asked when he had finished eating.

'In Bahia,' I said, 'about five or six hours ride from São Salvador.'

'Ha, Bahia!' he exclaimed with some delight. 'Are you going there, or coming from it?'

'Going,' I said.

'Then, permit me to join you,' he said. 'Company and conversation will make the journey shorter.'

I readily agreed, seeing that his speech suggested that his

background was similar to mine. I offered him a selection of clothes from my bundle but it was soon clear that nothing would fit him.

'Ah well,' he said, 'I've been naked for many months now, and clothes will only make me feel funny. Maybe I can wrap a shirt around my waist when we enter Salvador.'

I offered him Jari's horse which he accepted gratefully. Jari, of course, was most put out and sulked for most of the journey. As we began to make our way to Salvador, I briefly described who I was without saying anything about having lost my plantation.

'And now, sir,' I said, concluding my remarks about myself, 'perhaps you will honour me with an account of your life.'

'Me? Ha! The world knows me and yet no one knows me. I am a Brazilian in my heart and my soul and yet I am a foreigner. I have known greatness, but what do you see, a shrivelled old naked body. I am a subject for historians, for in my story is the story of Brazil, and yet no one would have cared had I perished in the backlands. Well, perhaps one or two might have shed a tear, and perhaps some people might have remembered. But ha! Mankind forgets its failures. My name is Antônio Rapôso Tavares. I was born in Alemtejo in Portugal sixty years ago. When I came to Brazil with my father I was already older than you are now. You see me now as one who has lost everything. The only thing I have, as you can well see, is my own body. Nothing else. Yet, I have a great deal more that you cannot see. If you were to go to São Paulo and mention the name of Antônio Rapôso Tavares, people will open their houses to you, they will embrace you and honour you simply because you announce that you have met me. For I am a man of some prestige in my country. The *Paulistas* have seen me commit patriotic acts of the highest virtue. Why, it was almost twenty years ago now that I fired the minds of a hundred and fifty *Paulistas* with the notion that it was their duty and their privilege to defend Brazil, and paying them out of my own pocket, I enlisted them in my own little army and up we came, crossing through this very land, to Pernambuco to fight the Dutch. There were some at the time who said that Portugal should have sent the soldiers to fight the Dutch, and I've even heard people say that Portugal cares nothing for Brazil as long as it gets the sugar and the brasilwood, that Portugal spends all its money trying to establish itself in India. But I said at the time and I say it again, no, no, and no. Portugal, I say, is wise in letting us look after our country. And what a country! We don't even have it as yet, we don't even know where it begins and where it ends. What will make us into a country is first the fact that we should be able to defend it ourselves. We showed that with the Dutch, we managed to get the Dutch out without Portugal's help. But it took courage, it took the maniacal zeal of people like my hundred and fifty soldiers. I profited nothing from the venture and yet I profited more than any man can. What I earned was honour and the thrilling knowledge that we Brazilians could get together from as far apart as São Paulo and Pernambuco and feel that we were the same people. The second fact which we must realize is the need to define our frontiers, to know exactly where the country becomes foreign. There is something about a land, Gregório, which is that land and none other. This is difficult, how shall I explain it? When I was your age, I travelled across from Portugal to Seville. There was a river which divided the two lands. On each side of the river the nature of the land was the same and to an outsider, a Frenchman, say, there could be nothing to distinguish one land from the other. But to me at that time to look towards Portugal was more pleasing than to look the other way. I felt glad in my heart, my body swelled with pride. And this is what I now feel about Brazil. Let me tell you something, Gregório. I have seen *all* of Brazil!

'Ha! You look as though you don't believe me. You don't know anything, you've never before been to Salvador, you don't even know which is the way to São Paulo, you haven't looked at the ocean, so how could you know about me? Ha! When a famous man meets the ignorant he realizes how

215

empty is his fame. You mock what little vanity I have left in me. But let me tell you, Gregório. I've come across people in villages who've told stories about me! And a lot of fantastic rubbish some of the stories are, too. According to one story, I crossed the great mountains of the west, the Andes, I travelled across Peru and entered the Pacific Ocean, brandishing my naked sword in the air and calling to the ocean to submit itself to the rule of the King of Portugal. Well, the story does nobody any harm and does me a great deal of superficial credit. I've heard people describe how with a few men I have encountered and defeated mighty Spanish armies. Some people will swear to you that I found an Inca kingdom which even the Spaniards never discovered, that I ransacked this kingdom and, collecting twenty tons of gold, sailed down the Amazon, taking the gold straight to Lisbon. So, let me tell you the truth, Gregório. Though, in telling you the truth, I have to admit that in recent years I've heard so many stories about myself that some of the stories have become real in my mind. This is always the problem with mankind as you must know by now. What you hear and what you think become part of your experience; even what you imagine and even your obsessive dreams take on a subtle reality of their own. Finally, there is no reality; each one of us expresses his own version of the possibilities of experience, each one of us is, in the end, an approximation. So, the truth, whatever it is, now is in my mind which has not been without its hallucinations.

'Well, some ten years ago, in the winter of 1648, I headed an expedition of twelve hundred men down the river Tietê. Two hundred of the men were Portuguese, and the remaining thousand were Indians who had been subjugated and who were now properly armed. Our objective was – Brazil! Of course, this was not my first expedition. I had made several forays into the interior, especially hunting for Indians. My favourite type of expedition had been to enter a Jesuit reduction, the kind where Jesuits run a little community of Indians whom they're trying to Christianize by making them sing hymns and do agricultural labour. Ha! Some of these Jesuits

216

make me sick. First they persuaded Lisbon to pass a law forbidding reduction Indians to be used as slaves and then they either make them their own slaves or quietly sell them. But the raids I carried out were among the piously run reductions where the priests were downright stupid. It was an easy matter to destroy a reduction and to capture the emasculated Indians. And a good profit it always was, too. But now we were not out hunting Indians; there was something much more important on our minds. We did, indeed, attack a reduction or two on the way, much to the despair of the Jesuits who feel so damned fanatical about civilizing Indians, but these attacks on the reductions were simply a matter of maintaining the morale of my twelve hundred men by giving them something attainable to do. Of course, it was good booty, easy loot to sell to landlords.

'But we were going for something much more difficult, something worth real honour. We were going to show our heads over the top of the Andes where the Spaniards could see us. But don't imagine that it was simply a matter of marching across the land and getting to the top of the Andes. We wound our way through the São José range, climbing through the thick dry vegetation only to come down into a burning plain and then to enter a sodden marsh parts of which swallowed men like a whale swallows small fish. There was the mighty river Paraguay to cross, and the Rio Grande. In this region my men began to die of the plague if not of starvation. Already a year had passed since we had left São Paulo, our food supplies had long been exhausted, and we were in the wildest interior of this country, worse than what we were later to experience in the Amazon region, for the Amazon has its savage Indian tribes, the Amazon has fish and its banks offer a variety of wild life. But now we were in that part of the interior where we must have been the first people to violate the virginity of the land. Certainly, we came across an Indian tribe from time to time, but fortunately this was a very rare phenomenon. I say fortunately, for the tribes here were the most ferocious that I have experienced in the whole of Brazil. If famine and plague were not daily destroying my men, these Indians would descend on us like locusts and take great chunks from the extremities of the diminishing tree which was my army. The plague would strike a man with a burning fever, his body would explode in a rash and his skin would become like the dry earth of a land which has been stricken by drought. And what do you think was left of my army of twelve hundred? No more than two hundred by the time we reached the Andes!

'The Andes, ha! If you ever see the Serra out from São Paulo to the Atlantic, you'll think the sheer dizziness induced by the height will kill you. There are parts where you've simply got to hold on to the roots of trees to inch your way up or down, and many is the man who has given his trust and his life to a root which has had no more strength to hold him than a straw. Well, if you see that Serra, imagine something ten or twelve times higher, imagine a creature which lies before you seeming to be tame and possessing the lassitude of a well-fed dog and suddenly without warning changing into an enraged panther. Imagine the thick hot air gradually thin out and become freezing cold. Fog has its home there, curling around those upright trees, fog which is like gunpowder to a deaf man, suddenly exploding in his face, and you know that you must go on to escape it and that if you go on you're likely to put a foot somewhere where there is no floor for seven or ten thousand feet. You come out of the fog if you're lucky, but now the earth is becoming more and more patched with ice, the trees which had been like ghosts in the fog now seem to vanish as though plucked away by frost. And the hands of frost have a jaguar's claws which keep pawing at your chest. The ice thickens, and above you are the peaks, white as Jesus Christ, and the sky is a blue which must be the most perfect blue in the world.

'Well, my young friend, it was there that I discovered a route into the land of the Incas. Except that the blood of the Incas had drained into the ocean a hundred years before I entered their land. And their gold already gilded the cathedrals of Spain. Ahead of me lay Potosí, and a little to the north La Plata. Had my army not been reduced to about a hundred and fifty able men, I think I would have been tempted to have a go at Potosí and to get those silver mines for Brazil. Ha, who knows what might not have happened if I had succeeded in attacking Potosí! Perhaps a war between Portugal and Spain, who can tell? Small incidents alter history. But my scouts found the two towns well defended, and it would have been suicidal to attack. In any case, this much of my mission had been successful. We had made sure that the Spaniards knew that we'd come across the Andes, that we considered the Andes a definitive border.

'I marched my men back down the mountains, an even more hazardous undertaking than the ascent had been. The poor bastards thought they were going home, and they held out courageously, but no sooner were we again in the dry plain than I headed north. Up we went to the Guaporé river and then on to the Madeira. Now we were in swampy desert land and now in a thick, dark jungle where the Indians would appear as suddenly as a swarm of insects when you unwittingly disturb them in a bush. And let me tell you one of the weirdest things that has happened to me. Once we came to a tribe of Indians whom we succeeded in befriending. This was lucky for us since we had not eaten anything for several days apart from some roots and the bark of trees, and I managed to convey to the chief that we would greatly appreciate some food. His eyes lit up and he seemed to indicate that he would be happy to be our host. Well, we were tired and so near starvation that we simply lay back and waited for the food. Soon enough it was ready, and it was none of the usual nonsense of herbs and roots either, but real meat. We all enjoyed it enormously and left expressing our profuse gratitude. We had hardly gone a mile when we realized that three of the men were missing and suddenly all of us were violently sick. Can you imagine the two of us on an expedition and you find me missing one day and realize you've eaten me!

'The Madeira river took us directly into the Amazon. We

were mistaken if we had thought that we'd seen all that was fantastic and unbelievable in this world. For we came upon an incredibly savage people who for some fortunate reason were not interested in extending their savagery to us. Perhaps they found us curious, like a child with a new toy, guarding it jealously from its friends. These people were called the Hipupiaras, and we lived among them for a week. It was the most miserable week that I've spent in my life. Some of their warriors had gone out hunting and when they returned I was amazed to discover that what they'd killed were not animals but Indians! They came back carrying the corpses of three Indian males, two women and five children, and what's more, they came back with the same triumphant glow on their faces as when people return from the sea having caught some lovely fish. As you might expect, a feast was called for. Well, I thought, the good Lord never meant me to acquire a taste for human flesh, but what can I do? And so I prepared to take part in the feast by telling my mind that there was no alternative. But I had a surprise, a most hideous, a most sickening surprise. For what was served was not the flesh of the Indians, but their eyes and noses! And this as a special favour to me! For apparently, the Hipupiaras considered the eyes and the noses a great delicacy, and since these were limited, most of the tribe had to eat the meat while the chief and his wives and I as the principal guest had the honour of eating all the eyes and the noses. And don't think that these organs were disguised in some lovely sauce, no, they were there absolutely raw on a broad leaf placed in front of me by a young man who seemed to think I was a most fortunate man. Can you imagine it, Gregório, two eyes looking up at you which you're supposed to pick up and chew slowly and with a lingering enjoyment? And the nose, oh, God! There was blood around it and the nostrils needed to be picked. Believe me, I would have been prepared to starve for a week than eat such a meal, but right there I had no choice. I could not offend my savage host. The memory of that meal makes me want to vomit, so you can imagine what I felt at the time.

'I was glad to say farewell to the Hipupiaras, but I must tell you of one strange sight I saw there before I left. It was at night and I must have woken up to satisfy some bodily need. It was a bright night, I suppose there must have been a moon. Anyway, I sleepily stumbled towards the nearest tree to do what I had to do. I was just about to get on with my business when I realized that I stood beside a hammock in the tree and that a woman lay in the hammock with a baby at her breast. The woman, of course, was naked and the baby, asleep at the breast, seemed unconsciously to be suckling in a slow rhythm. Now, that is a sight I've always enjoyed, a baby at its mother's breast; and, being a man, I'm always interested in the size, shape and texture of the breast, and my glance naturally fell on the woman's free breast. Well, it wasn't free at all. A great, long, fat snake, a *snake*, Gregório, had coiled down from the tree and was feeding itself at the free breast.

'After my experiences among the Hipupiaras, all subsequent hardships were child's play. The Amazon provided us with one problem after the other and we came across all sorts of fantastic sights. Perhaps the most interesting thing I saw was a boa constrictor that lay dead across a path, his belly blown into an enormous size. We cut him up and discovered that he had swallowed a deer whole. That provided us with a little feast, the deer, for it seemed to have died only recently. And the most intriguing thing we came across was a type of lizard which produced a most extraordinary sweet smell, a smell sweeter than musk. On killing one and examining it, we discovered that the smell came from its testicles! Nature is full of jokes, Gregório.

'In the Amazon I did what had been considered impossible: led my party downstream without mistakenly going up – as has been the fate of almost every navigator on the Amazon – one of the many, many affluents of the river. The adventures I had on the Amazon are so numerous that I must relate them to you at some other time, for we seem to be approaching the capital of our country. But let me tell you something, Gregório. The expedition I led was a serious affair. Living in Brazil, I had to go and discover what there was of Brazil, what, in other words, had not already been grabbed by the avaricious Spaniards. To discover, too, what mineral wealth there might not be in the country; and in this respect, I'm sorry to say that although Brazil is the most wonderful country in the world, it still keeps its gold and silver in its secret bosom. But these were the public reasons for my expedition. I had, however, a private reason and now that my expedition is almost at an end, I can tell you what it was. It was to see, simply to *see* the great spectacle that is this country. And I alone of the twelve hundred men who left São Paulo ten years ago have come back to tell you this!'

Rapôso Tavares hastily concluded his narrative now that we were entering São Salvador do Bahia. Children from the outlying settlements ran up to us and followed us at a little distance, many of them laughing and calling out rude names. I had become so accustomed to the fact that Rapôso Tavares was naked that I had ceased to think about it and had forgotten to give him a shirt to tie across his waist. As I was about to stop and take a shirt out of my bundle of clothes, six men on horseback came riding up to us. They wore uniforms and I supposed that they were soldiers on duty at the gates of the city.

'Where do you think you're going?' one of the soldiers asked Rapôso Tavares.

'To see the Governor General, who else,' said Rapôso Tavares. 'My name is Antônio Rapôso Tavares and I've just come to the end of the longest expedition any Brazilian has made into the interior. Twelve hundred men gave their lives to this expedition, but the good Lord demanded that I give only my clothes to it!'

'Your name may be Pedro Álvares Cabral,' said the soldier with an insolent smirk on his face, 'but before you see the Governor General you'll have to reside in one of our special houses.'

The others laughed at this, and one of them said, 'We'll see how his balls stand up to the rats.'

222

'And you? Who are you?' the first soldier addressed me.

Offended by the impudent manner in which the question had been put, I replied with a deliberate show of my superior background: 'I am a gentleman from northern Bahia, master of a plantation with over a hundred slaves. And let me inform you that you are making a grave mistake not taking my companion seriously. He is, indeed, Antônio Rapôso Tavares, and when the Governor General hears of the way you have treated him and the rude manner in which you have addressed me, you will have a lot to pay for.'

'And what may your illustrious name be?' the soldier asked.

'Gregório Peixoto da Silva Xavier,' I said, holding my head high and looking straight ahead at the street.

'Well, well, isn't that something?' the soldier said, exchanging smiles with his companions. 'Just as Mr Cardoso described him, seeming to be arrogant but really a very silly young man, those were his words, were they not? Well, Mr Gregório, you too are going to enjoy the loving company of the rats. You, we expected. That you would come in the company of a naked madman, that we admit has been a surprise. Still, the more the merrier, there's always room, the rats are most accommodating.'

My slave Jari and my two horses together with my bundle of clothes were confiscated, and I was thrown into jail. My only solace was that Rapôso Tavares was also imprisoned, although unfortunately he was put away in a part of the jail where I could not communicate with him; I did not doubt, however, that soon word would reach the Governor General that the leader of the famous expedition was in Salvador. I expected Rapôso's release to expedite mine. But the days passed and I remained in the dark filthy cell with five other indescribably dirty prisoners, each one a criminal with swollen blood-shot eyes and wild hair. When I was thrown into this cell, I must have appeared to these characters as a pretty young girl, for soon I had to learn to defend myself against the revolting attentions two of them insisted on paying

223

me. One of them, Mariano by name, sat in a corner much of the time merely looking at me like a beggar stands looking through the doorway of a shop. The other, Simão, was quite uninhibited and was for ever uttering obscenities. 'Come on, princess,' he would say, 'let's see what you've got between your legs.'

'Look, scoundrel,' I would tell him, glad that the three other prisoners seemed to be permanently asleep and woke only when food was served, 'the Governor General is going to come here any time in order personally to have me out of this fucking place, and I'll have you hung if you try anything.'

I learned that people who utter obscenities are best answered in an obscene language, for a kind of equality is established and they refrain from taking advantage of one. The threat of my potential power suggested by my conviction that the Governor General was going to help me worked for a couple of days, but later became a joke from which I suffered severely.

It was impossible to sleep on the first night. Once I shut my eyes and felt something scratching my cheek. Opening an eye in the dark, I saw a rat had climbed up my face, and I could feel his tongue on my mouth for he was poised to nibble the end of my lips. I jumped up, involuntarily giving a shout, and the rat fell away. I sat up for a few minutes, beginning to sob quietly to myself, for I saw that there were other rats encircling me and watching me. While I grieved over my fate, I became aware of a slight pinching on several parts of my body, especially the legs, and discovered that tiny bed bugs were sucking at my blood. I could not help giving out a scream as I jumped up to my feet and began beating at my thighs where the bugs were concentrated. It was inconceivable that I would ever sleep in these circumstances, and I began to shout through the window, begging to be let out. My fellow prisoners seemed quite oblivious to my shouting, except for Mariano who came up to me and gently stroking my shoulder as if I were a cat, said, 'Come and lie next to me, I'll keep the rats away.'

224

'No,' I cried aloud, pushing him away strongly since his stroking hand had made its way down my back to my buttocks and I could sense a certain excited pressure in his touch.

My shouting became somewhat hysterical and presently I heard footsteps out in the corridor. A broad-shouldered guard came up rubbing his sleepy eyes, and I observed that there were two others with him, one carrying a lantern and the other a shotgun. The first guard opened the door and the other two gripped my two arms and dragged me out.

'It's our gentleman,' said the first guard, locking the door again. 'Our pretty young gentleman needs a soft bed for the night. We'll give him one, won't we? We're kind men, aren't we? The gentleman is a man of some means and will pay for a good mattress.'

There was raucous laughter from the three as I was taken to a room which was evidently their room, for there were three beds in it and it was obvious from the disturbed bedclothes that they had been lying in them. The two guards who had been dragging me down the corridor now hoisted me up and threw me on one of the beds.

'Let's see now,' said the guard who had carried the lantern. 'The gentleman needs relief from the bugs first. Obviously, they've got into his clothes.'

The three of them stooped over me and pulling at my clothes had me completely stripped in a minute.

'Oh ho, what do we have here?' said the one who had the shotgun. 'A little water pistol!'

'Oh that's my favourite toy!' exclaimed the first guard.

'That's no water pistol,' said the second guard, 'that's a stick of candy, and it's far better than any sugar candy because you can suck and suck and it never finishes. Let me show you.'

I was horrified as the man knelt down beside the bed and bowed his head towards my thighs. I turned over and began to wriggle my body and to beat my arms and legs.

'Oh ho, here's something else,' one of them said, and I felt a hand pinch my buttocks and a finger insert itself in the passage there. 'Hmmm. How do you like that? A secret chamber.'

His hand moved from my buttocks to my hip and gripping me tightly, he pulled at me so that I was again flat on my back. Simultaneously, the other two soldiers gripped me, one at the shoulders and the other at the ankles, and the soldier who had knelt down beside the bed and had talked about sucking candy now began to demonstrate what he had meant. I started to scream but the man who held me at the shoulders quickly slapped me across the mouth, a hard stinging blow, which shut me up. I was powerless to resist. While the hairy grunting mouth worked at my groin, his mouth dribbling over what it encompassed and then letting his teeth scrape along the flesh as he attempted to swallow the object whole, I observed with horror that the man who held my ankles had dropped his trousers and was climbing into the bed, his monstrous organ like the handle of an axe. When the candy fanatic had received a mouthful from me, which he spat out on my stomach much to my disgust, I was rudely turned over and pulled up on to my knees and in a moment felt as though my buttocks were being split open with an axe. I cried, I yelled, and again was slapped across the face. The man behind me seemed to be suffering a hideous pain, for while he worked on me, he groaned and made long drawn-out moaning sounds. When he finished, I was allowed to collapse on my stomach, but I was mistaken if I thought that the worst of my ordeal was over. By now I had completely lost what strength I had, and could do nothing except sob helplessly.

'One thing our gentleman will have to learn,' said the man who had been holding me at the shoulders, 'is to get used to rats coming up to his mouth. You know how it is when you're asleep and your mouth falls open and you snore in blissful oblivion, well, that's when the rats come and get into the mouth. Our gentleman will have to get used to that, so let's give him a little practice.'

The revolting swine could not have thought of a worse

perversion to perpetrate on my helpless body, for while the two who had had their pleasure of me held me in an appropriate position, this man dropped his trousers and, pulling at my jaw to hold my mouth open as if he wished to extract my teeth, inserted his rat into it. God, I thought I would choke if I did not die of sheer disgust.

'Gently now,' he said softly as if to a lover, 'don't bite, just grasp it with your lips, just roll your tongue around the tip and draw it all in. I can tell you, you won't be visited by a friendlier rat.'

I stared wildly at the hairy abdomen which beat against my face, and closed my eyes, making a strong effort to think of something pleasant. But my mind was so filled with disgust at what had been and was still happening to my body that it seemed to want to disengage itself from the physical world and live in some purer sphere. I felt the man's thighs straining against my face while my face itself was straining to reject all the sensations which violated it as well as to find some breath with which to survive. Finally, the man came, ejecting his mess into my mouth and mercifully withdrawing. I held the mess in my mouth and just when he drew back, I spat it out on his face. His eyes were suddenly inflamed with anger. He passed a hand across his face and wiped it clean and swung the same hand at my face so that not only was some of the stuff transferred on to my face, but my jaw seemed to collapse, so hard was his blow. And this was not all, for he proceeded to batter at my face with clenched fists as if I had done him some serious wrong. I was rapidly losing consciousness, for after the perversities suffered by my body this brutality was destroying what little strength survived in me. The other two guards decided to join their friend in aiming fierce blows at me. I don't remember when I passed out, for the next thing I knew was that my head was in Mariano's lap and I was lying on the floor of the cell. Mariano was stroking my hair. Thrown by one group of perverts into the arms of another was no consolation, but still to be tenderly stroked by Mariano was like being returned to a friend and I sobbed

227

quietly for the misfortune which had befallen me.

This early experience in the jail toughened me, made me fight back with ferocious hatred and as the weeks passed, I found myself become as brutal and degenerate as my companions. I found, too, that the more obscenely I talked and behaved the less attention was paid to me by the guards who began to take me for just another criminal. I realized later that with the passage of time I must have lost whatever physical attraction I possessed for the men, for I grew emaciated. My shoulders stooped and my chest seemed to become caved in so that I had the appearance of a hunchback.

I wondered what had become of my illustrious friend Rapôso Tavares and asked a guard about him one day. I was shocked by what I heard. Apparently, the prison officer, just to be on the safe side, had sent word to the Governor General that they had in custody a man who called himself Antônio Rapôso Tavares, who, as everybody in Salvador knew, was the great Brazilian adventurer, a *bandeirante* who had led an expedition to the borders of Peru, even, as some believed, to the Pacific Ocean. The Governor General had made investigations and discovered that Antônio Rapôso Tavares was residing happily in São Paulo, having returned triumphantly from his *bandeira*. Clearly, the man I had met was either a fraud who hoped to win favours from the Governor General by passing himself off as a famous man, or he was a madman. How was it, I asked, that he knew so much of Rapôso Tavares's *bandeira*, for the man could not invent the topography which Rapôso Tavares had travelled through since he had described it with such vivid accuracy. The answer which was generally accepted was that he had been one of Rapôso Tavares's men on the expedition and had left it at a late stage, having thought up the scheme to pass himself off as Rapôso Tavares and consequently to win favours in Salvador. What he had not known was that the real Rapôso Tavares had better knowledge of the country and, taking a shorter route, had already visited Salvador on his way back to São Paulo. Well, it was a

228

sad story, I thought, since the man had been so interesting, and it was disappointing that the presumed famous man who had befriended me was a fraud who was now free to engage his fantasies in the appropriate atmosphere of a lunatic asylum.

The worst aspect of this story, however, was that now I had no way of escaping my miserable situation. I had not been summoned before any judge, I had not been told why I was being kept indefinitely in jail, and no one would answer my question as to when I would be released. In fact, my question invariably elicited a mocking laughter among the guards and the people in my cell. The weeks began to turn into months. One day, realizing how used I had become to the unspeakably bad condition of my existence, taking for granted the rats and the bugs as if they were the clearest air, I asked a guard if I could speak to one of the prison officers. His answer was painfully offensive: 'If you're bored, try buggering a rat.'

Slowly, the months began to pass, and a depression overcame me which created a great emptiness in my mind. I simply sat there, hunched on the floor in the corner of the cell, incapable of listening to the foul nonsense my companions talked, hardly touching the wretched food which was pushed in my direction. The depression alternated with times when I raved like a maniac from the extremity of my despair. My companions learned to suffer me, and the noise I made was no novelty in the prison, for similar noises were often heard from the other cells. In one moment of sanity, it occurred to me that if nothing were done, I would remain in my present situation for ever. The thought only brought on an attack of loud raving, and my companion Mariano did me the favour of knocking me unconscious; if he had not done so, the guards would have come and given me a greater beating. The depths to which I had sunk can be measured by my submissiveness to Mariano who, once he had succeeded in seducing me, used me for whatever perversity occurred to his fancy. Neither he nor I seemed to care that we had an audience of fellow prisoners in the cell; indeed, sometimes our companions sat watching our performance and commenting to each other on the finer points of oral and anal practice and, at other times, simply turned away out of boredom. On two occasions I had permitted Simão a little gratification, but it was soon established in the cell that I was exclusively Mariano's lover.

The extremity of the degeneracy to which I had been reduced can be measured by the eagerness with which I began to anticipate Mariano's perversions. I knew then that were a young man to be thrown into our cell, I would be the first one to rape him, so corrupt and sinful had I been rendered by remaining in that prison. The longer I was kept there, the more dependent I became upon depression and despair, for moments of sanity were my worst enemy since they reminded me of my wonderful past and only made my subsequent misery worse. I began to think that a time would come when I would completely have forgotten my past, when the only reality I knew about myself would be one of being depraved, when I would unquestioningly believe that I, too, was a criminal.

The prison officer summoned me one day. I was taken out of the cell and escorted down the corridor. I could hardly walk properly since we had been allowed no exercise. Staggering and putting an arm up to support myself against the wall, I reached the prison officer's room. A well-dressed man sat beside the officer at a desk. I seemed to recognize the man; the wart on his right cheek was familiar and yet I could not remember his name.

'You are lucky,' the prison officer said when I entered, 'one of the most distinguished men of Salvador has come to visit you. Perhaps, Mr Cardoso you would prefer to be alone with the prisoner? Please feel free to use my office for as long as you like.'

Cardoso! The name came back to me and I was stupefied to realize how much I had forgotten. Domingo Cardoso, my own former agent, sitting there like a bishop, giving the air of doing me a favour!

'Gregório,' he said, 'you've done a very wicked thing, try-

230

ing to steal two horses and a slave from an estate to which you no longer had any claim. I hope your stay here has provided you with a salutary lesson. You realize, don't you, that unless someone is good enough to intercede on your behalf, which is to say, good enough to pay out a reasonable bribe to the officer, you would languish here until you died? This country is too young not to be ruthless and brutal to its criminals. Since I have a great affection for the memory of your father, I am prepared to help you.'

'*Help* me!' I cried. 'You have a lump of horseshit for a face, your mouth is dribbling with cat's piss, and you're going to help me? You're a two-faced cunt, Cardoso, you ought to go and spend a night in one of the cells here and you'll get screwed the way you deserve.'

No sooner had I finished abusing him than I regretted what I had said, for much as I detested him, I realized that he was the only one who could possibly help me. It suddenly came as a shock to me that I had no one else in the world.

'This place has taught you to be rude and unmannerly,' he said. 'I'm willing to overlook your insulting behaviour if you will listen to my offer.'

'What the hell can you offer?'

'Your deliverance from this hell, Gregório.'

'I'll listen,' I said, ashamed inwardly that I had fallen to this low level where I had no choice but to listen to one who had been responsible for my destruction.

'Good,' he said, 'I thought you'd come round to my point of view. Well, what is better, to live in this hole or be out in the open where the rivers flow freely and the sky is full of stars at night?'

'Obviously, the latter,' I said.

'And,' he continued, 'when one has no choice, isn't life in the open preferable under any circumstances? To be unconfined even if it means to work hard for one's freedom?'

'Yes,' I agreed. 'Whatever you say, get me out of here.'

Well, he arranged for my freedom that very day, but it was a very brief freedom that I enjoyed. Before we left the prison,

231

he persuaded me that I should apply all over my body a black grease which he had brought with him so that I might protect my skin against the sun.

'You've been in the dark for so long,' he said, 'your skin will burn and you'll suffer terribly if you go out without this protection.'

Outside the sun was so hot and blindingly bright that I asked for a handkerchief to be tied round my eyes since I feared I might go blind in that light. Feeling the heat, I thought at the time that perhaps he had a good point in making me apply the black grease to my body. But very soon I realized that I was mistaken to think that any act of Cardoso's could be charitable, for he presently disposed of me with some profit to himself. It was clear that he had cunningly planned both my imprisonment and the subsequent spurious liberation. From the prison, he took me straight to a square near the harbour where a slave auction was in progress and immediately put me up for auction. That, of course, explained the black grease. The bastard. I suppose I must have looked half-dead, squinting my eyes cluelessly in the sunlight, for the price paid for me was so unflattering that I have no intention of revealing it. I must say that it hurt me to see middle-aged Negroes bought for greater sums.

An iron collar was put round my neck and I was loaded on to a wagon which contained other slaves, each with an iron collar. A long chain was passed through a loop in each collar, and the ends of the chain were hooked on to the side of the wagon and padlocked. Our ankles, too, were chained in a similar fashion.

Thus ended my visit to the capital of Brazil. I had seen nothing of it, except for the darkness of the jail and the blinding light when I left it. The villas and the mansions that I had heard of and the great ocean and the ships docked in the harbour, all that might as well have been something in a fairy story. The black slaves around me had recently arrived from Africa and looked worn out by the experience of crossing the ocean. No one knew where we were going; no one knew what kind of master awaited us. We were seated very close together, and the chains which bound our ankles and our necks permitted no movement.

The journey took several days and ended in a plantation in northern Bahia. Our chains were removed once we were inside the guarded gates of the plantation. I did not like the sight of the armed guards at the gates, for they suggested that the master of the plantation had not succeeded, like my father, in achieving a harmonious understanding with the slaves and consequently deemed it necessary to rule like a tyrant. I was not wrong in my judgement, for the master, determined to get the most out of his investment, appeared, whip in hand, as soon as we were freed of the chains and put us at once to work. It was harvest time, the cane needed cutting, and we were not even given time for the sores on our necks and our ankles to recover. I, for one, was the weakest of the batch of new slaves and I had not spent ten minutes in the afternoon sun, hacking at the cane with a sickle, when I collapsed from extreme exhaustion. My body was still stained black from the grease Cardoso had so thoughtfully let me apply to it, and I must have looked a pathetic sight stretched out in the cane field. Any human being would have pitied my condition and ordered me to a month's wholesome food and rest, but not my master. Assuming that I was merely feigning and had not fainted at all, he proceeded to whip me. The whipping certainly brought me back to consciousness, for I had never before been whipped in this fashion and screamed now for mercy like any common slave. My master had no intention of being merciful, but suddenly he stopped and looked frightened. I understood afterwards what had happened. The lash of the whip removed the black grease on my back and the resulting streak of white was far whiter than the mark left by a whip on the back of a Negro; add to this the fact that the grease made the end of the whip go black, and it can be imagined how petrified the master was when he saw it all. Since he had no intention of seeing his newly-bought slave perish, he left me, instructing a Negro slave to attend to me. I was taken to a large hut which accommodated thirty or forty slaves and there put to bed on the straw-covered floor. I must have passed out of consciousness, for the next thing I remember is being wakened by a voice which called, 'Gregório, Gregório!'

I opened my eyes and saw the beaming face of my own slave, Jari.

'What are you doing here?' I asked him.

'I was sold soon after they put you into jail,' he said. 'And you? How come you're all black?'

I explained my recent history to him, and he said, 'There's a river, come, let's go and bathe in it.'

'I want to eat something first,' I said.

'I'll get food, too,' he said. 'We'll have a pretty picnic. You want me to bring you a nice Negress, too?'

'No,' I said. 'Not yet anyway. You seem to have organized yourself quite adequately by the looks of it.'

'It's barbaric here, I tell you,' he said. 'The master's a maniac. It's like a jail here. It makes me think of old Mr Rodrigues and your father, now they were kind masters, they must be rare. But, Gregório, you look in a bad shape. You need taking good care of. I'll get you a good woman to take care of you.'

It was early morning, I realized as we walked out to the river some half a mile away. While we walked, Jari described the harsh ways of the master and said that he had almost completed planning his own freedom.

'How are you going to do that?' I asked.

'Go to a *quilombo*,' he said.

'What's that?' I asked. 'A *quilombo*?'

'A bunch of *macombos*,' he said.

'Oh, come on,' I said, 'stop playing games with me.'

'That's the Lord's truth,' he said.

'But what the hell is the simple truth?' I asked.

'Well, a *macombo* is a village full of runaway slaves, and a *quilombo* is a whole bunch of *macombos* together. The more the better, the bigger the *quilombo* the easier it is to defend

234

it against the whites who come to capture the Negroes back for slavery.'

We removed our clothes and began to bathe in the river. The water blackened slightly around me, and soon I felt clean and refreshed. It must have been the first time in six months that I felt so clean. When we were sitting on the river bank, chewing dry bread and cold beans, I said, 'Jari, can I come to the *quilombo* with you?'

'You aren't black,' he said.

'I was sold as a black slave,' I said.

'Yeah,' he said, 'that's it, that completes my plan.'

'What are you talking about now?'

'Well, you're white. You could walk right out of the gates without the guards challenging you. All you've got to do is to stop by them as you get out, abuse them like any white man does, call them maybe mother-fuckers, they'll like that, for that's what it is to be black, always to expect to be called foul things and to be relieved when someone in fact does so, it clinches the blacks' status. And then you walk right away. Maybe you can even take a horse out. Five minutes later, you turn back, greet them black guards again, calling them horses' arses this time, just to be a bit more friendly, and tell them, Well, damn it, I forgot my son of a bitch, no good, cunt-grabbing slave, and I better go and fetch him before he screws all the cows. You do that, Gregório, and I'll take you to the *quilombo.*'

'All right, when do we go?'

'This very morning before people begin to get used to your face.'

'There's one snag,' I said. 'The guards will know that I never entered this plantation.'

'Hell, they won't, because they change from day to day.'

'Well, we can try,' I said. 'Suppose it doesn't work?'

'We'll remain slaves,' he said. 'Nothing worse can happen, can it?'

I accepted his argument, carried out his plan, observing that the sceptical faces of the Negro guards became friendly as soon as I called them foul names, and by mid-afternoon, the two of us were well on our way towards freedom, riding hard on two splendid horses. The *quilombo* was in western Bahia across the dry barren land which few people dared and fewer cared to cross. The hot, arid plain was the best defence the Negroes had. It was a totally inhospitable land. A determined party could no doubt have crossed it, but the expense of equipping one to do so was such that it was cheaper to buy new slaves than to chase those who had run away. Also, it has to be said for the Brazilian landlords that they rather respected the Negroes who ran away and developed their own colony in the interior, for a man who valued his freedom so much that he was prepared to risk his life seeking it was someone to be admired. Of course, the landlords did not encourage the expression of noble ideals among their slaves and if runaway slaves were caught they had to suffer the consequences which were grave; it was only when the runaway slaves were beyond being recaptured that the landlords privately wished them well.

It took us a week to cross the bone-dry land which was so covered with cacti that there seemed to be an army of crudely constructed toy soldiers placed on the absolutely flat land as on a table-top. Putting our shirts across a cactus, we managed to create a little shade in which to sleep during the hottest part of the day, and rode as much as we could in the nights. We did not find any water on the way, but Jari knew of ways of cutting open a cactus to extract its juice. It was Jari's knowledge and his good humour that kept me going. At the end of the week, we arrived at a river which had a little water in it. Beyond the river was the *quilombo*.

They must have seen us from a distance, for as we approached the entrance to the settlement a group of Negroes on horseback trotted up to us and immediately surrounded me.

'He's all right,' Jari told them, 'he's a slave, too.'

'You shut up, boy,' said one of the Negroes. 'You're going to come, too, to the master.'

'The *master*!' I cried. 'I thought you all came here because you wanted to be free of a master.'

'You shut up, white spy,' I was commanded.

I was soon to discover that when slaves free themselves, they ardently attach themselves to a harsher tyranny.

Chapter 8

THE NEW SLAVERY

The master's name was Adriano Zaballos. He wore feathers in his hair and painted white lines on his face. A charm hung round his neck and an ivory bracelet adorned the wrist of his left arm. He sat on a high stone seat outside his hut, holding a spear in his right hand.

In retrospect, I do not think he had a clue about what he was doing, and seemed to be carrying out in a haphazard fashion a rather confused notion of an African chief; perhaps he had some dim memory from his childhood of what a tribal chief looked like, or perhaps he had improvised as best he could. The charm, the bracelet and the feathers were sufficient, however, to mark him out as someone special since the rest of the blacks went about nearly naked, having only a strip of cloth across their waists. I was delighted to observe that the women, too, were no more dressed than the males, a point of considerable satisfaction to me since my early sexual experiences had led me to establish a clear preference for the Negress body. Although Adriano Zaballos was outwardly stern and tended to frown in a studied manner whenever he spoke, I could not help detecting in him an emotional softness as well as an intellectual bewilderment. Jari must have noticed this, too, for we were soon calling him Adri the Padri. Later, we simply referred to him as the Padri.

Our first interview with him was not altogether a slight matter, for his frowning face looked down upon us while we were made to lie prostrate in front of him, inducing not only a considerable trepidation in us but also making us most uncomfortable. Jari, always confident whatever the immediate danger, explained the circumstances of our arrival, describing how I was as much a slave as anyone else and that consequently I had as much right to seek liberation as a black man.

'No,' said the Padri loudly, frowning and screwing up his eyes as he looked at me. 'There is no place for a white man here. You say he was your master once. How do you know that the instinct of the master will not again make him want to dominate you? You are a fool, a disgrace to the black people, to think that you owe anything to your former white master. We blacks have to make our own society, our own culture. If we take one white man in, we stain ourselves.'

'Excuse me,' I said, 'may I have permission to speak? Thank you. I am white because I look white. It's the colour of the skin I was born with. It's the first impression you have of me, and, as is common knowledge, first impressions are most deceptive. As Jari has told you, a white man painted me black and sold me as a slave. That's what a white man did to me. Do you think I have any more respect for whites after that, when they can take one of their own kind and sell him as a Negro? No, on the contrary, being painted black and being sold as a black, changed my entire outlook. It made me *think* like a black man, and what you think is what you are. In my soul I am as black, even blacker than anyone else here. And it is my soul which is crying out for liberation. Will you not look at my soul? See its delicate black wings trying to flutter, trying to rise above the white heat! Look at its little black eyes wobbling in their white sockets, searching for the purity of the black night!'

I must confess now that I spoke a lot of nonsense, but adversity makes subtle hypocrites of us all and I was no exception at that time. I went on with more meaningless phrases about my black soul, my voice taking on the burden of suppressed tears. It had a hypnotic effect on the audience and even Jari watched me open-mouthed. When I was convinced that he, too, was taken in, I stopped and looked down at the earth, giving the impression that I was shedding solemn black tears. The silence which followed my speech had a sacred quality about it, and then Jari said, 'And another thing, your supreme majesty.'

I thought he was over-doing it, but the Padri seemed quite pleased to be given a fancy attribute, and Jari went on: 'Gregório has a black son.'

This, I was convinced, was a mistake, and I silently cursed Jari for his tactlessness; for a race hates nothing more than to be told that its women have been violated by another race, and sure enough the Padri frowned again and shouted out: 'So, you want me to accept a white man who has spent his youth violating black women! You offer as a recommendation the fact that this white scoundrel took advantage of his superior position to rape a black girl and give her a child! There is only one thing I would do with such a scoundrel. Gather all our women folk together and let them stone him to death.'

'No, no,' said Jari, 'not at all, your highness. It was not what you think. I never said anything about raping. He was not like the master who uses the black women for his pleasure, no, no, please don't get that hideous impression. Gregório must be the first man in the history of Brazil to take as his wife, while he was the master of a plantation and had the choice of the richest heiresses in Pernambuco, to take as his wife a black girl whom he chose from the slaves of his own household. Had the moneylending crooks of Bahia not cheated him of his property, he would still be running the plantation with the greatest fairness to the blacks of whom he had made himself one through marriage. Ah, I still remember the lovely day when the son was born, how proudly Gregório called the black people together and proclaimed the beautiful black baby as his heir.'

'Jari,' I cried, interrupting him before he could elaborate a story too wild for belief, 'do you have to torment me with these memories? Do you have to remind me that my beautiful wife, the rarest virgin from Angola, died giving birth to my son and heir? Do you have to bring tears to my eyes in front of these kind people? Oh Jari, you're tearing my heart apart

240

in front of these gentle people! Poor Aurelia, how I loved her!'

'And the presents of silks you brought her from Salvador,' said Jari. 'The gold bracelets you had made for her in Lisbon!'

'Enough, Jari, enough! Oh, Aurelia, are you watching all this from heaven?'

I had worked myself up to a fine hysteria and began to shed tears into the earth. I seemed inconsolable, for one of the women in the audience, so moved by my apparent suffering, came up to me and patted my head and made sympathetic sounds. Another woman appealed to the Padri, 'Let him stay, master, let him stay.' Her statement became a chorus and soon many people were shouting, 'Let him stay.' The Padri raised a hand, commanding silence. He stood up and looked frowningly up at the heavens.

'The people say that you should stay,' he said, speaking so loudly he could have been addressing an army of ten thousand men. 'Very well, you shall stay. But there is one condition. You have proved to us that you are black in your soul and that the greatest happiness in your life has been your marriage to a black woman. Therefore, the condition we set is that to maintain your blackness, you marry a black woman from our tribe. If you agree, the ceremony will take place this evening. If you don't, you will leave within one hour, after which, should you be found within a mile of the farther bank of the river, you will be speared to death.'

'I agree,' I said, thinking how illogical the Padri's conclusion had been. First he had been against admitting a white man at all, and now he was committing himself to the production of at least half-white children in the tribe. My agreement led to a jubilant cry, and I could see in the eyes of the women that they were more delighted than the men, for the latter must surely have seen me as a potential threat: since I was unique in being white, I was bound to become a desirable object among the women.

There were some elders in the settlement who had assumed the role of priests. I thought that it was somehow typical of the intellectual confusion among these people, who were so determined to work out their own destiny in the country's general environment of a spreading and a dominating white culture, that they should attempt to revive something of their African past and yet not be able, for fear perhaps of vexing the most recent god they had been compelled to believe in, to abandon Christianity. The priests wore crosses and yet chanted in high-pitched nasal tones phrases which were incomprehensible to me and, I have no doubt, to a good many people in the settlement – and incomprehensibility, I have since realized, is the strength of religions which always have a stronger hold among the ignorant. The rhythm of the priests' voices was African, the words came from various sources, for the priests did not all come from one tribe in Africa, but from different tribes in different countries, and each insisted on promoting what he could remember of his own culture. Angola, Guinea and the Sudan were echoed in the chanting which had also absorbed lines from Christian hymns. The result seemed at first to be a cacophony, something like four horses going in different ways to pull the same carriage, but soon began to capture one's mind with a strange fascination. I have to admit that over the years I grew very fond of that sound; it became for me the sound of Brazil.

The priests' invocations that day to the composite god of their imagination were for my benefit, the chanting being a preliminary act of devotion in order to propitiate the elements to make my union with a black woman a happy one. One of the priests had dressed me earlier, making me wear feathers on my head and a loose robe in which I looked ridiculously small. He had smeared my face with charcoal dust, rubbing the dust on those parts of my body which were not covered by the robe.

'Why are you doing this?' I asked.

'The gods demand it,' he said. 'A black woman may only marry a black man. That is why you're getting married after sunset.'

'But the gods won't be deceived,' I pointed out.

'The gods are not interested in deception,' he said somewhat enigmatically. 'It's appearance which counts.'

'And not reality?' I asked.

'The gods are kind,' he said, evading the point completely.

'I don't doubt that,' I said, 'but surely, they're also infinitely wise?'

'Their wisdom is greater than the seven seas,' he said solemnly.

'So, they'll know what kind of a black man I am, won't they?'

'Only blackness brings out the brightness of stars,' he said.

'True,' I said, deciding not to pursue this insane dialogue, and watched him rub the charcoal dust on my wrists and hands.

I had wondered during the afternoon who my wife was to be, but my questions had elicited no answer. Instead I was told that a man may not look at his wife until the gods had extinguished the fire in front of which they were united. Well, the moment now came for the ceremony to commence, for the priests, their piping voices reaching a shrill climax, had lit the fire in front of which I was made to sit. Two boys began to beat on drums and the Padri emerged from his hut, leading a veiled woman in my direction. Perhaps she was heavily robed, but I thought that she looked rather plump. Well, what does it matter? I said to myself. This is not to be a binding marriage as far as I'm concerned. This irreverent thought was perhaps audible to the gods for at that very moment I suffered a pang of pain in my groin and was reminded of the fact that I had not been able to see a doctor about my condition and that Salvador, instead of providing me with some treatment for my disease, had only worsened matters by bringing me into contact with some of the most diseased men in Brazil.

The Padri, looking sternly at me, screamed out some phrases in a language which I could not understand. I understood that he meant well, for the people gathered for the ceremony applauded and the priests began to encircle the

243

bride, each one patting her head in turn. The Padri withdrew and, turning his eyes to the stars, began to scream again. Throughout my stay at the settlement, I was always startled when the Padri suddenly burst out in this fashion even though I soon learned that screaming was his way of giving an authoritative voice to his sentiments. One of the priests asked me to repeat some phrases after him. I did so but had no notion as to what I was uttering since the phrases were in an alien language; just when I had become used to repeating the phrases automatically, paying no attention to what I was saying since I was certain that the priest himself had very little idea of what he was asking me to repeat, he suddenly said, 'For better and for worse,' which I repeated automatically before realizing what I had said. This phrase, in a language which I understood, came as a shock, but inwardly I had begun to enjoy the comedy of the situation: for it was clear to me that the priests, in their desire to regress racially to their African past had not altogether succeeded, having forgotten the precise verbal formulae of their culture. If there were many such *quilombos* in Brazil, then, it occurred to me, their existence was bound to contribute an admirable informality and confusion to the future of the country. As my thoughts wandered among these matters, I was promising to cherish and support the woman beside me. Suddenly I realized that the name Eudoxia was being mentioned by the priests; it was no longer simply a black woman I was marrying, for the name now gave her a particularity, made her real. Eudoxia, a strange name, I thought, I had never heard it before. Well, Eudoxia, I said to myself, be prepared to receive a good dose of Brazil's most popular disease, laughing to myself and thinking that if this damned ceremony did not end soon I would go hysterical with disbelief at the phoney attempts to revive a dead past. The next thing I observed was that one of the priests was sprinkling incense into the fire, making it smoke and produce a sickening smell. Then, another began to spill water on the fire until it began to die out.

244

'Now,' said one of the priests, 'Eudoxia, blessed by the master, Adriano Zaballos, first and eminent chief of free men, watched over by our Father who is among the stars, open your eyes to your husband, Gregório.'

I did not immediately ponder the implication of Eudoxia having been blessed by the Padri, for I was eager to see what she looked like. A moment before I saw her I recalled all the fantasies I used to have when I had first become aware of sex, how I would think of the day of my wedding to a delicate white virgin from a leading family in Bahia or in Pernambuco. Instead, I viewed in a most matter of fact, if not cynical, manner what I was convinced was a mock marriage and turned to look at Eudoxia in the spirit of one acting out a comic drama.

I saw her eyes first which were bright and black, reminding me of the glint in Aurelia's eyes which had so much excited me. Her hair was woolly and short, and there seemed to be a frown on her forehead. She had thick lips forming more a snout than a graceful entrance to her mouth, and there was a wide space between her upper lip and her short, flat nose. There were creases at her neck and her breasts were not those of a young girl but hung down to her stomach. I realized that the frown on her forehead was no temporary creasing due to nervousness, but well-formed wrinkles which proclaimed that the woman was well past thirty and old enough to be my mother. I had never thought that I would ever need to descend to the level of a woman's navel in order to kiss her breasts.

My thoughts were abruptly terminated by the dancing which commenced. Again, we had a mixture: half-naked bodies going wildly round in circles and chanting incomprehensibly to the beating of the drums, and the slower rhythmic pacing of the kind white Brazilians carried out in couples.

I did my best to imitate the frantic pacing and circling which was going on, thinking that the blacks themselves were carrying out an imitation of something in their imagination; still, it was an exhilarating experience. I noticed that the priests, too, were hopping around. They carried little batons which they tapped on Eudoxia's shoulders as they went past her. When we were all exhausted by the dancing, we sat in several rows outside the Padri's hut and were served beans and roast pork. A drink followed the food, a liquor which I later learned was made from the juice of cacti and which smelled strongly. It had a revolting taste and I sipped it holding my breath so that I could somehow consume my allotted share without undue suffering. Since I was the principal guest at this feast, I was allotted more than anyone else. The Padri, who sat on my right, asked me questions about my plantation and particularly wanted to know what plans I had had about reforming the condition of my slaves. I answered him as satisfactorily as I could and realized that I was actually describing what I had seen on Mr Rodrigues's plantation.

'It is a great pity,' the Padri shouted, 'that a man of your advanced convictions had to lose his plantation. If only one landlord could show the way to emancipate the slaves, we would have a new nation.'

We certainly would, I thought to myself, for the blacks would outnumber the whites and Brazil, which was slowly receiving the benefits of civilization, would become another savage Africa.

In front of me sat my wife, Eudoxia, and I must say that if there was one woman in that party who was not worth looking at it was Eudoxia. Behind the Padri sat five young women, two of them no more than fourteen or fifteen, and these I learned were the Padri's wives. He had certainly had the best pick of the settlement's women.

'What factors,' I asked him, 'governed your choice of Eudoxia for me?'

'First,' he said, 'that she is faithful. Second, that she is so jealous that she will make sure that you, too, are faithful. Third, that she is sterile and we will not have any half-white children here.'

'How do you know all this?' I asked.

'The master has great wisdom,' he shouted.

The master also happened to be a right old bastard, as I discovered later, for I learned that Eudoxia had been his first wife and that although she had been compelled by the priests to allow the Padri to take on more wives for the reason that the gods demanded the chief have many sons, she had refused to leave his side. At one time, the Padri had even discussed with the priests the idea of instituting religious sacrifice in order to get rid of Eudoxia, but the priests had seen bad omens and declared that the gods were against sacrifice. The younger wives naturally hated Eudoxia, for she insisted on sharing the master's bed even when the master was amorously engaged with another wife. Also, Eudoxia believed that the younger wives were the master's passing fancies while she alone had permanent claim to him. The master had offered a reward to any man who could seduce Eudoxia away from him, but no one had succeeded. Now, however, flattery succeeded where bullying, cajolery, prayers and connivance had failed; for the Padri had said to Eudoxia that since she was the senior woman on the settlement, he wished her to be the first to have the choice of marrying the white young man who had just arrived. What had made Eudoxia so determined to stay with the Padri had been the notion that she had distinction, being the master's first wife; and what induced her to leave him now was the flattering notion of the new distinction of being the wife of the only white man on the settlement. Well, I must say that my first night with her was far from pleasant; my plight can be imagined if I say that I thought nostalgically of the perverse attentions of Mariano.

The trouble with having as my wife a woman twice my age was that she lived under the illusion that she could recover her own youth if I made love to her frequently. I was sufficiently under the influence of liquor to humour her on the first night even though it made me feel nauseous to have to touch her loose-skinned body and to have bearing down on me her snout of a mouth with its vile breath. Her actions indicated that she had observed the Padri in strange juxtapositions with his younger wives and that she now wanted me to engage in similar experiments.

'Not tonight, Eudoxia,' I told her gently, refusing to remove my pants.

'What's up?' she demanded, her hand at my thighs.

'Nothing's up,' I said, 'and that's the problem.'

'Come, I know how,' she said. 'Otherwise this is no marriage and the gods will be angry.'

With anyone else I would have been curious to find out what she meant by knowing how, but with Eudoxia even the prospect of novelty was not without the element of disgust. I wished she would blow out the lamp and go to sleep and disappear by next morning like some bad dream. But her hands were powerfully engaged in a battle to remove my pants and I realized that it was not sufficient to humour her superficially, I would simply have to commit myself to some action if I were to get any peace.

'Eudoxia, let me tell you something,' I said, letting her pull my pants off at last.

She did not hear me, for, with a sigh, she began to examine what she had now revealed, saying, 'Oh my dear, we have a small one here, a darling little baby one. And what's this on it?'

'Precisely what I was trying to tell you,' I said. 'Enough sores to turn your inside into a little garden of sores. I wouldn't even touch it unless you want to go blind.'

'Ah, this is nothing,' she said, grabbing hold of it with her bony hand and bringing down that great snout of hers to inflict a repugnant little torture. 'When I was a slave girl in Bahia, the first man to have me was the master, and his was so far gone that it was like a thorn tree. And he gave it to me all right, I had the garden you talk about when I was thirteen. But don't worry, Gregório, I'll cure it for you. I've learned things. I know of a potion, a mixture of strong liquor and a herb, that'll save you.'

Holding and looking at and talking to what she called 'my little baby', she interrupted her monologue with explosions of her snout on its tip. I expect that it suddenly became big not out of any desire on my part but out of sheer annoyance, like a lizard distends a pink skin at its neck when it feels

248

threatened. She took this to be a triumph of her art and quickly pulled herself up to mount me.

'Oh, Saint Anthony!' I cried, and she took my cry of despair for an expression of ecstasy.

Luckily, I came quickly, and with it, passed out altogether and knew nothing until I woke up the next morning to see the fat, loose flesh of her right arm across my chest. I pushed it aside and got out of bed, noticing that she had tied a bandage round my delicate member. I discovered later that when I had passed out, she had commenced the treatment which after some months of application was to relieve my condition. A full cure, it seemed, was going to be impossible.

I found Jari blissfully asleep in a hammock outside my hut, and woke him up. He seemed highly amused by my predicament, and said, 'Who would have thought, Gregório, that you'd be married to the senior woman of a *quilombo*!'

'Cut out the fucking jokes,' I said.

'Be careful how you talk to a black man in black man's land,' he said, laughing.

'But what am I supposed to do?' I asked.

'Ask the Padri to have mercy,' he said, continuing to laugh.

'Look, Jari, do I have your serious sympathy or am I to stand here being laughed at?'

'Well, Gregório, you have a serious problem. You'll have to bear it until we can think of something. One thing you must not do and that is to show that you're fed up with the whole business. You've got to make out you're loving every minute of it. That'll make the other women jealous of your loving wife and that'll give you power over her.'

'Shit, it'll only make her more possessive.'

'No, no, as long as you appear content and loving in public, you can be as rude to her in private as you like. If she wants public dignity and you give it to her, she'll accept any amount of private humiliation.'

While I reflected that he had a point, an armed man on horseback rode up to us and demanded what we were doing.

'Why,' said Jari, 'wishing each other a good morning. What

business is it of yours?'

Holding the reins with one hand and the gun in the other, the man said, 'Go on, stand against that wall.'

'What's up?' Jari asked.

'Go on,' the man shouted, aiming his gun at Jari, 'before I shoot your damn brain out. And you too, white man.'

Both of us stood against the wall of the hut, and the man, advancing on us and keeping his gun aimed at the blank space between Jari and me, said, 'Now listen you fresh turds, this isn't a playground for kids. I am officer Gonzales. There are nineteen other officers in this *quilombo* and our job is to keep order. There are laws which must be obeyed or you'll be whipped, even shot.'

'I never heard of any laws,' Jari said.

'Watch your tongue,' the man shouted. 'Any more rudeness and you'll be sent to the compound where they'll keep you tied for two days to the whipping post, let your skin flake off a little in the sun and then give you twenty lashes. The law you were breaking just now was the one which forbids people to stand around gossiping after sunrise.'

'No one told us of it, officer,' I said.

'You have to find out for yourself,' he said. 'When we were shipped across the ocean from Africa, no one told us anything. We had to learn with each stinging lash of the whip. The white man didn't tell us he was going to pack us in the ships like timber, he didn't tell us that we were going to shit where we ate, and when we were sold in the square in Bahia, the master didn't tell us he was going to keep us out in the sun cutting cane until our bones hurt.'

'Excuse me, officer,' I said, 'but why take revenge on your black brothers for what the white man did to you?'

'What do you know about the blacks, you white turd? What business is it of yours to interfere in the way we run our land? Any more of your racist insults and I'll report you to the master for execution.'

'He didn't mean it that way,' Jari said. 'You must forgive our mistakes, we're new here.'

250

'I've told you already being new is no excuse.'

'Can you do us the favour and tell us some of the laws here?' Jari asked. 'It will be very kind of you,' he added, for the man was clearly being most menacing.

'I told you, no gossip from sunrise to sunset. Each man must go to his work at sunrise and not return until sunset. Anyone found slacking will be sent to the compound for three days. Everyone who passes the master's hut must bow to the door whether the master is inside the hut or not. No man may talk to another man's wife unless the wife's husband is also present. Everyone must be present for military drill on the days appointed for military drill. No one except the master and his twenty officers may ride a horse.'

'But we brought our own horses,' Jari protested.

'They've been confiscated. Anyone on horseback who is not authorized to ride a horse will be shot. All the master's laws must be obeyed. The master is good. He is wise. He knows. Now you'd better get to work.'

'What kind of work?' I asked.

'Go to Fonseca, his hut is next to the master's. He makes the plans, he'll tell you. Remember, in future you won't be warned.'

Fonseca asked me if I had done any work in my life, adding sneeringly that all the work whites ever did was to seduce innocent black virgins. I refrained from telling him that I was getting tired of hearing derogatory remarks about my race, and said that I had some experience of cutting cane – for I recalled the ten minutes I spent at that occupation when I arrived at the plantation as a slave from Salvador.

'Ha!' Fonseca said, spitting through the doorway of his hut. 'Cutting cane! I can just see you cutting cane. You couldn't cut a blade of grass if you tried.'

'I don't wish to contradict you, sir,' I said, deciding that I would simply have to put up with endless ridicule and sarcasm on this damned settlement, 'but the truth of the matter is that I do know how to cut cane.'

'I don't like that, the way you called me sir just now. Your

251

tone suggested you didn't honestly mean to call me sir. I'm not going to suffer your impudence.'

'Forgive me, please,' I pleaded. 'I mean no offence at all. Please believe me that my father taught me to respect all people whatever their race or colour.'

'Who's talking of colour?' he shouted back. 'I said nothing about colour. You don't have to bring in ideas of your white superiority every two minutes.'

'I believe that all men are equal before God,' I said.

'You hear that?' he asked Jari. 'He can't open his mouth but he must insult our race.'

'Look, Mr Fonseca,' Jari said, 'if there ever was a black white man, then it is Gregório. The master wouldn't have accepted him otherwise. The master accepted him. The master is good. He is wise. He knows. And that being the case, Gregório is one of us. So, please tell us what our job is to be and we'll go and do it.'

Jari's forthright manner and his references to the master hit the right note with Fonseca who immediately directed us to the cane fields.

'What a shit,' Jari said as we walked away.

'I don't know what's the matter with your people,' I said. 'Everyone seems to think that I represent everything contemptible in this world. It's bad enough having to suffer fucking Eudoxia all night. If I'm to be insulted by one and all throughout the day I might as well give up and go back to Salvador.'

Jari let me go on abusing his race, swearing at the world, and generally relieving a great deal of irritation and anger which had accumulated in me since the previous day.

A guard on horseback greeted us at the cane fields. We told him of the work Fonseca had allocated to us. I was to cut the cane and Jari was to load it on to an ox cart.

'We have enough workers here,' he said, 'you should go to that field there.'

He raised a hand and pointed at a distant field with his whip. It was a good mile away.

252

'You go on ahead,' he said. 'I'll come and see you and tell you what to do when you reach there. Better start running, I want to see you there in ten minutes.'

'Oh, come on,' Jari said, 'it's damned hot.'

'Did you say something, son?' he said, his whip already raised.

'No, sir,' Jari said, beginning to walk away quickly.

'Just wait,' the guard called. 'Remember the rule. All workers must be at their work *before* sunrise and must commence work as soon as the sun rises.'

'Yes, sir,' said Jari.

'There'll be no talking, no slacking. Remember, you're being watched by the guards all the time. You have a five minute rest break every three hours when you will be given water and asked to stand in a line while the guard talks to you.'

'Yes, sir.'

'You will be given a meal at midday which you will eat sitting down, your face in the direction of the master's hut. Anybody who has his back to the master's hut while eating will be sent to the compound for three days. While you're eating, a guard will talk to you.'

'Yes, sir.'

'There will be rest breaks in the afternoon every two hours. You will be given water and asked to stand in a line while the guard talks to you.'

'Yes, sir.'

'Now run.'

We ran. What I had thought to be a confused, comical settlement was now turning out to be a highly organized camp run by an authoritarian master and his viciously efficient guards. I had never known a white landlord treat his slaves as savagely as these people treated their own kind in the name of freedom. What came as a shock to me was the fact that the people in general did not think that they were being treated savagely, for they believed that their regimented existence with its endless rules represented a good life. They worked

253

harder than I had ever seen Negroes work on a plantation; they were made to suffer far more severe punishments than any Negro had experienced on a plantation; they were given no time at all in which to do what they liked, for all their entertainment and even their religious activities were communally organized. The rest periods at work, when we stood in a line and received a few drops of water from the guard, were simply times in which we were reminded again and again that the master was wise, he was good, and he knew. All this should have been enough to make a people rise in bloody revolution. Instead, the people on the settlement were convinced that they were free. The only aspect of the regimentation which I found entertaining was the military drill. Everybody on the settlement, except for the very young and the very old, spent one day of the week training under one of the officers. There were a variety of exercises, from simply swinging one's arms about to running for half an hour. The chief reason why I found all this entertaining was that on the same day that I trained there was a group of some fifty or so girls of my age who also trained. It was a wonderful sight to see so many beautiful girls with nothing to cover their growing breasts train with such determination. Like us, they learned techniques of physical combat and some of them were superior to the men in dealing with threatening situations without any weapons.

As for the work on the fields, I found it hard at first: not because it was difficult, but because it was physically exhausting and the guards riding up and down kept urging us to put in more effort. But as the days passed, I began to enjoy the work since my body went through the actions without my having to think or to make a special effort. There were mornings when, walking out at dawn, I looked forward to the smell of the sugarcane and to the stickiness in my hands induced by the mixture of sweat and the juice from the cane being cut. When the sugarcane had all been cut, I was given other work. There was a plan, devised by Fonseca, to cut a canal from the river in order to irrigate a barren field where rice could be grown, and I was put in the party which was given the job of digging a narrow trench as an experiment before a wider canal could be constructed. Jari and I had little opportunity to talk except at night when we sat outside my hut and shared some liquor.

'When you think of it,' Jari said, 'this life is good enough. You work, you eat, you sleep, what else can you want? I could do with a woman, but I'm not taking chances yet.'

'But don't tell me you're free,' I said. 'Were you better off or worse when you were my slave?'

'Ah, that was a game, that wasn't life.'

'Nonsense,' I said.

'But what is freedom?' he asked. 'Not to work but to live on the labour of others? Not to marry but to screw every woman on the plantation?'

'I'm sure I don't know the answer, Jari. All I've experienced are different types of tyranny.'

'No, here we're all equal,' Jari said.

'Don't tell me that the guards have convinced you with their idiotic repetition about the master's wisdom.'

'No, it's not that,' he said. 'What made us slaves on the plantation was the fact that you *owned* us. You could make us work or whip us because that was your pleasure, because you earned money from making us do what you wanted us to do. Often, we served only your vanity. Do you remember that once you whipped me because the girl I brought for you I'd screwed myself and that made you mad? Here, we're not whipped for that kind of thing, but breaking rules which are of some consequence to our survival here. Here we're not made to do anything for the master's pleasure or profit. He gains nothing. By making us work, all he does is to make sure that we all have enough to eat. And we do. As long as we don't break the rules, we don't suffer anything, neither hunger nor the whip. And everybody works and what is produced everybody eats. The idea of money doesn't come into it and that makes us all absolutely equal. Do you follow me?'

'Yes,' I said, 'but what happens in the end?'

255

'What do you mean?'

'I mean what happens, do they all keep on doing the same thing again and again? Doesn't anybody ever advance? Or do people just fade out?'

'I still don't know what you mean.'

'Let me put it this way, then,' I said. 'Are you content here? And if so, do you think you'll continue to be content indefinitely?'

'Maybe,' he said, and added after a pause: 'And maybe not.'

'That's a great answer!'

'Look, Gregório, let me say this. If you decided to get the hell out, which will be difficult without horses – and why do you think horses are forbidden? – but if you decided, say, to go up the São Francisco to live among Indians like some missionaries, or to go on an expedition to Peru like that madman we met, well, I'd be damned glad to join you. But you know right now you can't. Right now you're a wanted man and so am I. And I guess we better stay put here for a year or two.'

Jari was right in respect of his concluding remarks. And also, when I thought of my own condition, although it certainly lacked the splendour of the brief period when I had been my own master – a splendour which could never be recaptured even if I could be free – my present life was at least wholesome: I worked hard and ate and drank well. Really, Eudoxia was the only painful element in my life. Slowly, I learned to suffer her; the physical exhaustion after a day's labour and the strong liquor helped, and with time I became quite brutal towards her and on a number of occasions beat her rather than submit to her disgusting demands. She was so utterly degenerate a creature that she actually enjoyed the beatings; and that in a way eased my problem, for during the year or so that I was forced to suffer her companionship, I must have beaten her ten times for every one time that I made love to her. In this fashion of my hating the life on the settlement and at the same time finding a deep contentment in it, the time passed.

One day, perhaps about a year after Jari and I had arrived there, the settlement was attacked by a party of white raiders. I could not understand by what extra-sensory knowledge the guards discovered several hours before the party appeared over the horizon across the river, but they had alerted the entire settlement and had armed all the available men either with guns or with bows and arrows and spears well before the raiders, some fifty strong, reached the river.

As we were massed in rows on the slope beside the river, I noticed that the army of girls had been positioned at the rear. I did not see them until I was in the position to which I had been ordered – right on the front line (and I should add that I had hastily rubbed some charcoal dust on my body in order not to present myself as too conspicuous a target). Being lined on the slope, we seemed to be arranged like some terraced vegetation. For some reason, I looked back and that was when I noticed that the final two tiers of this formation consisted of the girls. I must say that they looked extra-ordinary, wearing only short skirts, holding their chests out and carrying spears. I was reminded of the happy time I had just watching them do their weekly training; and if I now had any doubts about which side I was fighting on, they were instantly dispelled on seeing the girls, for it occurred to me that if these beautiful and tender creatures were so devoted to the idea of their settlement that they were prepared to give their lovely little lives for it, then their example was a sufficient inspiration. I had had doubts for the understandable reason that I wondered to myself whether I should take part in an offensive against people who were of my race. Needless to say, I had no choice in the matter, for every worker on the settlement was expected to fight. I had been given a shotgun since I had maintained that I would be lost with a primitive weapon. My choice of weapon had been a mistake, for I now saw that the men with the guns were the first line of defence.

The Padri commanded us from a hut built in a tree. The order at the moment was to wait silently while the enemy committed itself to a first move. As we waited, I saw the enemy arrange itself on the opposite shore. The men were mainly Portuguese and I could tell that most of them were of the adventurer type, prepared to take monstrous risks in order to make a quick profit. I guessed that they had mounted this expedition not at the behest of those landlords who had suffered from slaves running away but because they expected to capture slaves whom they could sell for money. It occurred to me that so much of existence in Brazil was a gambling of one's own life: to live at all you had constantly to take the risk of dying.

The Padri shouted out an order which I found incomprehensible, and waited to see if my line made any move. The men around me remained still, but somewhere behind me drums began to beat and suddenly everyone began to chant out aloud:

> Let us take the enemy by the throat.
> O! O! Let us take the enemy by the throat.
> Let us cut him up
> And drain out all his blood,
> O, let us take the enemy by the throat.
> This ancient land that we have made our own
> Will bear the fruit of seeds that we have sown
> And anyone who calls us a slave
> Will tumble into his grave,
> Oh, we'll make certain the enemy's overthrown.

The chanting came abruptly to an end. There was a moment's silence before the Padri yelled out another order. I saw arrows flying over my head and go shooting over the river to come showering down upon the white raiders. Although the arrows struck many of the raiders, not one man fell, and I saw that they wore quilted jackets which were specially designed to ward off arrows. Even their horses appeared to have some kind of protection. Suddenly they fired back at us, and the sound of their gunfire was something I had never heard before. Obviously, they had come meticulously prepared and were equipped with the most recent arms imported from Europe; for there was an explosive power to their firing which knocked about a dozen men from the front line with one blast. I was not hit, but I fell involuntarily to the ground as if I had been knocked down by the sheer force of the explosion. Once on the ground, I decided that that was the best place for me. Those who still remained up began to fire back and it was obvious that our firing power was much weaker than theirs, for when they returned the fire, it served us another shattering blow. Three more rounds of this firing, I thought, and our first two or three lines would be completely destroyed. There were too few of us left to fire back, and for some time a silence ensued; it occurred to me that if the enemy's intention was to capture slaves, it was not in its interest to kill too many of us. The raiders' aim could only be to make us surrender. It was clear that this was going to be no battle, that sooner or later we were going to be overcome. All we had was a strength in numbers, but we knew that the raiders could decimate us at their pleasure, such was their superiority of arms. There was only one means at our disposal for resolving this confrontation: trickery. And, having an idea, I went to the tree which harboured the raving Padri. Two of the guards challenged me on the way, threatening to shoot me for breaking my position and I had to convince them that I simply had to speak to the Padri in order to help win the battle. They let me go grudgingly. Now, having reached the tree, to talk to the Padri was no easy matter, for he was a good thirty feet up, and the guard who stood below absolutely refused to let me climb up the ladder.

'You're a traitor,' the Padri shouted down at me. 'You've left your position, you want us all to be killed. You have a white heart.'

'I have a plan,' I shouted back. 'Let me come up and see you.'

'Yes, yes,' he yelled down at me, 'I know your plan. To kill me here where the enemy can see you do it and so become a white hero. I know the dirty tricks white men think of.

259

You'd better get back to your position or I'll get the guard to take you prisoner.'

'Look, listen for a change, will you?' I called back not without some anger in my voice. 'We don't stand a chance against their guns, they'll only butcher us if we tried.'

'That's what you'd like, isn't it? You'd like us to be butchered or you'd like us to surrender. Go on, get back to your position, I shan't warn you again.'

'I'm not talking about what I'd like,' I cried at him. 'I'm telling you the obvious truth, you have seen their guns in action. What I'm offering you is a plan which might save us. I know the minds of white men, you have to admit that.'

He thought for a moment and then called down, 'What is your plan?'

'The girls,' I shouted. 'Let the girls drop their spears and cross the river. That will make the white men crazy.'

'Ha, you're telling me to start an orgy, is that it? You'd like to see a mass rape of the black people, wouldn't you?'

'Keep race out of it, if you can,' I said. 'Just try and think of the power fifty girls will have over the men. Just let them go and let us retreat. The girls will do it, they're our only chance.'

'Do what?'

'Why, get those damn guns of theirs.'

'I see.'

My plan was presently put into action. The Padri allowed me to climb up to his hut from where the two of us watched while all the other men were ordered to retreat to their huts until they were called by the beating of drums. A couple of guards on horseback remained below the tree to take messages to the settlement. I looked at the party of raiders across the river to see what effect the slow marching of the nearly naked girls was having on them. The girls swayed their hips a little as they marched and jerked their shoulders with each step, so that their breasts wobbled – no one had instructed them to march in this fashion, but I suppose that they instinctively realized what was expected of them. I must say that I wished for a moment that I were on the other side. As the girls entered the river, the men all ran up to the bank as if they did not believe their eyes – an action which confirmed that the men were Portuguese in their blood, for it is doubtful if you will find men from any other part of Europe lose all sense of responsibility when faced with bare-breasted women. Yet, I did not think that they were so stupid or naïve as to believe that the girls were being sent to them as a friendly present, for they must have realized that a people who had at first lined up a comparatively huge army was not going to give up and send its prettiest maidens as a gift. But they behaved as though they might be stupid or naïve, for I could see laughter among them as they jumped into the river and could well imagine the coarse jokes which they must have been exchanging.

My principal fear was that they would indeed assault the girls or simply put iron collars around their necks and take them away.

'Let me tell you, white man,' the Padri yelled into my ear, 'if anything happens to those girls, you will pay for it with your life.'

'Come on,' I said, 'you agreed to the plan, you made no conditions when you agreed.'

'You have been here for a good year now,' he said. 'You now have a good idea of how we work as a community, what our defence is, and so on. The information you have will be valuable to white men. I have had reports of how dissatisfied you are here, and I know of the kind of thinking you've been trying to spread among my people. I must tell you that I've kept you under close observation. And everything I've heard about you points to the fact that you'd give anything to sell our lives for your own freedom to be back among the white people.'

'This is a fine time to be telling me all this,' I said. 'I think you're over-obsessed with power. I think that in the name of your race and in the name of freedom, you've established a most tyrannical system here simply in order to inflate your own self, to make yourself into a king.'

'You're talking too much, white man.'

'Indeed, I am,' I said, and was about to say more when our attention was caught by the girls who were now almost across the river and within a few feet of the men, who, gone quite crazy, were splashing each other and seemed to be behaving with a raucous hilarity. I must say that I was not altogether overjoyed at this moment, for it was quite clear that the men intended to assault the girls with the least delay; and, as if to confirm this thought, the men now began to remove and fling away their shirts. I did not know whether I should at this moment assassinate the Padri, fight it out with the guards below and make a dash for the river, too, or whether I should submit to whatever my fate was to be at the hands of the angered blacks. I looked at the Padri. He was watching with keen eyes and a vein was throbbing at his neck. I looked down at the guards and noticed that they could not have a clear sight of me in the tree-top hut if they wanted to shoot me, that, on the contrary, I would have the advantage since there were cracks in the hut through which I could shoot. I looked back towards the river once more. The girls were within an arm's distance from the men. The men moved towards them. The girls came to a dead stop. The men, seeming to act simultaneously and giving the impression of being one man in front of one girl caught between parallel mirrors, lifted their arms to reach for the girls. Just then, the girls took a step back, moved sideways and jumped up on to the river bank. The men quickly turned round, one or two slipping, and the girls laughed aloud, a laughter not of playfulness but one of vicious mockery. The men made for the bank and received thumping kicks in the face. There the joking seemed to come to an end. For the men now realized the seriousness of the situation and succeeded in making their way to the bank without any more kicks. But the girls were far too good for them, having been thoroughly trained in physical combat. Within five minutes, simply by keeping their eyes alert and moving quickly, they landed so many precise blows on the men, that the men were completely stunned. Next, they picked up the guns and began to walk back to the river.

'You can thank me later for suggesting the plan,' I told the Padri and climbed down from the tree. He stood there, admiring the girls as they crossed back to our side of the river, leaning out of a window in the hut and clapping his hands. As I reached the ground, I said to the two guards, 'What you need in your master is someone who has sense and knowledge of how other people think, and not someone who merely keeps screaming all the time.'

I don't know what made me say that, for it was obviously a foolish statement likely to get me into trouble. Perhaps I felt elated that my plan had succeeded; perhaps I thought that I was entitled to a little triumph after all the abuse I had had to suffer. At any rate, I thought, now that I had made the rather conceited statement, that, since people already knew (who could have missed all that shouting at the tree?) that it had been my plan to send the girls across the river, I would have popular support in any confrontation with the Padri.

But my thoughts were superfluous, for now a most extraordinary thing happened. While I was with the guards, we heard a shot and saw a man who had got up from where the girls had left him, found a gun and looking across the river had seen one target: the Padri who, seeing the girls succeed in their venture, had disregarded what precautions he had previously taken and was leaning out of the hut to cheer the girls back. The shot hit him between the eyes; he must have died instantly.

Since this happened a moment after I had said what kind of master they should have, the guards fell on their knees and bowed their heads to me. I realized what this indicated. I appeared to them as a prophet, and they were now proclaiming me master.

'Go back to the settlement. One of you tell the people who their master is and why. One of you return with a chair. Four girls will carry me and install me on the master's stone.'

They went away, bowing repeatedly until they mounted their horses. I leaned against the tree and watched the girls return, smiling to myself.

Chapter 9

GOLD!

For ten years I ruled as the undisputed master of the settlement of free Negroes, and watched its population grow to
over five hundred souls. One of my first acts was to give a
name to the settlement: I called it Zaballos in the memory of
the first master – a gesture which won popular admiration for
it showed my magnanimity, honouring someone who in his
final hour had proved incompetent. I increased the number of
armed soldiers to fifty and introduced several reforms: every
Sunday, the entire population was required to assemble in an
open area created for that purpose and to sing a hymn to the
master of Zaballos. Apart from this one occasion, the people
were forbidden to gather in groups of more than six, and the
soldiers were instructed to send to the compound for whipping
those who broke this law. All males, from the age of ten until
their death, were expected to work; I appointed overseers to
assist the soldiers in seeing that the work proceeded efficiently.
Jari was given the task of inspecting the overseers. The most
productive workers were honoured at the Sunday morning
assemblies when they were called out to come and shake my
hand.

I do not need to give a detailed account of the prosperity
my rule brought to the settlement of Zaballos. It was a stable,
productive time, and for me to describe it all now would be to
give the impression of boasting. It is sufficient to say that the
people enjoyed a good life under my rule, and I cannot say
that I was not content, for one of my first satisfactions had
been to rid myself of Eudoxia by making her the mistress of
the small army of girls so that they could continue to be

264

trained and their force increased by the recruitment of younger ones. In my own life, Eudoxia was replaced by a succession of young women, and at no time during the ten years did I have a wife older than eighteen.

Something happened to me after the ten years, something which was inexplicable. Perhaps it was simply that I grew tired of remaining in the same place; or perhaps a nostalgia for my own people which I had successfully suppressed all these years now would not leave me at peace. Ten years of one's life is a long time to give in service to another people. I was nearly twenty when I became the master, and now at thirty I realized that the best years of my life would soon vanish and I would merely be an old ghost if I returned to my people. I felt like someone who has been banished to a far-away colony for many years and who, on returning, discovers that the world he left has changed beyond recognition. I grew melancholy, uninterested in what was happening about me. Even the Sunday morning hymn and the devotion with which the people brought me fruits did not thrill me any more. I lost interest in my latest wife. My children, of whom there were seven, irritated me by their presence. I realized that I would go mad if I did not get away from Zaballos.

It had never occurred to me to leave before, and even now I did not think that I would abdicate my position and return to people of my own race. Without any prior thought, I found myself telling the people during a Sunday morning assembly: 'People of Zaballos, you are unique in Brazil in that you enjoy freedom while others, the vast majority, of your race are enslaved. I had a vision last night in which the gods spoke to me, urging me to help the still enslaved Negroes, calling me to go to Salvador and speak to the Governor General, crying to me to rise and cut the chains from the necks of thousands of your brothers and sisters.'

The people were greatly moved by this speech, and began to urge me to go and accomplish my divine task. I appointed a deputy to rule in my absence, and taking Jari with me, left for Salvador on the following morning. I suppose I had every intention of returning, for I was not at all sure of what I was going to do in Salvador. And I suppose all I wanted to do was to see a street full of white people just to rediscover what it was in me which rejected the existence in Zaballos.

Once again I was fated not to see Salvador, for when we were a little way outside the famous city, we came across an expedition on its way south. A large company of men had camped for the night and welcomed us to the meal they were having. An elderly man of about sixty years was quite obviously the leader of the expedition, for I heard the men refer to him as the Captain Major. I had not heard his name before although his men spoke the name with great reverence; I was never to forget his name: indeed, all of Brazil was soon to learn of his name and to place it prominently in the history of the country to shine there for ever. His name was Fernão Dias Pais Leme.

He told me that he had grown up going out on one *bandeira* after another and that, although he was sixty-four now, he was impatient of the comfortable but mostly inert life of the cities. He was a man of some fortune, but now he had risked all his wealth in order to finance this expedition.

'You say that you've been on a few expeditions yourself,' he told me. 'You must have come across Indians from time to time who have described untold riches in the interior. Gregório, it is now about a hundred and seventy years since Álvares Cabral set foot on the coast of Brazil. Ever since then, both gold and precious stones have eluded us. How can it be, I ask you, that Mexico to the north of us has great deposits of silver, that Peru to the west of us has silver and gold? And can it be possible that this land which is part of the same mass of land is without the same blessing from heaven? Say what you like, I don't believe it. The Indians who have been on this land for centuries know that there is gold, they just don't know where. Wherever I have gone into the interior, I have come across the legend of the lost city. Somewhere in these mountains, Gregório, there is supposed to be a great city whose streets are paved with gold and yet it is empty, aban-

266

doned as if there were a curse on it. Of course, I don't believe such a legend, but what I do believe is that it could not have come into popular currency without there being something behind it. I believe that somewhere in the interior are to be found untold riches and I believe that I am going to find them.'

'Is it gold you're after?' I asked.

'No, I have no reports of gold in the area which I'm going to explore. I'll look for that later. What I'm searching for now is something I do have some information on, even though the information is the hearsay of Indians who are not at all reliable since they have the subjected people's habit of saying what their masters like to hear.'

'What is it?' I asked.

'Green emeralds,' he said, his eyes lighting up with the words. 'If you want to be in the first expedition to discover green emeralds in Brazil, you're welcome to join me. I could do with a strong man with some experience of the interior. Let me know tomorrow morning, for it's time we all went to sleep if we're to get anywhere tomorrow.'

I talked to Jari about the proposition, and we finally concluded that we should join the expedition. One of the men told me the next day while we were on the march that Fernão Dias had a special commission from the Governor General to search for emeralds and that it was the Governor General who had bestowed on our leader the title of Captain Major. If we found the emeralds, we would all be rich and famous in Brazil but most of the treasure would be taken by the state.

It was clear that our Captain Major had no lust for riches himself; what he lusted after was the satisfaction of achieving something which had frustratingly eluded everyone else: what he was in love with was the *idea*, which he desperately wanted to prove, that there were riches in the great Portuguese colony of Brazil as there had been in the Spanish empire. I believe that there was something simple in his heart, whatever visions burned in his mind: he seemed happiest when marching on or riding, his eyes proudly glancing at the horizon as if he walked on his own estate. Sometimes, when I was near him, he would break the silence with, 'Are you looking, Gregório? *All* this is Brazil.'

Once I asked him, 'What is Brazil?'

He stopped and stared at me as if the question was an incredibly naïve one. He alighted from his horse, and stooping, scratched at the ground and presently stood up and extended his hand to me, saying, 'This is Brazil. All of Brazil is here. Not in your cities, not on your plantations. You can have cities anywhere in the world. You can grow cane on the islands in the Atlantic. But this earth and what it contains, and remember that, Gregório, *what it contains*, this is Brazil. The cities will rise, each will reach its peak and each will finally decline. A time might come when man will no longer need cane and so your planters will have to grow something else. But what this country becomes, how it develops, will depend entirely on what's contained in this earth. Were I not so old, I would do without a horse, for I would plant my own two feet on this earth.'

Also in the party was a man of my age who was referred to as the Little Captain, and I soon discovered that he was the Captain Major's son. While the father was firm without being harsh of manner, coldly ruthless without needing to raise his voice, and an undeniable leader of men, his very presence having an air of authority about it, the son was short-tempered and loud-mouthed as if all he needed to be a leader were an abusive tongue, a fist all too ready to strike and the constant flattery of his companions.

An idealist though he was, the Captain Major was not an impractical man. Whenever we came to a particularly fertile area, he would order us to till the ground and plant crops, reasoning that we would thus easily find food on our return journey. Seeing how well prepared he had come on this expedition and how carefully he had thought out both the route and the manner in which we should proceed, made me think of my first expedition with Veríssimo which now struck me as one of the most insane and clueless actions undertaken

268

by a set of Brazilians. We had simply ventured out thought-lessly whereas here was an expedition led by a man who had first discovered the nature of the geography of the land and come prepared with the tools with which to cultivate the land and also to seek water.

Water was not really a problem, for we mainly followed the southward course of the São Francisco river, that is to say, we followed it upstream since in this part of the interior the river ran in a north-easterly direction until it reached Pernambuco where it swung right and ran east into the ocean. We were marching towards its source until we came to its major tributary, the Rio das Velhas.

'Now,' said the Captain Major, consulting his notes, 'we should soon come to an area bounded on the east by the Doce river. That is where we will find the emeralds.'

His confidence was most reassuring, for the months were passing and much of our enthusiasm had worn off. The men were becoming querulous, and seemed vexed at having to do hard labour whenever we camped for any length of time. Some of them complained among themselves that they were doing the work of slaves, tilling the fields, when they were supposed to be taking part in a heroic *bandeira*. Sometimes I wondered whether Fernão Dias was not the same type of madman as Veríssimo. I knew, of course, since I had heard many tales of his heroic exploits from some of the members of the expedition, that he had led successful *bandeiras* through the most savage parts of the interior; but he was over sixty now and I could not help wondering whether his vision was still to be trusted, whether he indeed knew where he was going or whether he was not pursuing some chimera. What I could not doubt was the ruthlessness with which he punished the slightest recalcitrance: once, two men quarrelled over some matter and came to blows; many others thought this was good entertainment and soon formed a ring round the brawling two, cheering them on. The Captain Major stood outside the circle, fired a shot in the air and said very calmly, 'Next time I see anyone fighting I'll hang him.' His threat seemed to have been forgotten many days later when the same two men, their quarrel still smouldering in their bodies, again began to fight. The Captain Major had them hanged on a tree, and told us all to stand at attention in the area in front of the tree and to watch the two men die. Nobody questioned his authority for a long time after that.

We came to a place near the headwaters of the Doce river where the Captain Major decided we should camp. We were now among the mountains, many hundred miles west of the coast. I watched our leader look at the towering mountain ranges which formed our horizon as if he wanted to draw out the emeralds with his eyes.

We stayed in this camp not just for a few days or a few months, but for four years. When I look back on it, it seems an incredible amount of time to have spent in that solitary wilderness, but at the time one thing or another kept us there for another week and then another week until the years passed. Our chief occupation was to make forays into the different mountain ranges, searching for the emeralds. I must say that I was distinctly disappointed, for in my imagination I had thought that one day by some happy miracle we would arrive at the foot of a mountain which would be strewn with emeralds just as a child's cot is strewn with toys. These four years were a time of extreme hardship. The crops we planted did not grow during the first year, for we did not plough the land well enough: the first heavy rain of the summer washed away the thin layer of the soil. The rainy season produced at first mild chills among the men and then delirious fevers. There were panthers in the forest which once mauled to death two men while they were out exploring. When the rains ended, we were all struck by dysentery which, coming on top of the fevers, killed several men, and made the rest of us so weak that we had no energy left for exploring into the mountains. The great Fernão Dias himself looked as if he would not survive the winter. But he did. Indeed, as the years passed and more and more men died, I was almost willing to believe that he alone was indestructible, that he was one of those men who will not die until they have achieved what they set out to do. During the last year at the camp, he looked decidedly weak and almost broken in spirit; but his eyes had not given up, the sun lit up his eyes each day as if without them the sun itself would shed no light. I could see that even if his body lost all its strength and his mind gave itself over to fantasies, all his life would still be concentrated in his eyes. I admired him and yet pitied him. I recognized in him that quality which marks out some men for greatness, and I saw that quality to be not only one of never giving up a belief but also one of expecting the universe to live up to their expectations; and it was the first time in my life that I had perceived this quality in a man. I learned from observing him that life was not a matter of seeking material advancement but one of looking beyond horizons. He taught me, not with words but merely by his presence and the manner in which he made that presence felt, that a faith in one's perceptions mattered more than any other faith. Now he was an old, dying man; and yet I have never known a more *beautiful* man.

Weak though he had become through illness and hardship and greatly saddened by the loss of so many men, he had not lost any of his ruthlessness, his severe authority. During the third year at the camp a revolt broke out among the men. A dozen or so men, led by none other than the Captain Major's son, woke us up one day by shooting in the air. We opened our eyes to see the camp encircled and the Little Captain call out: 'Listen, all of you, I am taking over this camp. We have had enough of dawdling here, looking for a dream. There is no treasure in these mountains. There are panthers in the mountains, yes, and there are hard rains which strike at your skin like the arrows of Indians, and there is a cold which makes its home in your bones, but of treasure there is none. We have been here for three years and not found anything resembling an emerald. What do you want to do, stay here until one by one we're all dead?'

Certainly, the Little Captain had a point, and it seemed as though he would win the rest of us and leave his father completely isolated. But the old man stood up and took a step forward.

'Don't move!' his son called out. 'I will shoot anyone who moves.'

'Even *me*?'

'Yes,' he said, 'even you. You have led us here and look at us, hungry and at the mercy of the weather and the animals. If anyone is responsible for our wretched condition, it is you.'

'In that case,' the Captain Major said, 'you have no business to be with us. We do not want people who give up hope.'

'I don't think you have any right to keep anyone here,' the Little Captain said.

'No, none at all,' the old man agreed. 'Simply allow me to say this. You are my son and like all sons you will never learn the meaning of patience. You believe that I am in your way, that the world would be wonderful if only I was not there insisting you come my way. Well, my men, some of you have been with me when we have gone into the interior from São Paulo, have I ever let any of you down?'

'You'll never let us down,' his son cried. 'We'll just die here.'

'We must all die, my boy,' the Captain Major said. 'If you want to die in bed, then you don't belong to an expedition.'

'Hear that, men!' the Little Captain shouted. 'That's an old man talking, and an old man can afford to say that. What does it matter to him? He'll soon die. But some of you are young. Some of you have wives you want to see again.'

'Oh, you talk like a sentimental idiot,' the father said. 'I have no time for that. If I'm to hear such talk, I'd rather hear it from a woman on whose lips it sounds natural. A fine country Brazil will be if all its young men were like you, worried about dying! Now, I ask you all to drop your guns and stop this childishness.'

But the rebellious group just stood there, the guns still raised.

'Enough!' the Captain Major said, raising his voice a little.

'I am warning you men. My authority on this expedition comes from the Governor General himself. I will have each one of you shot when we return to Salvador.'

But the men did not care about such a threat and stood their ground.

'All right,' the Captain Major said, 'you leave me no choice. I will deal with you as any common rebels deserve to be treated.'

I did not understand what he could mean since he was clearly surrounded and had no power to carry out his threat.

'Come on, then,' he called. 'Which one of you wants to take me prisoner? I warn you I am dangerous if you don't tie me up.'

He extended his arms as if asking for his hands to be tied up.

'You?' he asked his son. 'Let us see our new leader take the first step. Come on, where are your chains?'

The Little Captain, perhaps angered by this mockery, walked up to him. This was a mistake, for what we observed now was a father-son confrontation which no man, even the rebels, wished to interfere with. The old man's arms were still extended when his son reached him.

'Bring your chains, boy,' the Captain Major said, 'not your gun. Any coward can pull a trigger, it requires a man of courage, a leader, to take another leader prisoner.'

By continuing to talk in this fashion, the Captain Major was providing a subtle distraction to his son, for when the Little Captain was close enough, the father easily knocked the gun out of his hands and simultaneously struck him two blows, one in his right eye and the other in his groin. It occurred to me that some weakness in the son's character, a sudden failure of nerve perhaps or the final moment's inability to do injury to his own father, led to his defeat; for he collapsed on the ground and the father, taking up the gun, pointed it at the group of rebels and commanded, 'Drop those guns!'

The men's hands were tied and they were all, including the

Little Captain, made to stand in a line. Some of us were made to pick up the guns from the ground.

'Once men fail in a rebellion,' the Captain Major said, 'they will try again. Or, their disease spreads to other men, their equals in weakness and cowardice.'

He made those of us who had picked up the guns stand some ten paces from the men and ordered us to execute them.

'Including your own son?' some asked incredulously.

The Captain Major turned away, saying, 'If there is any other sentimental fool in this camp, he can line up with the rebels, too. Go on, shoot!'

All the rebels, including the son, were executed, and the old man never spoke of the incident again. He was not interested in people who did not believe in him.

About twenty men were now left in the party, so that what exploring was left to be done among the inscrutable mountains was now done by all of us together. Although the Captain Major was visibly suffering from some ailment, he led us on each excursion. One day we came to a lake which no one had discovered before. The water of the lake was a blackish green, a colour I have never again seen in any lake. There was a smell in the air which was so repulsive that one wanted to run away from it. The smell seemed to fill one's lungs like the fumes of a badly fermented liquor and made one's eyes smart. Clearly, it was more than a smell, for it had a physical body which was imperceptible to us and which none the less brought on attacks of nausea among the men. I do not remember what compelled us to struggle through this foul and thickening atmosphere, but we all felt that we had to get to the shore of the lake as if some spirit pulled us in that direction. In any case, the Captain Major was walking dauntlessly ahead of us, taking long strides, his head held high, and no one could think of not following him. When he reached the shore, he was about twenty feet ahead of the rest of us, and we saw him fall as though he had been overcome by the atmosphere. When we reached him, we, too, saw what he had seen: the shore was littered with green emeralds.

We all fell, too, and lay prostrate on the lake's edge, wallowing in the wonderful precious stones. Nobody could say now that Fernão Dias Pais Leme, Captain Major by the special appointment of the Governor General in São Salvador do Bahia, had not known what he was doing.

He now bid us rise and return with him to the camp. We did so, except five of the men. They lay there, not admiring the newly-discovered treasure, but dead, overcome by the poison in the air which came off the lake. As we marched back, two more men collapsed and died, making the rest of us terrified; some kind of vindictive magic seemed to be at work as if it had been decreed that no one would come to discover the rich secret of the lake and if anyone did, then he would die for breaking the supernatural taboo. We hastened back although the thick air was tying chains round our ankles and, with the evening falling, the sky seemed to be going black as if it were going to turn into a vast sheet of iron and crash down on us. I did not see if anyone else fell, for I walked blindly on.

When we were back at the camp, there were ten of us left.

'I would like,' the Captain Major said a day later, 'five or six of you to take back the specimens to Salvador. I don't think I want to travel yet. Who would like to go?'

Almost everyone volunteered. The Captain Major looked a little disappointed, for it appeared that he was going to be left alone.

'I'll stay behind,' I said. 'I will return with you when you're ready to go.'

'Me, too,' said Jari.

And thus it happened that only Jari and I were to be left with the old man. The remaining seven men were ready to leave by the next day. Fernão Dias wrote a letter to the Governor General, describing his find and giving the location of the lake, and instructed the men to go straight to Salvador and not to spend any more time in the interior. I think what he meant was that they were not to fall into the temptation of returning to the lake in order to collect some sacks full of emeralds for themselves. As it turned out, that was exactly what the men attempted to do. Not one of them survived. Jari and I came across their bodies while we were exploring in the region of the lake.

Fernão Dias decided that we should move our camp, and we made our way to the river das Velhas.

'Now that we have found the first precious stones in Brazil,' the old man said, 'don't you think the earth will show us something else?'

As the idea of something new to believe in entered his mind, his eyes seemed to regain the lustre they had temporarily lost after the fulfilment of finding the emeralds. But it was a false indication that he might be regaining his strength, for one day, sitting by the river, looking hypnotically into its racing waters, he died as quietly as a man dozes off to sleep after a heavy dinner.

After we had buried him, Jari and I wondered what we should do. One thought was uppermost in our minds: we alone knew where the emeralds were. On the one hand, I felt it my duty to go to Salvador with the specimens left behind by Fernão Dias and to announce the discovery; on the other hand, I was well aware that I was no longer a young man, being now past the age of thirty-five. Years of hardship in the interior had aged me, working into my skin deeper lines than a normal life would have produced in the same time. It was not hard to convince myself that a bag full of emeralds would provide me with riches in Salvador. Jari, being more superstitious than me, did not want to go at first, saying that we should remember what had happened to the others who had been similarly tempted. Finally, however, I persuaded him to come with me. So we travelled back in the direction of the river Doce. As it turned out, we never reached that mysterious lake with the emeralds on its shore.

We reached the river Doce and camped on its banks. It was spring-time, and there was a cool freshness in the air which was exhilarating. It was so beautiful on the bank that we decided to stay there for a few days. We bathed in the river several times each day, and then entertained ourselves by catching wild fowl and roasting them over fires. One day, we decided to leave this beautiful life, go and gather the emeralds and make our way back to Salvador where, we were convinced, glory and riches awaited us.

'Why don't we take one last dip in the river?' I suggested.

It was the most valuable suggestion I have ever made, and it changed the entire history of Brazil. For it was during this parting dip in the river, to which I might never have returned, such is chance, that I discovered gold.

Chapter 10

WAR IN VILA RICA

Locusts riding on a hurricane across a continent are slower than the flight of rumour. The instant in which lightning strikes in a tropical storm is of longer duration than the time taken by rumour to strike in every corner of the country. Gold, gold! The word was on the lips of Brazil. It seemed that Jari and I had hardly taken that historical plunge into the river Doce before the entire country was descending upon the region.

I had no wish, of course, to keep my discovery a secret; and in any case, the fact of the matter is that gold in itself was worthless to me unless I could trade with it, and to do that, I would have needed to reveal my secret sooner or later. Also, this was a time when many explorers from São Paulo were scouring the area between the river Doce and the Rio das Velhas; these explorers were lesser men than Fernão Dias and Rapôso Tavares as far as character and a far-reaching vision were concerned, but they were men of immense courage and an intense lust for power. They had marched out to the Andes in the west and the Amazon in the north; they had journeyed south to the Rio de la Plata; seeking everywhere to tame the wild country, to harness the Indians and to discover the elusive precious metals and stones which were presumed to be embedded somewhere in Brazil. It was not surprising that they, too, found the emeralds and the gold.

Alas for Fernão Dias, the emeralds turned out to be a trick of nature and not emeralds at all. With the news of these discoveries spreading rapidly, more and more people began to arrive in the area: not only the adventurers, not only the vagrant poor who saw in the brutal exploitation of the land a chance to compensate themselves for the years of struggle and penury, but also men who were expert in matters of geology. One such geologist took a cursory glance at the so-called emeralds and laughed aloud at our ignorance: what we had found and what some of us had died trying to clasp to our bosoms had not been emeralds but a worthless rock called tourmaline. The wilderness had merely provided us with a comforting illusion and what we had thought to be the rightful reward for the hardships we had endured was now a mockery with which nature laughed at man's cupidity. I was glad that Fernão Dias had not lived to suffer this moment of humiliation, that he had died satisfied with the belief that he had achieved what he had set out to do. And it was important, I thought, that we held our beliefs to be truthful as long as there was no evidence to the contrary: the human intellect's capacity to believe – not blindly but in a general context of educated doubt – is a measure of mankind's wisdom.

So: the news of the discovery of gold shot through the country like an epidemic, bringing blight to the sugar plantations; for now, almost everyone, fired with ideas of instant riches, abandoned his trade or estate and came down to the gold mines in an undignified haste. Why labour on the land for year after year when one day on the banks of the river would give you more wealth than you could accumulate in a year? Also, landlords, harassed by debt, found that they could sell their slaves at premium prices to the miners who desperately needed them. Spontaneously, towns sprang up. In valleys, on hillsides, wherever people built shelters for themselves, the early improvised huts quickly developed into houses, and clusters of houses soon became well established communities: Sabará, Vila Rica, São João del Rei. And in Lisbon, the moment that the Crown had been anticipating with diminishing hope for a hundred and ninety-three years at last came. Within two years of my discovery, Vila Rica had become the most important city in Brazil, and the royal agents had arrived to establish the Crown's privilege of smelting the gold and taking a fifth of it to send to Lisbon.

It was in Vila Rica over the next few years that I was once again a man of distinction, family and wealth. And it was not gold that made me wealthy – though gold certainly made me rich. In the early fever for the gold, I said to myself: Think of it, Gregório, you can't eat gold, you can't tell gold to go out and bring you a sack of wheat, you can't make love to gold. These fundamentals had been forgotten by most of my countrymen. I decided that I would put Jari in charge of the gold-mining aspect of my business while I myself would pursue what I was convinced would be more profitable in the long run: cattle, slaves and women. I established connections in Pernambuco for importing cattle and in Rio negotiated for supplies of slaves. The newly enriched miners needed what I had to supply and were prepared to pay a high price, and in the early years I had a near monopoly in the business. Once my fortune had been secured, I sent Jari to Olinda to find me a wife from the best family in Pernambuco. She doesn't have to be the greatest beauty, I told Jari, for by now I've known just about every kind of woman to know that beauty is one thing I am prepared to overlook provided the social and material circumstances are acceptable. Your commission, Jari, is to bring back a young woman of a distinguished family which has a fortune and a name worthy of the wealthiest man in Vila Rica.

Jari did not disappoint me. After three months, during which he communicated with me via messengers so that the marriage was arranged without my meeting the family, Jari returned at the head of a colourful procession. My marriage to Heloisa Helena Pires de Almeida was the occasion for a week's celebration in Vila Rica. And nor was I disappointed in my wife. Heloisa was sixteen, of a fair complexion, and had the smallest nose I ever saw on a Brazilian woman. Our first child was a daughter whom I named Sônia after my dear sister, and a year later Heloisa presented me with a son, whom I named Alfredo. I was content, and although I was aware that Brazil still needed many more sons from the ruling class,

I believed that by now I had made a most generous contribution.

Happy with my family, my life now turned to those pleasures which are more satisfying in middle-age – business and politics – and in these affairs I was at first respected and honoured and later abused and maligned, for there is no saying what ill-will is not engendered by the envy of one's neighbours.

A gentleman from the north, a solemn-faced man with the illustrious name of Manoel Nunes Vianna who owned cattle ranches on the São Francisco river, had also established himself in the region of which I could be said to be the master by virtue of my wealth. And if one were to accept the laws of nature, the fact that I had been the earliest arrival in the region ought to have given me greater social eminence. Certainly, no one in Vila Rica could dispute the fact that I had donated more money to the building of the cathedral than anyone else. The gold which made the altar so resplendent with the glory of God came from my mines. Wherever men met, there was talk of vesting authority in someone who would have the power to establish order; for this was a time of lawlessness, and no man's life was safe were he to venture unaccompanied outside the city. And even in Vila Rica, people who could not afford more than half a dozen slaves found it difficult to defend their properties against burglars and bandits. Clearly, if we were to have law and order in Vila Rica and in the neighbouring towns, the authority would need to come from among the eminent citizenry of the region. We did not want to appeal to Salvador, for that would only have brought into our midst the petty officials who would have soon established a system of corruption to benefit themselves at the expense of the leading miners. Wherever men talked of wanting a leader in the community, my name was the first to be mentioned. I expected a deputation to arrive at my house any day to offer me the leadership which seemed my right.

One day I was standing inconspicuously beside the door of a house which I owned, an establishment which my foresight

281

had led me to open as soon as I had realized that in a predominantly male society the availability of women would produce high profits. I had gone to considerable expense to obtain mulatto girls from the cities in the north-east, girls of that wonderful brown skin of a smooth, velvety texture which Brazilian men prize over every other kind of woman, girls who have a European subtlety in their limbs and a Negro fire in their blood. While I stood there in the shadow of the doorway, I heard a group of men standing not far from the door talk about the very subject that I had on my mind.

'Sure, Gregório is the richest man in Vila Rica.'

'He comes from a great family and has married into an even greater family. To my mind, he's well qualified.'

'He has the experience, too. Before he came to this region with Fernão Dias's expedition, he had been on a great expedition to the west with Rapôso Tavares. He was with Rapôso on the Andes. He has seen Brazil. I would choose him.'

I was about to clear my throat loudly to indicate my august presence when the desire perhaps to hear more flattering things about myself, even though some of the things were mere gossip, persuaded me to remain quiet. I could not recognize any of the voices, and reflected that praise was all the sweeter since it came from people unknown to me. The mass of mankind, I thought, is obliged to be a passive spectator and when it applauds the principal actors in the human drama, then it is expressing a morally significant approbation. With these thoughts I was heightening the tenor of the flattery that I heard when a new and a rather sombre voice spoke, beginning with that most destructive of words, *but*.

'But,' he said, 'the richest man is not always the best. We first need to question how he acquired his riches.'

'What do you mean, Gabriel?' asked someone.

'Could your candidate stand up in church and truthfully declare that his wealth had been acquired from an honest trade?'

'Come, come, Gabriel, you know very well that Gregório has paid for the building of the church. The gold on the altar he gave freely.'

'I suppose,' Gabriel persisted, 'that you think that heaven is like the opera house in Salvador at which you can buy a reserved seat. Some of our priests may be silenced with money, but do you think you could bribe God as well? Shame on you! And, pray tell me, what is this house in whose shadow we are standing? Can you not hear the squeaky giggles of the sinning women? Have you not yourselves squandered more gold here for a few minutes of pleasure than could sustain a family an entire winter? And whose establishment is this? Gregório's, your candidate for our leader! That will be wonderful for our sons and daughters, a whoremaster for our ruler!'

The others presently began to agree with Gabriel, and one who had praised me earlier was now heard to say: 'They say he was the first to discover gold in this area, but we all know what a great liar he is.'

My first impulse was to go out and to take Gabriel by the throat and make him choke on his words. What restrained me was the knowledge that violence was one's worst ally; politics and subtlety were the way to advantage, and I advised myself to subdue my passion and to listen. Soon, Gabriel began to suggest the name of Manoel Nunes Vianna and sing his praises. Vianna was virtuous. Vianna was kind. Vianna spent his time reading religious books and working on great writings. Vianna had the money to run the most sumptuous brothel in Brazil, but Vianna preferred to use his money to help the poor.

And so on. So that was the game! A most transparent piece of propaganda which was going to convince nobody. But within the week, Vianna's name was on everyone's lips. Convinced that Gabriel was some sycophantic hireling of Vianna, I had one of my servants follow him to discover what he could about him. But it turned out that Gabriel was not personally acquainted with Vianna, that Gabriel himself was some kind of scholar who despised money. I engaged three of my men to spy into the affairs of Vianna, for I did not believe that there could be any man whose existence had not at some stage been tainted. My men came up with nothing, not even a mistress. The man was incredibly virtuous, and appeared to want power for no other reason than to carry out his own ideas about justice. I found all this activity had a strange effect on me; at first I was so angered with Vianna's presumption that he considered himself a candidate superior to me that I was determined to spare neither the expense nor the labour in attempting to destroy his chances. Gradually, however, and much to my own surprise, I began to like the man. There was something of the visionary in Vianna; at least his eyes had the same searching intensity that I had seen in Fernão Dias's. He spoke softly and yet with authority; every sentence of his seemed to be uttered as a fact of profound knowledge which was being revealed to mankind for the first time. When he visited my house, at my invitation, I had the notion of offering him some prestigious position in my business, a scheme which entailed getting him to compromise himself. But no sooner did I welcome him to my house than I was so struck by his simple manners and the aura he had of being some kind of a prophet among a corrupt people that I wondered at the evil which had counselled me to devise a trap for Vianna. And when, soon after the dinner, my one-year-old son Alfredo would not stop crying – Heloisa said that he was teething – Vianna begged to hold him in his arms. Heloisa, as if hypnotized, gave him the baby; little Alfredo at once stopped crying and began to make merry sounds and to paw at Vianna's chin with his tiny hand.

'You're like a saint to him,' Heloisa said to Vianna. I was astonished that she should have hit upon a word which had also come to my mind.

'Oh, nonsense,' Vianna said. 'He's never been in a stranger's arms before. He's quite amused, which is lucky. Some children only cry all the more when a stranger picks them up.'

He kept Alfredo in his arms for an entire hour while he settled down to talk with me. And Alfredo, instead of soon beginning to protest, maintained a bemused interest, smiling from time to time while he watched Vianna speak.

'I need not presume to tell you, sir,' Vianna said, 'how important the child's first years are to his subsequent development. Let him pass his childhood in an ordered house and he will grow up to appreciate the values which nurtured his infancy. Let him grow up in a house in which the parents quarrel and the servants steal, and he will later expect the world to be a battleground of dispute and vice.'

'Very true,' I said, not at all sure whether he was returning my hospitality with a cunningly calculated abuse, but I was soon relieved to hear that he intended no malice towards me.

'Does not,' he asked, 'a country have its period of infancy? What is Brazil now but a child? Here we are sitting on ground that only five or six years ago had never been trodden upon by any civilized man. Indeed, we do not know if any man had ever stepped on this earth before explorers like yourself came to this region. Oh, but the country is not even born yet!'

'What can you mean?' I asked.

'What is it, two hundred, well, very nearly two hundred years since Cabral discovered what we call Brazil. And what has been Brazil for the best part of this time? A few captaincies, and then a few more families with their sugar plantations and cattle ranches. That is not a country. That is only property in a few hands whose allegiance is only to their own piece of land.'

'Ah, but what about the time when we in Bahia and Pernambuco got together to drive out the Dutch? Were we not being Brazilians then?'

'But only to safeguard our plantations, our wealth,' he said.

'I must insist on disagreeing,' I said. 'Men like Rapôso Tavares who were not at all threatened by the Dutch still mounted forces against them because they saw the Dutch as an enemy against the country, not just against the north-east.'

'Permit me to surrender to your greater truth,' he said graciously. 'But the truth in my mind is not the least diminished in consequence. What I proposed to suggest, if I may humbly do so with due deference to your superior knowledge and experience of the country, was this. That it is the discovery of the gold and the precious stones of this region which is going to create a Brazilian people out of us. It has not escaped your notice that every class of man, from the aristocrat in Olinda to the petty merchant in Rio, has found his way here. This is where the infant Brazil has its cradle. And if the voices around this cradle are the raised ones of those engaged in a quarrel, then what hope is there for the child?'

At this point, Alfredo gave him a deft undercut across the chin and beamed with pleasure.

'Isn't it strange,' I said, seeing in my mind his finger pointing clearly towards a certain idea, 'that whenever we Brazilians meet, we talk of nothing but Brazil. Brazil is our philosophy. Brazil is our entertainment.'

'Yes, indeed,' he said. 'Brazil is both an idea as well as a merry-go-round. In Europe people talk of the weather or of political economy. They argue over the latest comedy or the latest tragedy they've seen at the theatre. Here Brazil is the one continuing drama. No, I wouldn't say it is strange. Rather, I would say that there is something special about man's relationship with the earth here in that all that truly and passionately interests him is Brazil.'

Alfredo now settled down to watch him quietly while Vianna proceeded to expatiate on the subject of Brazil. I was perhaps too amused to observe Alfredo's attentiveness to be altogether attentive myself, but it was a general talk on the subject of patriotism and nationalism which I had heard before.

Vianna became a frequent guest at my house. What had appeared to be a contest for power at first, turned out to be no contest at all. I believe that if I had really wanted to I could have won power, for I had enough money with which to influence opinion; but on discovering a friend in Vianna and on realizing that one does not have to be an appointed or an elected official in order to exercise power, I let the burden of authority fall on him. Indeed, no appointment was made nor an election held; it simply happened, with more and more people appealing to Vianna whenever there was a dispute, that he came to be accepted as the leader of the community. I was going to say the political leader, but, really, he was not a politician; perhaps I should call him a moral leader, but that, too, suggests something that he was not, for he was a man of commonsense and of considerable humour. So, plain leader will have to do. He kept anarchy at bay, and the lawlessness with which the region had erupted into existence in the early days gave way to order. That is not to say that people walked about upright as if they wore some kind of spiritual armour; of course, there were disputes over mining claims, of course people were murdered in their homes and children were kidnapped. Except among the Indians in the dark interior, I have not known mankind anywhere restrain itself from committing atrocities upon fellow humans. All that can truthfully be said about Vila Rica and its neighbouring towns late in the seventeenth century is that the presence of Vianna had a subduing influence on a very violent people. And I dwell upon this, although more interesting matters concerning my own story are pressing themselves to be narrated, because a chronicle of this nature must pause to salute those Brazilians who, living in an environment of manic greed and ravenous cupidity, have attempted to show mankind that there is a greater beauty and richness in a voluntary submission to order.

Some cynic will no doubt wish to know how I can reconcile these noble sentiments with such matters as running the establishment of mulatto whores. It will have been noticed that I have refrained from using the word brothel when referring to this house. The truth is that it was not a brothel in the ordinary sense. I had seen such houses on visits to Rio in connection with my slave business. These were gaudily and cheaply furnished; the principal effect seemed to have been created by painting the walls blue and by hanging red curtains across the windows. The beds not only creaked but also seemed to be overrun by bugs; three or four experiences were sufficient to convince me that there was as much pleasure in lying beside an ant heap. The whores were mainly Negresses, recently arrived from Africa, thin and weak, who were destined as soon as they ceased to attract the cheapest customer to be sold to miners in Vila Rica for such labour as cleaning latrines. The very few mulatto whores were exorbitantly priced and were still in such demand that unless one visited the house early in the afternoon, one was liable to get a woman so exhausted that she merely went through the motions and made no attempt to please her client.

What my house provided in Vila Rica was something else. There was the essential service, certainly. But, remembering the time when I was briefly the master of the plantation after my father's death when I had a small Negro orchestra to play music while I was served dinner by naked Negresses, I introduced a band into the house. The customer entering the building heard the wonderful music which only Negroes seem to play well in our country. The band was in a long, low-ceilinged room which had no windows and was consequently dark and cool. Here the visitor was invited by Maria Carneiro, an adventuress from São Paulo who had lost all her money and whom I had employed to run the house for me, to take a seat and to accept a drink which was presently brought to him by a young Negress. At first I had thought of having these Negress waitresses completely naked, but realizing that it would be foolish to sate the appetite of the customers with a visual feast, Maria and I had decided to have the waitresses dressed in a manner calculated to excite and to incite the eye; so that they wore loose robes which, revealing too much only incensed the beholder into thinking that they concealed too much. After his drink, the visitor proceeded with the main business if he lacked leisure; but if he was not pressed for time, he was invited to visit the gaming room where he could play a game of cards or simply sit and enjoy a smoke. No women were allowed in this room. I have always observed that men, when in exclusive male company, tend soon to turn

to the subject of women and to narrate exaggerated stories of
their former conquests – each one, of course, being a tribute
to their handsomeness, virility and wealth; and this is what
happened in the gaming room where the stories invariably
were either of conquests or of being cheated by some whore
in Salvador or Rio. The effect of spending some time in the
gaming room was to make the visitor gain a mood of confidence as well as recklessness. I had plans to introduce other
elements into the house. One was to build an extension at the
back of the house where a doctor could open a consultancy
office, for there could be no doubt that many of the clients of
the house would have been glad to have a doctor so readily
available; and working according to the universally acknowledged truth that prevention is better than cure, the doctor's
services would have been most popular. Another idea was to
convert one of the larger rooms into a classroom and to have
some poor scholar like Gabriel give lectures on the history of
Portugal and her conquests. Obviously, I would need to wait
until Vila Rica became a more established society which
would be eager to go beyond the basic bodily pleasures and
would come to my house for a comprehensive entertainment
of body and mind. These ideas alone would have made the
house an extraordinary establishment and not just a simple
brothel. But I believed that I was providing Vila Rica with a
valuable social service; oh, not just giving men the opportunity they so desperately need in the wilderness of frontier
existence to empty out their lust, but something much more
important. One of my rules was that none of the girls should
be less than fourteen nor more than twenty-five years old. Of
course, such a rule meant that I lost money, for anyone with
any experience of brothels will know how many pitiable
women of forty, and more, are often painted up to look
twenty years old. And I will say nothing of those houses
which offered girls of ten or eleven as a special excitement to
men whose appetites had been jaded by an excessive possession of older women. No, I refused to allow girls who had not
come to maturity and, therefore, made fourteen the youngest

age at which they could be employed; and as soon as the girl was twenty-five she had to leave. And that meant that she was free of any contract with me and could now find herself a husband. And since there was probably a twenty to one ratio between men and women in Vila Rica, a girl at my house had only to be twenty-four when she began to receive offers, so that often the day she left the house was also very nearly her wedding day. What pleased me most of all about this arrangement was that a girl who, at one time or another during her ten or twelve years at the house, had given the profoundest and most intimate pleasure to almost the entire male population of Vila Rica ended by becoming the devoted wife of one. There was something very gratifying about this, for it seemed to create a bond among the families.

My own wife, busy with Alfredo and Sônia, took no interest in my business affairs. Having grown up in a family in which the woman's role did not demand her to express any curiosity in her husband's business for the simple reason that it was assumed to be either the management of a plantation or some gentlemanly pursuit, Heloisa never questioned the source of my growing fortune. Perhaps she assumed that it all derived from gold; it is more likely, however, that it never occurred to her even to wonder what my business might be. And, of course, when I returned home in the evening, I was anxious to hold Alfredo on my knee and to have Sônia playing beside me. I had no notion how many children I had fathered, and although at Zaballos I had seen my children grow up, I had never before Sônia was born been attached to my children. Heloisa enjoyed observing me find so much pleasure in our children, and was content that she had brought me this happiness. She was a quiet woman, rarely talking unless she was talked to – at least in the early years of our marriage. After Alfredo's birth, I had, as I have remarked, retired from the business of procreation. Heloisa had not questioned my decision, for it just happened that I was satisfied with caressing Heloisa and concerned myself less and less with making love to her. Aware that she was not yet twenty, I knew that from time to time she would want me to come to her, but she never made any demands and I took her reticence on the subject as a tacit agreement that she understood my reasons for withdrawal. I must have been getting old, for I had never before made such a mistake about elementary human psychology, *female* psychology at that.

Heloisa had a maid named Josefina, a girl of eighteen, black as coal but with a Negress's wide hips which I have rarely been able to see without wanting to pass my hand across them. Jari had once told me how he had seduced her, describing how she had willingly submitted to some perversion that he had proposed.

'She has a snake's mouth,' Jari said, concluding his story.

It was not the first time that Jari had described one of his affairs to me. We had been close enough for most of our lives to share such idle talk, but for one of the very few times in our friendship I was angry with Jari. I scolded him for playing with my wife's maid, and he was so surprised with my reaction that he was lost for words. I wondered later why I had been angry. It occurred to me that I could well be jealous that Jari had taken what I inwardly desired and saw as having a rightful first claim to since I owned the girl. This thought so vexed me that I sent Jari away to Rio, telling him that I could no longer trust our agent there and that he was to negotiate personally with the slave importers for new shipments. I could see that he resented going, that he suspected that I was trying to get him out of the way. If I was trying to banish him from Josefina's presence this was not because I intended to make her mine. True, she stirred the deepest desires in me, but I loved my wife and children and was not really interested in seducing her. It was pique, perhaps, for it certainly pleased me that Jari no longer enjoyed her.

One day when Heloisa and I had retired for the night, she said: 'What is your business, Gregório?'

'What do you mean?' I asked, for the question was clumsily expressed, almost as if she had wanted to ask what was my pleasure. I was on the point of stroking her cheek to

291

give her some little gratification, when she said, 'I mean business. There are the slaves and the gold, that I understand without seeing, but what else is there?'

'Why should you want to bother your pretty head with business, Heloisa?' I said.

'What is the house in town?' she asked suddenly.

'Oh, that!'

'Yes, that!' she said in an irritated tone of voice.

'Come now, Heloisa,' I said, 'this is no time to be discussing my business.'

'Please, Gregório, I want to know.'

'Well, what do you expect?' I said. 'It's a house where men come to find women.'

'A brothel,' she said, making me wonder if she thought that I used up all my sexual energies there.

'All right, a brothel,' I said. 'It's good business.'

'Is that where you spend all your days?' she asked, but went on bitterly: 'My husband is busy, he's working hard at the brothel. And when I write home to my mother and father, what news should I give them? I'm sorry, dear father and mother, Gregório has been too busy to see me recently, you see he's been working very hard at the brothel. And when I go to confession, I've had evil thoughts, Father, because I've been alone at home since my husband spends all his time in the brothel.'

'Heloisa! Stop this nonsense!'

'Nonsense?'

'Who put such ideas in your head?'

'You have certainly said nothing.'

'Well, it's not what you think,' I said, trying to explain my establishment to her. 'And I don't spend all my time there,' I went on. 'There's the gold mining to attend to, there is correspondence with agents in Rio and Salvador to see to. Please don't get the idea that I spend all my time surrounded by dancing girls. You should know, too, that it's the best service that can be provided for the male community. You should see the other establishments in Vila Rica, using old

292

worn-out Negresses who've been thrown out of the brothels of Rio. That is evil, that is degradation, and you should see the pitiable creatures who haunt these places, miserable failures who've found no gold and have come to the end of their resources and can find some solace only in liquor and depraved, cheap sex. What I provide is something which brings order to Vila Rica.'

'If you owned a bar, would you not take a little drink from time to time?' she asked.

'I know what you mean,' I said. 'The honest answer is no. A man who owns a bar in order to make money doesn't touch the stuff. For the good reason that he'd only be doing himself out of profit. Look, Heloisa, I love you and I love our children. You've given me contentment and peace, and I don't want it any other way now. Everything I do out of this house is to make money.'

For the present, Heloisa was sufficiently convinced to go to sleep, but I think some doubt lingered in her mind. Thinking that it was more difficult to convince people when telling the truth than when elaborating a subtle lie, I, too, went to sleep. Some days later, Josefina entered the room where Heloisa and I were sitting together with the children. It was after dinner and the children were begging to be allowed to play on a little more before being sent to their bedroom. I saw Josefina look at me and then at Heloisa and then back at me; and when I looked at Heloisa, I noticed that she was staring at me as if she expected to see something revealed in my face. She quickly turned her eyes away and said something superfluous to Alfredo. Josefina soon left the room, and Heloisa and I proceeded to take refuge in the children's games.

Alfredo was playing with some clay figures, brightly painted cockerels and peacocks, and I found myself saying, 'Careful, Alfredo, you don't want to break those lovely toys, do you?' While we talked thus to the children, we thought of something else. At least I was trying to puzzle out something that had begun to form itself in my mind. Could it have been Josefina, I asked myself, who had told Heloisa about the brothel?

Perhaps Jari had visited Josefina before leaving for Rio . . . no, I could not work it out yet. But still the question persisted and suggested other questions. Was Josefina trying to take revenge on me for taking Jari away from her? No, she could not be so subtle, for she would only see it as a business decision. Did Josefina, having lost Jari who was considered in the house as second only to me, now have her sights on me? No, I had not remarked any such ambition in her, she probably saw me as an old man; on the other hand, she must surely have observed me noticing her with a keen masculine interest, and must know of the advantages of doing the master of the house an intimate favour. Oh – ha, Gregório, you're getting slow in your old age! Could Heloisa, despairing of my not making love to her, have confided her feelings to Josefina and could Josefina have advised her to make me jealous?

No, it was getting too confusing, and I had no way of arriving at any kind of definitive answer. But why was Heloisa staring at me when Josefina came into the room? Could it be that she suspected something and wanted to read my expression so that she could discover what effect Josefina's presence had on me?

While this domestic drama was beginning to express its themes in mime too obscure for me to comprehend, the first act of a larger drama had commenced in Vila Rica. There was a merchant from São Paulo known all over the town simply as Coelho. He had run a shop in São Paulo with modest success and like thousands of others had abandoned everything and come to Vila Rica in the hope of making his fortune in gold. Now, while there was gold, and diamonds too, in the region, not everyone who came here was fortunate enough to discover it. Poor Coelho had no luck at all and degenerated into a drunkard who could be seen at evening uttering obscenities outside one of the cheaper brothels. There was nothing remarkable about this since he was not alone in such despicable circumstances. One day, however, his abuse at the world took a menacing turn. He was naturally proud of being a *Paulista*, like many from that famous city, and remembering that the *Paulistas* had been pre-eminent in exploring Brazil and had shown the greatest courage in the interior of the country, he began to say that the gold mining region rightfully belonged to the *Paulistas* who had lost more sons than any other Brazilians in finding it. Well, this was only half a truth since I had been the first to discover the gold even though I had taken no public credit for my discovery. In any case, it was the kind of nonsense no one was likely to take seriously, for it was laughable for anyone to suggest that the citizens of São Paulo as opposed to those who came from Salvador or elsewhere had a natural right to the gold mines. Minas Gerais, as the region around Vila Rica came to be called, was part of Brazil; we were all Brazilians; so, there was no question of anyone having a better claim. This is the way I saw it, and Vianna agreed wholeheartedly with me.

One night, however, a wealthy planter from Salvador, who had made his fortune in gold, was murdered in his house and the word *Emboaba* was written across the white wall of his house in large black letters. Coelho was not the only *Paulista* who felt cheated of what he was convinced was his right, and his utterances had attracted a group around him. The murder was a deliberate act of aggression. The *Paulistas* had banded together and had begun a war on the others who had been named *Emboabas*. None of our lives was safe, and a grim tension hung over Vila Rica as if we were on the verge of a civil war.

Meanwhile, quietly and insidiously, a civil war had begun in my house. One day, arriving home early so that I might not run into a band of *Paulistas* in the dark, I heard a screaming from the bedroom. I found Heloisa beating Josefina with a cane; she had apparently torn the back off Josefina's frock and was whipping her ferociously. She stopped when I entered and, dragging Josefina to the door, pushed her out. Presently, when her fury had abated, she explained to me that Josefina had broken some serving dish which she especially prized since it came from Lisbon and had been brought to Brazil by her ancestors. I accepted her explanation and tried to offer her my sympathy, but thought to myself that the dish was only a convenient alibi, for I had been reminded of the way my mother had beaten Aurelia and systematically mutilated her body. Oh, the Brazilian wife! She was the same from one generation to the next in her expression of sexual jealousy. Poor Josefina! I'm glad I had witnessed what must have been the first or second occasion of her suffering. Another month, and her mutilation would have begun in earnest, and what might not have been served in my dinner for meat? The thought made me cringe; and yet there was nothing I could do to prevent whatever Heloisa intended for Josefina. I could not very well tell my wife that she had no cause for jealousy, for she would not have believed me. And even if her own commonsense and observation were to convince her that I was faithful to her, she would still destroy Josefina for the fact that I no longer made love to her – as if it were a sacrifice she needed to make in order to bring me back to her bed. Once or twice, I made a deliberate attempt to make love to her, but it was a most inconclusive, insipid affair with both of us seemingly playing a game with the most unconvincing acting and, worst of all, I failed in the crucial matter. Perhaps this only convinced Heloisa that I no longer loved her. The truth is that I loved her more than I have ever loved anyone, but there was no language in which I could convincingly convey this to her.

'There is something women do,' I said to her one night when I had again failed. 'They mix things in their husband's food. Promise me, Heloisa, you won't do *that*.'

It was a pathetic attempt to communicate to her my horror at having to experience what my father had once undergone from my own mother before I was born. She did not answer, and perhaps I made my appeal worse by adding, 'You know what women do with their monthly blood, and how they introduce a strange meat in their food.'

She laughed aloud. It was not her usual laughter. It was artificial and calculated to mock and despise me.

'I have no more faith in such remedies,' she said bitterly.

'What do you mean?' I asked, uncomfortably aware of her

meaning.

'I've *already* tried what you talk of,' she said triumphantly.

'Heloisa! What have you been feeding me?'

'Oh, go to sleep, Gregório, you couldn't do it even if I gave you my womb to eat. God knows I've tried everything else.'

My horror was so intense that I could say nothing but simply suffer an excruciating sickness choking at my throat. From that day I began to take my meals out of the house. When I think back on it, it was a ridiculously absurd situation. I wanted nothing more than to continue to love my wife, and she probably wanted to possess me more than anything else, and yet we had begun to behave like enemies. Since I now spent more time away from home, I did not follow the details of Josefina's degradation. I felt particularly helpless towards her, knowing that if I were to intervene and attempt to persuade Heloisa that she had committed no wrong, Heloisa would not believe me and only make her punishment more severe; and knowing, too, that if I did nothing, the poor girl would suffer without anyone in the world acknowledging her innocence. This gnawed at my conscience until one night when I felt compelled to try and tell Heloisa the truth. When I had concluded what I thought was a persuasive statement, she laughed aloud and said, 'It's too late, Gregório, she's no longer in the house.'

'What have you done to her?'

'Go to what you call the cheaper brothels. At one of them, you can have her for what it costs to buy a banana. But please spare me your lies about her innocence. She was born with wide open legs.'

'But not with me, Heloisa, please believe me, not with me.'

'Of course, I believe you,' she said.

'Heloisa, what are you trying to say? You've sent a girl to a most degenerate existence, you've destroyed what humanity she possessed, and now you tell me you believe me.'

'I believe what you tell me about yourself,' she said. 'Gregório, I'm not blind. You spend most of your day out and all of your night in bed here beside me. Josefina used to spend all her day here. How could I suspect anything between you two? Please don't take me for a mad woman.'

'Then, why have you done this to her?'

'I told you. Because she was sinful, because her legs were wide open for any boy of thirteen or anyone else. Gregório, I suffer for your sin. Whatever you call your house, it's a brothel, nothing less. Your sin hangs over this house. I had to purge this house, Josefina had to be sacrificed. If you can find nothing wrong in selling girls in your house, you should not in the least be concerned about Josefina, for somebody else is selling her. What difference is there? When she'd been sacrificed, I felt better for a few days, but the sense of sin still hangs over the house, Gregório, and perhaps there will have to be other sacrifices.'

'Heloisa, stop being so stupid about this.'

'Stupid? I don't think it's stupid. I don't think what my mother taught me was stupid. I don't think what the Church teaches me is stupid. You tell me what is stupid.'

'Look, Heloisa, do you really see no difference between those brothels and my establishment?'

'I've seen neither. All I know is that at each house there are girls and that men come and pay money to sleep with the girls. I see no difference. Perhaps I'd be a better wife to you if I offered myself for sale at your superior establishment. Perhaps it will give you pleasure to make money from me, too.'

I surrendered. I promised to sell the house as soon as I could find a buyer, which, I told her, ought not to be difficult considering there were people with more gold than they had use for and would be eager to invest it.

'But it will continue,' Heloisa said. 'The girls will still be there, the men will still come, pay their filthy money and sleep with the girls. No, Gregório, selling it will not change anything.'

'What do you want me to do, then?'

'Burn it.'

As it turned out, I did not need to give myself the trouble of setting fire to the house. By one of those strange coincidences which make one wonder whether some joker is not in charge of the universe, just when Heloisa and I were talking of the house, the *Paulistas* were setting fire to it.

Had the *Paulistas* burned down the houses of ten of the leading *Emboabas* in Vila Rica they would not have committed so criminal an offence as destroying the best house of pleasure in the town; for Brazilians can understand regional animosity, but to set fire to a house which offered the finest outlet to human passion was an outrageously vile and inhuman act requiring a special kind of barbarian to perpetrate it. The *Emboabas* reacted by attacking the properties of the rich *Paulistas*, and within two days it seemed that two warring nations had entrenched themselves in the region. Houses were burned down, rape became commonplace. With the poorer brothels also burned down, rape in fact became the commonest recourse to carnal satisfaction – which, I told Heloisa, was a fine irony, but she answered that since I had established sin in Vila Rica the town could only be purged by a universal suffering: she refused to see the civil war which had commenced as the struggle for control over the gold mines, seeing only God's punishment on a community which had sinned. My attempts to explain the real nature of the struggle only convinced her that I was trying to distract her from the truth which she felt she alone perceived. It occurred to me that a large part of the world never saw what actually happened but, receiving some vague impression in its mind, arrived at a totally alien conclusion for itself and then stubbornly held on to it as the only truth.

There is no doubt that the *Paulistas* were some of the bravest men in Brazil. I admired them and had I been an impartial witness, I would have applauded the courage with which they fought. But I had been labelled an *Emboaba* myself although I found the term opprobrious since the word had originated as a designation for the newly arrived Portuguese who had rushed to Brazil at the first mention of gold. There were five times as many of these *Emboabas* as all Brazilians put together, and once those Brazilians who were not *Paulistas* were also grouped among the *Emboabas*, the *Paulistas* were outnumbered by at least ten to one by those they had made their general adversary. Consequently, the greater military skill of the *Paulistas* was evened out by the greater numbers of the *Emboabas*.

It was a time of chaos, a time when new adventurers poured in from Portugal and men of a proud, independent spirit from the south swelled the ranks of the *Paulistas*. It was a time when people who did not lose their houses and families in the widespread arson lost their fortunes through an inability to see that the new anarchic condition of society required new rules of conducting business. Once again, men who thought that gold alone could make one's fortune were the poorest.

When my ill-fated establishment had burned down, I had sent a message to Jari in Rio to purchase quantities of arms. My idea was to equip some twenty or so of my slaves with the latest weapons so that my own property could be defended against a *Paulista* attack. Jari, being a shrewd businessman, obtained arms from both the French and the English agents in Rio and asked them to quote competitive prices, telling them that his master was in a position to place a large order for the *Emboaba* army. This was only a trick with which to get the cheapest prices from the agents, but when Jari came with the arms and asked me which ones I would like to purchase, telling me about the way in which he had played the French and the English against each other, I had the idea that Jari had not only saved me money on the arms which I wanted for myself but had suggested a scheme by which I could add considerably to my fortune. I sent him back to Rio with an order which would equip an army of ten thousand men. And why equip only the *Emboabas*? The trick would be to sell the English arms to the *Emboabas* at a reasonable price and then, demonstrating to the *Paulistas* that they lacked modern equipment, sell them the French arms at the maximum profit. This would only be fair, for a war in which one side is much more powerful than the other is an unjust war.

The civil war had only just begun, but I had no way of

predicting for how long it would continue. My problem now was twofold. By placing the order for arms, I had committed myself to an expenditure which would ruin me if the war came to an end before the arms arrived; by the time the order went to Europe, was executed and the arms arrived in Vila Rica, at least six months would have passed. This was one aspect of the problem. The second was that if I succeeded in having the war prolonged sufficiently for my investment to show a return, I would only be continuing the danger in which I and my family lived, the danger of being exterminated by the *Paulistas*. But no one, I said to myself, succeeds in business without taking risks and it is clear that the greater the risk the greater the subsequent profit if one succeeds.

One of the facts about business that I had learned was: give people an expectation of an unexpectedly high profit and they will not only nearly kill themselves working for you but will also be eternally grateful to you. To spur the French and the English agents in Rio to have the shipments effected speedily, I obliged them to sign contracts by which they would receive premium prices for the arms if they could deliver them within three months – which, of course, was a near impossibility – the prices diminishing markedly the longer it took for delivery until penalty clauses began to function and, if there were no delivery at the end of six months, the order would become null and void and I would be granted a substantial compensation. For them, too, there was an enormous risk and at the same time the thrilling chance of a huge profit.

At home, I busied myself with plans with which to prolong the war. I established a secret council of *Emboabas* with the ostensible notion of protecting the properties of the leading businessmen of our group, but with the hidden purpose of filling their minds with a continuing hatred of the *Paulistas* so that their ardour for war might not diminish. At the same time, I deputed one of my trusted slaves, a Negro called Fernandes Gama, to allow himself to become a spy for the *Paulistas*, so that he could pass to them every detail of importance from the meetings of the council of *Emboabas*. In this manner, the *Paulistas*'s passions could be kept continuously inflamed, too. This kind of intrigue, in which nobody, not even Gama, could know what I was up to, was not sufficient to keep the war going, and I had, from time to time, whenever a lull in the fighting (following Christmas or Holy Week, for example, when religious festivity established a temporary truce) seemed to prolong itself for too long, some atrocity enacted to renew the bitter struggle. Sometimes it was sufficient merely to spread the story that a young girl from a noble family had been raped by a *Paulista*, but often, if the story had been a fabrication, it would make little impact or the people's belief in it would dissipate itself fairly quickly. If, however, the event had actually taken place, the story would have a greater force – for physicality, I learned, moves people's imagination to a more vivid narration of the event to those who have not witnessed it. It was obvious to me, therefore, that situations which elicited the people's horror had to be performed where they could be witnessed. If a rape had to be committed, it would serve everyone's interests better if it were committed in front of ten witnesses rather than only one. To achieve such effects, I trained a group of slaves who served the double function of mingling among men in bars and public places in order to keep the idea of the war alive in their minds and, whenever an opportunity presented itself, of burning a house or of relieving a wealthy man of his sense organs, especially his eyes and tongue, and then of spreading the story as a piece of barbarism committed by the *Paulistas* or the *Emboabas*, whichever happened to be the more convenient accusation.

It was, of course, good for the country that this tension continued in Vila Rica, for nothing makes a people more God-fearing and obedient to the Government than to be living in a time of crisis. As a consequence of my careful manipulation of the situation, the war not only lasted six months, just before which the shipment of arms arrived, but continued for another eighteen months. The simple truth of

302

the matter is that once I had succeeded in simultaneously selling arms to the two sides, the *Paulistas* and the *Emboabas*, each convinced that it now had the power with which to destroy the other side, were immediately anxious to intensify the war. And since neither side knew of the new arms which the other side possessed, each suffered heavy casualties, and, wishing to avenge these fresh losses, became more determined to increase the intensity of the fighting. In the meanwhile, I had entered into a larger deal with the arms agents in Rio, convinced that for the next year or so I had only to sit back and enjoy the fruits of the bloodshed that raged around me. It was a triumph of business acumen over mankind's foolishness.

Since my slave Fernandes Gama worked as a spy for the *Paulistas* but was in reality working for me, passing on to them what information seemed necessary to maintain hostile tempers in Vila Rica, he needed to be extraordinarily inconspicuous. In particular, my other slaves, the ones who had been trained to mingle with men in bars and to spread stories, must not know of Fernandes Gama's activities, for I believed that the Negro slave worked best when his mind was not confused by the presence of more than one idea. You can tell a Negro to go and give a bone to a dog and he will understand that; but if you tell him to go and give a bone to a dog *and* a saucer of milk to a cat he will probably end up by giving the milk to the dog and the bone to the cat or by doing something else altogether, like going and milking a cow. Therefore, Fernandes Gama had not been given any insight into my operations either. All I expected him to do was to repeat to the *Paulistas* statements which I taught him, and that he performed effectively.

Well, one day Gama saw a commotion in the fields and, on investigation, discovered that three youths were raping a mulatto girl. Seeing that the youths were slaves from my household and having known them ever since they were born, he scolded them and sent them home, promising them a severe whipping. As it happened, the youths were from the group which performed the kind of service for me which they had been caught at. They came straight to me and described what had happened. I now know that what I should have done was to have given them money, asked them to say nothing and to take their whipping from Gama as if they thoroughly deserved it. Instead, I gave them money and told them to disappear into the distant town of São João del Rei. That was a mistake. For Gama soon discovered that I had helped them to run away.

He became suspicious, but as yet he did not know what to be suspicious about. He simply had a vague notion in his mind that something was not quite right. To make matters worse, the mulatto girl who had been raped was the daughter of a laundress with whom Gama had been intimate. I could see his great trust in me begin to diminish. I kept him discreetly under watch, knowing that a Negro's reactions are unpredictable, for not having a mind which makes rational deductions he moves by instinct and sometimes arrives at the truth when one least expects him to. And being a Negro, Gama could not think unless he thought aloud, which is to say unless he gossiped. All that he said was faithfully reported to me. He had concluded that since I had helped the culprits to run away, I therefore exonerated their behaviour; which implied that I wanted them to do what they had been doing. The girl's mother was a woman of no consequence, but she was an *Emboaba*. And this is what puzzled Gama. It took him days to proceed a step further along this logical path, but he was surely getting to the point of revelation where he would know what precisely was going on and what a dangerous role he himself was playing on my behalf. In short, Gama was becoming the most dangerous man in Vila Rica as far as I was concerned. His existence was a threat to my prosperity, indeed to my life.

In order to eliminate Gama, I had to hire some outsider, for it would have been insane to have asked another slave to perform this task. Well, I made the necessary arrangements. But I made another mistake. Trying not to involve too many people in my affairs, I hired only one man. When he made his

304

attempt in a dark street where I had sent Gama on a mission, Gama overpowered him, cut off his right hand and, coming to me, threw the hand on the floor, saying: 'Here is the hand you hired to have me killed.'

I feigned innocence, made a scene, abused him for taking liberties with his master, and asked him what he expected in a time of war but murderers at every street corner. My verbal violence was sufficient to confuse him for a day or two, for he had no proof of my complicity. The next day I announced that I was going to Rio on business, and ordered Gama together with two other slaves to be ready to accompany me on my journey.

When we had been two days on our journey, I found an excuse to send the two other slaves back to Vila Rica. I needed some papers, I told them, which I had forgotten, and it would be safer and pleasanter if the two of them went together. I was so precise in telling them which drawer of which desk to open with which key that neither they nor Gama suspected that the papers were quite unimportant. I also sent a letter to Heloisa, asking her to tell the slaves not to return. Alone with Gama, I had no difficulty in accomplishing what the assassin had been hired to perform.

I proceeded to Rio in a happy state of mind and thus the war between the *Paulistas* and the *Emboabas*, much talked about in our history books, came to an end. It was the year 1709, nearly a decade finished of a century which had given me nothing but riches and happiness.

The bountiful Brazilian countryside spread out around me. I felt as if I owned the entire land. The sun, high up in the sky, seemed to be sending down rays especially to illumine my head which wore the light like a crown. The air thinned in the mountains and filled my lungs with a new ecstasy; there was a luminous quality in the light which seemed to clothe me with gold. The trees bowed as I rode past. And there, as I came down from the mountains, far in the distance was the great ocean, blue and sparkling, making its eternal homage to the city of Rio de Janeiro.

Chapter 11

A FATAL FLIRTATION

My problem now was how to dispose of the arms which I had already ordered. There could be no cancellation at this late stage, and the quantity ordered was so large that all my considerable resources would not have been sufficient to pay for it all. I had never reckoned the exact worth of my fortune, but there could have been little doubt that I was one of the richest men in Brazil in the year 1709. And yet my own cupidity now had me cornered.

I made a secret return to Vila Rica to see if the war could not be continued for a few months longer, promising myself that I would retire from such ventures if I could come through successfully on the present one. But during my three months' absence, discord had died down – proving a country proverb that fires need to be continually fanned if they are to keep burning. Many of the *Paulistas* had left for their native state or, feeling again that the great interior beckoned them, had gone off on new *bandeiras* – the *bandeirante* spirit being irrepressible in the *Paulista*. There simply was no question of the war being renewed. To make things worse, Lisbon had sent many more agents to Minas Gerais; since the war had meant a reduction in the gold supply, for the men had not been working the rivers or the mines but fighting, Lisbon was determined to establish peace in the region. The Crown was apparently trying hard to assert its authority, something which, in the delight of being overwhelmed by gold, it had not hitherto attempted. I heard that Vianna was in the process of transferring the power he had acquired to the new administration and expected in a year or so to retire to his ranch on

306

the São Francisco where he hoped to work quietly on his books. A strange man, I thought. He could have demanded and received a governorship, for he commanded the respect of all the factions even though he had been helpless during the war; in spite of the power he could undoubtedly exercise if he chose, he preferred to withdraw into a world of his own.

What the presence of the Crown's agents meant for me was that questions were being asked and an enquiry was being conducted into the war; clearly, it was no time for me to be readily available, and I unobtrusively returned to Rio – much to Heloisa's disappointment, for during my brief return to Vila Rica I had been so overcome by my love for her that I had succeeded in overpowering my demon and had once again made her pregnant.

Leaving Heloisa and the children when I most wanted to be with them, I felt as if an impending misfortune was about to burst upon my head. I could not take my family with me for fear of attracting unnecessary attention, and nor could I make arrangements to dispose of my property and business interests. At best I could hope to have my family follow me to Rio later and to have an agent sell off all that I had built in Vila Rica. But the very thought of not being able to manipulate what was mine depressed me; and the added thought that my commitment to the arms deal was sure to bankrupt me and thus bring my activities to public notice filled me with despair. For once in my life, I did not know how to fight my way out. The journey to Rio gave me no pleasure at all. I felt none of the ecstasy that I had experienced on the previous journey, none of that delicious sensation that Brazil belonged to me, that every tree bowed like a peasant on the passing of a king.

But how capricious life is! Some it destroys as if they were ants in the path of a marching army and others it seems to protect as if they were jewels that must be kept in satin-lined boxes. My gloomy journey ended, I spent some days in Rio without seeing anyone, not even Jari, wanting only to breathe in the exhilarating sea air before my troubles began to asphyxiate me. I walked on the beaches, watching the slave

307

ships come into the bay. Or I lay on the hot sand, letting my mind browse idly among thoughts of human destiny. Sometimes I walked among the streets, finding the stench of human excrement in them sweeter than what I could expect after I had seen the arms agents. Many of the houses had slaves chained outside, slaves who had recently arrived from Africa and were kept in this fashion until buyers from the interior came for them. Naked and dirty, the slaves looked like a wild species of animal. Sometimes a house would have a dozen or twenty slaves outside it, and if anyone wanted to see how barbaric the Negro is in his original state, here was a perfect spectacle. At any time of the day, one could observe them sitting on their haunches and excreting, or one would suddenly pick on a woman, push her to the ground and proceed to copulate, or another be seen to be masturbating absent-mindedly. And yet when you see the same Negroes a year later on some plantation, the discipline of work seems to make them into civilized creatures. I was convinced that slavery was the greatest gift bestowed upon the African.

Thus, wandering about in Rio or lingering on its beaches, I passed a week or so, until I ran into one of the French agents with whom my extravagant order for arms had been placed. Now, an odd thing happened. He saw me just when I saw him; I was certain that our eyes met. And yet it was he who tried to pretend he had not seen me; it was he who *tried to avoid me.*

This is most strange, Gregorio, I told myself. Here is a man to whom I shall presently be accountable with my life after he has wiped away the last speck of gold-dust from my fortune, and he is anxious not to meet me. I pursued him to his shop where he sold silks from France. My curiosity had impelled my mind to work on its own while I walked some distance behind the man; he seemed to be aware that he was being followed and continued to behave as if he did not wish to see me; in fact, the hasty manner in which he walked indicated that he hoped to slip away into some side alley. By the time I caught up with him at the doorstep of his shop, my mind had resolved the answer, which was so simple that I was shocked at the way I seemed to have lost control over my affairs. The answer was that six months had elapsed and therefore my order was null and void! And the reason why he had wanted to avoid me was that there was a penalty clause in the contract which obliged him to compensate me handsomely for the loss of business – though I could not say why he should act so strangely and try to avoid me when I could easily visit him in his shop at my leisure.

Well, I made him as well as the English agent pay, and set up house in Rio. The shipments had not arrived. Recently arrived ships had brought stories of storms in mid-Atlantic and of many wrecks. We could only conclude the obvious.

And so life continued to keep me in a satin-lined box without the box being my coffin! I sent Jari to Vila Rica to bring me news of my family and also of any political gossip that he might pick up. My recent lonely state had provided me with ample opportunity for reflection; divorced from my great wealth, without which, I would have been prepared to believe a few months earlier, no existence could be possible, I now felt that I had lost nothing that I valued by not being in Vila Rica to control my business empire. If Heloisa and the children could join me in Rio, I would be perfectly happy to pursue a modest existence. Such clear perception of what one needs for one's happiness is rare; more often, one is engaged in reaching towards a variety of fantastic directions without ever seeing what happens to be right beside one. Ah, but we are a fantastic race, with minds so busily fabricating a multiplicity of futures that the present remains as unnoticed as a beggar outside one's house.

Before Jari could return, and God knows what delayed him, an expected event again changed the course of my fortunes. The ship with the arms from France which had been given up as lost at sea suddenly arrived one day. Flying the French flag, the ship was in the charge of Jean-François Du Clerc who sent emissaries out to enquire of the agent what he proposed to do with a ship full of guns and ammunition. At least that is what I heard, for I kept out of the way, knowing that I could suffer from a disclosure of my original complicity in the deal. Another rumour was that Du Clerc had made up his mind to win glory for himself even before he arrived in the bay, that he did not even care to find a plausible excuse. Whatever his thinking, Du Clerc unexpectedly attacked the city one morning. We woke up to see French soldiers marching down the streets and shooting at whatever target caught their attention, whether it was the slaves chained in the streets or the open windows of houses. Everyone looked to the governor of Rio, Francisco de Castro Morais, to bring out his troops and to put an end to the intrepid Frenchmen but the governor seemed petrified by the alarming situation.

A handful of citizens, with more pride in their city than the governor, took to the streets armed with nothing more lethal than kitchen knives. It was a ridiculous situation, and these poor defenders of the city were quickly massacred even though the French, who seemed to love to dramatize and exaggerate what was really very ordinary, tried to make the miserable little resistance look like a powerful defence and screamed orders at one another and gesticulated wildly before they managed to kill the dozen or so people who had rushed at them with knives.

Perhaps this scene finally made the procrastinating governor come to a decision, for anyone could see that given the sight of fifty properly armed soldiers, the French would probably go berserk at the thought of having to meet so enormous an army. Well, a larger force than fifty soon bore down on them and pushed them back to the water-front. A brief battle ensued in which there was less bloodshed than there were comical scenes of Frenchmen falling into the sea, flinging their arms and screaming loud oaths. It was this fate that saved Du Clerc from being killed, and when he was fished out he seemed to resent being arrested while his clothes were wet. It was obviously an affront to his dignity. Looking greatly vexed, he protested and asked for a towel and a comb. When he had dried his face and hair, he carefully combed his blond locks, returned the towel and the comb with a most gracious gesture, smiled at everyone around him, and looked absolutely delighted that he was being arrested. It appeared that he did not mind what happened to him as long as he was properly groomed.

When the governor had him imprisoned in the Jesuit college, Du Clerc was greatly offended and wrote lengthy letters to the governor in a language which was abusive without being discourteous, letters which were in no sense an appeal or a petition, saying that it was incorrect protocol to keep a French officer confined within the walls of a Jesuit establishment. Instead of requesting superior treatment, he pointed out to the governor that as a nobleman the governor was showing very bad taste in inflicting an indignity on a fellow nobleman, thus suggesting that the governor was showing very bad taste for his class or – and this was Du Clerc's subtle suggestiveness – could it be (God forbid!) that the governor was not a nobleman? The governor was puzzled, confused and vexed by these suggestions, being one of those people who appear to be very sure of their position in the world and yet eagerly allow themselves to be influenced by people who question their behaviour; forever trapped into playing roles which other people devised for him, the governor was thus never the same person. Because he was so dependent upon other people to shape his personality at any given time, he was incapable of making decisions which affected the city. He somehow expected things to fall in their rightful place by themselves. While he procrastinated about Du Clerc's demands, the latter was constantly thinking up other ways of getting out of the Jesuit college. He tried bribing his guardians but to no avail, not because the holy jailers were incorruptible but because the proffered bribes were theoretical since Du Clerc had no money. It was almost as if one had to consider oneself extremely fortunate to have the opportunity to free Jean-François Du Clerc, his suggestion being that the honour of so doing would be so great that one could hope for no greater worldly advancement. But the holy guardians were not convinced by these abstract considerations and they continued to uphold the sacred principles of high-minded virtue as long as Du Clerc continued to be without hard cash. Du Clerc tried other means of escape, disguising himself as a priest one day or as a tradesman on another, but failed. It seemed that every day he was engaged in composing a letter to the governor, having long conversations with the Jesuits on the spiritual value of helping the nobility of France, and devising some disguise. When all these seemed to offer him no hope, he began on a new course: he started to write letters to the various leading families in Rio, and knowing that the women would be curious to see his letters (for he assumed that women all over the world had a secret passion for a Frenchman), he wrote his appeals in so poetical a language that presently the women were convinced that the poor man needed their personal help. The governor was persuaded by a deputation of Rio's leading women to move Du Clerc to one of the finest mansions on a hillside.

Once installed in the mansion, he was provided with servants and soon all the tradesmen, from the butchers to the tailors, were vying with each other to offer him freely all that he desired; so much so that if a shopkeeper could display a sign that he served Du Clerc, he won the business of the leading families. The mansion became a kind of court where elegant society assembled, and not to be invited by Du Clerc became a sign of social disgrace.

I met him by chance late one morning while he was strolling in the gardens of his house. I had climbed up the hill for no better reason than to enjoy the view of the bay, an excursion which had long been recommended to me by my acquaintances in Rio but which I had not before undertaken. It was certainly a beautiful view, the blue sea hazily disappearing in the distance while the bay sparkled brilliantly. I had not, however, expected the climb to be so arduous and by the time I reached the most advantageous position from where to enjoy the view I found myself beside Du Clerc's house in a state of exhaustion and extreme thirst. Introducing myself to the man in the garden, I wondered if I might not obtain a drink of water. I had not seen Du Clerc before and when he bowed courteously and made excessively flamboyant gestures while inviting me into the house, I knew at once who my host was. Of course, even before we had reached the door, he had introduced himself. I expressed both an exaggerated astonishment and a profound delight which he no doubt expected and which gave him a great deal of pleasure.

'You caught me at my principal preoccupation,' he said when we had sat down in the drawing-room which had windows looking out to sea. 'I spend hours strolling in the garden with my eyes turned in the direction of France. Ah, what would I do without my memories of France! I am like a man whose mistress has forcibly been taken away from him. You cannot tell how wretched I am.'

A servant entered and served us with wine which I discovered to have come from France.

'Do you love your country that much?' I asked.

'Miguel,' he addressed the servant, 'a few olives and some cold beef will not be too inappropriate at this hour to offer our guest, don't you think? Please excuse me,' he said to me when the servant had gone, 'your Brazilian servants are so backward, they have to be instructed at each step. Ah, the love of one's country! Is that your subject, sir? Alas, no one can know what it is to love one's country unless he has been born in France.'

He turned a sad eye to the window which faced east when I answered: 'Allow me to protest on behalf of Brazil if not the rest of the world.'

'My dear sir, please save yourself the labour of so doing,' he said. He paused as the servant came in with a bowl of olives and a dish of sliced cold beef and placed them beside me on a small table. 'If you possessed a most beautiful duchess,' Du Clerc continued, 'would you listen to my description of a peasant's daughter?'

'But you have not seen Brazil.'

He placed his left hand in the palm of his right hand and

examined his nails, taking a minute look at the middle finger, while he said, 'What may I want to see? Rio, all of Rio I can see from here, and I believe it is at its most attractive from this height and distance, for I am not unfamiliar with the smells of your streets. Is Salvador any better, is Olinda?'

I confessed that I had not seen these cities, and for a moment was reminded of my own miserable days in the Salvador jail.

'You will perhaps wish to sing the praises of your interior,' he went on, dropping his hands to his lap and looking up at me. 'I have no desire to encounter jaguars and snakes let alone the Indians. There is nothing in your interior but barbarism. The New World is only a great wilderness seething with violence. There is no Brazil that I am aware of as yet. A country is not a country until it has won wars against its neighbours, and a people has no national identity until it has refined its manners, established an elaborate class order and acquired a palate so delicate that it can be pleased only by the most subtle sauces. But what do you have here? Chaos. A man comes from Lisbon where he was nothing, a street vendor perhaps, goes to Vila Rica and strikes gold and begins to dress like a nobleman and to give himself the most superior airs. Please don't expect me to show deference to any such upstart. You will find it a useful rule in interpreting your experience of the world, that a society may be judged by the behaviour of its women. Foolish though they are universally, the women in France at least appreciate the advantages of discretion in matters of amorous intrigue. In Rio, the women are going to considerable pains to solicit invitations to my house, and once here they appear to be eager to win my affection. There seems to be a competition going on among them. And why do they prize me so highly? First, because I'm a Frenchman. There is not a woman in Rio who is not convinced that a Frenchman is a born lover who somehow has extraordinary sexual powers and is specially endowed by nature to dispense orgasms. And secondly, because they have no established social order among them, they find highly

314

attractive someone who comes from a country with a high sense of social order. I doubt if any of your women if asked the colour of my eyes will be able to tell you that they are blue, my point being that they've not looked at me but only at a Frenchman whom they desperately wish to possess. Such behaviour shows a most regrettable vulgarity. No, sir, a country without a monarchy and a ruling aristocracy is not a country. Brazil is only an outer limb, not a limb even, but a root of Portugal, feeding Portugal with the sap of gold. Brazil, as Brazil, doesn't exist, and if it does, it's of no importance whatsoever.'

'I have not,' I replied in a most deliberate manner, 'your experience of the world. Nor do I have your education and breeding. Also, I am grossly lacking in the ability to present a logical argument, not having your sophistication in the articulation of ideas, and I cannot hope to match the subtlety of your intellect. But if you will permit me to express in my untutored, clumsy way a few observations on this subject, then I will say this. According to the considerations which you have mentioned, I agree that Brazil is not yet a country. But I have seen the land that is Brazil. These feet of mine have trodden upon thousands of miles of this land. I was born in the house of a planter and if you go to Vila Rica and ask whose property the greatest mansion in it is, you will be told that is the house of Gregório Peixoto da Silva Xavier. Mine. And yet much of my life I have spent sleeping on the bare Brazilian earth. I have been among the Indians in Amazonia and I have lived in a colony of runaway Negro slaves as their ruler. I have walked with great explorers, I have been confined in a prison cell with the greatest criminals and perverts as my companions. At one time a priest saved me from death, at other times whores have succoured me. What I have seen is something vaster than what you can comprehend, what I have experienced has been so varied that your imagination would fail to grasp a tenth of it. The Old World does not prepare you for the immensity of this land. The wheels of carts going along the same muddy road soon

315

make ruts which the carts which follow find it difficult to avoid, and soon anyone driving a cart assumes that the only way to go is by keeping the wheels firmly in the ruts. *That* is what I think of the Old World. And when people like you come here from the Old World, you find that there are no ruts and you immediately conclude that there are no roads! In other words, if you have an order, as you call it, you are not prepared to look at the rest of the world through any other point of view except the narrow one of that order.'

'Forgive me interrupting your most wonderful flow of rhetorical banalities,' he said, flicking away some fluff from his sleeve, 'but let me establish one point. We assume that there is such a thing called civilization, do we not?'

'Well, yes.'

'And we are agreed that in all the contemporary world the most civilized countries happen at present to be in Europe, are we not?'

'I will have to take your word for it, for I really do not know.'

'Come, come, how else do you think France and England, Spain and Portugal have acquired such dominance over the world? You've had other people who've attempted to conquer the world, but none succeeded as these European powers appear to be succeeding. And why do you think this is happening? Because these European powers have the ships, a greater knowledge of navigation than anyone in the past, they have the weapons before which the rest of the world must either submit or be wiped out, and, most of all, these countries have that intellectual maturity which the world has never possessed before. And how did they arrive at this maturity? As soon as Aristotle began to systemize ideas, to put them into categories in which their complexity and unity could analytically be observed, that is one source. As soon as the caveman drew a line across the wall of a cave is another. As soon as Galileo looked through his telescope is one more. Most of mankind merely lives in the world; in the Old World we not only live in it but we also *know* what it is all about.

316

And the degree of a culture's knowledge, as you must know, depends on the quality of its language. If Europe, instead of Asia, now dominates the world this is because Greek and Latin were capable of defining more of the knowledge available to human perception than Persian, Sanskrit or Arabic were. And because we already know more than the rest of the world, other people will forever be behind us and will, forever wanting to catch up with us, never have any fresh perceptions of their own because they will simply be trying to make sense of the perceptions which we've already had. In the meanwhile, we shall continue to see more and more and to build up a complex body of science which to the rest of the world will be meaningless until many years later by when we will have gone still further. You see, we've had civilizations in the past, we all know about China and Egypt and India, for example. But however advanced these civilizations were, they lacked in one essential: an equally advanced language which could accommodate a complex theory of the world, and, lacking this, the old civilizations, even at their most glorious moment, remained intellectually naïve. With Greek, for the first time, we have an intellectual language, and *that*, permit me to say, has made all the difference. We have been running while the rest of the world continues to crawl on all fours.'

'I accept everything you say,' I said, 'but you make the mistake of those wise men who think that everyone else is an idiot. Brazil is neither in Asia nor in Africa but at the present a root, as you say, of Portugal. It is, therefore, starting with an advantage. What is to stop Brazil from acquiring the best of the Old World and creating, because Brazil has the space and it has the gold, a greatness which is now inconceivable in Europe?'

'Tell me,' he said. 'You've hinted that you're a man of wealth and influence. Have you ever – please forgive the delicacy of the question – but have you ever murdered a man because he was in your way?'

'Why do you ask?'

'Have you?'

'Don't tell me it doesn't happen in Europe!'

'So you have! Of course, it happens in Europe, but we have a legal structure which attempts to keep it in check. What do you have here? Barbarism, anarchy. This may be the great land of opportunity where you've only got to touch the soil and out pop the diamonds. This may also be the great land of the future, but it can only be an imitation of Europe. No new country is going to grow up without taking the facial character- istics of Europe. We've gone too far for the rest of the world to have any choice. We've created universal inequality. We are the leaders, and the world must follow. We make the rules, and the world must obey. Because if it does not, then it can expect no emancipation from savagery; the price of emancipation, however, is a permanent subservience to our way of existence. You must know that very few people actually *see* the world, for the majority of mankind is content to accept the versions presented by poets or prophets or poli- ticians. Europe is the world's prophet now as well as its political dictator and its poet. The world will reject its own vision in order to create an approximation of European civilization. There are societies which believe in many gods; they will even abandon their gods and accept the one Euro- pean God in order to call themselves civilized – even if we in Europe tend to be cynical about *Him*! Allow me to fill up your glass. This excellent wine which comes from France is the most precious thing I have, fortunately succeeding in saving it from my ship. A sip from it is sufficient to prove that the rest of the world has no idea of what life is like.'

After over an hour of such argument, our tone at times that of two bitter adversaries engaged in a vital struggle, we parted the best of friends. He pressed me to visit him again and I promised to do so. He struck me as an interesting man but too obviously full of the conceit of the European who comes to the New World determined to demonstrate the splendidly ordered virility of the Old. I could not help detecting a slight hypocrisy in him, however, for here was a man who had been

318

guilty of attacking Rio, killing some twenty people in the process, and he behaved as if he were the innocent victim of some vicious conspiracy. The fault, I suppose, was ours, for instead of hanging him from the nearest tree we had established him in the finest house in the city and allowed him to treat us as if he owned us. Someone not familiar with the circumstances of his presence – imprisonment is a ridiculous word for the situation – in Rio would have thought him to be a prince. All of Rio seemed to pamper him by fulfilling his every wish and all he did in return was to abuse us and to lecture us on our inferiority. Why did he not take the opportunity, which was there, to escape and go back to France?

I visited him again several times, having little else to entertain me in Rio. It was during this time that Jari finally returned with the news that Heloisa had given birth to another son, and that she planned to join me with the three children as soon as the baby was strong enough to travel.

'But I will go to her,' I said. 'I want to see my new son.'

'Oh no, you won't,' Jari said. 'Why do you think I was away so long? The King's men are asking questions. Remember how you very cleverly decided to give the French guns to the *Paulistas* and the English guns to the *Emboabas*?'

'Yes, what about it?'

'Well, the King's men want to know how is it that your slaves are armed with the same guns as the *Paulistas*.'

'God, could I have been that stupid!'

'I told them,' Jari said, 'that we captured the guns.'

'Jari, you're a genius.'

'But wait. Some of your slaves are idiots. A couple of them quickly said, No, we didn't capture them, our master gave them to us. I tried to tell the King's men that the slaves didn't know the difference, but I guess they're still pretty suspicious that something's not quite right. So, as I said. You stay right here for the present.'

And in Rio I remained, the best entertainment I could hope for being a visit to Du Clerc. I had become such good friends with him that I often arrived unannounced at his house. One day, as I walked up the hillside, a thick mist hung around the house and floated away in ribbons across the distance. The mist had probably been there since early morning and was gradually dispersing. I stood in Du Clerc's garden, entranced by the mist while it curled about the plants, now massed itself against the house and now thinned out so that the house appeared to be there one moment and not there the next. Looking down towards the bay, I became absorbed in the mist's indulgent manner of rubbing itself against the hillside, rising and coming down again as though some duty called it away and yet it could not make itself go away and must submit itself to the temptation of lingering a moment more and then a moment more. Consequently, the sea, which caught the full face of the sun, glittered through the patches of mist and provided a most beautiful sight. I stood in the garden, lingering, like the mist, enjoying this extraordinary sight. Suddenly, there was a commotion in the house and three masked men came running out. I did not see them until they were on the path some ten yards away from me where the double coincidence of the mist having thinned and their spontaneous action of removing their masks revealed their faces to me. They did not see me since I had instinctively moved behind a tree and in any case the mist was floating about too rapidly for the men to be the least aware of my presence. I looked hard at their faces to make sure that I would recognize them again; one of the faces struck me as strangely familiar: I could not actually identify him, but I felt as if I had known him all my life. The men ran away and, deciding that it would be useless as well as probably foolish to give them chase for whatever they had done, I went into the house.

Du Clerc lay in his bed in a pool of blood, murdered. Presently, the servant Miguel appeared, shivering as if he suffered from a severe fever and sobbing. Obviously, he had been terrified for his own life and had stood hiding himself while the murder took place and was now afraid that he would be held responsible for his master's death. I told him to go and drink some of his master's wine and to lie down, and,

drawing a sheet over Du Clerc's body, left the house in order
to go and make a statement to the governor. On my way down
the hill, I was myself overcome by shock; it seemed to be a
delayed reaction, for while I had been in the house I had gone
about in the practical manner of one who in the midst of
tragedy must do the commonsensical thing. Now the impact of
the loss of my friend struck me with a nauseous force, and on
reaching the town I went into a bar to sit down and have a
strong drink. I sat down at a table, holding my head in my
hands, and it was not until I was lifting the glass to my lips
that I noticed that the three men were sitting at the table next
to mine.

I could not concentrate enough yet to distinguish what they
were talking about, but their conversation was of the boisterous sort that goes on among men who have had some daring
success like a sudden discovery of gold. Since it was early in
the day, there were only two other men in the bar; both
looked weary and disconsolate, and I thought to myself that
at this time of the day the only people who needed a drink
were the dejected or the exultant. The three murderers became more boisterous and while ordering a new round of
drinks, the man whom I had thought I recognized decided to
invite everyone else in the bar to join his group's drinking.
I had recovered from my sense of shock sufficiently to think
that I could only gain more information by joining them, and
shortly two tables had been pushed together and we were
sitting in close companionship, drinking and sharing a nonsensical hilarity. I kept observing the man whose face seemed
familiar. The conversation was inconsequential, consisting of
anecdotes at the conclusion of which the entire bar echoed
with the company's laughter. It would have been most enjoyable did I not know that what had given occasion to our
coming together had been the murder of my friend Du Clerc.
The talk turned to the relative merits of the different parts of
Brazil. Needless to say, this subject was begun by a *Paulista*
who not only sang the praises of São Paulo but also of the
supposedly brave character of the people who come from

there.

'To hell with São Paulo,' said the man whose identity still eluded me though I became more and more convinced that I had known him in the past. 'What I have against the *Paulistas*,' he went on, 'is that they're so damn keen. Give them a plate full of meat and beans and rice and a bowl crowded with bananas, they will, instead of accepting that, go out into the fields and start digging up roots as if that was the only thing left in the world to eat.'

Everybody laughed at this exaggerated comment on the *Paulistas*' industriousness, but the man from that city said, 'We're an independent lot. We want to work for our food. Not like the Bahianas and the Pernambucans, who wake up at midday, give three strokes of the whip to the nearest slave and convince themselves they've done a hard day's work.'

'I think I must defend the northerners, being one myself,' I said, speaking for no other reason than that I thought that I should contribute something nonsensical to this mediocre conversation. 'The northerner not only feels he's done a hard day's work after he's weakly whipped his slave, but he's also convinced that by doing so he's done his duty by the King and the Church.'

Incredibly, there was laughter at this statement, making me think that everyone had drunk himself into the mood of believing that none of us was capable of saying anything which was not extraordinarily hilarious. So that I went on, 'Why, I once met a man who was convinced at the age of thirty that he'd aged prematurely because he'd been whipping *two* slaves a day. His only consolation was that he was sure of his place in heaven.'

'That's nonsense,' said the man whose identity still puzzled me.

'It's as true as the bay of Rio is beautiful,' I said. 'I ought to know, I come from there.'

'I not only come from there,' he said, standing up in a menacing manner, 'I belong to one of the best families there.'

'Excuse me,' I said, also standing up and noticing that the

322

company had stopped laughing, 'but I too, come from a leading family. I inherited one of the largest estates you're likely to see on either side of the São Francisco.'

He hesitated for a moment, seeming to be searching my face as if he saw some writing there which he as yet could not clearly read.

'How did you come into your inheritance? By murdering your family?'

'That's an insult,' I said. 'I do not wish to discuss the subject of murder on which you may well be a greater authority than I, for I confess to be totally ignorant in the matter. But if you must insult me and the name of my family, perhaps you value your honour sufficiently to defend it tomorrow morning on the beach. Your name, sir?'

'Francisco Peixoto da Silva Xavier. And your name, a name to which you will have no breath to answer by tomorrow, your name?'

I stared at him for a moment, wondering whether I should pretend not to know him or whether I should reveal myself, but before I could come to a decision, I found myself compelled by some sentiment within me saying, 'Why, Francisco, you old bastard, this is a great surprise! How long is it since you left home, some forty years?'

'What are you talking about?'

'I am your elder brother, Gregório!'

My choice of the phrase 'elder brother' was unfortunate, for I noticed that something jarred within Francisco for a moment before he took the hand I had extended to him. Thus, the tension in the bar finally broke and the general hilarity commenced once more now that everyone was convinced that we had greater reason than before to get drunk.

That evening Francisco and I dined together at my house, and he told me his story. Apparently, his life had been as varied as mine though I could not help detecting in him a suspicion of the world, as if it had been created in order to thwart him at each step. I realized, too, that he considered a form of gangsterism as the only mode of advancement. He

323

talked amiably, however, and it was only twice or thrice during the evening that he found it difficult to repress a tone of bitterness – as if I had once deliberately cheated him of his rights. In this respect, his memory seemed to have distorted our common history, but I decided not to argue this point with him.

As we sat after dinner, drinking wine on the verandah, a soft cool breeze coming from the bay, we were overcome by that feeling of well-being in which one is compelled to express one's secret thoughts or to reveal those bits of information which in another mood one would keep to oneself. And it was in this mood, late in the evening, when we had revealed a good many private things to each other that I found myself telling him that I had seen him come out of Du Clerc's house and that I had been on my way to the governor's and would have given a detailed description of the three of them had I not stopped for a drink at the bar. I suppose I expected Francisco to melt with warmth towards me and to express his profound gratification. Instead, he seemed most annoyed, the mood of well-being left us, and soon he took his leave, weakly trying to cover up his annoyance with some trite jokes. He agreed to call on me again, but on the next day I received a short letter from him in which he said that he had to go away to Salvador on some urgent business. He was obviously once again going out of my life. I wished he had come to see me before going so that I could have reassured him that he had nothing to fear from my knowing of his involvement in the murder of Du Clerc.

The Frenchman's death was mourned by all the ladies in Rio. The city gossiped idly for some weeks about the motive of the murderers and while it was believed, after the servant Miguel's testimony, that there had been three murderers, no one was actually apprehended. There were no clues, and the motive seemed obscure. Some believed that the murderers had been hired by husbands who had grown jealous on observing their wives devote too much attention to Du Clerc. Others were convinced that the murder was politically motivated, for

Du Clerc's presence had begun to be an embarrassment to the governor who had been asked by Lisbon to explain why was it that a foreigner who had led a murderous attack on Rio was being treated like a prince. There was probably as much truth in these theories as in the hysterical assertion of one of the ladies that Du Clerc had not been murdered but that he had killed himself because he found life intolerable without her; were it not, she announced, for her tyrannical husband who knew nothing of true passion, she would have committed her sin for all the world to see rather than let Du Clerc die of grief. Of course, the other ladies were furious, and they succeeded in persuading the bishop to excommunicate the lady, an act which made her husband believe that he was justified in casting her out of his house and taking up a mulatto mistress.

While I observed this bizarre comedy in progress, I kept my information to myself. It occurred to me that there was no purpose in revealing the identity of the murderers, and although I too wondered what the motive could have been, I did not wish to deprive Rio of an engrossing topic of conversation. And while the city still amused itself with speculation about Du Clerc's death, a new event plunged the city into the greatest tragedy that it had known.

The new event was the arrival of another Frenchman, René Duguay-Trouin, a young dare-devil from Brittany who was determined to avenge the death of Du Clerc. I suspected that Duguay-Trouin was out to win glory and a fortune for himself and that, hearing of Du Clerc's death, he was simply using that as a convenient excuse. Fortunately, after the fiasco of the governor's hesitant attempts to meet the challenge of Du Clerc's attack, Rio was prepared for this new intruder; I say fortunately because for a few days while we observed Duguay-Trouin slowly make his way towards the bay we were comforted by our preparedness and were convinced that he was sailing right into the mouth of a monster which awaited to devour him, for our forces commanded by Castro Morais and Gaspar da Costa Ataide were ready to destroy him at any moment once he was inside the bay. And for these few days, Rio was full of excitement, its atmosphere gay and festive: people climbed up the hills every morning hoping to see Duguay-Trouin's moment of truth. Bands roamed the streets all day, intoxicating the air with their rhythms; the streets were like veins running with a wildly excited blood. Women who normally remained indoors could not resist the attraction of the streets and seemed to abandon themselves to the general excitement. By the third night Rio seemed to have lost all sense of decency and morality; the masses of bodies which appeared in the streets expressed a ritualistic sexuality in their public dancing and as the night progressed the ritual became with many a reality. There was something pagan and elemental, ecstatic and intense in its physicality about the manner in which men and women gave themselves first to celebration and then to each other that night. It was a long night which elated the spirit and exhausted the body. In the meanwhile, Duguay-Trouin, almost forgotten in these celebrations, lay at anchor just outside the bay.

After that long night, the morning was slow in coming. For many it never came. A mist hung over the city and by the time the sun finally peeped through Duguay-Trouin had taken his chance: he had captured the Ilha das Cobras, the tiny island in the middle of the bay, and sent a troop to establish positions on a hillside. And by the time the sun had completely chased away the mist, Duguay-Trouin was bombarding the city from his two positions. Our two leaders, Castro Morais and Gaspar da Costa Ataide, stunned by the sudden surprise, their forces already dissipated after the night of debauchery, could do nothing to defend the city. Each sent messengers to the other accusing each other of incompetence and weakness. Duguay-Trouin, making the most of the element of surprise, kept up the bombardment, setting Rio aflame where it did not simply collapse into great craters.

He let Rio burn for a week after which he sent his conditions to the governor. He wanted nothing less than one hundred chests of sugar, two hundred head of cattle and over

326

half a million cruzados in gold. Otherwise, he would raze the city, make a dust-heap out of it, and leave not a soul alive in it. The governor had sent messengers into the interior and hoped that the great soldier Antônio de Albuquerque would come to his rescue, and, playing for time, he answered Duguay-Trouin with the subterfuge that he did not have that much gold to give him. Duguay-Trouin showed what he thought of the answer by beginning the bombardment again. After some more destruction, Duguay-Trouin again made his demands. Our resistance had completely broken down, and people prayed for Albuquerque's arrival.

But Albuquerque did not arrive. The rains had broken out and everyone believed that they had slowed Albuquerque's march across the mountains. The governor decided that Duguay-Trouin could no longer be persuaded to wait and ordered an evacuation of the city, believing that Duguay-Trouin was serious in his threat of exterminating the population.

I was astonished by this decision, but most of Rio, eager to escape Duguay-Trouin's wrath, willingly co-operated. The evacuation took place at night while the most savage thunderstorm answered Duguay-Trouin's guns; a torrential rain fell all night, finally silencing the guns but creating additional misery for the people. I sent Jari to Vila Rica, instructing him to tell Heloisa to remain there with the children, for this was no time to be coming to Rio.

Evacuation, I thought, was a despicable and a dishonourable way of surrendering to an enemy. I could not make myself leave the city. I, who from infancy had been brought up to love Brazil, who had possessed so much of it with my senses, who had ruled over a part of it, could not abandon one of its cities to a foreign adventurer. If there was misery in the lives of the people that night there was a greater misery in my heart.

In the early hours of the morning, the rain still falling heavily, I made my way towards Duguay-Trouin's ship. It was not easy to be granted an audience before this outrageous bully, but I found that French notions of honour and discipline tended to be vague as soon as a few gold coins were produced. Bribery, however, is not easily accomplished, for even when the recipient of one's coins is eager he nevertheless feels obliged to go through a ritual of indignantly protesting his incorruptibility. It took me the best part of the morning to work my way through the successive posts of French soldiers guarding the sacred person of Duguay-Trouin.

He sat at a table, his eyes moving about as he glanced from one dish to another while he held a leg of mutton in front of his mouth. He heard me enter but, in the fashion of men who have a high opinion of themselves, took no notice of me and, dipping the leg of mutton into a bowl of some sauce, proceeded to chew at it. His thin lips glistened with the sauce and his moustache and beard shone with grease.

The table was of the kind used in monastic refectories, large enough for a dozen monks to sit around it, and it was covered with more food than a dozen monks would wish to consume without suffering from self-guilt. Once again Duguay-Trouin dipped the leg of mutton into the bowl of sauce and took another great bite off it, more sauce being rubbed off on his moustache and beard; and just when his mouth was full and his hands held the mutton some distance from his lips so that they appeared to be coated by fat, he looked up and said something. I could not understand what he said, for his mouth was full and the sound I heard was some kind of animalistic grunt. However, I took that as an indication of his good manners and assumed that he wished me to sit down. So, I took a chair opposite him. Seeing this and being again at the point of taking another bite of the mutton, Duguay-Trouin let go of the mutton in the manner of one who cannot believe what he sees, the mutton crashing on to a vast plate in front of him, sending various bones earlier deposited there flying in several directions; simultaneously Duguay-Trouin clenched his hands and brought the two fists banging down on the table, rattling the plates and making some bits of food bounce about, and screamed aloud a number of words which I again failed to understand because again his mouth was full and the words in any case, being spoken in what was obviously a rage, were uttered more to convey his anger than any meaning. I stood up and bowed, noticing in the corner of my eye that a glass had turned to its side when Duguay-Trouin had banged upon the table and that the glass now lay precariously on the edge of the table far to Duguay-Trouin's right. Having bowed, I said, 'Allow me to introduce myself, Gregório Peixoto da Silva Xavier, former landowner in Bahia, explorer of Brazil, discoverer of gold, the richest man in Vila Rica and, therefore, in Brazil.'

Having said this, I sat down and, picking up a fig from the table, put it into my mouth in the manner of one tasting the rarest delicacy. Just then the glass fell off the table and was shattered to bits, but Duguay-Trouin paid it no attention. Ah well, he wants to know more, I thought, and went on: 'You want, what is it, half a million, a little more, cruzados of gold? The governor of Rio can't produce that without coming to me. And for me, half a million, even a million cruzados is neither here nor there. My dear sir, you may think that politicians and noblemen rule this land. Allow me to inform you that the power is with the people with the gold. If I were to decide against placating your wishes, I would only need to expend some ten thousand cruzados and we could raise an army to destroy you. What am I talking of? What army do I need to raise to destroy you? We need only to leave you here after you have childishly destroyed Rio. What will you do then? You won't have the provisions with which to go back home. No, sir, if gold is your objective, you should talk to me.'

While I spoke, he stared at me as if I were some priceless diamond at the centre of a red satin cushion. When I paused, he looked round at the table and his fancy being taken by a baked fish which lay in an oval dish, he picked the fish up with one hand, clutching it as if it were a sheaf of papers, and began to tear at the flesh on the two sides of the fish with his other hand and to stuff his mouth with it. I do not know why he insisted on talking only when his mouth was full, but gradually I began to understand what he was saying, difficult though this was at first; and I hardly need to add that I am never more revolted by mankind than when it is performing in this manner at a table.

'I came to take revenge,' he said. 'Jean-François Du Clerc was killed by Rio. He was a great man and a close friend of mine.'

'He was my friend, too,' I said, surprising him. 'Nobody of any consequence comes to Brazil without wishing to be introduced to the richest man in Brazil.'

'I must apologize,' he said and I could see how he had fallen for my bluff, 'for not having availed myself of the introduction to you which Jean-François had sent me before his death. You will appreciate the pressures under which I live.'

'Of course,' I said, gratified that now we spoke on equal terms, a position arrived at with subtle falseness on each side of which I have no doubt that he was as much aware as I was.

'Rio killed Jean-François,' he said mournfully. 'And now Rio is burning for it.'

'Is that not enough?' I asked. 'Why should you want gold and sugar and cattle as well? What does that have to do with Du Clerc's death?'

He had by now finished with the fish and I noticed that although he had torn at it savagely, he had worked at the fish in such a way that he now held the bone perfectly whole and clean. He contemplated it for a moment and then threw it over his shoulder. It hit the wall behind him and fell to the ground. He poured himself a glass of wine, tipped it all into his mouth at one go and, looking up at me, said, 'Forgive me, I am most inhospitable. You must have some wine. FRANÇOISE!'

The last word was shouted so loudly that the room seemed to vibrate. I was surprised to realize that women, or at least a woman, accompanied him on the ship. Perhaps an old servant, I thought, when Françoise entered. Well, I have known some beautiful women in my life, but I had never seen a creature of such delicate beauty as to find a perceptible change in my own breathing. She could not have been more than sixteen, and her skin was so perfect and white that it could never have been exposed to the sun. Her hair was a mass of auburn ringlets, a fringe of them falling across her high forehead. Her cheeks, slightly sunken, suggested an infinite sadness about the face, an effect heightened by her drooping, dark green eyes which flashed when she looked up momentarily. Her lips were moist and pink, held slightly apart to show the glint of sparkling white teeth. A very slender neck gave an immense dignity to her bearing and stood in fine proportion to her sloping shoulders. She was dressed in a red silk blouse which was deliberately made to fit her loosely, thus creating a most provocative effect about the bosom. She wore a green skirt which came to her ankles, but just when she entered the room, she lifted the skirt so as not to trip, revealing not only a pair of beautiful gold slippers but also gently curving calves. God, Gregório, you're going to die!

'Monsieur?' she asked timidly on entering.

'A glass, Françoise, for the gentleman.'

As a matter of fact, there were three other glasses on the table and there had been no need, as far as I could see, for Françoise to have come and picked one up to place next to me, for I could have done so merely by stretching my arm. But I must say that I was delighted to have her walk behind my chair, her skirt brushing against it, a dizzying perfume from her body momentarily creating a wild desire within me.

'Oh, don't just stand there, Françoise!' Duguay-Trouin shouted at her.

'Well, monsieur?' she said softly, hesitating.

'Shit, Françoise, do I have to instruct you at each step?'

I wished I could take her away from this brute of a master and hold her close to my heart, but he went on, 'What do you think should go in the glass, you tit!'

'Wine, monsieur,' she said, seeming to brighten up with the idea, and went round to Duguay-Trouin's side in order to pick up the bottle which lay next to his plate. While she stooped to pick up the bottle, Duguay-Trouin stretched out his hand and struck it right across her face, shouting, 'Christ, do I have to put up with your imbecility? *Ask* the gentleman first which wine he prefers, don't just assume he's going to put up with whatever you're going to serve him.'

Françoise looked up at me. Tears stood in her eyes. At that moment, I could have cried for her, I could have killed Duguay-Trouin, I could have given away all my gold to go away with her to some small island where I could hold her in my arms and kiss her fragile mouth. But remembering my mission and remembering the name of a wine I had drunk at Du Clerc's, I said, 'There's a château some fifty miles south east of Bordeaux, I forget its name, perhaps it's Durat, or it could be Seurat, but it produces a memorable claret.'

'Go and get it, you stupid cunt,' Duguay-Trouin shouted at the precious object of my sight. 'Ask Jean-Baptiste for it.'

When she had gone, Duguay-Trouin poured himself another glass, drank it all down, picked up a roast rib and began to nibble at it but threw it away in dissatisfaction, turning to a ham which he sliced by hacking at it as if it were a tree which he wanted to chop down. Françoise returned, poured from the bottle which she had brought, and left before Duguay-Trouin could shout any further obscenities at her. I sipped the wine, finding it delicious.

'Well now,' said the brute. 'To the memory of Jean-François.'

'To my friend Du Clerc,' I said, raising my glass.

'He was a great Frenchman,' he said.

What a race, I thought, if such adventurers were representatives of its greatness, but said, 'I'm not likely to forget him.'

After the expression of such civilities, we now turned to business.

'Rio is still burning,' I said, 'but our friendship can put out the fire.'

'What is our friendship worth?' he asked, folding a large slice of ham in his hands as if it were a handkerchief and

332

putting it into his mouth.

'You will stop bombarding Rio at once. I will be your ambassador to the governor, and tell him that you have decided to become Brazil's friend instead of its enemy and will depart in peace if Rio will give you sufficient food supplies.'

He raised his eyebrows at this, but I went on, 'But you will get the gold. *I* shall give it to you.'

What I did not tell him was that I could thus buy time, which the governor could not, in which to procure the arrival of Antônio de Albuquerque and his troops.

'Why should you be so generous to me?'

'Because I would have to give the gold in any case. As I said earlier, the governor has no gold, he'll have to get it from me. Now all you want is gold. And what I want is the honour of my country. If I give you the gold you want, you will be content. And Brazil will be delighted that I have persuaded you to depart in peace and will, therefore, consider me a great patriot and will probably give me a noble title. Do you see the advantage to both of us of this scheme?'

My glass was empty, and Duguay-Trouin now rose, walked round the table up to me, picked up the bottle of claret, filled my glass, and, putting the bottle up to his mouth, began to guzzle the wine like someone who has just crossed a desert, much of the wine spilling down his beard and chest. He threw the bottle away to a corner of the room where it broke into fragments, and holding me by the shoulders kissed me on both my cheeks. His breath was foul.

Presently, we were both laughing and joking about many trivialities like two old friends, although he had again sat down and continued to stuff ham into his mouth.

'You know, Gregório,' he said in a most comradely manner, 'if I had the most beautiful mistress, I would give her to you. There! What greater token of agreement can you expect from a Frenchman?'

'You have her here,' I said, the words slipping spontaneously out of my mouth, for I had certainly not had any prior notion of making such a demand.

'What can you mean?' he asked.

'Your mistress,' I said. 'She's beautiful enough for me.'

'You mean Françoise?' he asked as though he did not believe me.

'Who else?'

He laughed aloud as if he had heard the funniest joke. I did not see the joke, but laughed lightly with him.

'But Françoise is only a servant, a little plaything.'

'We were talking of beauty,' I said. 'I find her beautiful.'

'All right, you may have Françoise.'

He shouted for a servant and asked him to take me to his own bedroom and to send Françoise there. I do not know what madness had overcome me, I who was now over sixty years old really had no business to make love to a young girl; indeed, I had no business to be thinking of making love at all, but there I was in Duguay-Trouin's sumptuous bedroom waiting for Françoise.

Tapestries, depicting erotic scenes, hung from the walls, the curtains across the window were of red velvet, a brocade awning hung above the bed. In the other room I heard another bottle go crashing to the floor when Françoise entered, closing the door behind her. I had never been more excited in my life, and in that moment, various episodes of my life went through my mind, particularly my first night with Aurelia. No, this was a greater excitement, and I wished to prolong it for as long as I could even though it was producing a strange ache in my breast.

I held Françoise softly by her hand and led her to the bed. She sat down on the edge and, as if performing a duty according to strict instructions, put a hand to unbutton her blouse.

'No,' I said, 'not yet.'

I wished her to lie there in the middle of the bed where I could enjoy seeing her first, where I could let my eyes love each invisible part of her, where my hands could begin to play about the soft flesh of her cheeks and find their way towards the openings in the clothes, exploring first, scouting the terrain over which I must finally ride in triumph.

I lay next to her and turned her body towards me in a relaxed embrace. Gently, gently now, I said to my pounding heart and to that other vital organ which too was wanting to burst. I touched her soft hair and, leaning forward, kissed her forehead, her eyes, her nose. And her lips, oh, the sweetest lips I have ever kissed. Softly now, calmly boys, I said to my vital organs again, for Françoise's kisses were driving me to another world where only intense ecstasy and sensuous sweetness existed. I slid a hand to her hip and slowly stroking her thigh, drew up her skirt so that I could stroke the tight flesh of her legs. Taking one more long, lingering kiss from her mouth, I lifted myself and looked down to her exposed thighs, the skirt heaped around her waist. I bent down and kissed her knees, and, playing my tongue along her flesh, kissed more and more of her thighs, the tight, glistening flesh of her thighs. My kissing was driving my mouth closer and closer to the centre of her body but I withdrew, saving up that pleasure for a few more moments, and again lay next to her, again embraced her and kissed her wonderful, sweet mouth. My hand still stroked her thighs, going up and down and around the thighs, but with a great willpower keeping away from the exit of her body's heat. My other hand, coming from behind her neck and over her shoulder as I embraced her, reached for the opening at her blouse – another pleasure which I had so far forced myself to postpone. Now, simultaneously, while one hand reached for her breast the other drew itself at her thighs towards the point of heat. My heart beat wildly, but still I spoke to it, Calmly now, softly. It was a moment I could delay no longer. With my two hands reaching for the two points of attraction and my mouth tight against hers, I made the simultaneous move.

It is difficult to describe a heart attack, especially if the ferocious moment of the attack is also the moment of one's death. To say an explosion takes place within one's breast would be to give a very vague approximation of the experience; to add that a moment's fire rages in the breast at the

335

same time as the explosion would make the description a fraction more explicit without really conveying the essential experience. So, let me simply say that I had a heart attack and died just when my lips were forced against Françoise's and my hands, which had slowly been approaching their destinations, held the objects which produced the violent shock: my left hand which had anticipated stroking and squeezing a girl's small breast with a hard little nipple clutched instead balled-up rags and my right hand grasped a boy's erect penis.